Bryce

— CORAL CANYON COWBOYS —

LIZ ISAACSON

The Young Family

Welcome to Coral Canyon! The Young family is BIG, and sometimes it can be hard to keep track of everyone. **This is updated through Bryce (November 7, 2023).**

Here's how things are right now:

Jerry and Cecily Young, 9 sons, in age-order:

1. TEX

Wife: Abigail Ingalls

His son: Bryce (28)

Children he and Abby share: Melissa (10), Carver (6), Pippa (4)

. . .

2. TRACE

Wife: Everly Avery

His son: Harry (23)

Children he and Ev share: Keri (5), Clay (4)

3. BLAZE

Wife: Faith Cromwell

His son: Cash (21)

Children he and Faith share: Grace (5), Celeste (4), Tyrone (1)

4. OTIS

Wife: Georgia Beck

His daughter: Joelle (Joey / Roo, 19)

Children he and Georgia share: OJ (Otis Judson, 8), Anaya (5)

5. MAV

Wife: Danielle Simpson

His daughter: Beth (16)

Her son: Boston (18)

Children he and Dani share: Lars (9), Emilia (5)

6. JEM

Wife: Sunny Samuelson

His kids: Cole (15), Rosie (12)

Children he and Sunny share: Ladd (5)

7. LUKE

Wife: Sterling Boyd

His daughter: Corrine (14)

Children he and Sterling share: Ryder (5), North (3)

8. MORRIS

Wife: Leighann Drummond

Children he and Leigh share: Eric (13), Rachelle (8), Skip (4)

9. GABRIEL (GABE)

Wife: Hilde O'Dell

His daughter: Liesl (13)

Her daughter: Lynnie (22)

Children he and Hilde share: Canyon (6), Brant, Cort, Tanner (2.5)

1

"Come on, you old man." Bryce Young smiled at his golden retriever as Lucky moved only his eyes. The rest of his body stayed perfectly still on the end of Bryce's bed. "I'm gonna eat breakfast myself then."

Lucky lifted his head at the mention of food, and he did heave himself up and off the bed. After a big doggy stretch, he trotted past Bryce, who pulled his bedroom door closed.

He'd lived in the big farmhouse on his enormous horse rescue ranch now for five years. He loved everything about his life—except how lonely it was to come home to an empty house at night and wake up alone in bed—sans the dog—every morning.

He'd attempted a few dates here and there over the past several years, but getting his ranch in operational condition, caring for the horses, applying for the grants he needed, traveling around to various farms and ranches and picking up new animals, and dealing with his big-and-still-growing family had taken all of his time.

He hardly thought of Bailey McAllister anymore, and he didn't know what to do with that as he made coffee, squirted some salmon oil in a bowl for Lucky, then added dry dog food, a couple of spoonfuls of green beans, a tablespoon or two of warm water, and then a whole container of wet dog food.

Yes, Lucky was spoiled. Bryce would like to have someone make him a meaty, delicious breakfast every morning, but he usually made toast and grabbed a protein shake on his way out the door. The toast would be eaten by the time he entered the first barn, and he drank the protein throughout the morning as he fed, watered, rotated, and cleaned up after twenty-seven horses.

Yes, he had twenty-seven horses now, and he smiled to himself as he mixed everything together for Lucky and set it on the floor next to his bowl of dry dog food. "There you go, my friend."

He poured himself a cup of coffee and doctored it up with sugar and cream before he sat down at the dining room table. It held six people just fine, and if he put the leaf in it, he could host Kassie and his family with an extra seat to spare.

His dad had three little kids—Melissa, who was ten now, Carver, who was six, and Pippa, a bright, if not a bit rambunctious, four-year-old. When the five of them came to the farm, it was all hands on deck, and they loved him as much as they loved Kassie, who always took the kids out onto the farm and let them do almost anything they wanted.

Bryce definitely felt like an outlier in his family, but at the same time, he fit perfectly. He couldn't quite describe the feelings he sometimes had, and he usually put his head down, got down on his knees, and worked through the problem with God.

The Lord had a special way of unbraiding the parts of Bryce that didn't make sense. Then he could see them, examine them, and make a plan for what to do with them. That was what Bryce always wanted to do—make a plan. Go over the plan. Execute the plan.

He'd taken this almost desolate piece of land and made it flourish again. He'd helped over one hundred fifty horses get back on their hooves and back out into the world, onto ranches and farms and small family plots of land where they could feel the measure of their creation.

He and Kassie nursed sick, abused, and abandoned horses back to health, and they both loved it with their whole hearts. Kassie had started dating Stockton Whittaker, but that hadn't worked out. She'd tried with another cowboy in town, but he'd left Coral Canyon after a few months, and Bryce couldn't remember where he'd moved to.

His thoughts meandered to the blonde woman who'd given Lucky a bath and a trim once-upon-a-time. Codi Hudson. He'd never asked her out, because she'd been one-hundred-percent right. He'd been completely overwhelmed by his move here, all the tasks that needed to be completed, and everything with the horses.

He gave Lucky his baths now, usually with the hose and then a wrestling match with a towel and brush. Bryce had looked up Codi's mobile grooming bus, but he hadn't been able to find it.

She'd moved on too. Left Coral Canyon for something else, and he hoped, something better.

"Thank you, Lord," he murmured as he finished his coffee and went to make his toast. He stood in front of the appliance as it warmed and toasted the bread, his head bent and his eyes closed.

"Thank you for this new day. Bless me to make the best of it, to be a servant for Thee if possible, and to stay safe out on the farm. I'm real grateful for Thy guiding hand in my life, for the miracles I've seen today and throughout my life, and for my daddy."

He paused for a moment. "And Abby. For Kassie, and all she does around here to make my life easier and better." He took a breath, expecting the toast to pop up at any moment. That always signaled the end of his prayer, and Bryce reasoned that he spent far more time on his knees at night. This morning prayer could be short, as long as it was meaningful.

"Thank you for my family, and for creating horses, and for the gift of repentance. Bless me to fix any wrongs I've done and help me to know where I stand with Thee."

The toast popped up; Bryce's eyes popped open. "Amen," he said, and he reached for the toast to butter it.

He did know where he stood with God, and it was right beside Him. God had told him that plenty of times, and Bryce didn't doubt it this morning as he slid open the back door and let Lucky exit first. The dog turned right around and sat, his happy face begging for a bite of toast.

As per their routine, Bryce gave him a bite, and Lucky took off for the edge of the deck. It needed to be re-stained and resealed, and it was on Bryce's list of things to do. Taking care of a home, a yard, a deck, the dozens of buildings here, the land, the animals....

Bryce had learned early on to make lists and schedule things if at all possible. He'd learned to humble himself and ask for help. He'd learned to find grants and volunteers that would come help with big clean-up projects. He'd learned to listen to his body, take care of himself mentally, and be sure to feed himself spiritually.

As he faced a new day, with plenty to do and lots of challenges, he turned his face into the almost-summer sunshine and smiled.

"Maybe I'm ready for something romantically," he said out loud. The sky did not answer back—but a horse nickered from somewhere on the farm, probably upset Bryce hadn't arrived to feed him yet.

LATER THAT AFTERNOON, BRYCE LAUGHED AS GOLDEN BOY, the horse he was currently working with, tossed his head and sent the water in the pond rippling away from him. The equine loved to swim, which made Bryce's job of trying to get him strong enough to go back out on a farm all the easier.

Lucky barked as he ran toward the pond too, and Bryce didn't bother to try to stop the dog. That would be impossible, as Lucky loved to swim too. Plus, the sun had been beating down all day on the farm, the dry ground, and the state of Wyoming, and Bryce actually thought *he* might get in the pond to cool off for a few minutes.

Truly, he wouldn't, because he wore jeans, and no one ever wanted to be wearing wet denim for long. He had to get everyone back to the barns and house, and it was at least a forty-five-minute ride.

So no, he would not be getting in the pond. Lucky and Golden Boy seemed to be having a race from one side of the pond to the other, but there was no way for the canine to win. He barely seemed to be moving as the horse went by him.

Bryce grinned and grinned at them, and while he knew he couldn't let his animals play in the water for very long, he gave them a couple of minutes to enjoy themselves.

"Come on," he yelled when they needed to go. "Let's get on back now."

Lucky got out of the water first, while Golden Boy tossed his head and nickered again.

"Yeah, you're swimmin'," Bryce said, as if the horse understood his human English. "But we have to go. Come on. Let's get." The horses did know those last two words, and Bryce bent to pick up Golden Boy's lead.

He wasn't strong enough to wear a saddle or be ridden. He'd been neglected and underfed for years. He'd had wounds on his legs that hadn't been attended to, and when Kassie had found him, he'd backed himself into a dark corner of a barn and wouldn't come out.

He did for her, though, as she possessed one of the calmer

equine spirits in the world. He went right with her, no lead needed, and he got on the trailer with bleeding legs and plenty of ribs showing.

Bryce had to work hard to tamp down his anger and frustration at people and commercial operations who kept horses they couldn't care for. Or didn't know how to care for. Or were too stubborn or lazy to care for.

He knew how much work it took to keep a horse healthy and happy, and getting one who wasn't in those categories to a state of existence that didn't include suffering? It took even longer. Months and months. Years.

He owned twelve horses that lived on the farm permanently. He and Kassie had done their best, but they were either too skittish or too old or still too unwell to go back to a farm or ranch.

The other fifteen existed in various states of readiness, and as Golden Boy lifted his beautifully golden body out of the pond and shook himself dry, Bryce had the very real feeling he'd be saying good-bye to this amazing horse very soon.

"Good boy," he said to the horse as Golden Boy plodded toward him. He was a Tennessee Walking Horse—a show breed who'd never shown or learned to show—in a palomino color— light brown or gold, with a white mane and tail.

He was like a king to Bryce, and he stroked both hands down the sides of Golden Boy's head as he lowered it to press against Bryce's shoulder. "You don't muscle me," he told the horse, holding his ground. "I'm in charge here."

Horses were like big babies, and they did need to be told

and shown who was boss. If they could get away with something, they did, and Bryce had quite a few mischief-makers right now. Golden Boy sometimes went along with the herd if he could, but most of the time, he let his gentle spirit show through.

Golden Boy never tried to push Kassie around, but he did try to get his way with Bryce. So he looped the lead around his neck and said, "You walk with me."

The horse did what Bryce wanted him to, and he looked around for but didn't see Lucky. He whistled, and the dog barked from somewhere to his left.

Bryce's heart fell to the bottoms of his cowboy boots. Left—north—led to the unplanted fields, and unplanted fields held a lot of dirt.

"Let's go," he said to Golden Boy, and he picked up the pace to try to head off the muddy mess that was going to be his golden retriever. He pushed through the vegetation that grew around the pond and arrived on the edge of the field only a minute later, but it was sixty seconds that Lucky had enjoyed rolling in the dark, rich earth.

Bryce could only blink at his dog, and he wanted to laugh but couldn't when Lucky stood up, his trademarked golden retriever smile on his face, and shook himself.

Hardly anything came off, because the dirt had suctioned to the water in his heavy coat, creating clumps instantly.

Bryce changed his plans just as instantly. "Let's get you to Kassie's," he said. Her house sat deeper on the farm, but she had a dirt lane that led right to the highway, and there were even a few pizza joints and restaurants that would deliver to her house.

And right now, her garden hose was about three times closer than Bryce's.

By the time they arrived, the outer mud on Lucky's body had started to dry, and he was barely walking. Bryce had no idea if Kassie would be home or not, and he came here all the time even when she wasn't. He threw Golden Boy's line around the tethering post at the edge of her backyard and said, "Come on, you silly dog," as he headed for the hose connected to side of the house.

Lucky whined but came with him, and Bryce heard an engine out in front of the house. Perhaps Kassie was arriving home right now. He'd get Lucky at least a little cleaned off before he went to see, and as he reached the hose, the dog lifted his head.

He barked and ran past Bryce and around the corner of the house. "Lucky, no," Bryce said, because while Kassie loved dogs —she had three of her own—he still had chores to do that day, and he'd already detoured from his plans by allowing the equine-canine swim party in the pond at all.

Sighing, he followed his dog. Before he rounded the corner of the house, he heard a woman say, "Holy baked potatoes, what happened to you?"

Bryce turned the corner, only half-expecting to see Kassie. That wasn't her voice, though.... It took him two more steps to realize the blonde woman staring in horror at his dog was none other than Codi Hudson.

Her white school bus with dozens of painted dogs on it sat in Kassie's driveway, and she lifted her eyes to Bryce's just as Lucky barked and jumped up on her.

"Lucky, no," Bryce said again, this time just as fruitless as the last time. Time froze, he froze, everything froze—except for Codi as she stumbled backward and fell with a muddy Lucky on top of her.

2

Codi Hudson had been bowled over by plenty of dogs. Tugged, pulled, licked, even partially buried once, as she'd taken her dog to the beach, and Gator hadn't been able to stop digging for more than five seconds.

She missed that dog sometimes, but for the most part, she didn't think of her life in Boise all that much anymore. Idaho was ingrained in her though, as evidenced by her use of *baked potatoes* as a form of cursing.

"Lucky!" Bryce Young called as he ran toward her. Yes, she knew it was him. No, she hadn't forgotten about him—or his golden retriever—though they'd only met once, what? Five years ago. Maybe six or seven now.

So much of Codi's life had been blended together, shaken up, poured out, and then re-blended. She had milestones she could cling to, but all the bits and pieces in between were

15

blurred, and she wasn't really sure where they existed on the timeline.

"Lucky, get off her." Bryce pulled his dog back, but the canine got one more lick in.

Codi sat up, wiped her now muddy and salivated-on face, and started to laugh.

"Sit down," Bryce said. "Lay down. Lay. Down." He pointed at the ground, and Lucky reluctantly slid forward on his forearms to a lay. His tongue lulled out of his mouth, and he squinted his eyes at Bryce in a very cat-like move of, *If I don't see you, you can't be mad at me.*

"Stay," he commanded, his eyes coming to Codi. She wasn't sure if he meant his dog or her, but she did see the concern and embarrassment in his face. She schooled her laughter as he knelt in front of her.

Oh, that wasn't fair. Him coming to her level only made him more attractive, and the simmering buzz of attraction that told her a good-looking man was in the vicinity started to vibrate through her whole body.

"You okay?" He reached out hesitantly, then pulled his hand back. "He doesn't usually jump at people. I'm sorry."

"It's not the first time a dog has knocked me over." She started to get up, and Bryce offered his hand to help her. She looked at it—seeing so much more than last time she'd met him. He'd grown up, though he'd definitely been a man before.

He seemed...older now, and not just in years. Wiser. More mature. She could see the years of work in his hands somehow, and she slid her palm along his and then gripped. Pure fire licked through her now, and as soon as she stood on her feet, she pulled her hand back to brush off her clothes. "Thanks," she said.

"What are you doing here?"

"I came to get my new dog." She indicated the house. "The woman who lives here sold me one of hers."

His mouth dropped open, but Codi didn't get it. With horror at all of the attraction still humming through her, she realized what she obviously already knew—she wasn't at Bryce's house right now.

Or was she?

"Let me guess," she said, her heart drooping behind her ribs. Praise heaven the Lord had put that organ in a place no one could see what it did. "Your wife sold your dog and didn't tell you?"

"Which one?" he asked, not answering her question. He looked up to the house as displeasure rolled off him. Great. So he was married. Of course he would be. The way Codi's luck with men went, he'd have to be either married or willing to cheat on her with someone who was.

Because of her last boyfriend—fiancé—she hadn't dated in almost seven years. She knew that milestone, and it would be seven years in June. Next month. Heck, June was next *week*.

"Which dog?" she asked. "You have more than one?"

Those gorgeous eyes came back to hers. "I only have one. Kassie has three, and I told her if she wanted to get rid of Pentagon to tell me. *I* want him."

Codi had no interest in getting involved in a small-town canine ownership spat. She hadn't technically paid for the beagle yet, but the cash sat in the glove box of her bus. Before she could decide if she should offer to let Bryce buy him or tell him "Tough luck," a woman's voice called his name. She sounded like she was outside too, probably in the backyard.

"I can't believe this," he muttered. "Stay here, okay? I want to talk to you before you leave." He didn't wait for her to agree to stay, and irritation fired through her at his arrogance as he took the steps to the front porch two at a time and walked right into the red brick house.

Yep, he lived here—or had at some point—and his wife had just tried to sell his dog out from under him.

She looked at Lucky, and Lucky panted back at her. "Come on, you," she said to the dog. "Let's get you cleaned up." Codi took the dog around the corner of the house where Bryce had come from, where she found a hose and spigot. She heard Bryce and Kassie talking in the backyard, and then their voices went quiet, presumably as they entered the house.

Codi turned on the water and marveled that Lucky held so still for the cold spray she turned on him. She'd only got to groom him that one time, and he'd been good then too.

She'd only been in Coral Canyon for a year—barely long enough to start having steady clients and a steady income— before her mother had fallen ill. Codi had packed her whole life in less than twelve hours, put everything she could in the bus or a small trailer she'd towed behind the bus, and left Wyoming.

Another milestone, and she'd thanked the Lord her mother's cancer diagnosis had come in August—a very moveable month for Wyoming. She'd been living in California for the past four years, at which point her mother had finally succumbed to the awful disease that had plagued her for so long.

Her daddy still lived on the potato farm where she'd been raised outside of Boise, but Codi couldn't go back there. At least not for longer than it took to visit, to tell her daddy she loved him, and to see her brothers—one of whom now ran the potato farm with his wife and two sons.

Codi had drifted though Utah, Arizona, and Colorado for the past year, living on her momma's inheritance and the grooming jobs she could pick up in random cities through social media.

When she'd finally come out of the haze her mother's death had cast over her, she'd sat down and asked herself, "Where do you want to be?"

Coral Canyon had been at the top of the list, and she'd returned only two weeks ago. She hadn't even started taking on grooming clients yet. She'd lived out of her bus until she found a place to rent that wasn't infested with spiders—and that was harder than she'd anticipated.

She'd only been in the place for four nights now, and she wanted a dog of her own. She loved rescuing dogs, but the shelter in town only had big dogs, and well, her basement rental unit only allowed dogs up to thirty pounds. She had a yard for him to play in and everything, and she'd started looking in the classifieds for dog owners trying to rehome their pets.

And she'd found Kassie and Pentagon, who was apparently a lovable, high-energy beagle who needed a stricter owner. Kassie said he was so smart, but she just didn't have the time to train him, and they'd agreed on a price of five hundred dollars.

The dried mud slipped from Lucky's fur with the water and Codi's strokes, and she rinsed him the best she could. "Maybe your daddy can be my first customer here in town," she said to the dog—only moments before he shook, drenching her in less than five seconds.

Codi simply stood there and took it, her eyes squeezing shut lest there be any errant mud, weeds, or who-knew-what-else in the water droplets.

"Codi?" Bryce called, and she told herself not to get excited that he'd remembered her name. Still, it had been a long time, and she certainly didn't remember everyone she'd met one time in the past six years.

She did remember Bryce, though, and she said, "Right here," as Lucky turned and trotted toward the corner. She followed him and found Bryce standing on the front lawn with a blonde woman with more honey in her hair than Codi had in hers. Hers seemed to drink up the sunlight and turn white instead, and Codi told herself to be nice.

Be nice, be nice, be nice.

"Kassie says you were gonna pay her five hundred for Penta."

Codi nodded and held up both hands. "Yeah, but I don't want to get in the middle of you guys." She looked between Kassie and Bryce, dying to look at their left hands just to confirm that they were indeed married. "I'll just go. I rinsed your dog with the hose, so he's not super clean or anything."

Bryce looked down at Lucky as if just realizing he was there. "Wow, thanks, Codi." He grinned at her, and Kassie elbowed him. He jolted away from her, frowned, and said, "Hey."

Kassie smiled at Codi, and she just wanted to leave. "Can I

have a few days to talk to Bryce about Pentagon?" She glared at him in the nicest way possible. "He knows he can't take care of another dog, but he needs some extra convincing." She spoke with a slower lilt than Bryce, and Codi suspected she wasn't from Wyoming.

The South. She definitely spoke like she came from Georgia or North Carolina.

"You can't take care of him either," Bryce shot at her.

"That's why I put him up for sale." Kassie rolled her eyes. "I hope we're not keeping you from anything." She did seem like a nice person, but Codi knew looks could be deceiving. Even the way a person behaved could be totally contrary to who they really were, what they really thought and believed, what they were willing to do or not do.

"No," Codi said. "Let me know if I can have him. If not, I'll keep looking." She nodded to Kassie, who smiled and nodded almost like a doll. Then she turned her back on Codi completely and practically smashed herself into Bryce's shoulder, clearly saying something to him.

He ducked his head, using that sexy cowboy hat to conceal his face and all of Kassie's head. Codi *really* didn't want to be here now, and she started to give the pair of them a wide berth on her way back to her bus.

Kassie left, and Bryce said, "Codi, can I talk to you for a minute?" before she could escape the situation. She paused only a few strides from her bus and looked up into the clear blue almost-summer sky.

"Sure," she said. "Why not?"

Bryce had turned in the same spot on the grass, and he pocketed his hands as he looked at her. "Uh, do you have the same phone number?"

"Yes," she said. "I can book you for Lucky right now if you'd like."

"Yeah, okay, sure," he said. "But I was, uh, wondering if you —ahem—might—if *I* might be able to use your number to find out what your *personal* schedule is like." His face turned a ruddy shade of red that made Codi's blood heat too.

"Your dinner schedule," he said with more confidence.

Codi had started to take out her phone to book his grooming appointment, but now her motion stalled. "You're asking me out?"

"Yeah."

Fire seethed inside her now, and not the pleasant kind. "In front of your house? Or I guess you don't live here anymore. But she's your ex, right?" Codi didn't dare look away from those bright brown eyes, because she didn't want to miss anything. "This whole thing is weird. No, you can't use my number to ask me to dinner."

"I have never lived here," he said, his eyebrows puckering down. "She's not my ex."

"She's—what?" Codi had all the wrong dots, and the picture sure wasn't coming into focus. "But you know her."

"Yeah, I know her," Bryce said, taking a step forward. "Let me explain it all to you. Tonight. At dinner." He fixed a smile on his face, and oh, the cowboy knew that was a game-changer. A deal-sealer. That smile had gotten him what he wanted many times in the past, Codi was sure of it.

She wasn't sure why she didn't trust him, and if she didn't, why she wanted to say yes to dinner. As she stood there staring at him, trying to formulate a response, he pulled out his phone.

"You know what? Shoot all the stars down. I can't tonight." He looked up. "I forgot I'm having dinner with my aunt and uncle."

"Are you an orphan?" she asked, because while she'd remembered his name, and knew she hadn't come here to bathe Lucky before, she actually knew very little about Bryce Young.

He chuckled and shook his head. "No, but I'm pretty close with all my aunts and uncles. Otis and Georgia particularly. They're—nothing."

Codi's eyebrows went up, and she had no idea what to say. His aunt and uncle meant a lot to him, but they were nothing?

"I have a lot of complicated stories," Bryce said, finally showing another round of nerves as his feet scuffed the grass and he dropped his gaze to watch them do so.

"I'll say," she said.

"So...dinner?" he asked. "I'm free tomorrow night." He looked up just enough to be able to see her from under the brim of that maddening hat.

Codi reached out and plucked it off of his head, which, oh, he did not like. She quickly handed it back to him as she said, "I don't like not being able to see who I'm talking to." The eyes said so much, and Codi had to make sure he wasn't a wolf in sheepskin.

He held his hat at his side, his expression open and unassuming. "I'll tell you all the stories—at least the interesting parts."

"You're going to try to convince me that you should get Pentagon."

He grinned, and this one held twice as much wattage as the last one. It had probably won him a lot in the past too. "Not at all," he said, stepping closer. "But see, I need your help with Kassie. She just bet me I wouldn't be brave enough to ask you out, and I have to win this one."

"You have asked me out," Codi said, having to look up at him now, because he stood so close. "So you win."

"But I actually *want* to go out with you," he said. "I'm crazy-busy, but I'm not as overwhelmed as I was before, and I think we'd have a good time." He laughed lightly. "Of course, I thought that about Kassie, and our first date was like being out with my sister."

Codi folded her arms. "So she *is* your ex."

"Nah," he said. "We never even started anything. She's my best friend though. We own this farm together." He seemed… happy about it. Not prideful, and that made a thread move from Codi to Bryce, where it attached itself, bonding her to him whether she liked it or not.

"So?" he asked. "What do you say?"

Codi didn't know what to say, and she couldn't read anything nefarious or off in Bryce's expression. This whole afternoon *had* been weird, though, and Codi honestly wasn't sure if she should say yes or no.

So she stood there, considering her options, as the seconds ticked by—and Bryce wasn't going anywhere.

3

Bryce watched Codi, not super pleased with the indecision raging across her face. Or her silence. At his side, Lucky nosed his hand, and he finally broke his gaze on the pretty blonde in front of him and looked at his dog. "Yeah, we need to get goin'."

He glanced over to Codi again, noting that she'd styled her hair a little differently now. He reasoned it had been six years since he'd seen her, and women cut bangs all the time. She still made his pulse quiver, and he'd never been happier that he had bones, muscles, and skin hiding that from the outside world.

"I have to get my horse back to my house," he said. "Do you want to meet Golden Boy?" He wasn't sure why he asked. Surely she couldn't just wander around his farm either.

But her face lit up, and Bryce sensed in her a soul who loved animals as much as he did. The fact that she owned a dog grooming business spoke to that too, and he looked at her big, white bus in Kassie's driveway.

"I can drive you back over here once we get to my house."

Codi nodded and said, "Sure. A horse named Golden Boy has to be something, right?"

Bryce grinned at her. "He's something special, all right." He started for the corner of the house, glad when Codi came with him. "We got 'im from a ranch on the Colorado border, and I can't wait to see how he'll do with a saddle."

They walked through the shade on the side of the house, and then the backyard opened up. The Hammond twins ran a lawn-mowing business, and both Bryce and Kassie used them to keep their grass trimmed and their leaves raked.

"This place is nice," Codi said.

"Yeah," Bryce said. "It's been through a renovation or two. It was kind of a mess when Kass and I bought it, but we've worked hard to get 'er up to speed."

"You co-own it? Fifty-fifty?" Codi looked over to him, and the weight of her gaze made him nervous for some reason. Sparks popped between them, and Bryce recognized it as attraction.

"I own more of it," he said. "I do all of the administrative work, like filing the grant paperwork, hiring ranch hands, keeping the horses fed, scheduling the vet, all that kind of stuff. Kassie works with the horses. She's got the good job." He grinned and looked up into the pure blue sky. "I get to work with the horses too, and I don't mind everything else."

"You love this place."

"One hundred percent." They reached Golden Boy, and

Bryce unlooped his lead from around the post. "Hey, you. I brought you a new friend." He looked over to Codi. "How familiar with horses are you?"

"It's been a while since I've been on one."

"He's—" Bryce cut off when Codi lifted up her hand and held it a few inches from Golden Boy's nose. A pause filled the moment, and then Golden Boy pushed into her palm.

"There you are," she whispered to him. Then, she leaned her head against his, and Bryce wanted to take a series of pictures so he could see this peace in both the woman and his horse whenever he wanted to.

She stepped back, breaking the moment, and Golden Boy lifted his head.

"Yeah, you can walk with her," Bryce said, and he handed Codi Golden Boy's lead and then led the way back out into the fields. "He needs the exercise, which is why I'm on foot with him. He's not strong enough to be ridden yet, so I'm walkin' with him everywhere."

"He's real pretty." Codi moved effortlessly at his side, though her legs were far shorter than his. "Good spirit."

"Yeah," Bryce said, glancing over to the gentle giant. "He does have one of those." He grinned at his horse. "We try to get them back to full health. Train them and teach them so they can go back out on ranches and farms. Heck, I even sold one to the Border Patrol several months ago. There's this prison program, and—"

He cut off when Codi looked over to him, her eyebrows almost up under her bangs. He couldn't help being eager to talk to her. He loved his Rising Sun Ranch, and he could talk to anyone about it for hours.

Instead, he cleared his throat and said, "I talked to the horse trainer at the Honor Farm, which is only a couple of hours down the highway. He let me bring a couple of my horses to their auction last fall, but I only sold one. They capture mustangs from public land and use prisoners to train them. It's rehabilitation for both horse and man."

He swallowed, wishing he had a drink. Bryce normally had water with him, but he must've dropped his bottle somewhere or left it at Kassie's. Something. As close as Codi stood right now, he couldn't really remember.

"That's interesting," Codi said. "I didn't know they did that."

"Yeah," Bryce said, refraining from telling her they had prison programs to train and sell horses in several western states. "I got Goose a good partner, and they're down in Texas now, working. Sheriff Lancaster sends me photos sometimes."

Bryce tilted his face toward the sky and absorbed some of the afternoon sunlight as they walked. He wasn't going to try to talk Codi out of buying Pentagon, though he would take the beagle in a heartbeat.

They simply walked through grasses, along dirt roads, and then beside a fence until the main part of the ranch came into view. "This is where I usually am," he said. "We've got four stables here; twenty-seven horses. We categorize them into health pods, so the Blue Stable is our horses that are getting really close to being able to be rehomed. The Yellow Stable is where Golden Boy lives."

The horse tossed his head at the use of his name, but Codi didn't seem to mind at all.

"Yeah, you live there, don't you?" Bryce asked the horse, grinning at him. Only when his gaze dropped to Codi's did he realize that he'd spoken out loud. To a horse. He spent so much time with them, he talked to them like friends, like people.

Embarrassment squirreled up his spine, and he focused forward again. "Those horses aren't quite ready to be considered for rehoming, but they're not in bad shape. That's the Red Stable, and our newest, most injured horses go there."

"What's the fourth stable for?"

"My permanent residents," he said without missing a beat. "I've got twelve of them, and while we still work with them, they're not really candidates for rehoming."

"I understand that," Codi said almost under her breath. She walked with her eyes down on the ground, and Bryce wanted to lift her up so badly.

"Barns," he said instead. "Feed sheds. Chicken coops. I'm not sure you can call yourself a ranch if you don't have chickens." He chuckled, glad when Codi smiled too. "We've got dogs, cats, chickens, and horses here."

"Probably some rats too," she teased.

Bryce grinned at her. "Are you insulting the cleanliness of my operation?"

She smiled at him, and oh, that felt like God Himself had pulled back the curtain on the full glory of the sun. Beams radiated from Codi Hudson, and Bryce knew—he just *knew*—he had to have her in his life.

He'd felt like this about Kassie too, and then on their first date, he'd taken her hand in his and felt...nothing. He'd known then too, that he and Kass would not be sharing sizzling kisses beneath the moonlight. But maybe he and Codi could....

He let that thought sit there in his head while he opened the door to the yellow stable. "This is where the wash stations are," he said. "Golden Boy took a bath in the pond today, so he's got to get rinsed down before he can go back in his stall."

"I can do it," Codi said. "If you'd like." She looked at him with pure hope in those blue eyes, and Bryce wouldn't have told her no anyway. "You said you have a lot of other things to do."

"Yep," Bryce said easily. "I'm gonna go feed my Green Stable, and then I've got to get into my garden and do a little planting."

"You're planting a garden? Like a vegetable garden?"

"Yes, ma'am," Bryce said without any extra heat crawling into his face. "I like eating out of my garden come autumn."

She nodded, her voice definitely set on surprised when she said, "Yeah, I mean, who doesn't?"

Bryce wanted to lean in close and say something flirty about how she should come eat with him when he finally pulled the produce, peppers, and potatoes out of his garden. But he didn't. He stayed flat-footed and reached up to salute her with two fingers against the brim of his cowboy hat.

"Come find me when you're done. He goes down in the one with his name outside it." He pointed down the aisle a little bit, and then he swung his attention back to Codi and Golden Boy. The horse stood there with his flaxen eyelashes hovering halfway closed. Completely nonplussed, when normally, he glared Bryce to dust if he had to get a bath after a dip in the pond.

"You be good for Miss Codi," he said to the horse. His heartbeat bumped through his chest strangely when he looked at Codi. "Do you have my number? I don't know if I should leave you here with him alone."

At the very least, she should be able to call him if she had a problem. She released Golden Boy's lead, and the horse just stood there. Didn't so much as shuffle a hoof. "I don't think I have your number still," she said. "What is it?"

He recited it as she typed, and she goes, "Oh, I do have it." Her cheeks pinked up as she muttered, "Let me update your name...."

"What did you have as my name?"

"Nothing." She pulled her hands closer to her body, making it impossible for him to see her phone. Curiosity dug at him, but Bryce said nothing.

She definitely blushed as she tapped, and then she met his eye. "Got it."

"He just needs to be rinsed and brushed down. You can do that?"

"I've brushed down a horse before."

"You said it had been a while."

"I can do it."

"Okay." Bryce believed her, and he moved out of the way as Codi eased Golden Boy into the first wash stall. He wanted to stand there and stare, but he didn't dare. For as glorious as Codi could smile and call down the sunlight from heaven, that same fire could burn as well.

So he turned his back, almost praying he could withstand the heat of her gaze, and left the stable. Outside, he picked up the pace to get over to the Green Stable, and he prayed, "Lord, I don't know what You had in mind for me today, but putting Codi Hudson in my path? Was that deliberate? Should I be paying attention to these racing thoughts, the way I want her to like me, and how I'm literally planning our first date already? Like, what is this?"

He looked up toward the clouds, the skies, the heavens. God did not answer him directly, but his thoughts didn't cease through his evening feeding of his permanent resident horses. He didn't exactly hurry, because he liked to move down the line and talk to every horse there.

"I met a woman today," he told the first horse, a tall, dark chestnut named Rebel. He stroked down the equine's neck. "She's really pretty, but she never did say if she'd go out with me...."

Bryce honestly wasn't sure he was ready to be going out with someone again, but he figured he had to try again some-time, and he did feel better than he had in years. So he gossiped with his horses, then headed over to his vegetable garden, his thoughts zeroing in on one that simply would not go away, though Bryce didn't like it.

Talk to Georgia and Otis about it tonight.

He didn't want to involve his aunt and uncle in his love life, though the only other people he was closer to were his own parents and Kassie.

"I don't want to talk about it in front of OJ," he muttered as he stepped into his backyard shed and started gathering the seeds he needed to plant pumpkins that evening. "Guide me." Bryce sighed. "Yeah, just...guide me."

He sometimes hated that he didn't know what to do, but even when God didn't directly tell Bryce what to do, when he opened his heart to be guided, he'd never been led wrong. So if the Lord wanted him to talk to Otis and Georgia about Codi... maybe he should.

4

C odi stroked the brush down Golden Boy's side, taking comfort in the steady rhythm she'd found, the soft silence around her, and the pure vibe of this ranch. She needed something like this in her life, but every time she thought that, she worked just as hard to push it away.

She didn't want a job working for someone else. She wanted to set her own schedule, and the dog grooming business allowed her to do that. Still, she thought of her shrinking savings account, and she needed to get more than Lucky on her schedule.

Glancing over to where the golden retriever had laid down, Codi allowed herself to smile. She couldn't believe the dog had chosen to stay with her over going with his master, but he clearly spent some time in this stable. He had a bed in the corner, and he'd trotted right over to it, circled, and laid down.

"All right, Boy," she said to the horse. "You're all done." She reached up and ran her hand from the crown of his head—which she could barely touch—and down his neck and along his back. The horse stood absolutely still for her, and when Codi moved in front of him, she leaned her forehead against the side of his neck. "Don't hide who you are, okay? He can already sort of see it, so you're not foolin' him."

The horse huffed at her, and Codi grinned at him. "Maybe I'll ask him to let me come see you again." She wasn't sure she would, but if she really came to bathe Lucky, she'd be out here on the Rising Sun Ranch. She let that thought sit without trying to push it away, and when she exited the stable, the sun moved behind a cloud.

Shade got thrown over the land, and Codi took a long, deep breath of the pure air here. Everything seemed to move slower in Coral Canyon, and slower was exactly what she needed. It wasn't hard to keep following the road and end up behind the homestead. She paused as it came into view, a few rays of sunlight getting caught by the big bank of windows and being reflected back out into the world.

Bryce lived there?

Codi reached up to run her hand through her hair and realized she'd tied it back to work with Golden Boy. Pure horror streamed through her when she realized if she'd run into Bryce, he'd have been able to see the lacing of her wig.

She quickly pulled the band out and smoothed her hands through her hair several times to get it to lay right. She didn't wear a wig every day, but she did like having more hair. It always shone with the right color, and she didn't have to think so hard about how she could make the hair she did have look good.

Satisfied that she wouldn't embarrass herself, she continued toward the yard. A deck sat off the back of the house, with a perfectly trimmed lawn. Bryce had shrubs, bushes, trees, and flowers. She found him standing at the far side of a patch of dirt—his vegetable garden. He bent and pushed something into the earth, then straightened and wiped his gloved hand along his beard.

His eyes caught hers, and Codi marveled that they could do so from so far away. Her veins buzzed now, as if someone had poured baking soda in them and then followed that with vinegar. She might go volcanic if she didn't move, and her feet took her toward the drop-dead gorgeous cowboy who had more stories to spill than anyone she'd ever met.

To her surprise, she wanted to hear his stories too, and she wasn't sure what that said about him. Or her.

"Hey," she said when she stood about thirty feet from him. "He's all cleaned up and in his stall. Lucky stayed with me, so I brought him back."

"Yeah, I noticed." Bryce smiled as his retriever trotted over to him. He bent down and patted the dog, then looked at her again. "When can you come give him a proper bath?"

"Tomorrow?" Codi suggested. "I don't have any clients, so you tell me when, and I'll be here."

"Tomorrow." Bryce pulled off his gloves and tucked them under one arm. He retrieved his phone from his back pocket and started swiping. "I've got Uncle Luke comin' out in the morning to help with some pasture rotation...the vet's coming to look at Tiger's bandages at twelve-thirty."

He looked at her as she arrived only a few feet from him. "What about in the afternoon? It takes what? Three hours?"

"About," she said. "For a dog his size, with all that fur." She could still see the darker mud in his lighter hair. "And the mud." She grinned at him and crouched down in front of Lucky. "Why do you guys always go for the mud?"

"If you came in the afternoon and finished up close to five or so, we could just have dinner here."

She looked up at Bryce, and with the evening sun haloing him from behind, he looked like a cowboy king. Fine, Codi was attracted to him. She could admit it to herself, and that only sent her pulse flapping through her body with the wings of a pelican.

Could she ever trust another cowboy?

Codi stood slowly, feeling utterly exposed though she had no reason to. "You're asking me out again."

"Technically, I'm asking you to stay in with me," he said. "And Lucky."

"Do you cook?"

"Well, I've lived here by myself for about six years now, and I haven't starved." He smiled at her, and he should have to show a permit before being allowed to do that. He had a great mouth, with full lips and all those straight, white teeth.

Codi pulled her eyes from him and looked at the marker he'd put at the end of the row. Cabbage. She said the word over and over in her mind so she wouldn't look back at Bryce's mouth.

Cabbage, cabbage, cabbage.

"...okay?"

Codi clued in to the fact that he was still talking, and she managed to look at his shoulder now. "I'm sorry. What?"

"I was just asking if you were okay. You...got lost." He wore compassion in his gaze now, and Codi wasn't sure she wanted that. She may have needed it, and that only made the ragged parts of her heart bleed a little more.

"I have to get going," she said.

"Yeah, okay," he said. "I'm done here." He detoured into his shed to put away the shovel and rake he'd been using, along with the gloves, and then they walked around the house to the front of it. A big, black truck stood there, and he moved to the passenger door to open it for her.

"Let me grab my keys from inside. You might not want to get in yet. You might suffocate in the heat." He beamed at her again and then turned to go into the house. As she watched him retreat from her, the strangest feeling of sadness overcame her.

She didn't want to watch him walk away from her. "Then you better talk to him," she muttered to herself. He returned quickly, before Codi could come up with anything that would explain, and they got into the truck.

"Bryce," she said as the big engine growled to life. He looked over to her, his expression so open and unassuming. Codi couldn't stand being this close to him. He made every cell in her body vibrate in such a glorious way. She looked down at her hands, noting the way her fingernails weren't as clean as they'd been when she'd driven her bus along the highway between Coral Canyon and Dog Valley.

"I—I can come tomorrow at two and give Lucky his bath."

"Okay," he said. "I don't want you to be upset or uncomfortable."

"It's not you." She switched her gaze out the side window. "Well, it is you, but it's not your fault." She looked over to him, because he hadn't started driving yet. "My heart is delicate, you know? I...I had this fiancé, and then my momma got sick, and now I'm the one who's newly back in town and trying to build my business from zero."

"I know," he said. "I'm sorry I asked twice. I just—you're a beautiful woman. I couldn't stop myself." He put both hands on the wheel, his jaw tightening. "I won't ask again. I'm sorry to pressure you."

She nodded. "You didn't."

"I did." He put his truck in drive and got moving. He went past the house and around a circle drive to turn around. "I haven't dated anyone in a long time."

"How long?"

"Uh, let's see. Eight years now." He cut a look over to her, but he could've just been checking the road for traffic. There was none, and he pulled out and went further along the road toward Dog Valley.

"That's a long time."

"Yeah," he said. "When I see you again, I can tell you about my aunt and uncle, or my ex-girlfriend, or the job I had in Louisville before coming here." He flashed her a smile. "And you can tell me about your fiancé, or your momma, or how you came to own your big white bus."

Codi could talk about one of those, sure. "I haven't dated since the fiancé," she said, shocked she could admit it.

"What was his name?"

"Lester."

Bryce remained quiet for a moment, then two, and then something like a snort, or a shout, or a laugh filled the truck. She looked over to him, and he was definitely laughing. Or trying not to. He glanced at her, those dark eyes dancing with so much life. She wanted to get nearer to it, reach out and touch it, see if she could ever feel as vibrantly as his eyes looked.

"Lester?" he asked between chuckles. "Was he seventy-five-years-old?"

Codi's whole life brightened. "Hey," she said back. "Even Lesters deserve love." She pushed her hair over her shoulder. "Besides, he went by Les."

"I'm not sure that's better, sweetheart."

Codi pulled in a breath at the term of endearment, and she looked at Bryce with raised eyebrows. He grinned back and said, "My ex's name is Bailey."

She wanted to find something about her name to laugh at, but she couldn't. "Where is she now?"

"Montana," he said. "Is *Les* still in Boise?"

"I don't really know," she said. "I haven't kept tabs on him."

"Yeah, fair enough," Bryce said. He made a turn, and the big doggy bus and Kassie's red brick house came into view. "Tomorrow at two. If you happen to be hungry when you're finished, I can pour you a bowl of cereal." He got down and called back into the truck, "Just a sec. I'll help you out."

Codi wanted to tell him she'd been getting into and out of trucks her whole life, but she didn't. She did enjoy being taken care of sometimes, especially if the man doing it had dark, delicious eyes and hair that curled at the ends when it got too long.

Bryce opened her door and reached up for her hand. "It's got these oversized tires, and it's a bit of a drop to the ground. My little sister dang near broke her leg getting out last week, and my momma gave me an earful." He smiled, and Codi kind of liked how his mouth ran away from him. She liked how much he gave away, including how much he loved his momma, even when she lectured him about his sister's safety.

She slid her hand into his, pulled in a breath, and froze. While her muscles turned to ice, her bones and blood turned into liquid lava. His skin practically smoked where it met hers, and as Codi stared straight into his eyes, the feeling only intensified.

And he could feel it too.

"Well." He cleared his throat and gave her hand a little tug. That got her moving, and she did slide out enough to get her foot on the runner of the truck. From there, she stepped down, and Bryce still didn't release her hand.

"The first—and only—time I went out with Kassie, I touched her hand at the beginning of the date. We looked at each other too, but it was the opposite of that."

"The opposite?" Codi could barely think, let alone get words to form. His hand was so much bigger than hers, and warm, and a bit calloused, which she actually liked.

"It was nothing," he said. "We both knew it. She's like a sister to me and has been for years now."

"Okay," Codi said, not sure why he needed to tell her this.

"That was not a sister touch," he said.

"No," she agreed.

He dropped her hand then and pocketed his hands. "All right, then." He drew in a deep breath and blew it out steadily. "I'll see you tomorrow."

"Yeah." Codi half-stumbled and half-walked over to her bus, climbed the steps, and sank into the seat. She stared out the gigantic windshield for several long beats. Long enough for Bryce to go by and up the steps to Kassie's house. He didn't ring the doorbell or knock; he simply walked right in.

Codi didn't want to sit there and stare, though with the fizzing heat still boiling through her bloodstream, she couldn't do much else. She did manage to start the bus, and she finally backed it expertly away from the house. Away from Kassie. Away from Bryce.

At times like these, Codi really wished she had an older sister to talk to. She'd often relied on her momma over the years, but she was gone now too. Her two older brothers were both married, but Codi had been gone from Boise and the potato farm there for so long, she didn't have strong friendships with her sisters-in-law.

So she had to rely on herself as she drove in the shadows that became dusk that became twilight. She parked the bus on the street in front of her rental house and looked into the quickening darkness.

"You don't have to marry him tomorrow."

She was right. She didn't.

"Don't push him away either."

The way his skin had heated against hers...maybe she should physically push him just to feel that again.

"Be nice. Be open. Not every cowboy is like Lester."

In fact, she hoped the majority of them weren't, and he would've never, ever apologized for asking her out more than once. For anything, actually.

"Go to dinner with him."

Before she could talk herself out of it, Codi pulled out her phone and texted Bryce. *Cold cereal for dinner is one of my favorite things.*

Yeah? he came back with almost instantly. *What's your favorite kind?*

She smiled at her screen. *Don't laugh, but it's Wheat Chex.*

I see, he said. *You're the seventy-five-year-old.*

She could just picture that smile, hear that laugh. *BYOC?* She sent him. *Tomorrow, after Lucky's appointment?*

You don't need to bring your own cereal, he said. *I'll have the good stuff, Codi. See you tomorrow.*

She brought her phone to her chest, a sigh slipping through her lips in a way it hadn't in a long, long time. This wasn't a frustrated or irritated sigh. It wasn't one of contentment or contempt either. It wasn't laced with desperation or exhaustion.

No, this sigh had emanated from her heart, and it sounded a little lovesick, a little lonely, and a little bit like she was ready to get back on the dating horse again.

With one cowboy king, Bryce Young.

Now, all she could do was pray and hope and pray some more that he wouldn't re-break the pieces of her heart she'd managed to put back together.

5

Bryce pulled up to his uncle Otis's house to find Aunt Georgia sitting on the front steps in cutoffs and a red-checkered blouse. She lifted her hand to him in greeting, and he put the truck in park as two kids ran toward him.

His biological son, OJ, and his cousin Anaya. Bryce loved both of those kids—and Joey, who'd just come out of the house and joined Georgia on the porch—and his heart swelled and filled with love twice, three times, four times over.

OJ yanked open the door and said, "Bryce, come look at this new dog we got."

"Oh, boy." He chuckled as the boy ran off again and his younger sister crowded into the doorway.

"Bryce, did you bring Lucky?"

The golden retriever panted in the back seat, and Bryce hooked his thumb toward him. "You can let 'im out."

Ana grinned as she slammed one door, which made Bryce cringe, and then struggled to open the back passenger door. She'd been born about a month premature, and she'd been small her whole life. She wasn't disabled, but she did catch every virus and bacteria that came through town, and she'd been in the hospital four times in her short five-year life.

She'd be six this fall and going into kindergarten, which he knew his aunt and uncle worried about. Bryce got out to help her, but the back door opened before he'd closed his door.

"There he goes," Uncle Otis said in his rich, tenor voice, and Bryce's heart warmed again. "Don't make him play with Emerald if he don't want to."

The cowboy twang in his uncle's voice propelled Bryce around the back of the truck and into his arms. "Hey, Uncle Otis."

"Howdy, son." He clapped Bryce on the back a couple of times, and when they parted, Uncle Otis wore a bright smile. He'd always been less sober than some of the other uncles, but he had a fiercely protective streak, and he'd do anything for Georgia, his kids, or Bryce.

"You got a new dog?"

"Oh, Georgia brought one home from the rent-a-puppy that's been havin' problems." Otis smiled at the dogs and children on the front lawn, which a powerful set of porch lights illuminated as the sun went down. Bryce watched them too. "Ruby's gettin' older, and I think she's looking for a replacement already."

The rent-a-puppy had pretty coloring—brown, red, black,

and white—and as Bryce and Otis started toward the front porch, she jumped back from Lucky, bowed, and then *bark, bark, barked* in her higher-pitched voice.

Bryce only smiled at her, and Lucky's tail didn't stop swishing back and forth for a single moment. Aunt Georgia rose to meet him, and he hugged her as she asked, "You didn't bring Kassie?"

"She has a date tonight," he said, really hitting the Ts. He grinned as he stepped back. "I guess the veterinary assistant who's been bringing our medical supplies once a week finally asked her to dinner. They're goin' to some place up in Dog Valley."

"Good for her," Georgia said as she turned to go up the steps to the porch. "Neither of you have dated much since you moved here." She gave him a side-eyed look, and Bryce saw his way into the conversation he didn't really want to have.

A quick glance over to OJ told Bryce the boy wouldn't overhear anything he might say, and that the kids would be occupied with the dogs for a little bit.

"I wanted to tell you guys something," Bryce said as he mounted the steps after his uncle. He paused in front of Joey, who wasn't so skinny and straight anymore. In fact, the girl had graduated last year, gone to her first year of college with the goal to become a nurse, and probably dated more than he did.

"Roo." He drew her into a hug too, glad when she squeezed him back. "You're home for the summer?"

"And looking for a job," Uncle Otis said quickly. "You got anything she can do on the farm, Bryce?"

"Always." He grinned at her. "You'll want to get a good pair of gloves, or pass up the manicures this summer, though."

"I don't want to work on a horse farm," she said, shooting her father a look.

"You need the money," Uncle Otis said back.

Joey didn't argue with him again, though she probably could have. Uncle Otis had plenty of money, as Country Quad had found a way to live in Coral Canyon almost full-time and keep their country music careers. Bryce wouldn't be surprised if his daddy didn't sign another contract though. Dad had turned fifty a couple of years ago, but apparently there were female fans worldwide who liked a little silver on their cowboys.

Bryce grinned just thinking about his father, who did have such a natural performing streak inside him. Still, he also knew of the exhaustion after the concerts, and that Dad just wanted to settle down in his quiet small town and enjoy his little kids as they grew up.

"What did you want to tell us?" Georgia asked. "I can call the kids up now, or...."

Bryce's heartbeat spiked, and he sure was glad he hadn't been hooked up to a machine. The beep that would've caused. "I, uh." He shuffled his feet and looked down at the tips of his cowboy boots sticking up from beneath the cuffs of his jeans.

He raised his eyes to Aunt Georgia and Uncle Otis, the thought to tell them about Codi louder now than it had been earlier. *Here goes nothing*, he thought. *Stop me, Lord, if I'm about to make a fool of myself.*

God did not stop him, and Bryce leaned into the arms of Jesus as he said, "I met a woman today." He quickly shrugged one shoulder. "Well, I met her years ago, when I was home with Lucky before I even moved here. Obviously nothing happened then, but today...." His voice trailed off, as his body couldn't seem to compute the zings and tingles he'd felt when he'd held Codi's hand and keep speaking at the same time.

Uncle Otis smiled. "You've got that look on your face," he said.

"What's her name?" Aunt Georgia asked.

"Codi," Bryce said, once again checking to see what OJ was up to. "Her name's Codi Hudson, and she runs a mobile dog grooming bus."

Aunt Georgia and Uncle Otis exchanged a look, and Bryce watched them both. "Do you know her?"

"No," Aunt Georgia said, her voice pitched up maybe a bit too high. She smiled at Bryce, and she'd always been so kind to him. So loving. So inclusive. "Did you ask her out?"

Bryce sighed, the euphoria of that first touch with Codi fading away. "Yeah," he said. "But she's...skittish. She didn't say yes."

"Ouch," Otis said as he opened the door to go inside.

"She didn't really say no either." Bryce went past him and into the house, Joey right on his heels. "She's coming to bathe Lucky tomorrow, and I invited her to stay for dinner." He turned back to the three of them as the door closed and his eyes adjusted to the dimmer light inside.

The house smelled like he'd be feasting on roast beef and mashed potatoes, and he probably would be. He thought of tomorrow night's dinner, and his stomach did a somersault. "So I don't know."

His phone chimed, and he looked down at it. "Holy horses," he said. "It's her right now." His thumbs flew over the screen though Aunt Georgia demanded to know what she'd said.

Cold cereal for dinner is one of my favorite things.

Yeah? Bryce typed furiously, feeling strangely flirty and also like he floated outside of his body. *What's your favorite kind?*

Don't laugh, but it's Wheat Chex.

A huge grin came to his face. *I see*, he said. *You're the seventy-five-year-old.* He hoped he wouldn't scare her off with his potentially lame jokes.

"Bryce," Georgia said again.

He glanced up at her. "I think she's gonna stay for dinner tomorrow." He held up his phone. "She said cold cereal is one of her favorite things. I'd told her if she wanted to stay tomorrow after the dog bath, I could just pour her a bowl of cereal."

His phone chimed again, and he turned it so he could see, though his aunt and uncle and cousin had to still be reading. *BYOC? Tomorrow, after Lucky's appointment?*

You don't need to bring your own cereal, he said. *I'll have the good stuff, Codi. See you tomorrow.*

Then he shoved his phone in his pocket and faced his family. "I need to buy some Wheat Chex on the way home."

Georgia studied him, and Uncle Otis grinned in that way he had that made Bryce want to laugh out loud. Joey reached up and brushed her cornsilk hair off her face. "That's great, Bryce," she said, her smile full and beautiful. She glanced over to her parents and then linked her arm through his and led him away from them.

"You're brave to tell them," she muttered. "They're like pitbulls with this type of thing."

"What? Dating?" he whispered.

Joey rolled her eyes and tossed her hair again. "I went out with this guy this past semester, and I swear, my daddy called me every day."

"That's because his name was Tim Ryan," Uncle Otis said, practically shouting as he sidled up beside them.

Bryce's eyebrows went up. "Like the trucker who kidnapped all those girls in Montana?"

"Exactly like that." Uncle Otis raised his eyebrows at his nineteen-year-old daughter. "So don't give me grief for callin' my daughter to make sure she was still alive."

"Okay," Georgia said as she joined them in the kitchen. "Enough of that. She's not seeing him anymore, and we don't need to talk about it tonight." She gave Otis a severe look, and Bryce could only grin at them. "I'm calling in the kids and the dogs."

"Here we go," Otis said good-naturedly. "Come sit down, Bryce. Dinner's ready, and we just need to wrangle everyone into their seats."

"Kids," Georgia called out the front door. "Ruby, Emerald, come on."

The first one through the door was Lucky, and Bryce clapped his hands twice and bent down to run them along his dog's back. Lucky went right through his legs so Bryce could scratch his rump, which he did.

Emerald barked once in the house, and Georgia said. "Nope. No barking inside. Quietly." She crouched down in front of the Australian shepherd. "Quietly. Whisper." The dog made zero sound and focused on Georgia exclusively. Bryce figured she was probably a really smart dog who hadn't been able to run the way she needed to and who definitely could be trained if someone would put in the work.

Like Pentagon, he thought, and he knew he didn't have time to take the beagle. So, while Aunt Georgia put Emerald in her crate and tried to get both of her kids to wash up, Bryce pulled out his phone.

I can't take Penta, he sent to Kassie. *You should sell her to Codi.*

You sure? His best friend always wanted the best for him, Bryce knew. They'd had some words today, but that didn't mean they were any different than before.

Yeah, he typed out. *I'm sure.*

He looked up at his uncle as he lifted Ana onto the chair next to him. "Do you think I'm ready to start dating again, Uncle Otis?"

His uncle looked at him, right into his eyes. He'd always been able to see further into Bryce than anyone else, but he didn't look away. "I can't answer that for you, son."

"Yeah." He sighed and looked over to the boy who carried half of his genes. OJ had the dark shock of hair like Bryce, like Otis. His eyes hovered somewhere in the hazel realm, as Bryce's weren't exactly midnight like Uncle Blaze, and Bailey had had blue eyes.

"Bryce," he said, though OJ knew Bryce was his biological father. He never called him Dad or Daddy or anything like that.

They'd sat down and talked it all out, and they'd keep doing that as new things arose.

"What's up, bud?" he asked as Aunt Georgia set a huge platter of steaming beef, potatoes, and carrots in the middle of the table. Bryce's mouth watered, and he looked from the food to his boy.

"It's time to pray," Otis said, which silenced OJ from whatever he might have been about to say. "Your turn, son." He nodded to OJ, who leaned back in his chair and folded his arms.

He squinched his eyes closed, a V pulling his eyebrows closer together in the cutest way. Bryce grinned at him as he folded his own arms, but he didn't want to close his eyes as his son prayed.

OJ was only eight years old, which meant his voice hadn't deepened or dropped yet, and he spoke in the purest childlike voice Bryce had ever heard as he said, "Dear Lord, we're so glad that Bryce could come for dinner tonight. We're thankful for this food, and that Momma could make it for us. Bless us that there will be a lot of leftovers, so we can feed 'em to Emerald. Bless her that she'll be a good dog, so we can adopt her, and don't let Obsidian and Onyx be too mean to her."

Bryce glanced over to Georgia, who watched her son too. OJ paused, and the whole house seemed to hold its breath.

"Bless all the uncles and aunts and cousins," OJ said, more on track now. "Because Uncle Luke has that new baby comin', and I don't think they're ready, and what is Aunt Leigh gonna do with those twins?"

Uncle Otis and Aunt Georgia both cleared their throats at the same time, and it took all of Bryce's willpower to hold his laughter inside. Yes, Uncle Luke and Aunt Sterling were adding their third baby in four years, and Bryce couldn't imagine that either. Otis and Georgia had obviously talked about it, and the innocence of an eight-year-old didn't realize just how much he'd given away.

And Uncle Morris and Aunt Leigh were having twins, but their next youngest child was three already, so it wasn't like they'd have baby upon baby upon baby the way some of his uncles had.

"Did I say to bless the food?" OJ asked. "If I forgot, Lord, bless the food. Bless Ana to be healthy and bless Joey's momma up in Dog Valley. Oh, and speaking of Dog Valley, bless us that we can go to the Lion Lodge this summer, because Daddy says—"

"OJ," Otis barked.

"Amen," the little boy said, and he opened his eyes and relaxed his arms. He didn't seem to think anything had gone awry with his prayer, and he reached for his fork. "Momma, can I have extra carrots?"

"Yes, you may," Georgia said without missing a beat. Bryce could only grin at his son as he watched his momma pile on a few extra carrots with OJ's beef and potatoes. He tended to talk too much, let his mouth get away from him sometimes, and he could definitely see that trait in his little boy.

"You could take some leftovers for dinner tomorrow," Georgia said once they all had food. She sat directly across the table from Bryce, and he looked into her eyes.

"No," OJ said, glancing between the two of them. "We need 'em for Emerald."

"We can't load that dog up with roast beef and send her back to the office." Georgia flicked a look at OJ, but her attention came right back to Bryce.

"You said we could keep her and maybe adopt her," OJ said.

Georgia's mouth twitched, and Bryce looked at OJ now. He didn't know what to say, though, which was why he hadn't kept this child to raise. "How are we gonna go up to the Lion Lodge this summer with another dog?" she asked.

OJ's eyes widened with hope and maybe some shock. "They take dogs."

"They do not," Otis said. "And we have two already, and the cats, and you silly kids." He grinned at everyone at the table. "We have to find someone to babysit all the pets when we leave."

"If Bryce takes the leftovers," OJ said. "He can take the dogs too." He smiled like that was the solution to the world's problems, and Bryce loved him so.

"I bet there's enough for both of us," he said. "But I don't think I'll take any leftovers." Part of him craved a simple dinner with Codi, and something deep inside him told him she needed it to be casual. "I can take the dogs and cats for you if you go to the Lion Lodge."

"Onyx will filet off your flesh while you sleep," Georgia said, shaking her head. "With one claw. No. Not a good idea."

Bryce laughed, the sound truly leaving his body and carrying happiness with it. He couldn't remember when he'd felt like this. It had been a while. "Okay," he said. "But I don't need the leftovers, really. I for-sure pour cold cereal some nights."

Georgia nodded, accepting his refusal of the leftovers. "Okay," she said. "But I'm gonna tell your momma that."

Bryce laughed as he scooped up a bite of meat and potatoes. "You do that, Aunt Georgia. Momma gives me peanut butter puffs for Christmas."

Georgia looked like such a thing should land her best friend —who was Bryce's mother—in a jail cell. Of course, not everyone could give gifts the way Georgia could, and Bryce loved his cold cereal gifts. Groceries were expensive, and if he didn't have to pony up the cash for a cold-cereal-breakfast, he was grateful.

But he would be buying a box—maybe two or three—of Wheat Chex on his way home tonight, because that was his chance to see the gorgeous Codi Hudson again. And that was worth any price.

As he chatted with his family, and then played with the rent-a-puppy, Bryce never let Codi wander too far from his thoughts. When Uncle Otis hugged him goodbye, he held on tight and whispered, "I think you're ready for anything, Bryce." He pulled back and met Bryce's eyes. "Okay?"

"Yeah." Bryce swallowed. "Okay." He waved as he left the house to choruses of goodbyes, and he always felt so loved when he came to Otis and Georgia's house. He kept the radio off as he drove toward the grocery store, and he kept his thoughts caged while he bought the cereal and milk he needed for tomorrow's dinner date.

Then, on the dark highway home, Bryce finally let everything stream through his head, and as he pulled up to his house and the motion-sensor lights flared to life, he came to the same conclusion as Uncle Otis.

"I'm ready," he whispered to Lucky in the backseat, to the house which sat in still silence, to himself. "I'm ready to try dating again."

Now, he just had to wait and see how tomorrow night went with Codi.

6

Codi didn't have much to clean up in her new place, because she'd been there for such a small amount of time. She didn't have any clients in the morning, and therefore, she still lay in bed, reading on her phone, when it rang.

A number she didn't know sat there, and she realized her device read *forwarded* at the top. This was a client. Or potential client, who'd called her business number from her website.

She sat straight up and swiped on the call. "It's Poochy Keen," she said in the chirpiest voice she could muster. "This is Codi."

"Ah, Codi herself," a woman said, her voice registering on the friendly scale. "This is Georgia Young, and I'm wondering what your schedule is like for a couple of dog washes."

The woman's name rang like a gong in Codi's head. Georgia Young.

Bryce had called his aunt Georgia just yesterday. Coral Canyon was a small town, though it had grown over the years. Still, how many Youngs could there be?

She had to be related to him.

"Sure," Codi said smoothly. "Let me get some details. Can you tell me the breed and size of your dogs?"

"I've got a couple of mutts," Georgia said. "Ruby is about fifty-five pounds, and Isla is about thirty. I used to have this black lab, but he went to live on a farm a few miles south of here."

"Okay," Codi said, not sure why she'd told her about a lab that didn't need a bath. "You want them washed and clipped?"

"Yes," she said.

"Okay." Codi didn't need to open her calendar. She had Lucky this afternoon at two, and that was it. "Morning, afternoon? I come to you. I have a big white bus, and as long as there's a place for me to park, I can get the grooming done right on-site."

"Let's see," Georgia said, and Codi thought she heard the flipping of a page. "I'm not in the bookshop on Thursdays. Thursday morning?"

"Sure," Codi said, holding the information in her head. "Nine? Is that too early?"

"I have three dogs right now," she said. "A bird, and two cats. Three kids, and a cowboy husband. You could say five in the morning, and it wouldn't be too early." She laughed, and Codi really liked this woman.

"Good to know," Codi said. "Seeing as how I'm still lying in bed, I think nine is a good time for me."

"Nine it is." She sounded like she might hang up, and Codi leaned into her phone a little more.

"I just need your address," she said. "I've got your phone number from the call, but I have to know where I'm coming."

"Oh, sure." Georgia gave her the name and number of a street in Coral Canyon, and Codi typed it into her notes as quickly as she could. She should've gotten out of bed to take this call. She had a system for scheduling dogs, and it included a giant desk calendar, a real pen, and then an app where she transferred everything so she could have a digital record and find her way while out on the bus.

"Great," she said. "See you Thursday at nine."

The call did end then, and Codi pushed aside her comforter and moved into the second bedroom in her basement apartment, which she'd set up as an office. Well, if a folding table and chair, the desk calendar, an old laptop, and a lava lamp could be considered an office. For Codi, it was.

She jotted down the names of the dogs—she memorized those for her clients—the time, the address, and then looked at her phone for Georgia's number. Since she was still really new to Coral Canyon, the address didn't mean much to her.

After powering up the laptop, Codi put in the address to see where it was. "Only ten minutes from here," she murmured, zooming in on the map. "Looks like plenty of parking for the bus."

She opened her scheduling app, something that had been invented and developed for small business owners like her, and typed in all the information she'd just written on her physical desk calendar. Now AppointMate would notify her of her dog washing appointment and display the address for her. It would even navigate her there.

Feeling supremely satisfied that she'd gotten a customer—even if Georgia was Bryce's aunt—Codi felt more empowered to try to drum up more business. She posted on her social media, set a reminder to take a picture with the clean and fluffy Lucky that afternoon, and went to her website to make sure everything looked the way she wanted it to.

It did, because Codi had checked it so many times, she'd lost count. She tended to be a little obsessive about some things, and her dog grooming business was one of those.

She opened the graphic design site she used, moved the cartoon dog a fraction of a centimeter, then moved him back. She just needed to get these sent to the printer, and then she needed to hit the streets. She needed to find other small businesses who would put her flyers on their check-out counters, and she'd need to start attending the small business meetings in town.

Codi had grown up with technology, and she was smart and savvy with the clicking of a mouse and typing in search terms. Within a half-hour, she had a list of a dozen small businesses she could call, from the hardware store, to the furniture store, to this perfect little book shop on Main Street.

"Wait a minute...." Codi peered closer at her screen, her vision not as sharp as she'd like it. She knew she needed glasses, but she didn't want to get them. Contacts, maybe, but she also wasn't super keen on putting her finger in her eye every day.

"Beck's Books." She looked at her phone and swiped it back on to get to her AppointMate she'd just inputted. "Georgia

Young." But the Georgia Young on the phone had said she wasn't working at the book shop on Thursday. Hadn't she?

Codi clicked on the ABOUT tab on the book shop website, and a picture of pretty blonde woman came up. Not that Codi would know her until she showed up on Mountain Dale Road on Thursday.

But the name at the top gave it all away.

Georgia Young has owned Beck's Books since its inception, back before she married Country Quad superstar, Otis Young.

"Country Quad superstar?"

Codi felt herself falling down a rabbit hole, but there was no going back now. No parachute in the world could slow her down either, and her fingers ached and her stomach growled before she sat back from the computer.

Her shoulders, which she'd hunched forward for the last—

"Holy chili cheese fries." Codi swiped her phone off the folding table, slammed her laptop closed, and bustled out of the room.

She had to be up in Dog Valley to give Lucky his bath in an hour. She hadn't eaten, hadn't brushed her teeth that morning, had none of her equipment ready, and could absolutely not show up for her first dinner date with the handsome Bryce Young looking the way she did.

In the bathroom, she got a washcloth wet with the hottest water her sink would put out as she brushed her teeth. She washed her face and neck, instantly feeling better. Her stomach still pinched at her, but she looked at herself in the mirror and ran both hands through her hair.

She didn't particularly want to wear her wig today, not to do a golden retriever wash in the bus, but Bryce had seen her wearing it already. "Maybe I should go with a totally different style."

Across the hall, she faced her mannequin heads. She owned six wigs of varying lengths, styles, and colors. Most of them were blonde, because she had blue eyes and light eyebrows, but she did have a reddish-brown wig that fell in semi-curly waves to her chin.

She needed time to get this wig on right, and she needed more time to at least smooth out the texture of her skin, swipe on some lip gloss, and choose some clothes she wouldn't be embarrassed to wear in front of Bryce for as long as it took to consume a bowl of cereal.

In short, she needed more time.

So Codi picked up her phone and started texting Bryce. *Hey, I'm so sorry, but I'm gonna be a little late for Lucky today. I should be there by* 2:30.

That gave her an hour to get ready, and a half-hour to get her big white bus up to Dog Valley.

No problem, Bryce said, and she wondered if he was part golden retriever too. The thought made her smile, and then Codi got down to business. After all, this was her first date with a cowboy in over seven years, and she couldn't just show up with yesterday's makeup on.

"Heya, Lucky," she called as the golden retriever saw her and started running in her direction. Bryce walked yards behind him, but she waved her hand to acknowledge him. He waved back, his smile evident even from this distance. His cowboy hat curled up on the sides, and he wore a long-sleeved shirt and jeans, both of which had to be adding to the heat of the day.

She knew why he did, as she'd grown up on a farm too. Insects and the sun were a cowboy's biggest enemies in the summer, and long sleeves and jeans protected the skin. Still, she expected him to be a little sweaty when he arrived, and she cooed at his dog until he did.

Then she looked up at him, and he wasn't all that sweaty. He did smell like horses and dirt and everything pure and good about the country, and Codi could admit she liked that. She rose and tucked her hair behind her ear. "Hey."

"I don't think we've met," he said, his smile stuck to his face and those eyes dancing with pure delight. "The gorgeous woman I met yesterday had blonde hair. You know, bangs? Went down to about here too." He cut one hand across the middle of his bicep.

"Yeah," Codi said with a smile. She'd barely made it here by two-thirty as it was, because she'd maybe put on too much eye makeup for a single dog wash. Not only that, but she had a different blouse and a pair of ankle boots stashed away in the bus, and she planned to change before she knocked on Bryce's door and returned his fluffy, spotless canine to him.

"I like the darker hair," he said. "It's just...different. You look so different."

"It's a wig," she finally admitted, watching him for his reaction. "I didn't go to the salon this morning or anything."

His eyebrows went up, and that lethal smile slipped. "Oh."

"Yeah." Codi absently scrubbed along Lucky's ears. "I have hair. I'm not bald or anything, but it's...I don't like it."

"You don't like your hair?"

Codi didn't want to explain this to him, at least not right now. "Not especially." She squinted into the sun, her shades forgotten in the bus. "Can we talk about it later? Maybe over Cap'n Crunch or something? I'm already a little late, and I want to get going on Lucky."

"Sure thing," Bryce said easily. He struck her as a pretty easy-going guy, and Codi really needed that right now. He looked over to her bus. "I'll leave you to it. I'll be out on the ranch, but if you need me, just call."

"Will you hear a text?"

"Yes, ma'am."

She nodded, because Codi would rather text over call any day of the week. She wished she could text nine-one-one, because she totally would.

Bryce reached out and squeezed her hand. "It's good to see you, Codi." A fiery hot fizzle ran up her arm and zinged in her shoulder. Then he pulled back, that smile oh-so-glorious, and turned. "I'll be back about five-thirty."

"Okay," she called after him, and wow, the view of him walking away sure wasn't bad either. Codi schooled her thoughts and dropped her eyes to the dog at her knees, her face burning over her behavior.

"Come on," she muttered to the dog, and she led him over to her bus. She had air conditioning, but she'd still parked in the shade along his driveway, and she refused to let herself look out the big windows that faced the lane Bryce had walked down.

Instead, she focused on her job, her nerves vibrating a little harder with every minute that brought her closer to Bryce's front door and their cereal-for-dinner date.

"All right," she finally declared to Lucky. "You're all done." He grinned at her, his big, pink tongue lolling out of his mouth. "You look so stinking handsome." She managed a smile too, and she started cleaning up as Lucky sniffed around the bus. Codi found a bag of dog treats and gave him one, and he settled down to chew through the dried pig's ear with one paw on top and one beneath.

That gave her enough time to change her shirt, then prep her bus ready for another dog, though she didn't have one for a couple more days, and when she couldn't put it off any longer, she took Lucky up to Bryce's front door. The dog put both front paws up on the step, his nose right at the seam, clearly expecting her to just open the door and go in.

Codi couldn't do that, but she knocked. Bryce didn't come to the door. She rang the bell. Still nothing. Lucky whined and paced on the porch, and Codi didn't know what to do about him. He could run anywhere, so surely he didn't need to use the bathroom.

"Lucky?"

He barked and looked at the door, then her. He barked again, and the urgency of it sent a shiver of fear through Codi. Without thinking too hard, she opened the door. Lucky lunged through it, making it settle open more, and she called, "Bryce?"

Lucky's claws, though now trimmed appropriately, skittered

on the hard floor in the kitchen, and he barked again. Codi stepped up into the house, and that was when she heard the very horrifying sound of a human moaning.

"Bryce?" She hurried through the living room now, her heartbeat thumping hard at what she might find in the kitchen. She arrived, and she didn't have to wonder anymore.

"Bryce." She ran toward where he'd fallen to the floor, skidding on her knees as she got close. "Hey, wake up. Talk to me." She spoke in a firm, authoritative voice. She'd worked on a farm. She'd cared for her ill mother. She'd seen a lot of situations that involved blood, and she could tell Bryce had been injured out on the farm.

The blood trailed in from the back door, and his eyes opened as she leaned over him. "Hey, hey, hey," she said. "You've gotta wake up. Tell me what happened."

"That new horse," he muttered, his eyes sort of wandering somewhere past her. "Freaked...out...."

"I'm going to call an ambulance," Codi said.

"No." Bryce tried to sit up, and that caused a mighty groan to come out of his mouth too.

"Hey, don't move."

But he kept moving as he sat all the way up. "I just—" He looked around. "I passed out."

"Yes, you did." And the worst part was, Codi had no idea how long he'd been lying there, alone on his kitchen floor. "I really think you need to go to the hospital."

"I just don't like the sight of my own blood." He pressed his eyes closed. "Yours is fine. A dog, a horse, whatever. But my own?" He pressed his lips together and shook his head.

"Where did you get hurt?" He had blood on his face, his hands, his neck, and Codi couldn't locate the source of it.

"Kass and I got a new horse a couple of weeks ago. I've been working with him this week, and he is so not ready for me." He kept his eyes closed as he spoke, and Codi listened to make sure it wasn't slurred. Didn't seem to be. "His name's Dragon, and he is a beast. He body-slammed me against the wall as he reared up, and I got jabbed with a nail."

"Sounds like you could have some horrible disease from that," she said. "What is it? Tinnitus? Tech...tonic?" She grinned when he did. "Titanium?"

"Yeah," he said dryly. "I think I'm going to get a bacterial infection called *titanium* from a puncture wound." He actually laughed, and Codi gave herself a lot of credit for joining him.

He opened his eyes and met hers. "It's not bad. It just bled a lot, and I was fine until I got inside and saw it all down my side." He didn't look that way, but held his gaze on hers. "The nail wasn't rusty or anything. It literally just jabbed me good." He reached up with his right hand, sucked in a breath, and lowered it again. "Right in my lats there."

Codi sure wasn't a nurse, but she knew she had to either call an ambulance and ruin the dinner date, or get him into the bathroom, strip off his shirt, and fix the problem.

"All right," she said. "I'll see what I can do." She glared at him and leaned closer. "But if I think this is more than just a little wound, I *will* call the ambulance, and you *are* going to the hospital."

"You got it," he said, and then she stood so she could help him do the same. Codi wasn't overly emotional about things, especially since her momma had died, and she couldn't remember the last time she'd been to church.

But as she steadied Bryce and helped the much larger man get to his feet, all she could think was, *Please Lord, don't let this be too bad.*

Please, Lord, don't let this be too bad.

Please, Lord, don't let this be too bad.

Bryce eased himself onto the closed toilet, the guest bathroom just down the hall that led to the bedrooms suddenly the smallest room in the world. That, or he just felt like he'd grown ten feet and put on four hundred pounds, because Codi certainly wasn't taking up all the room.

She stood at the sink and appraised him. "Can you lift your arm?"

"Do I have to?"

"That shirt has to come off," she said. "You've got blood all down your pants too, but once we get you bandaged up, you can leave everything in the tub and change...in private." She took a step toward him, and she really was stunning with the dark reddish-purplish-brown hair. Bryce wanted to reach up and thread his fingers through it just to see what it felt like.

Maybe he had hit his head too hard, because his good hand actually moved a little like he might touch Codi in this tiny bathroom. Thankfully, he didn't, and she undid the buttons at the end of his sleeves, then moved in really close to him so all he could see was the floral print on her blouse as she made quick work of the buttons down the front of his shirt.

"Okay," she said. "It's coming off." She got it over his right side just fine, then shimmied around him to the left side, which was where he'd been hurt. He gasped as something pulled in the middle of his back, and she said, "Sorry, sorry. It was just—you had some fabric stuck to the wound. I got it."

She pushed the shirt down his bicep, sending licking fire along every particle of his skin. Heck, even his toes inside his cowboy boots blazed with the touch of this woman. He held very still while she tossed his shirt into the tub behind her.

"Okay, yeah," she said. "I see it. Let me get it cleaned up." She moved in front of him again, and Bryce kept opening and closing his fingers into a fist. Then not a fist. Then a fist. He just wanted to make sure his extremities still worked, and it gave him something to focus on besides him sitting half-naked and bleeding in his bathroom.

Codi took the warm, wet washcloth around him again, and he said, "I can face the other way."

"Okay," she murmured, and Bryce flinched as she touched his back. "I'm going to work toward it. Tell me if it hurts." She seemed to barely be touching him, and he started to relax. She straightened and added, "Yeah, turn around while I rinse this out. Eyes closed for a minute."

"Is it that bad?"

"It's—there's some blood."

He dutifully closed his eyes as she moved in front of him

again, and when she told him to, he turned and faced the tub and the back wall of the bathroom.

"Now you won't have to see it," she said. She also didn't have to move around him, and he held very still for her.

"I grew up on a potato farm," she said. "I've been nicked, kicked, and bruised more times than I can count."

He smiled but didn't say anything.

"I've got two older brothers," she said. "I've doctored them both up lots of times. This one time, Rand—he's my oldest brother—got hit with a stalk of corn that came whipping back. Gave him quite the black eye, and it was bleeding." She gave a light laugh.

"You grew corn on a potato farm?"

"It was in our family plot," she said. "But we do have to rest and rotate the fields."

"Yeah, we do that here too," he said, the thought he'd had yesterday about hiring her to work at the Rising Sun Ranch forming in his mind again.

"When my daddy stepped on a wasp's nest, he had stings up and down his legs, all over his back, everywhere. Me and my momma—" Codi's voice caught, and Bryce opened his eyes. His back felt a little numb, and he wasn't sure what she was doing back there. He looked over his shoulder but couldn't quite see her.

"Me and my momma spent hours on him," she continued in a much quieter voice. "Some of those stings would then weep, and they'd crack. It was so painful for him. He had so much poison in him, we eventually did take him to the hospital. They had to give him a series of shots. Saved his life."

"Wow," Bryce said.

"They told us there that we were very good nursemaids," Codi said. "That he might not have done as well as he did if we hadn't cleaned him up and dressed the wounds the way we did."

"So you're saying I'm in good hands."

"I have been told I have very good hands."

He heard the playful beat in her voice now, and he wished he could see her smile. Codi didn't laugh or smile as often as he did, but he reminded himself this was only the third time he'd been around her.

"I don't think this is too bad, actually," she said. "I'm going to clean it and bandage it." Those magic hands pulled away from him, and the next time she touched him, she put something foamy and hot on his back. He yelped and tried to get away, but Codi held his shoulder with one of those "very good hands."

He growled while she said, "It's the hydrogen peroxide. It's cleaning it all out. Hold still."

"It hurts," he grumbled.

"Yeah, I didn't think we'd be crammed into the bathroom to have a birthday party."

The stinging in Bryce's back ebbed away, and he managed to smile. "I do have some frozen birthday cake in my freezer."

"You're joking."

"I never joke about birthday cake. It's from our quarterly family party."

"I...well, I don't even know what that is," Codi said.

"My family is huge, right?" Bryce said, his tongue deciding it was his turn to talk. "There are scads and scads of birthdays, so my grandparents host a big quarterly family birthday party four times a year. We just had one oh, I don't know. Mid-April? And I got to bring home some of the leftover cake." He refrained from telling her that every single person he came in contact with wanted to give him some sort of leftover. He normally didn't mind, because he liked a hot lunch and a homemade dinner, but he didn't love spending time in the kitchen.

"We can have it after our cereal," he said.

"Do you need to finish up on the ranch?" Codi asked. "Where did Dragon get to?"

"I locked him in the Red Stable." Bryce rolled his neck, only feeling a tiny pull down in his lat. "So yeah, we've got to go back out and put him away properly."

"I can do it," Codi said.

"I don't trust him," he said. "We'll go out together."

She patted his back, about a couple of inches below where his arm met it. "I got it all tidied up."

Bryce stood and turned to face her. "Thank you, Codi." He saw the bloody washcloth, the wipes, the gauze wrappers, and the bathroom swayed again. He instantly squeezed his eyes shut, and Codi put both hands on his forearms.

"I'm gonna walk you into your room," she said. "You can get out of those dirty jeans and meet me on the back deck when you're ready, okay? Don't open your eyes."

"Mm." He moved when she tugged on his hands, and he kept going, trusting her every step of the way until she said, "Okay, Bryce. I'll see you outside."

He opened his eyes, and sure enough, he now stood in his bedroom. He undid his belt and pushed his jeans to the ground.

Even his boxers had been stained with blood, and he shed everything, wishing he had time to shower.

He didn't, so he dumped his clothes in the hamper and pulled on fresh everything. He could move his left arm okay, but it did hurt, and he figured it would be sore for a while. "Relief comes through Jesus Christ," he whispered to himself, something the pastor up here in Dog Valley had preached several months ago.

Physical pain? Christ had suffered through that. Emotional ailments? Christ understood those too. Mental illness? Sin? Heartache? Christ could relieve all of those—and more. The peace he needed, the release from a heavy workload, the soothing of a wound on his back—all of it could be relieved through Christ.

When he passed the guest bathroom, Codi had cleaned it all up so there wasn't a drop of blood in sight, and pure appreciation moved through Bryce. She'd tenderly cared for him too, and he found her in the kitchen, throwing something in his trash.

"You didn't have to clean up the bathroom." He looked at the floor, the walls, the door handle. "Or the kitchen."

"I know." Codi faced him, her eyes crinkling as a soft smile appeared on her face. "But I didn't want you to see it and pass out again." She nodded toward the door. "Should we go get the dragon contained? Then we can eat."

His stomach raged at him to put something in it first, but he really didn't want to go back out on the ranch once he and Codi sat down to eat. "Yeah, let's do this."

He led the way outside, and once Codi had followed him

down the steps from the deck to the backyard, he wondered if he could hold her hand.

To stop himself, he asked, "So you have two brothers? Older or younger?"

"Older," she said. "Both married. You?"

"I've got three siblings," he said. "Two sisters and a brother." That wasn't entirely true, but Bryce didn't want to get into all the half-things and how Abby was technically his step-mom. He didn't think of her that way, and he certainly wasn't going to spill his guts about his mom in Boise, not when he hadn't spoken to her in over six years.

"Are they married?"

Bryce chuckled and shook his head. "No. Melissa is ten. Carver is six, and Pippa is four."

"*Four* years old?"

"Four," Bryce said, grinning at her. "And she's the sweetest thing on the planet, but she will use whatever tactics necessary to get what she wants. She's got her momma's redheaded fire."

Codi simply looked at him while Bryce tried to look everywhere but at her. "Fine," he finally said. "But this is like your hair thing. I don't want to talk about this tonight."

"Fair enough."

"They're my half-siblings. My daddy got remarried when I was like, seventeen or something."

"Ah, I see." Codi stepped a little closer to him, and he wasn't sure if that was on purpose or not. "And how old are you?"

His hand brushed hers, and his breath caught in his throat. On the next step, he took her hand in his, rejoicing silently when she didn't pull away. Bryce cleared his throat. "Twenty-eight. You?"

"Thirty-two," she said.

He glanced over to her then, the evening light on her face golden and gorgeous. "I wouldn't have thought you were older than me."

"It's my height," she said. "Everyone thinks I'm a teenager."

"Seriously?" He hadn't thought that, not even for a moment.

She nodded, though. "Oh, yeah. Sometimes I get stopped at the grocery store and people ask me where my momma is to pay for all the stuff in my cart."

Bryce scoffed. "That can't be true."

She grinned at him. "It's true."

"Is that why you...wear the wigs?"

She shook her head. "No. My hair is just really thin. It never really grew well, and it's...well, it's white."

"White?"

"Pure white," she said. "I colored it all growing up, and I just got tired of it. Dealing with my momma and everything, I just started wearing wigs."

They neared the Red Stable, and Bryce slowed. He turned Codi toward him and offered her what he hoped was a friendly, kind smile. "You've mentioned your momma a couple of times. What happened with her?" She'd mentioned she was sick, and Bryce feared the worst as pure sadness entered Codi's lovely blue eyes.

"She died, oh, about fourteen months ago now." She drew in a long breath and looked to her left, away from him. "Cancer. She held on for a long time. I moved from here to California to tend to her years ago. After she died, I just...drifted. I've been living out of my bus, and just touring the western states."

Her eyes came back to his, and Bryce really wanted to dive into the depths of her and swim around. "Then I came back here."

He had so many questions for her, like if she was planning to stay in town, or if she'd been to Four Corners, or why she hadn't gone back to her family farm. Instead, he pulled her into his arms and held her against his chest. "I'm sorry about your momma," he whispered into her hair, thrilled when she wrapped her arms around him too.

They stood there in the dwindling near-summer light, and Bryce could do so for hours. Days. Months. He wanted to know so much more about this woman, and he wanted to see her hair and tell her how beautiful she was, and he needed to share some of the deeper secrets that lived inside him with her.

Instead, after several long moments, he drew in a breath, stepped away, and together, they faced the Red Stable. "Let's get this dragon put away," he said. "I'm starving."

He moved in front of her to open the door, and immediately, the hot breath of a horse snuffling met his hand. He pulled it back and dodged out of the way.

Dragon—the big, brown beast—started to come outside, but Codi held up both hands and yipped at him. "Go on," she commanded.

To Bryce's pure surprise, the horse settled and looked right at her. He dipped his head, almost bowing to Codi, and she lowered her hands. "Ah, yes," she said as she moved forward.

"Codi," he warned. But Dragon didn't charge. He didn't rear up. He certainly didn't body slam *her* into the wall.

As he watched, pure shock moving through him, she put her hand on the bridge of Dragon's nose and said, "Come on, now. You'll feel better in your stall." Then she stepped past him and entered the stable.

The horse turned to follow her, his hooves clopping on the cement, leaving Bryce standing several feet away, completely dumbfounded. As the horse's tail swished back inside, he launched himself into action too. He entered the stable in enough time to watch Codi lead Dragon—without a rope; without a lead—to his stall. She opened the door and said, "Go on. Get in there," and the horse just did it.

In so many ways, she reminded him of Kassie and her special ability with horses. As Codi closed the gate and turned toward him, Bryce knew he was going to let the words gathering in his throat burst from his mouth.

"You're incredible," he said as she neared. "I need you out here. What do you think about working for me? For the ranch? I lost my only full-time person when he got married a few months ago." Bryce gestured down the aisle, hoping that was a universal sign for *what just happened here was incredible.*

"Like, you want to give me a job?"

"Yeah," Bryce said. "I'm offering you a job."

8

odi frowned, because she'd been working for over a decade to get away from working for someone else. She'd grown up on a farm, didn't particularly want a farm, and certainly didn't want to have to report to a boss every morning at a certain time.

"I don't know," she said, her stomach doing a weird swimmy thing.

Bryce turned back to the house, ever the picture of calm, cool, and cowboy perfection. "Tell me what your objections are."

"I want to get my dog grooming business going again," she said.

"I'm hearing...you need flexible hours." He cut her a look out of the corner of his eye, and Codi wished he'd take her hand in his again. She wasn't sure she was brave enough to reach over and grab onto his, and in fact, she tucked hers in her pockets as a keen sense of self-consciousness flowed through her.

"Yeah," she said. "I don't really want to report to a boss."

"What if I said you could set your own hours?"

"Then I'd say you're a big, fat liar Mister Young." She grinned up into the evening sky. It had started to bruise, and oh, Codi loved it. "Horses are the biggest divas on the planet," she continued. "They want to be fed at the same time every day, and given treats, and put out into the sunniest, greenest pasture." She scoffed, really adding on some extra sound. "Set my own hours. Right."

Bryce grinned at her and slowed enough to stop. She went with him, because he possessed some strange magnetism over her. "What?" she asked.

"You're really good with horses," he said. "What if I said I'd do all the feeding, because I'm here on their regularly scheduled hours. But you could come—whenever you can; whenever you want—to work with the—" He glanced back toward the stable she'd just been inside. "The tougher ones. You really seem to know how to communicate with them." He rotated his injured shoulder and added, "Then maybe I won't get any more puncture wounds."

Codi wanted to say yes, if only to make him smile. Heck, he'd probably whoop into the night and sweep her off her feet. They'd twirl while he laughed, and she'd get to grip those broad, sexy shoulders.

"...take your time," Bryce said, drawing Codi back to the land of reality, not the fantasy world where she sailed off into the blissful sunset with Bryce on the second day she'd met him.

"Okay," she said. "Like how Kassie is trying to decide about Pentagon?"

"I told her this morning I can't take him." Bryce hung his head, and Codi didn't like that. She wanted him to cheer up, show her that smile, and tease with her some more. "So she'll probably be callin' you soon." He looked over to her. "Do you still want him?"

"Yeah, of course," Codi said.

Bryce nodded, and then he linked his arm through her elbow, as she had her hands in her pockets still. "All right," he said. "So you're gonna get a new dog, and you're gonna think real hard about coming to work out here upon your own whims, and we're gonna have great big bowls of cereal for dinner."

Codi did the most surprising thing of her life—she giggled. "Sounds about right," she said, wondering who she'd become in the past forty-eight hours.

Bryce grinned at her though, as if she hadn't done anything strange at all. "I got the Wheat Chex."

"Perfect." She removed her hand from her pocket and let her fingers slide down his forearm and settle between his. "I have to say, Mister Young, that I did a little bit of digging this morning."

"Digging? I thought you were renting a place."

"Internet digging."

"Oh, stars in heaven." Bryce actually tilted his head back and looked up into the twilight. "Lord, do not tell me she found any videos, okay? But of course she did, because my daddy is a famous country music rockstar, and I've been on tour with him." He let out a long sigh, like this was the worst thing he'd ever had to do—travel the country with his famous father.

She started to do that giggling thing again as Bryce said, "Well, at least help me with this conversation, would you?" He grinned, his steps slow and steady even as he kept his attention up in the heavens. "I kinda like this woman," he added in a mock whisper. "Don't let me mess up too badly, okay?"

He drew in a deep breath and looked over to her. "Internet digging?" he asked, as if he hadn't just had an out-loud, vocal conversation with God. "What does that mean?"

She gaped at him, her chest vibrating with every beat of her heart. "You know what it means," she said. She leaned up onto her toes for a step, then two, as she mock whispered back at him, "I found the *videos* of you playing on stage with Country Quad."

Bryce faced his house as they got closer to it again. Codi marveled that she'd found him passed out on his kitchen floor less than an hour ago. "Country Quad?" He chuckled as he added, "I really don't think so, Codi."

"Oh, come on, Bryce."

He grinned fully now, and Codi basked in his light. "Okay, I can answer anything you want about Country Quad." He took her up the steps to the deck, Lucky trailing along behind them. The dog entered the house first somehow, and Bryce gestured for Codi to go in after him.

"You're not Bryce," a man said, and Codi came face-to-face with a man she'd seen on the multiple album covers, the website, and the videos she'd watched online.

"I'm right here," Bryce said as he stepped inside. He pulled the sliding glass door closed behind him while Trace Young bent to pat Lucky. His smile completely transformed his face, and he chuckled as Bryce stepped into his arms and hugged him.

"I'm interrupting something, aren't I?" Trace asked, his eyes glued to Codi.

Bryce fell to his side, and with both of them facing her, she wanted to shrink back outside. "Uncle Trace," Bryce said with that trademark smile on his face. "This is Codi Hudson. She's Lucky's groomer, and today, she was my nurse, and an expert horse handler, and we were just gonna pour some cereal for dinner and maybe sit on the back deck and watch the sun go behind the Tetons."

"Mm." Trace Young didn't open his mouth to make the noise, and Codi got the impression that he played the serious part whenever he could.

"Codi, this here's my uncle Trace. He plays the best guitar in the band, and he helps Otis write a bunch of the songs." He glanced over to his uncle, who didn't deny any of it. "Oh, and his son is Harry Young. Did you happen upon him in your online snooping?"

"It was *digging*," Codi said as she gave him a withering look. When her eyes moved to Trace, she put a smile on her face. "It's great to meet you." She took a couple of steps toward him and extended her hand toward him.

Trace gave her a firm shake and said, "Likewise, Miss Codi." He looked over to Bryce, and Codi did too, and he practically shivered from heel to head.

"What did you need, Uncle Trace?"

"You said you were workin' with that new horse, and you weren't sure how it was going to go, and then you haven't answered your phone for a couple of hours." He raised his eyebrows at Bryce, who shifted his feet. Then Trace looked over to Codi. "You said she'd been your nurse."

His eyes scanned Bryce down to his toes and back. "So I'm guessing the nagging feeling in my gut to get up here and make sure you weren't dead somewhere wasn't completely without merit."

"I'm fine, Uncle Trace." Bryce moved into the kitchen and opened a cupboard. He got down a pair of bowls—not three—and put them on the counter.

"Yeah." His uncle peered into the trashcan. "All these bloody wipes look just *fine*." He raised only his eyes to Bryce, and Codi turned away to hide her smile.

"Dragon reared up and bashed me into the wall," Bryce said. "I got a little...." He glanced over to Codi.

"Impaled?" she suggested, and Trace's attention whipped to her.

"Impaled?" he repeated.

"Yeah, impaled," Bryce said. "That's a good word. I was bleeding a little, and I—"

"A lot," Codi interjected. "He was bleeding a lot, and when I got done with Lucky and brought him back to the house, Bryce had passed out."

"I'm calling your father," Trace said.

"Whoa, whoa," Bryce said, coming back around the peninsula. "Uncle Trace, I'm twenty-eight years old, not eight. I'm fine."

"It was a tiny puncture wound," Codi said.

Bryce turned and looked at her, his eyes blazing as he shook his head. "Can you not say things like 'puncture wound,' please?"

She grinned back at him. "I got him all patched up, and I got Dragon back in his stall."

"I'm fine, Uncle Trace," Bryce said again. "Codi got me all patched up, and she got Dragon back into the stall."

"Can I see your puncture wound?" Trace hadn't given him an inch, and Codi really liked this man.

Bryce released the biggest sigh Codi had ever heard a person sigh, and he swiped off his cowboy hat and tossed it onto the dining room table. She wondered if he sat there and ate his meals by himself.

He pulled his shirt up and over his head again, and Codi couldn't look away. The man clearly worked with heavy objects every single day, and he had muscles everywhere she looked. "See?" He turned his back on Trace and Codi. "It's fine. It's nothing."

Codi took a couple of steps toward him. "It's bleeding through a little bit, but I can change out the gauze." She arrived at Trace's side. "It really wasn't that bad."

"Let's change it now."

"Uncle Trace."

"Why didn't you go to the hospital?" Trace asked.

"Neither of us thought it was that bad," Bryce said.

"I'll get the stuff," Codi said. "You'll have to sit, Bryce. You're too tall for me to reach." She bustled off to get the medical supplies from his bathroom, and she heard him and his uncle start to talk in low voices behind her.

She took a steeling breath and looked at herself in the mirror before she went back into the kitchen. Bryce sat on the barstool, and Trace had already peeled back the other gauze pad. He held a paper towel to Bryce's shoulder, and he grumbled something Codi couldn't quite make out.

"What do you think?" she asked his uncle.

Trace's dark eyes devoured her, but Codi didn't know him at all, and she had no idea how to decipher his expression. "I think it's probably okay, and that you did a good job doctoring him up."

Bryce's shoulders shook slightly as he laughed, and Codi put a fresh pad over the wound as Trace pulled the paper towel back. She taped it into place and Trace picked up Bryce's shirt and handed it back to him.

"All right," he drawled. "I'll get out of your hair." He paused as he looked at Codi. "It really was great to meet you." He nodded his cowboy hat at her and headed for the exit.

"Don't call my daddy," Bryce called to his uncle, but only the closing of the front door answered back.

"It's not that bad," Codi said. "The blood that bled through was old."

Bryce stood up and faced her. "I feel like I have to disclose something." For the first time in the past couple of days, he looked nervous.

Cute too, but nervous.

"Go on, then," she said, her lips tipping up.

"That was my uncle, right?"

"Right."

"He's one of eight," Bryce said, reaching up and running both hands through his hair. "Not to mention my parents. With my grandparents, there are twenty adults—twenty, Codi—who like to make sure I'm okay. I barely cook, because I never eat here at home on the weekends. My aunts send me home with copious amounts of leftovers, and sometimes they just drive up here and drop off whole meals."

He paused only long enough to take a breath, and then his mouth ran away from him again. "I get no less than fifty family texts every day, and that's just on a normal Tuesday. If there's something—*anything*—going on in the family, it can climb into the hundreds."

Pacing away, he threw both of his hands up into the air. "It was a dinner date of cold cereal, for crying out loud."

Codi started to laugh then, and it seemed to take all of the past worries with it as it left her body. Bryce did not join her, which caused her to curb her giggles sooner than she would've otherwise. He stood in the kitchen, looking a little lost, and Codi moved over to him.

"I'm hungry, and someone promised me a sunset on a deck."

"You want to stay?"

"Why would I want to leave?"

"I can guarantee that my father will be calling in the next half-hour," he said. "An hour at the most." He pointed toward the front door. "And that was one of my least intrusive uncles."

"I liked him." Codi ran her hand along the top of Bryce's belt and continued toward the bowls he'd put out. "Spoons, spoons."

"They're right here." Bryce opened a drawer as he crowded into the kitchen with her. His house boasted plenty of space, and the kitchen was way bigger than the bathroom, but it still felt far too small.

He got out the milk, and then he started loading the counter with boxes of cereal. "The Wheat Chex," he said. "I like these frosted mini wheat squares." He put down a box of those. "My momma likes these Cocoa Krispies with cream, and she gives me these peanut butter puffs for Christmas."

Codi picked up the box of Wheat Chex, which hadn't been opened yet. She did that, pouring in only half a bowl. "I think I'll...." She plucked the peanut butter puffs from down on the end, ignoring his watchful gaze. She poured another half-bowl of cereal and reached for a spoon.

"You're *mixing*?" Bryce asked.

Her eyes met his. "Is there a law against mixing cereals?" She reached for the gallon of milk he'd gotten out of the fridge.

"I'm honestly surprised you haven't made a break for the exit," he grumbled. "Do what you want with the cereal." He poured himself a bowl of the mini wheat squares, doused them with milk, and said, "C'mon, Lucky. Let's keep our promise and show Miss Codi the sunset."

She grinned at the golden retriever who trotted over to the door, as if he knew Bryce was going to go outside. He went first, and Bryce once again waited for Codi.

He sat backward on the bench at the picnic table, facing the mountains. She joined him, and they crunched through their cereal for a few moments in peaceful silence. Codi sure liked being with him, and she never thought in a million years she'd feel like this with another cowboy.

She wanted to tease him about how he talked to himself, how he prayed right out loud, and how he let literally every emotion he felt show on his face. She had questions about his family, about Country Quad, about his life on this ranch and how he'd come to be here.

Instead, she finished her duo of cereal as the last of the sun dipped below the mountains in the west, making everything instantly cooler. The sun's rays jettisoned up now, painting the sky and the clouds in it in fiery colors that made her smile and lean into Bryce's side.

He took her bowl and nested it in his, then he put them both on the table behind him. Then he put his arm around her, and Codi truly sank into the warmth of his embrace.

No words needed.

9

ryce could practically feel the questions teeming inside Codi, but she didn't let a single one out. Dinner had maybe taken fifteen minutes, and they'd not spoken a single word. She knew about Country Quad; she'd seen the videos of him on tour with the band; he'd survived a chance encounter with Uncle Trace.

As the twilight faded to dusk, and the last of the sun's rays fully disappeared, he finally moved. Codi sat up, and the magic between them broke. He was tired, and he wasn't sure if that came from the blood loss or just because he worked like a dog seven days a week, but he didn't want Codi to go quite yet.

"I have a question for you," he said. "We can just have one each, okay?"

"One question?"

"Yeah." He nudged her with his elbow. "I know you're dying to ask me tons of things."

"Am I?" She smiled at him, a light laugh accompanying the pretty gesture.

"Yeah, you are." He leaned forward and rested his elbows on his knees and let his hands hang down. "Do you go to church, Miss Codi?"

She didn't jump right in with a *yes*, and Bryce moved his head the minimal amount possible to see her. "Not for a while, I haven't," she admitted. "You obviously go."

"It's obvious?"

"I think you've prayed out loud four times tonight alone." She reached up and tucked some of that dark hair behind her ear, and Bryce still wouldn't have known it wasn't real. "Okay, my turn."

"Here we go." He looked out across the backyard, though he couldn't see much. He could flip one switch inside and light the whole farm, but he didn't need to run the electricity all night long for no reason.

"Do you always talk to yourself?" she asked. "And say whatever's on your mind?"

"That's your question?"

"For tonight," she said, like there would be more of these nights. Bryce found himself yearning for such a thing, and he took a moment to gather his thoughts.

So, no, he didn't *always* say whatever was on his mind. But he said, "Yeah, about," because he knew he talked too much a lot of the time. "My therapist says I'm a verbal processor. If it comes out of my mouth, I have an easier time getting it to stay still long enough for me to think through."

"Interesting," she said.

"Which part? That I have to say stuff out loud, or that I see a counselor?"

Codi reached over and pulled his hand up and into her lap. "Both, I suppose."

In his back pocket, his phone started to vibrate, and Bryce cursed his family name—also silently, thank you very much. "This is gonna be...." He pulled his phone out of his pocket with the hand Codi wasn't holding and checked it.

"Yep, my daddy." He tilted it so she could see, and then he set the device on the bench next to him. "It's sometimes worse if I put him off. If I don't answer, he'll have my momma call."

"I also think it's interesting you call your step-mother your momma," she said, clearly fishing for more information without asking a question.

"That's a question for another night." He groaned as he stood and looked at her. "I want you to stay," he whispered. "But I'm exhausted. I got hurt today, and my daddy isn't going to give up." He glared at the phone as it started vibrating against the wooden bench again. "And I think I should quit while I'm ahead."

"Oh-ho, you think you're ahead?" Despite the teasing, Codi sobered in the next moment. They stood on the back deck, Lucky panting nearby, and Bryce's phone irritating him to no end as it continued to rattle.

But Codi reached up and slid her slim, delicate fingers down the side of his face, erasing everything but her. "Do you want to go out with me again?"

"One hundred percent," he said.

She smiled as she pulled her hand back. "You say that a lot too. I'm sensing a story."

He returned her grin. "When can we go out again?"

"I'm just *swamped* with appointments," Codi said, plenty of sarcasm in her tone.

He ducked his head, though he'd left his cowboy hat somewhere. "I get it. I'm the busy one."

She stepped away from him, and the world got even colder. "So look at what you have going on," she said as she reached for their bowls. "And text me."

"Okay." He followed her inside, locking the door behind Lucky. "You don't have to clean up."

"You left your phone outside."

"I'm aware." Bryce took the dishes from her and put them on the counter. "I'll walk you out." He was flirting with real danger now, but it would take at least twenty-five minutes for Daddy or Abby to show up at the farm, and Bryce just needed ten more.

As Codi descended the front steps to the sidewalk, he said, "Thank you for helping me with my puncture wound tonight."

"Oh, so we can say that again?" She threw him a flirty look, and Bryce caught it and stuffed it into his heart.

"Friday night?" he asked as the sidewalk ended and her bus beckoned. "I'll come get you, and you can show me your place. We can eat somewhere in Coral Canyon, or drive back up here. There's a really great Mongolian barbecue here in Dog Valley."

"You decide," she said. "I'm free on Friday."

"Six?" he asked. "Even with another puncture wound, I should be able to get to you by six."

She put one hand on his chest, and dang if it didn't brand him. He fully expected to have a red imprint in the size and shape of her hand there when he went to shower in a few minutes. "No more puncture wounds, Mister."

"No, ma'am," he whispered, his gaze dropping to her mouth. He quickly pulled his attention back to her eyes. "You drive safe. Text me when you get home, so I know this bus didn't get wrapped around an apple tree."

Codi pulled her hand back and ducked her head this time. She walked backward for a step, then two, and then she lifted her hand in a good-bye wave, climbed on her bus, and brought the engine to a rumbling roar that filled the country silence of his farm.

He stayed at the end of the sidewalk until she'd backed out and driven away, and then all the bravado and strength in his shoulders sank away. "You might be ready for a girlfriend," he told himself. "But you are nowhere ready to kiss her."

With that, he went through the house to retrieve his phone. Sure enough, Daddy had called three times and Abby once, and Bryce quickly dialed his father back.

"There you are," he said. "Abs, I've got him."

"Daddy, whatever Uncle Trace told you isn't true. I'm fine."

"He used the words *puncture wound*," Dad growled. "So start talkin'."

"I'm just saying," Bryce said. "He blew it up into nothing." He walked alongside his uncle Jem, with Blaze several feet to his left, keeping his girls out of the sharp nettles on the side of the lane.

"Daddy, look at the sunflowers," Grace said, and all three men looked over to the little girl. Bryce loved his cousins, and he had a whole heap of them younger than him.

Grace had turned five last fall, and her sister had just turned four this past winter.

"Stay on the road, girls," Blaze said. "You can see the flowers from here."

Bryce's ranch had whole fields of them, and while they grew wild, sometimes he thought the Good Lord had planted them just for him. They weren't the big, tall ones that grew seeds and caused the foot-wide heads to bow. But smaller, more delicate bunches of sunflowers that went on as far as the eye could see.

"Can we cut some and take them home for Momma?" Grace asked.

"Maybe." Blaze cut a look over to Bryce, who nodded.

"I've got them along my vegetable garden too, Uncle Blaze. She can get some there."

His rough, tough, rodeo champion uncle nodded. "So your shoulder is okay." He wasn't asking, which Bryce appreciated. He and Jem had shown up this morning with fresh doughnuts from the truck Aunt Faith had used to own, most of their kids, and plenty of questions.

To Bryce's utter surprise, Uncle Trace had not told his parents about Codi. None of his father's questions last night had been about her, and neither of the uncles he'd recruited to walk the fence line with him this morning seemed to know either.

So Uncle Trace kept his cool status, and Bryce would text him his gratitude later.

"It'll be fine," Bryce said. "Sleeping was a bit tricky, but I took some painkillers and got the job done." Plus, he worked sixteen hours each day, so his body sometimes had no choice but to fall asleep. "How's Cash doing in the rodeo?"

"Good," Blaze said, a smile touching his face. "He's going pro this year, and Jem and I are gonna head down to Vegas right after school starts. Work with him for a bit."

"You're not worried about him?" Bryce watched his uncle, because Blaze could turn from a puffy white cloud to a thunderhead in less time than it took to breathe. That, and he'd gone through a few surgeries in the past decade because of his time in the rodeo.

"I'm scared to death," Uncle Blaze admitted. Then he laughed, as did Jem and Bryce. "But I have an amazing older brother who's been through a scary thing or two, and I'm learning to take each day with faith." He looked away, watching his girls. "Still."

"Aren't we all," Bryce said.

"How'd we get talkin' about me?" Blaze growled. "Ask Jem something."

Bryce laughed, and Jem joined in with his chuckles too. Before Bryce could do exactly that, the growl of an ATV met his ears.

"Daddy," Cole called as he came driving up on the four-wheeler with his siblings. The three of them slowed and stopped as the roar of the machine would've drowned out anything they said anyway.

"What's up?" Jem grinned at his trio of children who rode the ATV. Cole was fifteen and gangly, so he could reach around Rosie, a twelve-year-old who still didn't have a single ounce of fat anywhere on her body, and Ladd, his almost-five-year-old son.

His wife was pregnant again and due in the middle of winter, when the days weren't anything like this glorious almost-summer day. Bryce didn't really have time to saunter down the dirt road, barely glancing at the fence around this pasture. At the same time, he always tried to do what mattered most, a lesson from a sermon he'd heard a few years ago.

So when his uncles and their children had shown up that morning, Bryce had asked himself, *What matters most?*

Sure, the fence needed to be checked. He'd already fed the horses, and honestly, he could use another day away from Dragon before he tried to take the smoke and fire out of that horse. Secretly, he hoped Codi would get some divine revelation that she should come work at the Rising Sun Ranch, and then she could start training and rehabilitating Dragon.

No matter what, the answer to his question had been clear: Family.

Family was what mattered most to Bryce right now, and therefore, he'd been walking in the rising morning heat with his uncles and their kids, talking about what had happened last night—without mentioning Codi—for the past hour.

"Ladd needs to go to the bathroom," Cole said. "Can I take him back to Bryce's?"

"Yep," Jem said, as he was definitely one of the more easy-going uncles. "Come on, Rosie-girl. Get down and let the boys go."

"Daddy," she drawled as she did what he asked. "You said I could drive the four-wheeler."

"You can, kid," he said. "We're not in a rush today."

She seemed to be, and she glared at her brothers as they left. Bryce smiled at her and said, "I heard you got a babysitting job, Miss Rosie. Come tell me about that."

Her face lit up, and since Rosie was part-sass and part-always-right and part-bossy, babysitting was the perfect gig for her. "It's for Uncle Shawn," she said.

"Ev's brother?" Bryce asked, looking past Rosie to Jem. They both nodded, and Bryce did too.

"Their baby is only one, but they've never left 'im," Rosie said. "They're goin' out tomorrow night."

"That's great," Bryce said. Shawn Avery owned a popular restaurant and catering business in town. Bryce's family used Pork and Beans for a ton of stuff, because Everly had married Trace, essentially bringing Shawn into the Young family too. Bryce knew her brothers well, though Reggie, the younger one, had been playing professional baseball in Seattle for the past several years.

He was three or four years older than Bryce—probably close to Codi or Kassie's age—and Bryce really only ever saw him on major holidays, and sometimes not even then.

"Where are they going?" Bryce asked, thinking he should probably put together a decent date if he wanted to impress Codi. His pulse thundered for a moment, and he very nearly word-vomited out something about her so Uncle Blaze and Uncle Jem could help him.

Uncle Blaze especially was very good at planning amazing dates.

"Same place the rest of us are," Blaze said, glancing over. "That new movie with Cameron Royce is premiering tomorrow. Faith and I have had tickets for months."

"Ah, yes," Bryce said. "The other Coral Canyon celebrities." He grinned at his uncles, because they hated being called celebrities. But they all kind of were. "Who's babysitting for you?"

"Lynnie and Joey are doing a big thing at Gabe's house," Jem said. "My kids—except for Rosie—are goin' there."

"Everyone is going there," Blaze said. "Lynnie, Joey, Boston, and Beth are in charge."

"Doesn't seem like they'll burn the house down then," Bryce said with a smile. "Boston...maybe. But those three girls will keep things in line."

They smiled together, and Bryce let a few steps go by where he actually did some work and checked the fence. Still intact, though there definitely had been some foxes or coyotes on his property in the night. He'd seen the footprints, and his chickens were all in a feathery fluff.

"Could I get tickets to that still?" he asked. "And what will the restaurant situation in Coral Canyon be like?" He tried to act casually, but he completely failed, if the way both of his uncles swung their heads toward him.

He walked in the middle of them, and that only squished

him between them. "Why?" Jem asked slowly. "You thinkin' of going?"

"Why can't I go?" Bryce asked him, looking him straight in the eye.

"Friday night," Blaze said casually, and Bryce needed to ask him how he achieved that tone. "Dinner and a movie. Sounds like something you'd do with a *date*." He didn't pull punches either, and the way his eyebrows slithered on up as he looked at Bryce only added to the death kill.

"Yeah, well, maybe I have a date." Bryce's voice broke on the last word, and he swallowed to try to get his voice box to play nicely with him.

"With whom?" Jem asked, coming to a complete stop.

"Nope," Blaze said, taking a couple of long strides toward them. He went past Bryce and stood between him and Jem. "No, we don't want to know."

"Yes, we do," Jem said, muscling his brother to the side and giving him a dirty look.

"No." Blaze glared at him and then Bryce. "Because his momma and daddy don't know." He looked straight into his soul, the way Uncle Blaze had always been able to. "Do they?"

"I haven't mentioned it to them, no," Bryce admitted.

"La la la la la," Blaze sang loudly. "We don't want to know. Come on, Jem. Let's go find some sunflowers for our wives."

"I want to know," Jem said, stumbling as Blaze nudged him to start back toward the house. "Bryce is a grown man. He can tell who he wants to tell."

"Girls," Blaze called. "Come on, we're headed back." His

little girls simply changed the direction they were skipping, no questions asked.

"Daddy," Rosie said as she turned around and started toward her father. "I want to drive the four-wheeler."

"If you tell me one more time," Jem bickered back with his daughter. "I'm going to drain the gas tank myself." He threw Bryce a hopeful look, but Bryce only lifted his hand to say good-bye.

"I'd avoid Coral Canyon," Blaze called as he walked slowly backward, waiting for his girls. "Or get reservations at the very least. The whole town will be out on Friday."

"All right," Bryce yelled back to them, and he stood in the middle of a remote dirt road on his ranch and watched his uncles and cousins walk away from him. As soon as he got back to a place with service, he'd call around Dog Valley and find somewhere...quieter for him and Codi to eat.

If he showed up with the beautiful blonde in Coral Canyon on the busiest night of the year, plenty of people would see them. It would get back to his parents, to everyone in the family, and Bryce wanted to keep his brand-new, budding relationship with Codi a secret for a little longer.

Plus, he figured she'd like something calmer, more peaceful, quieter. The truth was, *he* needed that, and Bryce didn't want to go into his first try at dating after all this time with both guns blazing.

So something quiet. Something amazing and meaningful, like the few minutes they'd had last night on his deck.

He took a deep breath and turned around to finish up the fence on this southwest side of the ranch. "Lord," he said, because there was no better place for a man to pray than out in the wild, beneath the shadow of the Teton Mountains, with plenty of blue sky overhead. "Thank you for this sky. Thank you for this ranch. Thank you for my uncles. Thank you for sunflowers."

He had the sudden idea to gather some for Codi too, and he suddenly couldn't wait to see her tomorrow night for their second date. As he walked along, he added one more plea to his prayer, this time silently.

Guide me with her, Lord. I'll do what matters most, if Thou will please just let me know what that is.

Especially with him and Codi. He could change; he knew that now, and he did want to be the kind of man his daddy was. He wanted to be a good father and a loving husband. He wanted little girls to skip along the dirt lane with him while they checked fences, and he really, truly thought he was ready to start this journey...with Codi at his side.

Please, just guide me.

10

Abigail Young looked over to her best friend in the whole world—Georgia. Her sister-in-law and the reason she'd come to be standing behind the sheer curtains in the master suite of a house she didn't own.

Georgia did, and she'd have to leave Abby for a few minutes to deliver her dogs to one Codi Hudson.

When Abby had first heard the name, it had meant nothing to her. Now, she felt like she knew everything about the petite blonde woman making her way up the sidewalk at Georgia's house to the front door. Down the hall, Ruby started to bark, and Georgia finally looked at Abby too.

"Okay," she said. "You sure you don't want to come out?"

"I wouldn't even if we were sipping coffee in the dining room," Abby said. She shook her head. "No, you just go give her the dogs. She doesn't know anything about how you're related to Bryce?"

"She didn't seem to on the phone," Georgia said.

"Are you going to tell her?"

Georgia wore pure worry in her eyes, and she lifted her hand to her mouth and chewed on her nails. "I don't know."

"Maybe I should just go."

"She's parked in the driveway," Georgia said.

"Yeah."

The doorbell rang, and Georgia spun toward the master suite door like she had no idea who had arrived. All of her canines went bonkers, and Ruby came galloping into the room. *Bark, bark,* she said, and then she turned tail and ran out. She'd go back and forth until Georgia opened the door and calmed her down.

Abby stayed right where she stood, because she didn't want her first meeting with Bryce's potential new girlfriend—the first one he'd had in almost a decade—to be at Georgia's house. He should get to introduce Codi to her and Tex when he was ready.

With that thought, she turned away from the window and took a deep breath. "What am I doin' here, Lord?" She shouldn't have come. At the very least, she should've told Tex. She could just hear him asking her all kinds of questions, and she knew she wouldn't be able to keep anything from him for very long. She didn't even want to do that.

At the same time, Bryce and Codi might become nothing. Just because he'd told Georgia and Otis about her a few nights ago didn't mean anything. Feeling calmer, and without a screaming warning from heaven, she turned back to the window about the same time Codi reached the bottom step. She had both dogs on leashes, and they both trotted along at her side like they'd been doing so for years.

Her blonde hair—Bryce had always been attracted to blondes—drifted in the wind, and she took the canines up the steps on her bus and closed the door. Georgia returned to the bedroom, breathless and carrying a cat.

"She's really nice," she said, almost panting. "The dogs loved her on first sight, so that's a good sign." She stroked Obsidian, who looked at Abby like he might eat her face off just for fun if she dared to stop Georgia from his rub-down. "She painted the bus."

"All those dogs and everything?"

"Yeah," Georgia said. "She said she's done some murals in Idaho, and she used to get paid to do art."

"I wonder if she could repaint the Bookmobile," Abby said, not sure what she was supposed to do now. Hang out for the next three hours until Codi finished with the grooming? "Did she say anything about Bryce? Your last name?"

"Not a word." Georgia turned away from the window, because there really wasn't anything to see. "I should've said something, right?" She sank onto the bed and put Obsidian down. He gave her the death glare now and picked his way up to the pillows, where he chose the highest one and laid down.

Abby joined Georgia on the bed. "I mean, I don't know? I think I'm going to tell Tex."

"Tell him what?"

"That—about...her."

Georgia frowned, and Abby knew that look. "I don't want Bryce to stop trusting me and Otis," she said slowly.

Abby gave her the fiercest librarian look she could come up with. Granted, she hadn't been in the library in almost a decade, and her children stopped pushing her buttons at a Look Level way below Librarian. "Georgia," she said. "He knows who his family is. There are no secrets here, even when people try to keep them."

"Maybe I should text him and say it came up...accidentally."

"What did? That you told me?"

"Yeah." She sighed, her shoulders going down. "Or I'll just tell him I told you, so then Tex is gonna know, and he'll probably ask about her, and...yeah." She finished almost in a whisper, and Abby knew exactly how she felt.

They'd been stuck between a rock and a hard place, and the worst part was, they'd *chosen* to be here.

"Okay," she said. "You text Bryce, and I'm going to text Tex." She took her phone from her pocket and looked at it. Her husband would call, guaranteed, and Abby wouldn't be able to lie to him. Not that she wanted to, but he always, always knew when she wasn't telling the whole truth. "I know what Bryce will say."

"This is nothing," Georgia said in a deep voice to mimic him.

"It's new, Daddy," Abby said, grinning. "I don't need you makin' a big deal out of nothing."

They looked at one another and both dissolved into laughter a moment later. As Georgia quieted, she said, "If it even is new, but he said he'd just met her. And he didn't expressly ask us not to say anything to anyone."

"I'm sure he also didn't mean for you to call her grooming bus and have her come over two days later."

"It's been three days," Georgia said, her chin rising a little in defiance.

Abby grinned at her. "Okay, we're both texting." Her heartbeat vibrated in a strange way, but Abby forced her fingers across the screen.

Georgia told me about a woman Bryce asked out earlier this week. Apparently, she's a dog groomer, and Georgia also hired her and asked me to come to the house when she came. So that's where I am now. Codi has the dogs in the bus. We're in the house. I didn't meet her.

"Let me see," Georgia said, and Abby handed her the phone. She took Georgia's and read her text to Bryce.

I hired Codi Hudson to come give Rudy and Ilsa a bath. Bryce, she's gorgeous and I see why you like her!

That text had already been sent, in fact. The one that hadn't said, *I told Abby about it, and she came over. She didn't meet her. Only I did, but we both feel kind of funny not telling you.*

"Send it," she said.

"Yours is good, but Tex isn't going to let you be friends with me anymore."

They switched phones again, and Abby smiled and shook her head. "He knows who we are," she said. "He knows where our hearts are."

"Yeah, and he also knows it's been killing you for six long years that you can't set up Bryce." Georgia touched her phone, sending her text off to Bryce. Abby read over hers again and had just sent it when Georgia's phone chimed.

She pulled in a breath. "He said, What color is her hair?" She looked at Abby with wide eyes. "What color is her hair? He doesn't know what color her hair is?"

Another chime. They both leaned over her phone now. Abby read, "Thanks for the heads-up. I'll screen Daddy's calls until I'm ready to talk about her," out loud.

Abby's chest froze. "Tell him he doesn't need to do that." She quickly got back to work on her phone. *We've told Bryce about our bad behavior, and I don't want you calling him. He doesn't need to be badgered about this.*

She sent the message and gripped her phone. It rang only a few seconds later, and she jumped to her feet. "Hey, baby," she said after she'd swiped on Tex's call.

"Oh-ho," he said. "You don't get to *hey-baby* me in that sweet voice."

Abby smiled even as she turned her back on Georgia and started to leave the bedroom. "I didn't go out there and pepper her with questions," Abby said back. "I observed her—"

"You *spied* on her," Tex said.

"I *observed* her from the window. Georgia says she's very nice. She's clearly good with dogs. Blonde. Both of those qualify her for Bryce's attention."

Tex said nothing, and Abby found another gray cat sitting up on top of a bookshelf in the living room. "I'm leaving right now. I'm not even going to talk to her. Nothing."

"Why'd you go over there, then?"

"Moral support," Abby said.

"Georgia." He said nothing more, though he loved Georgia. One hundred percent he did.

"Bryce tells them things he doesn't tell us," she said as she collected her purse from the island in the kitchen. "He gave her name. We're allowed to book dog groomers."

"You know what? I want some of that mint cookie ice cream from Waverly's."

Surprise jolted through Abby, and she blinked. Only a moment passed before she said, "Okay. I'll stop on the way home."

"Great, thanks, baby."

"You're—I'm getting whiplashed around here."

"I'm not gonna be mad about this. So you spied on a grown woman who Bryce is interested in. It's not like you stalked her at her home or anything, and when Bryce is ready to tell us anything, he'll tell us."

"Yes," she said, though she was still surprised Tex wasn't being a little more lecturey. The man loved to lecture, though he usually saved it for Mel or Carver, not Abby.

"He's callin' me right now, Abs. Talk to you soon." He hung up on her, and Abby supposed that phone call had gone as well as it could have.

"Georgia," she called. "I'm gonna go."

"Just a sec." Georgia came bustling down the hall, and she stepped into Abby's arms. "I love you. Sorry to drag you into this, but Bryce didn't seem upset."

"He called Tex." Abby stepped back and smiled at her. "I'm convinced my meddling will pay off one day—maybe today's the day."

Georgia laughed too, and then Abby left through the garage. Her SUV sat out of the way enough that the big, white dogified bus didn't prevent her from leaving, and she looked up through the windows of it to see Codi standing there with her back to Abby. Ruby had been tied to a platform, and the dog didn't move an inch while Codi worked on her.

She didn't come face-to-face with her. She didn't speak to her. She certainly saw the blonde hair though, and she got in her car and drove away, still wondering why Bryce wanted to know what color Codi's hair had been.

But she wasn't going to ask him. Oh, no, she was not.

11

odi paced back and forth in her apartment, her mind jumping from topic to topic. She should change her jeans.

The jeans were fine.

Maybe she should forgo the wig.

The wig was fine.

Did she have her wallet?

Yes, she had her wallet, a fact confirmed to her when she patted her pockets and found it there for the fifth time in as many minutes.

"What are you doing?" she hissed to herself as she made another pass through the living room. *It's fine,* she told herself.

It's not fine. Text him and cancel now.

I can't. He should be here any minute.

You can. Just go throw up and say you're sick.

She definitely felt a little queasy, but not to the point of actually throwing up. She'd not had a dog to groom today, but she had managed to get around to several businesses and talk to them about her flyers. They now sat on the counters at a bath and body works boutique that sold bath bombs, lotions, and more. The hardware store. A salon. A day spa. And a flower shop.

She'd skipped the bookstore for some reason, and as she paced, she knew why. "Gotta talk to Bryce about his aunt first," she muttered.

The doorbell rang, a horrible half-dead screeching cat sound that only lasted three seconds before it delved into a worse electrical buzzing that went on and on. It was still echoing through the basement apartment when she made it to the door and opened it.

Cowboy glory stood there, and his name was Bryce Young. She'd been struck dumb with the dark wash of his jeans, the deep indigo in his shirt, which had only been broken up by thin white lines to create plaid. He wore a black cowboy hat, no curls coming out the bottom anymore, and a smile the size of the sun.

"Miss Codi," he said with a cowboy twang in his voice. He reached up and touched the brim of his hat with one hand, the other carrying sunflowers. "You ready for this?" He looked down to her feet, where she wore tennis shoes. "You got my memo on the location, obviously."

"Yeah," she blurted out. "I did." He'd said he'd planned a quiet dinner outside, and to wear something where she might have to sit on the ground. She'd gone with jeans too, though hers were far lighter than his. Her black and white tennis shoes played well with her black-and-white striped shirt that had tight sleeves to her elbow.

"You look fantastic," he said, taking a half-step into her house as he slid his hand along her waist. "Are you starving right now? It's a bit of a drive."

She hadn't eaten since breakfast, and she said, "I'm hungry, yeah, but I don't think I'll starve or anything."

He grinned at her, seemingly so at ease. So comfortable with himself and where he stood and how much room on the earth he took up. Codi, though not a hair over five-foot-one-inch, felt like a giant, full of thick legs and bloated arms.

"We can have a sample on the way." Bryce leaned down and breathed in. "It's good to see you."

"You too," she managed to say, because she didn't want him to think she wasn't interested. She so was.

"I like the non-bang look too." He pulled away, his smile still etched in place. "I brought you these. They grow all over the ranch, and my little-girl cousins really love them."

Codi took the sunflowers from him, smiling at the bright yellow blooms. They calmed her for some reason, and she said, "Thank you," in a soft voice. She didn't own a vase, but she turned and went into her kitchen, aware that Bryce had entered her apartment.

As she put the flowers in a glass of water, he gazed around, and Codi's nerves amped up again. When she returned to his side, she said, "Ready," because she didn't dare ask him what he thought of where she lived.

"Can I?" He took her hand without protest from her, and he turned to leave the apartment.

Codi barely managed to pull the door closed, and she let him lead her up the steps to the sidewalk. "You sure clean up real nice," she said.

"You mean when I'm not dirty and bloody and passed out."

"Well, anything would be a step up from that, I suppose." She smiled too, glad she'd found a way past this lump of nerves in her throat.

He chuckled, the sound so careful and so cowboy that Codi let herself float on the happiness of it for a few moments while they walked to his truck. He opened her door for her and helped her up into the vehicle. She sat heavily in the seat, expecting Bryce to already be moving back to close the door.

Instead, he crowded in. "My aunt said your hair yesterday definitely had bangs." His dark eyes blazed—positively blazed—with energy, and Codi kicked against her nerves again. That hive had lodged right there in her throat, and she couldn't get anything past it.

He wasn't smiling now, and he tilted his head at her. "Breathe, Codi," he said. "I'm not mad." He closed the door then, and Codi sucked at the air, never taking her eyes from him as he rounded the hood of the truck and got behind the wheel.

"She called for a grooming appointment," she said.

"She told me." He started the truck and the air conditioning started to blow.

Codi trained it right on herself, wondering what to say next. "Okay, I knew she was your aunt. You said the name Georgia when I was out at Kassie's, and I don't know. It wasn't weird or anything. I picked up the dogs. I washed the dogs. I dropped off the dogs. She paid me for the dogs."

He looked over to her. "I've already spoken to her."

Her eyebrows went up. "Spoken to her? What does that mean?"

Easing away from the curb, some of his cowboy ire faded. "Remember how I said my family was big and loud? Well, they can be annoying too."

"I liked Trace—and Georgia too, for the record."

"Oh, they're all nice," he said. "No one's debating that. But well, my momma was there yesterday too, spying—oh, what was the word she used? Observing—you from the window."

Codi's blood ran a little colder. "Oh."

"It's fine," he said. "I just—they're very nosy, Codi. I haven't dated in a real long time, and I know they just want me to be happy. They're like these...this family of...cats. Like these really curious cats that can't help themselves. They just have to go after all the shiny things, you know? And then they find themselves up in this tall tree, and they can't get down."

Codi blinked, trying to comprehend everything he'd said. "Curiosity did kill the cat," she finally said.

"Exactly." He banged on the wheel a little. "That's what they are. *Cats.*"

"I like cats," she said next, starting to relax again.

"I like cats who are useful," he said. "You know, the ones who chase off the weasels trying to eat my chickens, and the ones who keep the mice out of my hay." He glanced over to her. "My momma? She doesn't do either of those."

"Bryce Young," Codi said with a grin. "You did *not* just say your momma wasn't useful."

He softened too. At least he didn't slap the innocent

steering wheel again. "She's useful. You should taste these French onion meatballs she makes. Which reminds me...." With only one hand on the wheel, he practically twisted all the way around to get something out of the back.

"Can I help you so we don't die?" Codi asked, her eyes trained out the windshield.

"There's not a single car on this road," he said. "I got it." He settled back into his seat with a brown paper bag in his hand now. "My grandmother packed dinner for us, and she made up this sample bag for us to try on the way there. It is about an hour from here."

"An hour?" Codi's stomach swooped and growled at the same time, and that was not a pleasant combination. "You should've let me come up to Dog Valley and meet you."

"My grandparents live right around the corner from you," he said. "In that fifty-five-plus condo place? I had to come down here anyway." He handed her the brown bag. "I didn't look at it. Wanna see what she packed? She's a pretty good cook."

Codi didn't know anything about a fifty-five-plus condo place, but she did know delicious-smelling food when she opened the top on the bag and the aroma came out. "I can see I'm not going to meet the cooking standards of your cat-family."

He laughed a little, which helped her relax. "There're no standards, Codi."

"No? You said your momma makes mean meatballs." She lifted what looked like a croissant in a cupcake liner out of the bag. "And this looks like a ham...sandwich...cupcake."

She looked over to him for help, and he glanced at the food in her hand. "Oh, those are the best." He reached for it and took it from her. "She makes this mustardy-mayo-magic sauce. And yes, it's ham and cheese." With zero hands on the wheel, he plucked the mini-croissant out of the cupcake liner and let it fall to the console. "It's two bites of heaven, Codi. Try it."

He gave her the first ham and cheese cupcake, and Codi wasn't one of those women who couldn't eat in front of men. She took the first bite, the mustardy-mayo-magic combining with the salty ham and the flaky croissant and the rich cheese enough to make a moan come involuntarily out of her mouth.

"Right?" Bryce chuckled, and with her second bite still in her hand, she reached into the bag and got out the second ham cupcake for him. As she finished hers, she peered into the bag again.

"This looks like...salad. Pasta salad?" She pulled out the container, wondering how Bryce was going to eat this in the car. "Oh, no. It's fruit." She popped the top on the plastic container and saw fruit kabobs. How convenient. And cute.

"My grandma has fed a lot of children in her life," Bryce said.

"Yeah, tell me how many cousins you have," she said as she lifted out one kebab for him. One square of watermelon, one huge green grape, one chunk of pineapple.

He took the kebab and stared at her blankly. "I didn't know I'd need to do math tonight."

She laughed, the sound just shooting from her before she'd even realized she thought what he'd said was funny. Codi hadn't laughed like this in years—way before meeting the wrong cowboy and falling in love with him.

Still giggling, she asked, "You don't know how many cousins you have?"

"It's a constantly changing number," he said. "Right now, two of my aunts are pregnant and a third is having twins. With those four new babies *this year alone*, I guess that would put us between Insanely Huge and Enormously Crazy."

"Ballpark me, then," she said, trying to decide if his family really irritated him, or if he loved them. She thought he loved them, because Bryce didn't strike her as the type of man to get irritated by much very easily.

"Number of cousins." Bryce shook his head and slid the watermelon off the stick with his teeth. After he'd chewed and swallowed, he said, "I can't believe I'm going down in flames on the second date over the number of cousins I have."

"Okay, fine," she said. "I have nine cousins. How's that?"

"I have nine *uncles*," he said. "Fine, eight, but it feels like nine sometimes." He grinned at her and pulled off the grape. Codi took her first bite of fruit, somewhat surprised that it still held a chill. The juicy watermelon made her pucker up for a moment, and then it turned blindingly sweet.

After he'd finished eating the grape, he said, "Ballpark on cousins: Thirty-five. I've got thirty-five cousins, Codi. And you know what? They *allll* live here."

"That's not true either, Mister Young," she said as she pulled off her grape. "I happen to know for a fact that Harry does not live here."

"He's here all the time," Bryce argued. "Plus the aunts and uncles. My parents and siblings. Kassie. All the honorary aunts and uncles and cousins. My grandparents. It's like eighty of us when we all get together." He looked over to her. "You realize there are some towns with a population less than that, right?"

Codi laughed again, quieter but with the same joy moving through her, as she shook her head. "The fruit is good."

"My grandmother can pick the best watermelons in the world." He finished his first kebab, with Codi only a few seconds behind him.

"Do you cook then?" she asked him.

"I can," he said. "A little. You?" He cast a look over to her and took the second fruit kebab she offered him.

She took the last one and put the lid back on the container. "Let's see, if we weren't going out tonight, I'd have made myself a bag of ready-rice. Does that count as cooking?"

"Ready-rice?" He filled his mouth with watermelon and didn't ask the next question.

"Don't get between a rice-lover and her ready-rice," Codi said. "It's ninety seconds to delicious, and I don't want to be teased about it."

"No, ma'am," he said, plenty of teasing in his voice. "I won't tease you about it."

"I'll convert you to the ways of ready-rice," she said. "Just you wait."

"I actually can't wait for that."

Once they'd finished their second course, Codi dug into the bag again and pulled out a square container that held two of the cutest glass jars She'd ever seen. She gaped at them, then Bryce. "This is some magic I don't know about."

He looked over to her. "Dessert. That's rice pudding."

Codi looked at the jars again. One was the palest of purples, the evening sunlight coming through the windshield at just the right angle to highlight it. The second one appeared clear, but it had bubbles all over the outside. A film of plastic wrap sat over each, with a teeny tiny baby spoon right down the side.

"Do you like rice pudding?" he asked. "My granny's is amazing." He reached for a jar, and Codi wanted to slap his hand back.

"They're so beautiful," she said.

He lightened the load by half and tore off the plastic wrap like it was, well, plastic wrap. "My grandma must've thought this was a special date," he said. "Because rice pudding is a lot of work, and she doesn't do stuff like this anymore."

Codi picked up the purple jar he'd left for her and lovingly swept away the plastic. "I'm assuming she wants the jars back."

"Yeah, I'm sure she does."

The delicious scent of milk, sugar, and vanilla met her nose, and Codi's eyes drifted closed. "My mom used to make this vanilla sugar cookie," she murmured, not sure where the story had come from. Probably prompted to the front of her mind from this similar scent. "It smelled just like this."

She smiled over to Bryce, who'd already taken a bite of his rice pudding. "We'd bake them together all day after church, and then she'd let me pick the frosting colors."

"That's a sweet memory," he said.

"I don't think I've ever had rice pudding."

"I don't think you can call yourself a rice-lover then." His quick wit made her more attracted to him, as if she needed another reason. He used his tasting spoon to take a micro-bite of dessert, and Codi pulled hers out too.

He'd said his grandmother must've thought this date was special, and she asked, "What did you tell your grandmother about tonight?" Then she put her first taste of rice pudding in her mouth. Her eyes widened at the creamy texture, the more savory flavors that she hadn't been expecting. It was sweet, yes, but nothing like a cookie with the subtle warmth of cinnamon.

"I told her I was going out with this woman I really like," he said in a near-whisper. "And that it was way too busy in town tonight to go to a restaurant, and I wondered if she might cater us a picnic."

"And she did." With rice pudding in glass jars that screamed family heirloom. "When did you ask her?"

"Last night."

Codi took another bite of her sample dessert, wondering what the main picnic would hold. "Be sure to tell her thank you from me," she said. "This is amazing food."

"She never lets me give her a menu," Bryce said. "She's kind of finicky about that sometimes."

"Well, she's probably earned the right," Codi said.

"That she has." Bryce finished his rice pudding, and Codi collected his jar from him. When she finished hers, she tucked everything away into the paper bag and set it at her feet.

As she straightened, she sighed, and she looked over to Bryce. "This is the best date I've been on in, oh, ever."

His attention flew to hers. "Ever?"

She gave him what felt like a melting-chocolate smile, one that oozed all over her face and felt gooey and warm. "Yeah, ever. I'm glad your grandma made a meal for two people who like each other a lot."

Bryce grinned and reached over and took her hand in his. "And this was just the sampler to tide us over until we get to the lake."

"A lake, huh?"

"Shoot," he said. "Me and my big mouth." He chuckled lightly, and Codi sure liked that he didn't take himself too seriously. She felt like she did, and that he could help her lighten up a little. "I want the record to show that I kept that a secret until...." He glanced at the dashboard. "Six-thirty-four."

She laughed again and said, "It's been noted on the official record." In her mind, which was clearly the official record, she put it right next to today's date and the title *Best Date With a Cowboy, Ever*.

And now, with the mention of a lake, Codi thought things could only get better from here.

12

Bryce pulled into the parking lot at Silver Lake, pleased by how few cars were there. He hadn't expected there to be a lot, despite it being a weekend at the beginning of summertime. "Let me come help you down," he said before he got out of the truck.

He went around to her side and opened her door. "I'm not sure I need to eat more," she said.

"Trust me, you'll want to eat more." Bryce's grandmother had texted him the full menu, and despite his protests that it was too much, she'd made it and packed it all. Codi slid to the ground, and Bryce moved to the back passenger door to get the picnic basket.

His grandma didn't skimp, and he had the full experience in his hands. Wicker basket. Red and white checkered cloth. Wet wipes for their hands. Heck, she'd probably packed a few ants to march across the blanket just to set the mood.

"This is one of my favorite places in the whole world," he said as he gazed toward the lake. The sun hadn't gone all the way down yet, and the remaining rays painted the lake in silver—thus its name.

"Silver Lake," he said.

"It's beautiful," Codi murmured. "It's really shining like silver."

He liked how she'd spoken with reverence, because he felt like that about this place too. He liked that she teased him sometimes, and that she'd told him some real things about herself too. He loved the longer wig tonight, this one without bangs but with plenty of pretty tendrils that she'd swooped back into a long braid that fell over her shoulder.

"Will you ever show me your hair?" he asked, not sure where the question had come from.

"Is that your question for today?" She faced him. "We get one every time we go out, right?"

"There's not a set limit," he said.

"Mm, I think there is." She put her hand in his and said, "Let's eat before the silver on the lake goes away."

He started up the path to the lake, where several picnic tables waited for mountain-goers. Bryce went past two or three to one that would keep them close to the lake but further from the path in case anyone else showed up.

Codi helped him spread the checkered tablecloth over the metal picnic table, and then he started pulling out food. "Chicken pot pie hand pies," he said, setting the golden-brown half-moons on the table. "Veggies and hummus. My granny knows I'm a hummus freak."

"A hummus freak," Codi repeated, plenty of smile in her voice.

"Cheese biscuits." He put those on the table too, another personal favorite. Grandma had made way too much food, and Bryce knew it was so he'd have plenty leftover. "And cookies. Oh, hot diggity dog. These are the toffee cowboy cookies." He looked up, his whole soul feeling like it had been dipped in sunlight and then silver, just like the lake.

Codi snorted. Scoffed. Maybe she was trying to hold back a laugh? Sure enough, only a moment later, a peal of laughter left her mouth, her face turning a bit red as she laughed and laughed and laughed. Bryce couldn't stop himself from joining her, because she was just so joyful.

"Hot—" She giggled and sucked in a breath. "Diggity dog." That unleashed another round of laughter while Bryce set out the wet-naps and pulled two bottles of his favorite lemonade from the basket too.

"It's a thing people say," he said.

"People?" she teased. "What people?"

"My boss in Louisville used to say it all the time," Bryce said. He straddled the picnic bench and sat down. Codi joined him, facing toward him while he looked at her. They sat on the same side of the table, and Bryce simply gazed at her for a moment.

His counselor often had him pause and identify how he felt in any given situation. Here, as Codi tucked her hair behind her ear and looked up at him, Bryce felt safe.

Safe.

He hadn't felt safe with a woman in a long time—not since meeting Kassie.

He felt strong, and that hardly ever happened around beautiful women. He felt powerful, like he could protect and take care of Codi should he need to.

And he felt happy. Not a single nerve buzzed at him, and with that came the knowledge that he knew who he was and who he wanted to be, and that God knew those things too. And God was pleased with the work Bryce had done to get himself to this place.

"I'll show you my hair," Codi said, breaking into his pause. "Maybe I can do it up nice for you one day?"

"That's totally up to you," he said. "I don't want to push you on it."

She nodded and picked up the hand pie he'd put closer to her. "How's your shoulder?"

"Good," he said. "Hardly a hole at all today."

"And Dragon?"

"Oh, that horse." He looked across the table to the lake, seeing the ripples in the silver now from something. A fish or a fly, maybe. "He wants you to come work with him. He doesn't like me much."

"What about Kassie?" she asked.

"She's bribing him with apples, and that's working okay." Bryce smiled and took a bite of his hand pie. The creamy sauce of the chicken pot pie always made him smile.

"There's something about this," Codi said, peering into the depths of her filling.

"Celery seed," he said. "But don't tell my grandma I told

you. She thinks it's a secret spice no one in the family knows about." He grinned and popped open the lid on the hummus. "And since there are no secrets in my family, we all know about it."

His throat closed around the food, and while Bryce would like to say he didn't know why, he'd given up lying years ago. He knew why, and he didn't want to tell Codi anything. Couldn't he just have his slow, summer night, with good food and a beautiful woman?

Maybe in another life, he thought. *If you were another man.*

But he wasn't. He was who he was, and he'd fought to be the Bryce Young he was today. He didn't have to hide that, and on his next breath, he drew strength into his core through his lungs. His ribs felt stronger, and his puncture wound pulled a little bit.

His shoulders lifted, and Bryce remembered who he was: a valued son of Tex and Abby Young. A devoted brother, cousin, and friend. A son of God.

"So," he said after he'd polished off his hand pie. With hummus, he could get through this conversation. "I wanted to talk to you about something."

Codi popped the last of her carrot stick in her mouth and nodded. "All right."

He told himself she'd shared some personal things about herself too. That was what he had to do in order to get to know a woman. So she could get to know him.

"One of my cousins," he said. "Is named OJ. Otis Judson Young."

She said nothing as she took another bite of her hand pie.

Bryce picked up a piece of celery and decided he might choke on the strings if he tried to eat it. He dragged it through the hummus anyway, his eyes tracking the move of the vegetable like it might come alive and attack him.

"He's my uncle Otis and aunt Georgia's boy. He's eight years old." Bryce suddenly wanted to pull up a picture of his son on his phone. Maybe Codi would be able to see the resemblance.

He swallowed, his mouth suddenly full of saliva. Codi simply watched him with those sapphire eyes, and he couldn't tell if she was curious or questioning or just waiting for him to drop the hammer.

"He's adopted," Bryce said, being careful not to blurt out the words or shout them. "They adopted him. He's my biological son. I'm his birth father."

Codi's chewing slowed to a stop as she gaped at him. He waited, which was akin to torture for him, as he just wanted to spew words all over the picnic table, the lake, the mountains. But Kassie's words ran through his head too.

You don't have to give her the whole story, Bryce. Just tell her and see what she asks. Tell her the truth based on what she needs clarified.

He'd never had to tell anyone but her before, and the stakes hadn't been that high. They were friends, and OJ being his biological son didn't affect Kassie's day-to-day life. But it might for Bryce's spouse.

Codi snapped her jaw closed and finished her veggies. "Wow," she said. "I—I don't know what you want me to say."

"Do you have any questions for me?" he asked.

"I...don't know."

"Bailey, the ex I told you about. She's the mother."

Codi nodded and gazed out to Silver Lake. "She's in Montana, right?"

"That's right."

"You...she didn't want the baby either?"

"It wasn't a matter of not wanting him," Bryce said carefully. He hated that talk of "not wanting" OJ. Of course he'd *wanted* him.

Codi's gaze came back to his, and Bryce realized how forcefully he'd spoken. Calmly, sure. But with conviction.

"For either of us," he said. "We loved him. We still love him. I was nineteen years old. No idea what to do with my life, what I even wanted to do with my life. And Bailey had a year of veterinary school left. We were not equipped to raise a child, either together or separately." He'd come to all of these conclusions through many hours of prayer, fasting, and therapy, and as the explanation came out of his mouth, he drew strength from it.

He studied the bench in front of him, pressing the tip of his finger through one of the patterned holes in the metal. "We knew that baby deserved more than either of us could give. We wanted him to have a life beyond what we could provide. We loved him so much, we decided to give him that life."

Bryce looked up, not sure what he'd find on Codi's face. She didn't exactly look horrified, but she didn't exactly not. That might not be the right emotion anyway. Bryce had a hard time reading other people, and he wished he could've tucked Uncle Blaze in his pocket to witness this confession.

Then his uncle could tell him what Codi really thought.

Of course, then his uncle would be a witness to this confession, and that sounded like an exquisite form of torture too.

"Otis and Georgia couldn't have kids. We sat down and talked to them about adopting the baby, and because we have a whole town in a single family, my uncle who's a lawyer did everything legally and properly, and they...they're his. He's theirs."

Codi nodded, but her neck looked a little rubbery. "And you go over there and eat with them all the time?"

"Not all the time," he said. "But yeah, enough. OJ knows I'm his birth father. He knows who Bailey is, though he's never met her in person—well, after the first five minutes of his life when we held him and hugged him and kissed him goodbye."

Bryce fell silent then, his memories of OJ's birth so vivid and so real inside his mind. It wasn't the sugar-cookie-afternoon kind of memory either, but one tainted with beeping machines, the scent of metal and blood, and the cries of a newborn baby.

Sometimes, when assaulted with memories like this, Bryce wondered if he'd truly been forgiven for the things he'd done wrong. Then the miraculous wash of forgiveness overcame him, and the many instances of when he'd felt the Lord's gentle hand, His whispered word of encouragement, His promise that Bryce was okay, that he'd done enough, that he was good enough, flooded through him.

But human beings weren't divine, and Bryce had never had to tell a romantic partner about OJ. Or Bailey for that matter. He had no idea if Codi would be as forgiving or as kind, and all he could do was lay out all the cards and pray she wouldn't say she didn't want to see him for a third date.

Probably shouldn't have driven her so far and then told her, he thought. Because if she was now uncomfortable around him? It was a long drive back to Coral Canyon.

Behind him, the snapping, popping, and buzzing of a light came on as the sunlight continued to fade. "We're going to lose the silver," he murmured, glancing out to the lake again. "It turns to oil in the darkness."

With the truth out now, Bryce reached for his hummus-covered celery and took a bite. He ate too much hummus with only the gentle lapping of the water and the crunching of his veggies lifting into the silence.

"Cookie?" he asked Codi, and she quickly cleared the food she'd put on the bench seat between them. Then, before he could truly process what was happening, she slid over and pressed herself right into his chest.

The natural thing to do was to put his arm around her, his hand resting on her thigh as he enveloped her in a partial embrace. So he did that, once again paying attention to how he felt. He wasn't hungry by any means, but he couldn't think of a single time he'd passed up a cookie if one was available.

Codi took one too, but she ate it without comment, without a moan of satisfaction, without a word.

The silence was going to suffocate him. "You don't have anything to say?"

She took a breath, held it, and released it. "I like the lake as a big body of oil just as much as I like it as a pool of silver."

"Not what I meant," he whispered, his gaze nowhere near the lake. He ducked his head, the brim of his cowboy hat coming to rest on top of her head. She smelled like vanilla and hand pies and chocolate, and Bryce could kiss her if she'd turn toward him even a little bit.

Panic reared beneath his ribs, and he straightened as she turned her head to look at him. "You're a beautiful man, Bryce," she said.

He sighed, because she wasn't saying anything he wanted to hear. He wasn't even sure what he wanted to hear, but not what she'd said.

"You process verbally," she said. "I don't. I think it to death, and then I come to a conclusion, and then I think *that* to death."

He smiled at her, because she was just so cute. So good. Probably too good for him. He did lean toward her again, but his lips landed on her cheek. "I can give you time to think," he whispered in her ear, satisfied when she pressed further into his touch. "If you don't want to see me again until you've thought everything to death, that's okay."

"I didn't say that," she whispered.

"Then what are you doing tomorrow?"

"Well." She drew in another breath big enough to lift her chest and her shoulders. "There's this cowboy I know who has a horse he can't control, and since I'm going to be picking up my new dog out his way, I figured I'd go by his place and see if I can help with the equine."

A smile bloomed in his chest and grew through his stomach, his throat, and out onto his mouth. It filled his soul and sprouted up into the sky. "This cowboy must be special."

"He's got a few things I like," Codi said. She leaned her head against his chest, their bodies making a T right there at the picnic table.

Bryce had not planned to meet Codi or start dating her, but he felt so many things in his life shifting to make room for her. His crazy schedule around Rising Sun Ranch. His relationships inside his own family. His assumptions about his future.

And while changes to his plans normally irritated him and caused him grief, this one simply didn't. This one calmed him, and he hoped he could be the champion she needed in her life too.

13

"Bryce!" Melissa yelled as she came flying down the side stairs. She still wore her church dress and shoes, and oh, Momma would be mad about that. It had rained during church, and surely his younger sister's shoes and socks were about to get muddy.

Mel had never cared about that. She loved going out onto the farm with Daddy or Uncle Wade, and she often came back covered in mud, bug bites, or both.

"Howdy," Bryce said as he reached her. She was ten, but he stood at least twice as tall as her and could easily scoop her into his arms the way he'd been doing for the past decade.

"Bryce," Carver called from the deck. "Kassie."

"Get back in here," Momma yelled, and Bryce grinned at his siblings, then his best friend, who'd come with him to the farmhouse for lunch today.

Even Pippa had come outside, and she didn't even have

139

shoes on anymore. Carver stayed up on the deck, but Pippa sure didn't, and that was how Bryce ended up with both girls in his arms as he climbed the steps to his brother, Kassie right behind him.

"Why am I the celebrity today?" he asked them. "And where's Franny?" His daddy's German shepherd always had a bark of a greeting for Bryce, and she usually beat all the kids outside as she had four legs compared to their two.

"Uncle Wade took 'er out to the stables," Carver said. "We got something for you."

"Something for me?" He set Pippa and Mel on their feet. "It's not even my birthday." He grinned at his more sober brother. He'd turned six a few weeks ago, and while he had a stubborn streak over what he put in his mouth, he was by far the mildest of Daddy's and Abby's kids.

"Come see," Mel said, pulling on his hand.

"Yeah, go see." Pippa moved behind him and started pushing.

"Hurry up, Bryce," Kassie teased, totally egging on the little girls.

"I'm goin'," he said with a laugh. "I'm goin' already." He entered the farmhouse to the scent of bacon—seriously nothing better—mingled with his momma's perfume.

"Hey, Momma." He stepped into Abby and gave her a kiss on the cheek. "Sorry to make such a big splash." He came over all the time, so he really wasn't sure what today was about. Even Kassie came out here with him often enough to make it normal.

"It's not really your fault," she said. "And just so you know, there are some things I can't control."

That didn't sound good, and Bryce looked past her to the dining room table that sat down at the end of the galley kitchen, against the wall.

His heart leapt straight up, smashing into the back of his throat. "Harry." He strode toward his country music-famous cousin and wrapped him up tight.

"Hey, Bryce," Harry said, pounding him on the back.

"Why didn't I know you were comin'? How long are you here?" He stepped away from his cousin. "Why aren't you staying with me?" Harry had been gone from Coral Canyon for about five years now, and he'd often stayed with Bryce when he returned. Uncle Trace and Aunt Ev had little kids, and a not-big house, and Bryce had bedroom upon bedroom he didn't use.

"Ev's having another baby," he said. "They wanted me to come for the announcement."

Bryce's eyebrows went up. "Wow, good for them." He glanced over to Abby as she approached and put something on the table. "I hadn't heard that. Must not have been on the family text."

"Not yet," Abby said.

"Harry," Kassie said, easing past Bryce and into his cousin's arms. "How's the South?"

"Already too hot," Harry said dutifully. He smiled at Kassie while Bryce watched. Once upon a time, he'd wondered if they'd had a little chemistry. A fizz of attraction. He'd asked Kassie about it multiple times, and she'd denied it over and over.

Right now, Harry didn't seem to be looking at her any differently than he looked at Bryce, and they were about a decade apart in age.

"Where's Daddy?" he asked.

"He went to get Aunt Leigh," Abby said. "He didn't want her driving herself with the twins being so close."

Bryce frowned, because things just weren't adding up. "But if Harry's here, then shouldn't Uncle Morris be?" He didn't travel with Harry full-time, because he had a family here—a wife and almost five children—but he had been with him in Nashville for the past two weeks, prepping for a summer season of choreography, working out, and song perfection before Harry's next tour, which began in September.

"He got really sick last night," Harry said as he backed up to put more distance between him and Kassie. "Couldn't fly. I almost didn't come either."

Concern spiked through Bryce. "So he's alone?"

"I flew home today," Harry said. "Gabe flew down there to be with him."

"Harry," Carver said, stepping into their huddle. "Will you teach me to play the guitar?" The little boy had his guitar out and everything, and Harry crouched down in front of him.

"We're gonna eat lunch, buddy, so I can't right now."

"Besides," Momma said. "Harry doesn't do lessons." She looked over to Bryce, who experienced a guttering of guilt.

"I can teach you," he said to Carver. "I used to teach guitar lessons, and I might be able to find some time."

Carver's whole countenance brightened. "Really, Bryce?"

"Bryce," Kassie said almost under her breath. Definitely not loud enough for anyone else to hear.

"Sure." He ignored his best friend and picked up the little boy to hug him, guitar and all. He hadn't wanted to do lessons here, because it felt like a Past-Bryce thing to do. He and Kassie had come here to do New-Bryce and New-Kassie things.

"Hey, hey," someone called, and that wasn't Daddy or Aunt Leigh, which meant more people had been invited to lunch. As Uncle Trace, Aunt Ev, and her brother Reggie entered the house, Bryce understood why Abby had said there were things she couldn't control.

Today's lunch was supposed to be his family, Kassie, and Morris's family. Now Harry was here, as were his momma and daddy, and they had three little kids between them as well.

A whole small town, he thought, and his plans to tell everyone about Codi started to wither on the vine. He reasoned they didn't have to. Uncle Trace had already met her, and Harry wouldn't care. In fact, he'd be keenly interested. Kassie knew as well, as did his parents, though it hadn't been Bryce who'd told them.

"Take it over to him then," Ev said, and Reggie drew closer. He wore his hair long, and it curled in sandy waves down past his ears and well along his collar.

"Heya, Harry," he said, and he seemed shy. For a professional baseball player, that struck Bryce as odd. Not only that, but Reggie and Ev's older brother, Shawn, had been coming to Young family parties for years. He shouldn't be nervous at all.

He held Harry's latest album. "My manager's wife is a huge fan, and when she found out I was gonna be in Coral Canyon here and there this summer, she begged me to see if you could sign this for her."

Harry grinned at the album—his second—and said, "Sure, Reg. No problem."

Bryce grabbed him a marker; Harry signed his name; Kassie asked, "Do you guys want me to get a picture of the two of you?"

"She'll freak out," Reggie said. "And maybe I won't get traded this year."

"I'm surprised you can be here," Kassie said as she held up her phone and Reggie and Harry moved in to pose together. "Isn't it high baseball season?"

"*High* baseball season?" Bryce teased. "As opposed to *low* baseball season?"

"Oh, be quiet, you." She took several pictures and waltzed the two steps over to Reggie. "I'm gonna need your number to send you this."

All the stars in heaven, he thought. Kassie was flirting with Reggie Avery right in front of everyone.

"We're here," another man called, and Bryce knew this voice like his own. Uncle Otis. "There he is." He laughed as he jogged through the kitchen to Harry too, and the two of them embraced and laughed together.

Kassie had just gone out with someone else a few nights ago, but Bryce watched as she and Reggie receded into the living room between the kitchen and the front door, and she was still standing way too close to him to be friendly.

What in the world was happening?

The front door opened, and Aunt Leigh walked in, her belly far bigger than it had been the last time Bryce had seen her. She seriously looked like she was about to topple forward, and he moved to help her.

"Your father needs help with my kids," she said. "I swear,

I'm going to get sick somewhere and have my sister fly in to stay with me until I'm better."

Bryce actually laughed out loud and went outside to help Daddy with Eric, Rachelle, and Skip. They were a bit on the wild side, Morris and Leigh's kids, but they were sweet as pie on the inside.

"Come on, you hooligans," Bryce called from the porch. "Last one inside doesn't get any hugs from me."

That caused squealing and running, at least from the younger two. Eric would be thirteen next month, and he sure didn't want anyone to know he might like a hug from his cousin. He wasn't the problem anyway, and Bryce swept Rachelle and Skip into his arms the moment they got to the porch.

"What about your daddy?" he asked them. "Are you prayin' for him?"

"Him not come home," Skip said as he put his hands on Bryce's beard. Eric had been really tactile as a younger child too, and Bryce was used to having little hands on his face. He didn't particularly like it, but he was used to it.

"He threw up all. Night. Long," Rachelle said. "Momma didn't even throw up that much with the twins."

"Wow, that's bad news bears," Bryce said.

"Bad news bears," Skip repeated as he wiggled to get down. Bryce set him on his feet, and both he and Rachelle ran in the house.

"Howdy, Eric." He held out his fist as the near-teen climbed the few steps to the porch.

"Heya, Bryce." They bumped fists, and then Bryce came face-to-face with his father.

"Definitely grayer today," he teased as he drew his father into a hug.

"As opposed to seven days ago when you saw me last?"

"Definitely," Bryce said. "Who else is coming?"

"No one," Daddy said. "Trace, Otis, Leigh, us."

"Harry, Kassie, and Reggie too," Bryce said, pulling away just as a round of laughter blasted out of the house. He pressed his eyes closed for a moment. Then Abby started yelling about the food being ready, and kids were eating on the deck, and Bryce followed his father inside without a word of complaint.

He stayed out of the way while people crowded into the room for the prayer, and then he stayed quiet while Abby told everyone about the food. Parents hustled their kids through the line and outside, and by the time Bryce found himself with a paper plate and a piece of barbecue chicken, plenty of side conversations had broken out.

He doctored up his baked potato while Kassie flirted shamelessly with Reggie in line behind him, and he sat down at the table, which had been pulled away from the wall to provide enough seats for the twelve adults there that day. With so many of them, they were using the corners, but they'd certainly fed a lot of people at this table before.

The moment Kassie sat down, she looked at Bryce. He recognized that glint in her eye, and he started to wave her off, their plan notwithstanding. "So," she said, not getting his subliminal message in time. "Bryce, I hear you're seeing someone."

The line got delivered with such a false brightness to her voice, and she'd practically screamed it. Yes, he'd asked her to help him segue into telling everyone about Codi, and he cursed himself for not changing plans mid-stream as effectively as he should've.

"Oh-ho-ho," Harry said. "Why don't I know about this?"

"Sounds like you came home for two announcements," Otis said.

Bryce looked at his uncle. Otis already knew about Codi. So did Trace. Kassie. His parents. Leigh didn't, but okay. He stirred his sour cream, butter, cheese, and bacon into the flesh of his baked potato.

"All right, yeah," he said. Clearing his throat only made him sound nervous, but he couldn't stop himself. "I'm—yeah. I've been out with a woman a few times now."

"Grandma made rice pudding for one of their dates," Joey said.

Bryce's gaze swept to her, sandwiched between the broad shoulders of her father and Uncle Trace. "She told you that?"

Joey smiled her perfectly symmetrical smile. "She's teaching me how to cook a few things. Did you like the rice pudding? It was my first time making it." She casually put a bite of chicken in her mouth, like his love life wasn't crashing down around them.

"Wow, rice pudding," Daddy said.

"It's not a big deal," Bryce said as quickly as he could.

"Rice pudding takes forever to make," Uncle Trace commented, and Bryce wanted to ask, *Yeah, so?*

"Why's Grandma catering your dates?" Daddy asked.

"It was the night of that big movie premiere," Bryce said. "The restaurants were insane. I simply asked her for ideas, and the next thing I know, she's telling me to stop by for a fully packed picnic."

"Sounds like Momma," Otis said.

"Where'd you go?" Kassie asked.

Bryce glared at her, and her eyes got big. "What?" she asked. "It's a normal question."

"Silver Lake," he said.

Kassie blinked, clearly getting it. Bryce wasn't sure who else would. "Oh."

"Real pretty up there," Uncle Trace said, so he didn't really get what Silver Lake meant to Bryce. Kassie did, though, and she gave him an encouraging smile.

Buoyed by that, Bryce said, "Her name is Codi Hudson, and yes, we've been out—sort of—a couple of times. Once, I guess, if we're being technical, but it's a—this—it's a *thing*. And it's really new, and I don't want to talk about it with y'all. I don't need to be asked every five minutes how it's going, and I don't need any advice. I'm almost thirty years old, and I'm—" He met his father's eyes. "I'm seeing how it's going."

A beat of silence filled the kitchen, then another.

"I think I can wait six minutes to ask how it's going," Uncle Otis quipped.

Bryce grinned at him. "You get six minutes. Everyone else gets six days."

"Six *days?*" Abby asked, clearly aghast.

"And no one is to call her up and start getting copious amounts of dog grooming, okay?" He gave his momma a glare. "Franny has never even had a professional bath, all right? She doesn't need to start now." He looked over to his aunt. "Aunt Georgia?"

"That was a one-time thing, honey," she said. "Promise, promise."

He nodded, about talked out—which meant a lot for him.

"Wait, I want to know what this all means." Leigh gestured between Abby, Georgia, and Bryce. "A one-time thing of what?"

"Oh, boy," Bryce muttered.

"I'll tell you later, Leigh," Abby said. Thankfully.

"We don't even own a dog," Aunt Ev said. "I think we should get ten minutes at least." She looked over to Trace. "He didn't even tell your momma and daddy about her when he found you with that puncture wound."

"Hold the front door," Harry said. "Puncture wound?"

"This is fun," Kassie said, taking a bite of her salad. She'd always loved his family parties, because no, they were never dull.

"I'm sure you'll still find a way to call her," Bryce said to Ev, ignoring Kassie and Harry.

"Wait. Did you say Codi Hudson?" she asked, swiping on her phone. She looked up, her blue eyes round. "Honey, she applied to the Small Business Association in town."

Trace started to laugh, and Bryce's stomach fell to the soles of his cowboy boots. "Of course she did."

"I set up an interview with her for Tuesday." Ev put down her phone. "This can't be held against me. *I* didn't reach out to her the way Georgia did."

"Bryce hasn't dated in a decade," Georgia argued back. "In

my defense, I'm really good at reading people, and I don't want him to get his heart broken."

"So fun," Kassie said again, and she was clearly enjoying herself.

Harry started to chuckle, and Bryce looked at him for help too. His cousin shook his head and said, "I'm just here for the ride, but I agree with Kassie. It's fun."

"It wouldn't be fun if it was you," he said.

Harry shook his head and took another bite of cole slaw. "Probably not. You're okay, though? The puncture wound?" They ignored the adult bickering around them.

"Yeah, fine," Bryce said. "A hazard of the ranch."

Harry reached over and covered Bryce's hand. "I'm glad you're doing this, brother. It feels like it's about time." His eyebrows went up, and while it was usually Bryce advising Harry, he had grown and matured a lot in the past few years.

"Yeah," he agreed. "It does feel like that."

"She's really pretty," Kassie said. "And she took Penta." She looked back and forth between Harry, Bryce, and Reggie in their little pocket of the table. "Oh, Pentagon, Reg, is this super-cute beagle of mine. But he's just too high energy for me, and Codi bought him. She's *amazing* with animals, and Bryce is trying to hire her at the ranch."

The last several words got shouted into silence as the other adults around them stopped talking.

"Smooth," Bryce muttered, glancing over to his father.

His sky-high eyebrows didn't settle Bryce, but he was done talking for right now. Maybe later, when it was just the two of them.

"I need to start dating too," Reggie said into the silence, sparing Bryce and surprising him at the same time. Ev swung her attention toward him, as did everyone else at the table. "Kassie, would you like to go to dinner sometime?"

"Oh, boy," Bryce said again, his smile widening across his whole face. Hers turned bright, bright red, and that meant only one thing—she liked Reggie already.

"How long has this been goin' on?" he asked, leaning closer but not trying to keep his voice down. "You're crushing on him *hard.*"

"Stop it," she said, pushing against his chest to get him to back up. Bryce did sit back, but he couldn't stop smiling.

Harry catcalled, but Reggie just sat there, grinning at her and waiting for an answer. The whole table, the whole house, seemed to be holding its breath.

Then she said, "All right, sure. I'd like that," and then the real cheering started.

At least I didn't have to deal with that, he thought. Of course, he did have plenty more aunts and uncles to deal with, and none of them—except Trace—had actually met Codi yet. And he started praying that once she worked through all he'd told her about OJ on Friday night, he'd have the chance to start doing that.

14

Codi brushed her fingers through her hair, the motion slowing as she got the side-part to land just the way she wanted it. She had an interview this morning with someone for the Coral Canyon Small Business Association, which she figured she might as well join. She'd bathed a dog yesterday morning, and she had two more appointments this week.

"You're going to go to that book shop today too," she told her reflection sternly. She reached up and fingered the wig again. Then she slid it off and removed the constraining wig cap as well. Her hair wisped off her head, and she could gather it up and make a tiny ponytail.

It really wasn't that she was bald. She had hair. No, not a lot, but she had some. What she really worried over was the color of it. Combined with the thinness and how it wouldn't grow past her chin, the pure whiteness of it caused people to look. They thought something was wrong with her, and Codi didn't like holding up the weight of their gazes.

She'd been wearing wigs for several years, and she rather liked the ability to have bangs one day and a side-part another. She liked that she could roll out of bed, pretty much a complete mess, and have perfect hair within seconds.

So, like she had many times before, she put the wig cap back in place, tucking in all the wispy ends of her hair and pushing it back to create a hairline. Then she positioned the wig back where she wanted it, pressed to activate the clip, and reached for her toothbrush.

Ready several minutes early, she looked at her phone, her desire to text Bryce climbing up through her whole system this morning. She hadn't seen him since Saturday, when she'd gone out to Kassie's to get Pentagon. Then, she'd stayed to help with Dragon.

He hadn't gone silent on her, which she appreciated. "He also hasn't asked you out again," she said, reaching for her phone. While her stomach cramped and growled, she tapped as quickly as she could.

I'm going to a meeting for the Small Business Association in town this morning. Then Kassie invited me to lunch at her house. I said I'd go. I'm wondering if you need an extra body working with the horses this afternoon? I could come. If you want.

Her anxiety forced her to read over the text again, and she deleted the last three words. She didn't need to make herself sound needy or nervous. Her self-invitation to his farm did that just fine on its own.

With that deletion, she sent the text.

Bryce seemed attached to his phone, but when Codi spent time with him, she didn't feel like he was. He sure did respond quickly this morning though. *Did you hear me praying while I waited for my toast to pop up?*

She smiled, because that was so Bryce. *No, sir. Just thinking about you.*

You can come work if you let me pay you. Otherwise, no ma'am. I'm fine on the ranch this afternoon.

Codi sighed, because while she didn't necessarily need the money, she definitely needed work that paid in real dollars. Her momma's inheritance could sustain her for several more months, but Codi was ready to start making her own way in the world again.

Okay, Mister Young, she said. *You can pay me.*

Great. Now, let's talk about you having lunch with my best friend....

Codi giggled, and she decided they could talk instead of text. She dialed him, and he picked up with, "I think I've died and gone to heaven, Miss Codi."

"Why's that?" she asked.

"Because you called, and you hate talking on the phone." The tell-tale sound of crunching toast came through the line, and Bryce said, "Go on, Lucky. We're already late."

Codi took a centering breath. "Kassie is a nice woman," Codi said. "She invited me when I picked up Pentagon, and she said she'd talk to you about it." She glanced down at the black, brown, and white beagle who perked up at his name.

"That little liar," he said good-naturedly. "I've heard nothing of a lunch between you two."

"I don't have any friends in town," Codi admitted. "Well, not of the homo sapiens variety, at least."

He chuckled and said, "Kassie and I have a very strong friendship. If she wants to have you for lunch, it's fine with me."

"Is it?" Codi bent and unlatched Penta's crate. "You aren't worried about what she'll tell me?"

"I am not," Bryce said with supreme confidence. "I trust Kassie."

Trust.

Codi nodded toward the hall, and Penta trotted ahead of her. "Bryce, I want you to know I trust you too."

He said nothing, and Codi wasn't sure what she was trying to say. She followed her pooch and opened the door for him so he could go outside and take care of his business. "I have that meeting this morning, like I said. Then I'll be out your way. Maybe—you said there was a Mongolian barbecue place that was good up there? Maybe we could go there tonight."

Another pause came through the line, and Codi could hear her own increased breathing as she climbed a flight of steps after her dog. "You've processed everything I told you about OJ?" he finally asked.

"Yes," Codi said. She watched Penta sniff and run and sniff some more. "I think you're an amazing person, Bryce. It couldn't have been easy to give up your baby for your aunt and uncle to raise. It can't be easy to see him all the time now. I—I guess I'm saying I don't think badly of you for it, and it's not going to be a thing between us."

"Someone really did hear my prayers this morning," he murmured.

Codi smiled as the sunlight stole across the grass where she waited. "I'm bringing Penta to the ranch, if that's okay."

"Totally fine," he said. "You two are getting along okay?"

"He's the best dog ever," Codi said.

"Listen, before I let you go." Something creaked on his end of the line, and it sounded like a big, barn door. "Your meeting this morning? At the Small Business Association? It's with my aunt Ev."

The air whooshed out of Codi's lungs. "You have got to be kidding me."

"I did warn you about us," Bryce said with another chuckle. "She's Trace's wife. You met Trace the other night, remember?"

"Of course I remember," Codi said, feeling like the ground might vanish beneath her feet now. "Big country music star? Cowboy hotness? Got a son in the industry now? It would be impossible *not* to remember." She shook her head, the length of the wig brushing along her shoulder blades.

Bryce fully laughed then, but Codi had a hard time absorbing the joy of it over the phone. Penta finished up, and she moved to the back corner of the house to pick up his throwing toy and ball. She'd run him a little this morning, then take him out to the ranch later.

"I'm gonna pretend the 'cowboy hotness' part was for me," Bryce said. "Not my fifty-year-old uncle."

"Age has nothing to do with beauty," she said.

"That it does not." He took a breath. "Okay, come find me when you get here, all right? I don't really know where I'll be."

"Sounds good." The call ended, and Codi shoved her phone in her back pocket. She suddenly felt like blue jean shorts and the flowered blouse she wore wouldn't be good enough for her meeting that morning. The problem was, blue jean shorts and a flowered, sleeveless blouse was the epitome of Codi Hudson. She wasn't going to wear something that represented someone she wasn't.

"It's fine," she told herself. Then she whistled through her teeth and pointed to the ground right in front of her. Penta came galloping toward her, and he sat down on a dime, his face up toward hers, eager to do what she asked.

"Good boy." She snapped her fingers and gave him a bit of liver from her other pocket. "Get it. Bring it." She spoke in short sentences, with clipped words, and she launched the ball out into the field of grass behind the apartment building.

Penta sprinted after it, grabbing it out of the foliage and turning back to her. "Bring it," she called, once again pointing to the ground. Bring it he did, and he sat down right in front of her. Another snap. Another treat.

He really was an amazing, smart, capable, easily-trainable dog. Codi played with him for several more minutes, and then she took him back inside. Kassie had not kept Penta in a crate, but Codi believed dogs liked having their own space, where they felt safe and comfortable.

He went into his crate easily, then turned right around for that piece of liver. Once he'd taken it, he lay down as Codi latched the gate. "I'll be back really soon, okay?" she told him. "And I'm not cheating on you and washing another dog today." She grinned at the beagle and left the apartment.

Her goal was to be able to bring Penta on all her jobs. She could put a bed or a crate in the corner of the bus, and he could accompany her around town. They still had a ways to go in order to do that, and Codi mulled over the idea of working for the Rising Sun Ranch—she struggled to think of herself as working for Bryce—while she built up her grooming business.

"Why can't I do both?" she wondered. Her grooming appointments sometimes came in erratically, but she could reserve mornings for those and give afternoons to Rising Sun. Before she knew it, she'd parked at the community center, and she didn't have much time to spare. She certainly couldn't sit around in her car, worrying over what Bryce would think if she went to him with an employment proposal.

"Anyway, *he* asked *you*," she muttered to herself as she got out of the car. Inside the air conditioned building, Codi got directed to where she needed to be, and a blonde woman probably a decade older than her appeared in the doorway of the appointed room before Codi could walk through it.

"You must be Codi," she said pleasantly.

Codi watched her look down to her feet and back to her eyes, but nothing but friendliness existed inside this woman. "I am. And you must be Bryce's aunt."

Her eyebrows went up, and she had the kind of blonde hair that Codi could only achieve with a wig. "He told you."

"Yes, he did." Codi shook the woman's hand with a smile. "It's fine. He said you Youngs are like a small town all by yourselves. I didn't really believe him, to be honest." She laughed a little as Ev went back into the room. Codi followed her, and as she sat down in one of the chairs, she added, "I do now."

"I own a dance studio here in town," she said. "I'm the president of the Association this year, that's all. It's my first time, actually, so you're just unlucky it's me." She gave Codi a bright smile. "But I'm thrilled to meet you. Trace said he met you last week too."

"Yes, we met. He was really sweet, concerned about Bryce as he was."

Ev lit up then, and she said, "He is sweet. He just likes to play that bad boy cowboy, you know? It's his image for the band."

"I kind of got that impression." Codi liked Ev Young, and she found that surprising too. "So I own a mobile dog grooming business," she said. "And I was taking around flyers to some businesses and asking them to set them out for me, and someone mentioned this Association."

"Who was it?" Ev asked.

"A secretary at this trailer rental place," Codi said. "I don't remember her name. It was down on the end of Main Street."

"Landon's been coming to our meetings for years, yes," Ev said.

"Right," Codi said, though she didn't know who Landon was. "Anyway, she said that y'all here often do swaps like that for each other. Like I might give out a coupon for the hardware store to my dog parents. Stuff like that. So I thought I'd find out more."

"Absolutely," Ev said, the folder in her lap just sitting there. "I'd take some of your flyers for my dance studio."

"Really?" Codi perked up. "I'd love that. I have some in the car, because, well...." She studied Ev for a moment and then tucked her hair behind her ear. "I knew Georgia was Bryce's aunt, and she owns the book shop. I didn't go there, because I was nervous, but I made a promise to myself to stop by before I head up to the ranch this afternoon."

Ev laughed, and it was a glorious sound. "We're going to keep the fact that Georgia scared you between us." She handed Codi the folder. "Application is in there. You bring it back here when it's all filled out, and you do need to have two people sponsor you for membership. But I'd be happy to, and I'm sure Georgia would. Hilde too."

"Hilde?" Codi flipped open the folder to find several sheets of paperwork inside.

"She owns the furniture store on the west side of town," Ev said. "The big one you see as you come in?"

"Oh, sure," Codi said, as she had passed it.

"She's Gabe's wife."

Codi's smile turned a little plastic. "And Gabe must be a Young."

"Yes," Ev said, her smile almost dazzling. "Hilde is amazing."

"Of course she is."

Ev only grinned wider. "Faith sold her doughnut trucks, but we all know Joe. He'd put some flyers on the Hole in One trucks for you. He'd sponsor you too, if you didn't want a whole Young wives sponsorship happening."

She closed the folder. "Still feels like I'm using the Youngs to get what I need."

"Mav's wife co-owns the flower shop," Ev said. "She'd sponsor you."

"Do any of you own the hardware store?" she asked.

Ev shook her head, pure delight radiating from her. "I'm

glad you're in town, Codi. The only pet grooming spot we have is called Clipped, and let me just say...someone that old shouldn't be anywhere near a pair of clippers."

Codi couldn't help laughing, and she decided it didn't matter who sponsored her. "Do you think there's a need for a business like mine here? Bryce said he hasn't used a groomer much. He just washes Lucky with the hose."

"Sure, you're gonna get that," Ev said. "It's a small town, but spread out. Lots of people have land, and horses, and small farms, so they just wash their dogs themselves. But I definitely think there's a lot of potential for you and It's Poochy Keen here in Coral Canyon."

Codi nodded, not sure why she needed this reassurance. "Thank you, Miss Ev."

She stood, and Codi did too. "We review applications in our third Thursday meeting, so if you want to be in by next month, I need that in the next couple of weeks."

"Yes, of course."

Ev turned back to her at the doorway of the room. "You're a delight, Codi. I see why Bryce likes you."

Codi studied her for a moment. "Did he tell you about us?"

Ev nodded. "He said a few things at lunch on Sunday. Then he put it on the family text."

"How many messages did it get up to that day?"

Ev's blue eyes sparkled. "Hundreds."

Codi nodded, swallowed, and ducked her way past the woman and out of the room. "I—okay. Thanks, Miss Ev. I'll get this application back in soon."

"Bye, Codi," Ev called.

She lifted her hand in a wave, smiled over her shoulder, and kept right on walking. In the car, she took several long, deep breaths, trying to decide why it mattered if Bryce had told his family about the two of them.

Of course he would. He couldn't keep her a secret forever.

"He likes you." She smiled to herself in the rearview mirror. "And you like him. So don't make this a big deal."

With that, Codi set her sights on the book shop downtown. Then, she had to head home, load up her dog, and get up to Dog Valley.

15

Kassie Goodman knew someone had arrived at her little red brick house simply by the way Gilligan lifted his ginormous head. He only did that if he'd heard something, and Kassie followed his gaze out of the kitchen and toward the front door.

"Is someone here, bud?"

The black-and-white great Dane sighed as he heaved himself off the couch. He was all leg as he walked over to the front door and put his big, black nose right on it. Kassie put the stack of small lunch plates on the table and went to see if Codi had arrived.

Her phone cheered like someone had smacked a home run right out of the park, which meant Reggie had texted. He'd gone home on Sunday night, because it was baseball season, and he had a job to do.

"Yeah," she said. "Standing in a field in striped pants. How is that a job?"

But it was, and Reggie made a lot of money wearing a ballcap and a baseball glove. He played shortstop for the Seattle Stingrays, but he'd confessed to Kassie via text that he was growing tired of it.

He was thirty-five years old, and he'd been playing ball for thirteen years. He had plenty of money in the bank, and if he was to be believed, he was lonely. Both of his parents had died years and years ago in a car accident, and his older brother and sister were both married now, with families of their own.

Gilligan barked, his deep voice filling the house and causing Stormy, Kassie's Pomeranian, to go into full small-dog attack mode. She *bark-bark-howled*, and Kassie rolled her eyes.

"Come on, guys," she said. "It's probably Penta, come to say hi." She opened the door, using her leg and hip to keep Gilligan back. Sure enough, Codi stood on the doorstep with Penta on a leash. The little beagle sat right at her side, his tail wagging against the cement.

"I knew he'd be perfect for you," Kassie said with a grin. She knew she'd been failing Pentagon, and she was just so happy that Codi could have him. She pushed open the screen door until Codi grabbed the handle. "Come on in."

"Hey, Kassie," the other blonde woman said, and there was something different about her today. Kassie couldn't quite put her finger on what, so she just iwatched Codi as she entered the house. She made Gilligan and Stormy sit down before she'd let Penta off the leash, and then they got to do their doggy sniffy greetings.

"It smells good in here," Codi said, looking toward the kitchen.

"I made my granny's buttermilk biscuits," Kassie said. She moved toward the kitchen, Codi flowing with her. She felt like a giant next to the woman, as Kassie probably towered four inches taller than her.

"How are things going with Penta?"

"So good." Codi sank onto a barstool though they'd be eating at Kassie's small dining room table-for-four. "Thank you for selling him to me. I love him."

Kassie got out three jars of jam and turned to face Codi. "You have no bangs," she said as she realized what was different about her. "Did you cut them? No, that makes no sense."

Codi brushed her hair back off the side of her face and gave her a smile. "It's not my real hair."

Instant heat filled Kassie's face. "Oh, I'm sorry, Codi."

"It's fine," she said like it was nothing.

"I say dumb things sometimes," she said. "Bryce is always telling me I put my foot in my mouth at least twice a day."

"That's funny," Codi said with a smile. "Because that man talks a lot."

"Right?" Kassie grinned at her. "He just has to get things out."

"I kinda like it," Codi admitted. "I don't have to guess about what's going through his mind."

"It's not always bad." She took the jars of jam over to the table. "We're eating over here."

Codi joined her and took in the spread. "Wow, Kassie. Look at all of this."

"My family is this old Southern…thing," she said. "We had bowls for the Fourth of July. Plates shaped like fall leaves in red, yellow, and orange. Platters for every holiday known to mankind."

"They're all flowers." Codi reached out and picked up one of the lunch plates. "They're cheery. I like them." She smiled at Kassie. "You don't like your family?"

"I do just fine," Kassie drawled. "Sometimes I miss them, but I really like living my own life up here."

"What did they do down South?"

"Racehorses," Kassie said, turning back to get the food out of the fridge. "I just wasn't into the family business, and when this opportunity came up, Bryce and I jumped at it." She got out the turkey and salami pinwheels, the sausage rolls, and the pimento cheese. "This is kind of a buffet. I put out little plates, and the idea is you just have a bunch of little things."

"Sounds good," Codi said. She possessed a good spirit about her, a calm spirit Bryce had called it. Kassie could feel it too, and she put down all the food on the far side of the table and took a seat kitty-corner to Codi.

"Bryce said you're working over on the ranch this afternoon." Kassie took a pinwheel as Codi picked up a pimento cheese pita.

"Yeah," she said. "I don't have anything else to do right now."

"Where are you from?" Kassie asked.

"Idaho," Codi said. "My daddy has a potato farm there. I grew up on it."

No wonder she knew animals and horses and hard work.

Kassie had wanted to get to know Codi from the moment she'd spoken to her about buying Penta. She just had something about her that Kassie sometimes felt with the equines.

Still, her mouth stuck together with the first bite of her pinwheel. She didn't want to offend Codi, but she hadn't asked her here just to get to know her.

They ate in silence for a minute or two, and then Kassie told herself to get the job done. "Codi," she said. "I'd like to work with you." She paused while the other woman lifted her eyes to meet Kassie's. "With the horses. I have sort of a system for how things go, and Bryce and I meet about the horses all the time. So I want to be your friend—Lord knows I have very few female friends here that Bryce is not related to—but I want to see if you and I can work together."

Codi nodded, the tips of her hair bobbing along her biceps. "Bryce offered me a job too."

"And...what do you think?"

"I told him I wanted to grow my grooming business."

Kassie nodded, the hope that had started to accumulate in her chest leaking away. "I see."

"I've been thinking about it," Codi said. "Which would be better? Me being out here in the mornings? Or the afternoons?"

Kassie blinked at her. "What?"

"I could do the grooming half-day," she said. "Work here half-day."

Kassie wanted to tell her that nothing about the Rising Sun Ranch was done halfway. Neither she nor Bryce had ever worked a half-day here; the very idea was laughable. But this was their ranch. They owned it. Codi didn't.

"I'd say afternoons, probably," Kassie said. "Bryce does a ton of feeding and moving in the morning. I can do the bigger, more general training in the morning, and then when you get here, we can niche down into what each horse needs."

Codi finished her pimento pita and reached for a sausage roll. "Is this going to make Bryce go nuts?" She looked up at Kassie through her eyelashes, and Kassie giggled.

"You know it will," she said. "But I don't care about him. I want you out here, because I think I could learn a lot from you."

"I don't have a clue what I'm doing," Codi said. "I can just...*feel* them, you know?" She looked out the back window, her expression lost for a moment. "It's like I know what they're thinking and feeling, and they just want someone safe."

"Our horses here especially," Kassie said, because she knew exactly what Codi was talking about. She'd always had a special connection with horses, in a way she couldn't describe any better than Codi just had. "As they heal, I heal a little bit."

Codi looked over to her again. "We all have a little bit of that to do, don't we?"

Rather than get into the disappointments and heartaches of her life, Kassie just nodded. "Okay, that's the business stuff." She took a deep breath, breaking the more somber mood. "I really do want us to be friends too, so tell me a fun fact about yourself."

Codi grinned at her. "I wear wigs."

"Boo," Kassie said, both of them smiling good-naturedly. "I knew that. Something I don't know."

"You go first," Codi challenged.

"Okay," Kassie brushed the crumbs from her hands. "I like

to put together a fantasy football team and play with my brothers in the fall."

Codi gaped at her, her blue eyes searching Kassie's for several long moments. "Well, I can't beat that," she finally said.

"Oh, come on," Kassie said. "It's not a competition. I mean, the fantasy football is, but not our fun facts." She picked up a biscuit and popped the top on the strawberry chili jam. "And my momma makes this jam from scratch. You're gonna love it. It's sweet with heat."

She pulled apart her biscuit, noting she'd gotten them just right. Her momma and grandmomma would be so proud.

"Sweet with heat," Codi said. "Yeah, I better try that."

Kassie buttered and then jammed her biscuit, and she slid it onto Codi's lunch plate. "I'm still waiting on that fun fact."

"All right." Codi straightened and gave Kassie a blinding grin, one that spoke of true happiness. "I like to sing in the shower."

"But are you any good? That's the real fun fact."

Codi picked up her biscuit, a serious look on her face as she took a sniff of the strawberry chili jam. "This is going to be good." She met Kassie's eyes. "And no, I'm tone deaf." Then she sank her teeth into the biscuit, her eyes drifted closed, and she moaned, "Oh, yeah. That's good," with maybe a few biscuity crumbs flying from her mouth.

"Fun fact," Kassie said. "She talks with her mouth full." She grinned at Codi and took a bite of her own newly jammed biscuit. "Which is fine, because so do I."

Kassie had never told Bryce that she was starting to feel lonely and alone here in Dog Valley. She really didn't have any friends except his family, him, and the horses. But as she and Codi giggled over biscuits and sweet-with-heat jam, Kassie truly hoped she could find a friend.

A female friend.

Someone she could tell about Reggie, and her worries and fears about him. Also, her hopes for the relationship, the excitement she felt when he video-called her, all of it. She had no one for that here, and Kassie really needed someone.

Plus, she wanted Codi to know there was and never had been anything between her and Bryce. She didn't bring it up now, because it didn't feel necessary, but she would soon enough.

As she got her biscuit down, her phone cheered again, and she set it between her and Codi. "Let's see what Reggie has to say." She looked at Codi with sparkles moving through her whole body. "He plays baseball in Seattle, and I'm gonna fly out there next month, during All-Star Week, because he won't be going to that."

"No?" Codi asked. "He's not an All-Star?" She grinned at Kassie. "Oh, I think he's an All-Star to some people."

Kassie couldn't argue with her there, and her stomach did a great big cartwheel as she thought about flying to a state and city she'd never visited before, to see her long-distance boyfriend. If that was even what Reggie was. They hadn't gone out. He'd only asked her, and she'd said yes.

Dating happens in a lot of different ways now, she told herself. She wasn't going to shut the door on something that could be great, she knew that. So she tapped on the video he'd sent, and she and Codi watched as he took them from the infield to the dugout and then inside the tunnel.

"Morning practice is done," he said. "I'm breaking for lunch, and then we'll be back outside in a bit." He turned the camera around, and Kassie caught sight of his handsome face, his sandy curls, and that lopsided smile. "How's your lunch with Codi going? Did she like the pimento pitas?"

Kassie looked at Codi, who reached over and picked up another pita. "She sure did," Codi said, and Kassie just knew they were going to be friends for life.

16

Bryce picked up an egg and put it in OJ's bucket. "Did you get those ones on the bottom there, bud?"

"Nope." OJ could get distracted walking a straight line, and Bryce smiled at him as he crouched down to get the eggs off the bottom row in the hen house. He came up with two eggs, both brown, and he put them in the bucket too.

"What are you gonna do with Grandpa Graham today?" Bryce looked over to the little boy, noticing his eyebrows droop down.

"I don't know," OJ said.

Bryce's pulse picked up speed. He so wasn't good at this kind of talk, but he'd committed to being open and honest with OJ about everything. He still took an extra moment to pull a couple of eggs from the next nest. "Do you not want to go up to the lodge?"

OJ looked at him, his eyes so open, so unassuming. "We might ride the horses."

Bryce smiled and nodded. "You like that."

"Yeah." OJ trailed behind him, not collecting the eggs. Bryce decided it didn't matter. Uncle Otis had brought OJ out to the ranch today, because school was now out for the summer, and they had a doctor's appointment with Ana in Jackson Hole.

Graham Whittaker, OJ's biological grandfather, was coming to get him in a few minutes, and he'd be staying with him and his wife, Laney, overnight. Bryce's heartstrings sang for the boy, especially if he didn't want to go.

"Hey, buddy," he said. "You gotta talk to me, okay?"

OJ looked at him again, right at him. No squirrelly-ness. No mouth moving a mile a minute. He looked almost like a subdued version of the boy Bryce knew him to be.

"Are you scared of something?" Bryce looked away to pick up the next egg.

"No." OJ bent down and gathered the eggs on the bottom row again.

"Tell me what's what," he said instead of asking another question. OJ didn't always know what to say, and answering questions usually got him talking more than leaving something open ended. But Bryce felt like neither was working right now.

"It's just my birth mom," he said. "I've been thinking about her lately."

"You have?" Bryce's eyebrows went up with the timbre of his voice. "Why's that?"

"We had to do these like, chain-thingys at school for the last week, and everyone had all these fun family vacations and stuff."

"You go on family vacations," Bryce said. "I know, because I'm takin' all those animals so you all can go to the Lion Lodge." He smiled, but OJ didn't see it.

"I just started thinking about her," OJ said. "Do you think she might ever come back here? Like, could I ever meet her?"

Bryce drew in a deep breath, his mind whirling a mile a moment. "I don't know, bud. I know she's been back to town a few times, but it's—it's really hard for her to see you."

"You see me all the time," OJ said. "It's not weird or anything."

"No." Bryce smiled softly, almost to himself. "It's not. But buddy, I've had a lot of practice. I've been to a lot of counseling sessions. I've worked really hard so we can be together." He paused in gathering the eggs and looked at his boy. His child. "And that's not because of you. It's because of me. It's because *I* needed to be okay with seeing you and not beating myself up for what happened."

"And she hasn't done that?"

"I don't know what she's done or not done, OJ." Bryce spoke quietly. "I haven't talked to your birth mom in a while."

"Grandpa Graham sees me all the time. It's not weird."

"Yeah, he and Grandma Laney love you." Bryce pulled in a breath. "OJ, I didn't mean for it to sound like that means your birth mom doesn't love you." He reached the end of the row and picked up the bucket. "Let's go outside."

The heat in the hen house didn't exactly make the smell very tolerable, and Bryce could get the rest of the eggs later.

Sometimes, conversations were more important than tasks, something his daddy had taught him.

They retreated from the hen house, and Bryce sat on the steps leading up to it. OJ did too, and he ruffled the boy's hair. "Buddy, your birth mom and I loved you so much. It was the only thing she wanted to do when she had you. She said to me, 'Bryce we have to make sure he knows how much we love him.'"

He could still hear Bailey saying so, all these years later, her voice pitched up and tinny with tears. He gazed at the sunflowers waving in the gentle breeze, and they infused him with hope, with vibrancy, and with bravery.

"But giving you away was really painful, even though we knew it was the right thing to do." He looked over to OJ, who picked at something on the end of his shorts. "You listenin' to me?"

"Yeah." He didn't look up, though.

"You hearin' me?" Bryce knew the difference between listening and hearing, but OJ might not yet.

"Yeah." OJ looked at him then.

"I left town," Bryce said. "Seeing you...it was hard. Even though I knew you belonged to Uncle Otis and Aunt Georgia. Even though I knew your birth mom and I had done the right thing. It was just...really hard. I had a lot to fix inside myself, and once I started doing that, it was way easier to come home and hold you, and kiss you, and celebrate your birthday with you."

He grinned at the boy, who smiled back at him. OJ crowded into Bryce's side, and he lifted his arm around the skinny kid.

"You can ask Grandma Laney about your birth mom, buddy. She'll tell you."

"They show me pictures," OJ said. "I feel bad, because Grandma Laney looks sad sometimes."

"She just misses her," Bryce whispered, missing Bailey keenly in that moment. "That's all. It's not because of you."

"Do you...?" He trailed off, and Bryce really wished he could get inside the child's head. He wondered how often his father had wanted this for him, and the thought made him smile.

"Do I what?"

"In our class this year," OJ said. "We wrote letters to military people who lived somewhere else. We sent them Skittles and stuff, and some of them wrote our class back."

"Mm hm." Bryce wasn't sure where this was headed, as OJ sometimes hopped topics like a jackrabbit.

"I was thinkin' of maybe asking Grandpa Graham and Grandma Laney if they'd help me write her a letter. They've told me her birthday is in July, and well, it's June, and I could maybe draw her a card with Ruby on it, or the grumpy cats, because she likes animals, right? Daddy says she's a vet."

"Yeah," Bryce said. "Yep." Part of him really wanted OJ to draw Bailey a card with super grumpy gray cats that scowled from the top of bookcases and write her a nice birthday note. He was sweet, and anyone would have their heart melted from such a thing.

But at the same time, Bailey had been pretty clear about how she felt about seeing OJ. It had been eight and a half years, and to his knowledge, she had not seen OJ one time. Not one single time. And if he drew her a card and wrote her a note, and she did nothing with it? No response?

His perfect OJ would be ruined. That would hurt so much, and Bryce absolutely did not want that pain in the child's life. He knew, because he had a mother who didn't want him, and it *hurt* in a way Bryce could not describe in words.

"And Grandma Laney could mail it to her."

"Yeah." Bryce nodded, wondering how to get out ahead of this.

"Do you think that's a good idea?" OJ looked at him with those half-light, half-dark eyes, and Bryce would not lie to him.

"I don't really know, OJ," he said. "Did everyone you sent letters to in the military reply back? Like, did they all send a card back to your class?"

"No."

"What are you gonna do if your birth mom doesn't reply back? What if you make her the bestest birthday card in the whole world, and she doesn't send you anything back?"

OJ ducked his head. "Yeah."

"That's—" Bryce cleared his throat as the emotion seeped up into his vocal cords. "Buddy, I just don't want you to get your feelings hurt." He pulled him closer. "Your momma and daddy love you. I love you. Our whole big family loves you. Uncle Tex and Aunt Abby. All the cousins. Grandpa Graham and Grandma Laney."

He wanted to ask why Bailey was so important, but deep down, Bryce knew why. It was the same reason why Harry hadn't been able to cut his mother out of his life either. Why

Bryce still yearned for the day his mother would call just to make sure he was still alive.

Moms were special. Only they could carry babies, and that mother-baby bond was absolutely real, and lasting, and powerful.

"You can ask them," Bryce said. "Okay? Let's see what they say."

"Okay," OJ said.

"Okay." He started to stand as someone asked, "Am I interrupting you?"

Codi came around the end of the hen house, about the most beautiful sight Bryce had ever seen.

"Hey, you." He left OJ's side and went to greet her. He took her right into his arms, glad when she melted into his chest pretty easily.

"Oh, so we're hugging already," she teased.

"I haven't seen you in days." He pulled back and grinned down at her. "We were just gathering eggs." He turned back to face OJ. "OJ, buddy, this is Codi Hudson. Codi, OJ. He's one of the thirty-five cousins. Sort of."

She knew exactly who he was, and she grinned at him. "Hey, OJ."

"Howdy, Miss Codi."

"Oh, he's a charmer too." She laughed, and Bryce really liked this happier version of her.

OJ came over to them and asked, "Did you know he's my birth dad?"

"Yes, sir," Codi said without missing a beat. "He told me all about you over the weekend." She crouched down and took him by one hand as she looked into his face. "Yeah, I see him in you. I see how much of a Young you are."

Bryce's chest hitched, and he had no idea why. OJ *was* a Young, and the Youngs were good stock. A big line. Plenty of people to know and love. He sometimes needed to be reminded of that too, because then it made the one person who didn't want anything to do with him less significant.

"Hey, hey," Graham Whittaker called, drawing Bryce's attention to the back deck.

"Grandpa Graham!" OJ whooped and ran toward the man. He had to go past the sunflowers and the garden, across the back lawn, and up the steps to the deck, but he made it easily.

Bryce took Codi's hand and asked, "Do you want to meet him? It's Bailey's daddy."

"Sure," she said easily, though he sensed some trepidation in her. By the time they reached the deck, Laney had arrived too, and the three of them talked over one another. When his top boot hit the deck, Graham looked up.

He nudged Laney, who likewise looked at Bryce. It sure wasn't hard to see Codi at his side, nor the way he held her hand. *Gripped* it might be a better way to describe it, and Bryce hadn't realized how tightly he held her hand until she slid her fingers out of his with a soft grunt.

"Hey, guys." He moved over to them alone and hugged Graham and then Laney. He faced Codi, and he hated how it was four on one. He'd done the same thing to her when she'd met Trace, and he mentally commanded himself to get on over to her side.

He did, and he took her hand again, his eyes never leaving

hers. "This is Codi Hudson," he said. "We're—well, we're not really dating, are we? Are we seeing each other?" He panicked then, because he didn't know how to introduce her. "It's a new thing, and—"

"We're dating," Codi said. "I'm working hard on getting this cowboy to take me somewhere *off* the ranch, but we've definitely had some nights I'd call dates."

Bryce gaped at her as she stepped forward. "It's great to meet you...."

"Graham Whittaker," Bryce shouted. "That's Graham Whittaker and his wife, Laney."

"It's wonderful to meet you," Laney said, her eyes dancing with an emotion Bryce couldn't quite name. It sure looked like the way his momma would look after setting him up with a pretty woman.

"Grandpa, can we ride the horses today?"

"They're already saddled, bud." Graham nodded at Bryce. "We'll text Otis about when to get him tomorrow."

"Yep." Bryce walked them out front, glad neither Graham nor Laney said anything more about Codi, and he waved from the front porch as they left. His shoulders seemed to fold in on themselves once he was alone, and as a ripple of pain ran from his puncture wound up to his neck, he shook his head. "What was that? Why can't I ever have the right thing to say? You say, just open your mouth, Bryce, and I'll give you the words, but then You don't."

"You're doing it again," Codi teased, and he spun back to the front door. She leaned in the doorway, that pretty smile on her face. "Talkin' to yourself."

"I was actually ranting at the Lord," he said. "Big difference."

"Is it?" She laughed, and Bryce loved the sound of it. He moved toward her and as she stood up a step, the difference between their heights didn't seem as large.

"I have missed you," he murmured, one hand sliding effort-lessly along the side of her neck and back into her hair. It felt like real hair, and his pulse went wild. His gaze dropped to her mouth, and Bryce had no idea if he could land a kiss right now.

"I haven't kissed a woman in a long time," he murmured, censoring nothing as it ran through his head.

"I haven't kissed a cowboy in a long time," she whispered back.

He took that to mean he could go ahead and kiss her, and his tongue darted out to wet his lips. With nerves screaming as loudly as they ever had, he lowered his head. His eyes drifted closed, and oh, he was going to mess this up so badly.

Still, he didn't stop, and when his lips touched hers, the bright lunchtime sun hanging over Wyoming doubled and then tripled in light, heat, and glory.

He pressed his lips there for a moment, and then he breathed, pulled back a hair, and as he realized that he hadn't completely crashed and burned, he kissed her again, this time like he meant it.

17

$\mathbf{C}$odi hardly felt like herself since coming to Coral Canyon. She certainly hadn't foreseen meeting a cowboy within two weeks of coming here, and even then, she'd only run into Bryce seven days ago.

Kissing him felt…good. Natural, like her mouth had been made to touch his. The very air fizzed between them, rattling something in Codi's brain. She ran her hand up the outside of his arm to his shoulder, where she held on to keep her balance.

Her other hand sat on his side, the warmth of his body seeping into her palm, into her skin, into her very soul. She wanted this moment to elongate, reshape, and start again, but Bryce pulled away. He didn't go far, and Codi didn't open her eyes, almost willing the sensation tiptoeing across her skin to stay a little longer.

"Not so bad, right?" he asked gruffly, his words catching against his lips.

Codi opened her eyes and looked up at him. "Not bad at all."

He smiled and pulled her into his chest, his arms encircling her completely. "I—I don't know what to say."

"Sometimes you don't have to say anything at all." She stood within the safety of his arms—and he did feel safe to her—for several long moments. Then she said, "I heard you talking to OJ."

"Oh, yeah?"

"What is he worried about? It sounded like he needed to ask someone something."

Bryce exhaled and stepped back. "Yeah. Let's go in, so I'm not air conditioning the Wyoming summer."

Codi grinned as she stepped out of the doorway. Bryce entered the house and closed the door, and it had gotten a little muggy inside from leaving the door open for so long.

"How was your lunch?" he asked.

"Good." Codi couldn't believe she'd actually liked it, but she had. "I don't, uh, this may shock you, but I typically don't have a lot of girlfriends."

Bryce cut her a look as he passed her and went into the kitchen. "Why would that shock me?"

"I don't know," Codi said. "I'm not really a tomboy, but I'm not really into makeup and shopping and lunch dates either."

"Oh, well, you and Kassie are like opposites attract then." He grinned at her as he stepped over to the fridge and took out a bottle of water. "I've gotta grab the eggs. You thirsty?"

She shook her head and watched him chug almost the whole bottle he'd gotten out for himself. He smacked his lips and took a noisy breath. "Yeah, that's better." They went outside, and he collected the white, ten-gallon bucket with chicken eggs in an array of colors in it.

"Those are so pretty," she said. "Some of them are blue."

"I don't want any laughing now," he said.

"Laughing?"

He handed her the bucket and climbed the steps. "One, OJ is not a great worker." He smiled down to her. "Two, my chickens aren't the run-of-the-mill farm chickens."

"Of course they're not." Codi followed him up the steps and into the hen house. She held the bucket patiently while Bryce quickly checked and rechecked for eggs. They came up with at least a dozen more, in beige, ecru, even a dusty rose.

"They're designer chickens," he said. "I love 'em."

Gazing down at the eggs, Codi could see why.

"Do you want some eggs, sweetheart?" he asked. "There's no way I can eat them all."

"Yeah, because you don't cook."

He chuckled and herded her out of the hen house. "I might make eggs in the evening sometimes."

"Not for breakfast?"

He shook his head. "I have toast and a protein shake for breakfast."

"No wonder you eat breakfast foods for dinner." Back inside, Bryce got out some store-bought egg cartons and started to fill them with his designer eggs. "I'll take some, yeah. I can scramble them up for Penta."

The little beagle lifted his head from where he'd flopped on the floor with Lucky. She smiled at him and re-focused on Bryce. "Kassie offered me a part-time job, and I took it."

He looked up; an egg fell down; a *crack!* filled the kitchen.

Codi sure did enjoy the shocked look on his face. His clipped voice as he said, "*I* offered you a job, and you said you'd think about it."

She shrugged one shoulder and reached into the bucket to hand him the next egg. "Her terms were much clearer than yours, Bryce."

"Oh, do tell me about the *terms*," he said as he ignored the blue egg in her hand and went to get a paper towel to clean up the one he'd dropped.

"Afternoons," Codi said. "So I can do my dog grooming in the morning. She's going to educate me on her protocols for the equine rehab, so I'm not just horsing around out here willy nilly."

Bryce tipped his head back and laughed, the sound flying up to the ceiling, where Codi felt sure it would get caught. "Horsing around. That's *punny*."

She grinned at him and watched as he swept the egg off the counter and into the garbage can with one swipe. His big hands sure got jobs done quickly, and Codi's scalp tingled where they'd touched her during that kiss.

"Penta gets to come with me, so he's not home alone all the time," Codi continued. "And the salary was super fair, in my opinion."

"Is anyone going to tell me the super-fair salary?" he asked. "Kassie has no idea about the finances of this ranch."

"She said you were paying someone named Evan almost fifty grand to be the foreman here. It's half that. I'm half-time."

"Mm." He didn't sound mad, and his face harbored no ill will when she studied him.

"Are you—this is okay, right?"

"Of course it's okay," he said, glancing at her.

"I mean, with us, and that kiss, and me working here? If it's too complicated, I'll—" She cut off, because she didn't want to reveal she'd give up this job for him. But she'd been about to say that.

"Whether we work together or not, it's going to be complicated," he said. "I don't mind it, and if there comes a day when either of us do, then it's just—done. Okay?"

"What's done?" she whispered. "Us or me working here?"

"Well." He ground his voice through his throat. "I hope not us, but while I love making and executing plans, I've given up on trying to boss the Lord around. Every time I try, it's like He drops a bomb onto just these two hundred and fifty acres and laughs at me from heaven."

He grinned, and Codi returned it. "Would you take me to church with you?" she asked.

That caused him to freeze again, but this time, he didn't drop any eggs. His eyes searched hers, but Codi decided she didn't have anything to hide from him. "I haven't been in a long time," she admitted. "I sort of...I don't know. Got mad at God when my momma got sick. We prayed and prayed. Fasted. Had the whole congregation praying and fasting and doing whatever they could to help."

She tucked an egg into the container now and set the empty bucket on the floor. "She didn't get healed. She still died."

"Oh, Codi, baby, I'm sorry." He abandoned the chore of cartoning eggs too and drew her back into his arms. "I sometimes go to church in Coral Canyon, with my family. But I really like the pastor up here better. He's the one I hear when I'm hurt, or upset, or don't know what to say to OJ when he asks about his momma."

Codi pulled away so she could see Bryce, and hear his voice come out of his mouth and not rumble around in his chest.

"He's the one who told me that Jesus Christ is relief, and if there's anything I need relief from, He can provide it."

"But *I* fixed up your puncture wound."

He smiled and leaned down to touch his lips gently to hers. A warm press, then gone. "You sure did, baby. But see, I believe He sent you to me. He made sure I wasn't alone that night. He provides medical centers, and doctors, and specialists. No, things don't always work out, but we live in a time where we've been blessed to have so many things that *can* help us find relief. I think those things come from God."

Codi liked how simply he put it. He didn't get too earnest, and he stepped back a moment later. "The pastor up here says good stuff." He cut a glance over to her. "I don't want to upset you about your momma's death or anything, but there have been some good sermons about relief, and I could tell you about some of them if you want. They've eased some of my fears about things, and his lessons have taught me a whole lot about how Jesus Christ works."

Codi's throat felt like she'd swallowed dust. "Okay," she said as she nodded. "I'd like that. But first." She reached up and slipped her finger under the edge of her wig, above her left ear. "Since we're gonna be working together and all, and it does get hot here in the middle of summer, and the job is outside—and you know, you kissed me—I want to show you my hair."

Her fingers trembled, and Bryce grabbed the three cartons of eggs they'd filled, and said, "Okay, let me put these away." He turned his back on her, and she slipped off the wig.

"Just stay there," she said. "Don't look at me yet."

"Codi, I'm not going to care."

"I know," ghosted out of her mouth. "You make me feel safe, Bryce, or I wouldn't show you. But just give me a sec."

He swung the fridge closed; Codi slipped the wig cap off and into her pocket. She looked at the mass of blonde hair, now discarded on the counter like it was nothing. She reached up and ran her hands through her hair.

"It's gonna be a little messy," she said, as she tried to finger comb it down the sides and back of her head. "I can usually tame it with some styling products, but...okay. You can turn around now." Her hands fell back to her sides and Bryce in all his cowboy glory turned to face her.

She couldn't help lifting her hand back up to smooth the hair over her ear. Bryce took a step toward her, then another. She locked her gaze on his, but his eyes moved all over as he took in her hair.

"It really is pure white."

"It's this rare form of albinism," she murmured. "My eyebrows and skin and eyes are okay, though I sometimes do feel like I get sunburned really easily."

Bryce's smile came softly, and it didn't spread his lips as widely as she'd seen some of his other grins. He slid that big hand along the side of her neck and up into her hair. "It's lovely, Codi."

His eyes finally sought hers and latched on. "I don't see why you have to hide this."

"It's just a thing I've always done," she said. "Not everyone is as kind as you, and can you imagine your thirty-five cousins? Kids don't mean to be mean, but they stare at anything and anyone different than them."

"Mm, you might be right about that."

She knew she was. "Wearing the wigs just became easier."

He tipped down and kissed her again, and Codi could lose some serious time with this man. Doing this. Wigless.

"Did you show Kassie?" he murmured as he pulled back.

Codi shook her head, unable to speak for how tender he treated her. How he spoke to her, how he kissed her. He wasn't anything like any other man she'd ever dated or met, and she folded herself back into his embrace.

"So you showed me first."

She smiled despite the hint of arrogance in this tone. "Are you jealous of Kassie?"

"One hundred percent," he said. "Now, come on. If we don't get out to the ranch, she'll come storming in here and blamin' me for keeping you and making her late." He stepped back and took her hand. "Do you need sunscreen?"

Codi's voice got stuck behind the emotion welling in her throat. She nodded, and Bryce released her hand to go get some out of one of his kitchen cupboards. He handed it to her, and to her horror, her eyes filled with tears.

She sucked in a breath, her mechanism for cinching everything tight and holding it in. "I'm okay," she said, though her voice suggested otherwise.

"Codi," Bryce said quietly. "Was Les...not nice to you?"

She shook her head and wiped her eyes. "No, he wasn't a very nice person." Her chest shook, and Codi once again tried to calm it with pure oxygen. "Really, I'm okay. It's silly that you offering me sunscreen made me start crying."

But it had, because it indicated that he was thinking about someone besides himself. He was thinking about *her*, and what she might need, and how *she* could be more comfortable.

"Yeah," he said, a bright glimmer of teasing entering those dark eyes. "I offered you water and got nothing."

That made her laugh, and that helped clear up the lingering quivers in her body. "I'll take some water now, cowboy. It's hot outside."

"Your wish is my command," he said, as if he really would jump to get her anything she needed. Codi had never, ever had that in her life, and she sure thought she could get used to feeling like she mattered enough for someone to care about, attend to, and try to make happy.

18

Luke Young whistled, expecting his dog and both of his boys to come running. The canine did, and Luke grinned and bent down to scrub along the full length of Black Hawk's body. "Yeah, you know to come, don't you, boy?" He stepped back and indicated the back seat of the truck. "Get in."

The Portuguese water dog always wanted to please Luke, and he fit just fine between the two car seats already in the truck. Soon, they'd have a third, and Luke had already admitted to Sterling that they needed a different family car.

He'd been looking at the big, able-to-tow SUVs, because he really didn't want a minivan. Just the thought of a cowboy driving a minivan.... No. Luke was going to hold his ground on this one. They needed something to tow the trailer anyway, and a minivan couldn't even get up to highway speeds without flooring it.

"Come on," he called to the kids, and Ryder came tearing around the corner of the house, making the noise of a race car. Of course. The boy didn't go anywhere without making some sort of locomotion noise. Plane, train, automobile.

Luke was actually looking forward to having another girl, because Corrine had never made noise with her mouth just to make noise with her mouth. Ryder never stopped.

"Where we goin', Daddy?" Ryder asked as he arrived and started climbing into the truck.

"We're meetin' Momma and Corrine for pizza, and then everyone is going to Uncle Mav's."

Sterling had taken Corrine to get a couple of new sundresses for the summer, and Luke had loaded everyone's bag into the bed of the truck.

"Daddy," North whined, and Luke turned away from his oldest son to go help his youngest. Tomorrow, he and Sterling would add their third child to their family in the past five years. They'd wanted a few children as quickly as possible, and the Lord in His mercy had answered them.

After this, though, they were done.

Luke grinned as he scooped his beautiful blond boy into his arms. North was this somewhat strange conglomeration of Luke and Sterling, and Luke loved his curly blonde hair and his midnight eyes.

"Oh, buddy, you're wet." He held the boy out from his body. "Is this water-wet, or pee-wet?" He looked at his three-year-old, who had been potty-trained fairly recently. But North wasn't usually accident prone.

"The hose is on back there," Ryder called. "I couldn't get it off, Daddy."

"Couldn't get it off?" Luke repeated. "How'd you get it on?" He set North on the floor in the back seat and said, "Go get buckled, North. I'll go check the hose and be right back."

He jogged into the backyard, noting that the boys had not closed the gate behind them, despite Luke's multiple reminders and lectures to do so. *It's fine*, he told himself. Sterling wasn't doing massages right now, and she didn't have clients coming and going through the outside entrance that sat just behind the gate.

The hose dribbled, and Luke cranked the faucet to turn off the water. "These boys are gonna be the death of me," he grumbled. He couldn't even fathom how his parents had had nine of them. *Nine.*

Luke had told Sterling two, and he'd never prayed as hard as he had leading up to this past ultrasound.

Back at the truck, he opened North's door to find the boy in his seat, buckled and ready to go. "Look at you, bud." He leaned over and pressed a kiss to the top of his son's head. "Ryder, why are you unbuckled? Get your belt on."

He rounded the truck and got behind the wheel. "All right. We're late, but we're going to pretend like we're not. Okay?" He looked in the rearview mirror. "Ryder, did you get muddy this afternoon?"

"No, sir," he said, though he absolutely had. Luke had stripped the boy down in the back yard and carried him to the tub before putting the evidence in the washing machine and starting it.

"Are we going to give Uncle Mav and Aunt Dani a hard time over anything in the next couple of days?"

"No, sir," North and Ryder chorused together, and Luke nodded.

"That's right. They don't have to let us come over there and jump on their trampolines or play in their basement."

"Uncle Mav says we're goin' camping!" Ryder yelled.

Luke smiled as he backed out of his driveway. He loved the house he and Sterling had made into a home, and he didn't even mind being further from everyone in Coral Canyon. As he lived in Dog Valley, he was the closest to Bryce, and Luke had spent a lot of time with his nephew over the years.

"Not the way we go camping, Ryder," Luke said. "Uncle Mav's gonna put up a tent in his backyard, okay? Are you gonna whine about it?"

Ryder took a beat before he said, "No, sir," though he clearly hadn't expected a tent in the backyard to count as camping. Luke took his family out into the mountains every year, and he loved his time with nature, without distractions, and with his family.

He made up some time on the apple highway between Dog Valley and Coral Canyon, and he and the boys met up with the female half of their family only five minutes after the agreed-upon time.

"Hey, baby," Luke said as he got out of the truck. He grinned at Sterling, who sat on a metal chair in front of the pizza parlor. "Bean, go help North, okay?"

Corrine stepped off the curb to do that, and Luke pulled open the back door where Ryder sat. His son was out of his restraints and ready to get down, which he did without assistance from Luke.

"Momma, Momma," he yelled as he ran toward Sterling. She grinned at him and absorbed his impact as she took him into her arms. "We caughted a frog in the backyard," he said. "It went ribbit, ribbit. Ribbit, ribbit."

"Is that right?" Sterling looked straight at the boy as he spoke.

"No," North said, nearly toppling over as he tried to step up on the curb in front of Corrine. Thankfully, she was like a thirteen-year-old mother hen, and she stabilized him so he could rush his mother too. "It was like, *crooooak. Crooooooak.*"

Sterling laughed, and Luke marveled that he stood on the sidewalk in front of three kids and a beautiful wife about to give him another one. He sometimes still felt like he'd switched places with a man whose life he didn't deserve.

"Ready?" he asked, reaching to give Sterling the stability she needed to stand. He didn't want to admit it, and he'd keep his mouth shut, but he was really looking forward to just the two of them in the house that night. All of the kids would stay with Mav tonight, for Sterling had an appointment at the hospital to deliver their baby girl at seven-fifteen tomorrow morning.

"Who's ready for pizza?" he asked, and both of the boys bellowed like they hadn't eaten ever, not once in their whole lives.

"Quietly," Sterling said, and the boys settled down as she got to her feet. Luke lifted her hand to his lips and kissed the back of it.

"You okay?" he asked in a low voice, the kids already entering the pizza joint.

"My feet hurt," she said. "My head hurts. My back is sore." She gave him a smile, and Luke loved and appreciated her so much for what she did to bring children into the world. *His* children. "I'm starving." She caught the door as it started to swing closed, but she paused and didn't go inside.

"I'm really excited about dropping the kids off," she whispered. "It'll just be me and you tonight."

Relief painted down Luke's throat. "I've been thinkin' the same thing." He pressed a kiss to her mouth and took a deep breath of her. "I love you, baby. Less than fourteen hours now."

"Less than fourteen hours," she repeated, and then she went inside, probably to make sure Ryder and North hadn't torn anything off the walls. Luke loved his family more than he'd ever thought possible, and not just his wife and kids. All the kids in the family. All of his brothers. All of their wives.

Momma and Daddy, who had really started to get older in the past year or so. Not only were they getting older, they *acted* older. Luke worried over them, but then again, Luke worried over everyone.

He survived dinner, and he told Sterling he'd see her at home. She got behind the wheel of her SUV, and he loaded all the kids in his truck now. "To Uncle Mav's," he cheered, and as his brother lived just outside of town off the highway that led to Jackson, Luke arrived only ten minutes later.

Mav came out onto the porch before Luke could even get the truck in park, because he had a long, long driveway with a circular pull-through with crunchy gravel in it. He smiled and tipped his hat at Luke, who said, "Everyone has to carry their own bag inside."

"Daddy," North whined yet again. "I can't do it."

"You don't even know what it is," Luke said.

"I'll help you, Northy," Corrine said, and Luke didn't argue with her. He wouldn't be the youngest in the family for much longer, and he was a tiny little kid, with skinny arms. Properly bagged up, the four of them went up the steps to Mav's porch.

"Howdy, brother." Luke hugged his brother tightly. "Thank you for doin' this."

"Yeah, of course." He opened the door for the kids. "Take your bags to the bedrooms downstairs, okay? Corrine, Beth isn't here yet."

"Okay, Uncle Mav," she chirped, and she hadn't given him or Sterling too much grief yet. She'd be fourteen in another month, and Luke had decided he might be able to keep the boys away if he prayed hard enough.

"What are you and Sterling doing tonight?"

"Going to bed without arguing with someone about it?" Luke guessed. Mav laughed, but Luke literally had an argument with someone about going to bed every single night.

"I don't miss that," Mav said. "Of course, now Dani and I argue with Boston about showering. And don't get me started on Lars and putting his bicycle away."

"Did you run over another one?"

"Yes," Mav muttered under his breath. "I just didn't put it on the family text, because Lars begged me not to. He was embarrassed."

"Maybe you should've," Luke said. "You know, like those

posts that shame dogs." He grinned at Mav as Black Hawk finally came up the steps from the front lawn, where he'd been taking care of his business.

Mav grinned. "Nah, but I've been using it to get him to put stuff away. 'Do you want me to put this on the family text?' I say that, and suddenly he hears me and can put his shoes in the cubby or his backpack in his bedroom."

"Whatever works," Luke said. "That's become my motto lately." He grinned as he followed Mav into the house. He took Black Hawk's bag of treats, food, bowls, and leashes into the kitchen and put them on the built-in desk. "Hey, Dani."

He hugged his sister-in-law around her shoulders, as she sat at the table with her mom and step-dad. "Hey Don. Susan. How are y'all tonight?"

"Just fine, Luke," Susan drawled. She played a card and beamed over to her husband. Luke didn't want to stay here any longer than he had to, so he turned and went downstairs to make sure the boys had gotten their bags in the spare bedroom with the bunk beds, and that Corrine hadn't claimed the bed that Beth would want to sleep in.

"Look, Daddy," Ryder said as Luke peeked into the room. "Lars set up a bear cave in here!"

Blankets had been draped from one side of the room to the other, and all three boys and Emilia, Mav's six-year-old, peered up at him from the floor. Luke's skin crawled, but he didn't have to deal with this tonight. "Looks awesome, guys. Come give your daddy a hug. I've gotta go."

Ryder and North crawled out of their bear den and into his arms, and Luke wrapped them up tightly together. "You behave," he said softly. "Mind your manners. Show respect." He kissed them both, and then went to find Corrine. She sat on a bed that clearly no one used, her head bent over her phone.

"Who are you texting?" he asked, and she looked up.

"Joey and Beth are almost here," she said. "They were asking what flavor of shake I want."

"Don't spend all night on your phone."

Corrine didn't have to roll her eyes for it to come through in her voice. "I know, Daddy."

"Okay, well, come give me a hug."

"When can I come see the baby?"

"I'll let you know." He wrapped his daughter in a hug and held on. "I'll be countin' on you to tell everyone in the family once we have her, okay?"

"Okay, Daddy."

"Love you, bean."

Luke turned the radio off in the truck to make the drive back to Dog Valley, and he enjoyed his time alone more than he thought he would. He pulled into the garage alongside Sterling's car, and the moment he stepped into the house, he knew something was afoot.

For one, Sterling had diffused orange into the air, and she only did that when she was trying to clear her mind to think through something troubling. "Babe?" He tossed his keys into the drawer and looked into the living room.

"Right here." She lifted her hand up from where she sat on the couch. He went that way, and he found Sterling in one of her maternity nightgowns. This one in lavender made her glow, and Luke sank onto the floor in front of her.

"The kids are good at Mav's."

"Thank you, Luke." She took his face in her hands, and Luke absolutely loved this woman. He'd given her his whole heart years ago, but it felt as exciting and as new as if he'd just done so yesterday.

"What do you need?"

"Just you." She pulled him closer and kissed him, and Luke happily obliged. "And a movie. And some popcorn. And maybe you can use your channel-flipping skills and find us a movie."

He grinned at her. "I can do all of that." A quick glance over to the diffuser had him turning back to her. "What's with the orange?"

"We need a name for this baby, Luke. And we're out of time."

He groaned, because they hadn't been able to come to an agreement on the name for their daughter. Naming the boys had been easy, but apparently, they had very different tastes when it came to baby girl names.

"All right." He sighed as he got to his feet. "Let's get all set up, and then we can hash through names." As the popcorn popped and he found a show he and Sterling could watch and talk through at the same time, Luke decided that if the hardest thing he had to do during the day was turn off a hose after a pair of curious boys and then discuss baby names with his wife, he had things pretty dang good.

"Thank you, Lord," he murmured as he salted the popcorn for Sterling, who couldn't seem to get enough of the stuff, on anything. "Thank you for giving me this life." He took the bowl over to Sterling and lifted it over the back of the couch.

As he went back into the kitchen, he continued, "Bless my wife that everything will go well with the delivery tomorrow, and while I'm askin' for things, can you please tell her that Ethel is *not* a good name for a baby girl these days? I'd really appreciate it."

He'd been batting a thousand for prayers coming true lately, and he figured he might as well try.

19

arry Young rolled over as his phone started vibrating. He pushed the black shirt off his face that kept the light out and allowed him to sleep past dawn. Squinting with only one eye open, he silenced the alarm and saw he had slept all the way to nine o'clock in the morning.

Sometimes he did, and sometimes he didn't. He liked to put in his workouts at night, and he had music lessons and practice starting after lunch and going until the work was done.

He still hadn't gotten out of bed when a message from Morris came in. *You up? Gabe says he's starving to death, and he's looked up this place with white chocolate pancakes, and I can't get him to stop talking about them.*

Harry called his uncle as he rolled over, his shoulders achy and stiff. "I'm up," he said when his uncle answered.

"I know you won't eat the pancakes, but they'll have some high-protein thing."

Harry had never cared about what he ate, and he didn't now. He'd taken a leaf out of the Country Quad book and committed to working out pre-tour, because singing, dancing, playing the guitar, surviving pyrotechnics, staying up late, traveling, it all took a lot out of someone.

"I can have pancakes," Harry said, his voice far deeper than normal. "But the white chocolate ones don't sound good."

"They come with macadamia nuts," Uncle Gabe yelled on Morris's side of the line.

Harry smiled up at the ceiling. "I need fifteen minutes."

"We'll meet you out front of your place."

"Will do." Harry let his uncle and manager end the call, and he put the phone back on his nightstand. He only had fourteen minutes, but he lifted his arms up and rotated his shoulders. He'd done arms yesterday, and he groaned as he sat up and swung his legs over the edge of his bed.

His daddy and Ev had come to Nashville to help him move into this apartment, after Harry had finally signed for three albums with Rebel Records. Cadence had tried to come in with a last-minute offer, but Morris had pointed out a pretty major clause that would require Harry to take whatever songs the record label wanted him to.

"You don't want that, Harry," Morris had said. So while Cadence Records had come in with more money, Harry had turned them down. He wanted pure creative license with his songs, and he met with his father and Uncle Otis about once a week during song-writing season.

The songs for this second album had been solidified and final for months now. Harry was still working with his music execs to identify the song they'd release as a single ahead of the album to drive pre-sales, and the order of the songs on the album had to be signed off on by the end of the month, or the printing of the covers and inserts wouldn't happen on time.

The days where Harry could roll out of bed and pull on sweats and go to his lame high school classes had ended when he released his first album, sold out venues from east to west and north to south, and became a household name for those in the country music sphere.

So while he'd showered last night after his weight training, he stepped into the bathroom and ran hot water over his face and through his hair. He brushed his teeth and swept his hair to the right and sprayed it to keep it in place.

He stepped into a pair of designer jeans his mother had picked out for him, pulled on his boots, and worked on his belt while he stood in front of his closet, examining his shirt options. He'd sort of made a fashion statement by wearing a couple of off-the-wall tees that the social media world had picked up on.

Which actually suited him just fine, as Harry would rather wear a shirt without buttons than one with them. He pulled a dark brown tee from a hanger and gave the chicken nugget on the front of it a half-smile. With that covering his torso, he grabbed his wallet and keys, pocketed his phone, and headed for the door.

A half-dozen cowboy hats hung by the front door, and he reached around to the back to the dark brown one to go with the chicken nugget shirt. He left the apartment, checked to make sure the door was locked so he could report to Ev that he did, and went down the steps to the street level.

A sleek SUV waited out front, and Harry crossed the sidewalk to it with only a few strides. As he slid in the backseat, Uncle Morris smiled over to him. "Morning, Harry."

"Hey, Uncle Morris." He bumped knuckles with his manager and looked up to their chauffeur. "Morning, Uncle Gabe."

"Where to, gents?" he asked, his voice clipping out with a slight British accent.

Morris didn't answer as he handed Harry a folder. "This is your agenda for the next month while I'm gone. I will be back for the start of your tour, and your father and Uncle Tex will be here tonight for tomorrow's meeting."

Harry flipped open the folder and scanned the first page. Morris always put the biggest things there, so Harry had the bullet points up front. He'd lived in Nashville alone for almost five years now, with Morris flying in and out when he needed to. With Aunt Leigh having twins in only ten days, he'd be leaving after tomorrow's meetings for Country Quad at King Country, and the collaboration Harry was trying to do with Rebel.

Sometimes he longed for the days when he could just set up his phone on a tripod and lean into the camera, a smile on his face, his funky tees and blue jeans just normal. *Here's a new song I wrote*, he thought as he'd have said it in the videos, and then he'd get to play something he'd somehow pulled out of himself.

Other days, he regretted thoughts like that, because he didn't want God, his daddy, his manager, or his record label to think he wasn't grateful for everything he'd been given in the past half-decade.

He honestly had no idea how long he'd keep up this career. He had enough money to retire back to Coral Canyon, find himself a nice girl, and raise a family right now. Truth be told, women scared Harry a little bit. He'd been popular enough in high school, what with his height, his father's rockstar status, and his quick mind. But out in the wide open world...women weren't the same as the girls back home in small-town Wyoming.

Harry hadn't found anyone he wanted to spend more than an hour with in Nashville, though he'd tried a year or so ago. When he'd been writing songs. Now, he was far too busy for dating, but he apparently had time for white chocolate macadamia nut pancakes.

His eyes caught on an item about halfway down the list. "I have to do the morning show with Julia and Kate?" He looked over to Morris, his eyes wide as wide could be. "Morris—"

"It's not going to be like last time," he said. "Besides, I've already hired you an escort—"

"An escort?" Uncle Gabe asked as he pulled out onto the street. "Morris, the boy is twenty-three."

Morris gave his twin a withering glare, but it wasn't like Gabe could see him. Morris sat right behind him, for crying out loud. "I hired you a *bodyguard* that day," he said, focusing on Harry again. "They've already got it on their site, and the discussion forums are already talking about how early people are going to start showing up to watch you walk in."

"By people, you mean women," he said. "Girls. Ten-year-olds." And they'd all be reaching for him, hoping to touch him.

"*People* of all ages like your music, Harry," Morris said. "I got Pumeni. He's as tall as you, and twice as wide."

"I like Pumeni," Harry said under his breath. He was a good bodyguard, and he'd make sure Harry got into the building and out without an incident. He ran down the rest of the list and closed the folder. "I won't have any last-minute meetings with Rebel?"

"Even if you do, I have a phone and a camera on my computer," Morris said.

"I can come down and act as him," Gabe said.

Harry grinned at his uncles. "I thought y'all didn't switch places anymore."

"We don't," Morris said. "Gabe, that won't work. I have a full beard, and you're a baby face."

"Baby face?" Gabe swung the SUV into the next lane over. "Say that when I'm not driving."

Morris only laughed while Gabe added, "And what? You think people don't shave their beards? Because they do, Morris. All the time."

"And then what?" Morris asked, still chuckling. "I show up two weeks later with it all grown back in?" He shook his head and looked over to Harry. "I have everything set up for you. The places you need to be, and when. Car services booked. They'll call you a couple of days in advance to confirm. All of it."

"I'm sure." Harry smiled at his uncle and reached over to grip his forearm. "Thank you, Uncle Morris."

"You pay him, don't forget," Gabe said from the front seat.

Harry laughed this time, and he too shook his head. The twins were the best of friends, and he often wondered what it would be like to have someone to be so close with. He had Bryce, but his cousin lived over a thousand miles away, and oftentimes, Harry felt more alone than ever, even when surrounded by tens of thousands of people in a crowd.

His phone ding-a-linged, and that was the sound for the family text. He pulled out his phone and looked at it, though he usually kept the family text silenced.

"Luke and Sterling had their baby," Morris said. "She's adorable."

The picture came up on Harry's phone a couple of beats behind Morris's, and sure enough, a newborn looked back at him. She had fluffy black hair that stood up in a mohawk, and someone had put a pink bow right along her hairline.

Harry didn't think newborns were especially adorable, and this one had the same smashed face he'd seen on most others. Still, he knew the magic of holding a newborn baby, and pictures could never do them justice. So his heart squeezed with love for this Young he hadn't met and probably wouldn't for a while.

We argued over a name for a long time, Uncle Luke said. *We finally agreed on Matilda Eve, and we're gonna call her Mattie.*

"Oh, that's modern," Gabe said. "He's been real worried about some of the older names Sterling has been coming up with."

"Matilda is pretty old-fashioned," Morris said. "But Mattie isn't."

"Eve is the first woman," Harry said. "Seems like they both

got their way." He tucked his phone under his leg, because he had no idea what it would be like to try to merge his ideas with someone else's. He hadn't always agreed with his father, but that was totally different than having to come to some sort of middle ground on literally everything.

"What are you gonna name your babies, Uncle Morris?" he asked.

Morris sighed like the naming of a person sucked all the life out of his lungs. Perhaps it did. Harry had been named after his great-grandfather on his mother's side, Harold Schwartz. His middle name was his father's, as was fairly common practice for families.

He bore the Young surname, and he knew it meant a great deal to those in his family. He'd been trying to live his life in a way that would bring them all honor, and as he looked out his window, he felt a very warm, clear presence flow over him.

He was doing okay.

"I'm not sure what we're going to name the girl," Morris said. "Why are they so hard?"

"Beats me," Gabe said. "We only had boys." He had four boys with his wife, Hilde, and of course, they'd both brought a daughter to their marriage. "We did have to name three of them at once, but we managed."

Harry couldn't even handle talking to three people at once, let alone having three babies. Aunt Hilde had been enormous, and she'd been put on bedrest for the last two months of the pregnancy. But then, right before Halloween a couple of years ago, she'd had the babies. All boys. All identical. They'd named them Brant, Tanner, and Cort, and since Harry wasn't around much, when he went to Coral Canyon, he couldn't tell them apart.

"I think we've landed on Ridge for the boy," Morris said.

"That's a good one," Harry said past his homesickness. He wasn't sure what God was trying to tell him, if anything. He thought of Coral Canyon sometimes, but it had been cropping up over and over lately.

"At least I got Leigh away from Remington. She thought we could call him Rem. You know, like the sleep cycle?" Morris shook his head as if such a name were preposterous. "Otis didn't want his kids named like dogs, and I didn't want Rem."

"I don't hate Rem," Harry said. "It's like Jem."

"Yeah, it's not so bad," Gabe said.

"I like Jessa or Sienna for the girl, but Leigh's not sold on either."

"Jessa's real cute," Harry said. "I'm gonna use that in a song." He smiled as music literally started to play through his head. "I can already hear it now."

"You and your mind," Morris said. "Hey, you never said what you thought of that songwriting seminar." He looked over to Harry, who, no, hadn't told his manager anything about it.

"It was good," he said, opting to go with vague. Harry already knew he was an excellent songwriter. When he worked with notes and words, he came alive, and he loved then taking what he'd created and making it sing with a guitar and his voice.

He wasn't real sure he wanted to be this famous country music star though. But songwriting? Once he had a reputation, he could do that from anywhere, and that included Coral Canyon.

"Just good? I get *good*?" Morris asked. "I'm not your daddy. Tell me how it went."

Harry sighed like this was the worst conversation ever. He told himself not to be petty or difficult, and that he only had to talk until they got to the restaurant. "I really liked it, actually. I learned a couple of things, and I don't know what you want me to say."

Morris watched him, a thoughtful look on his face. Yes, they'd talked about career alternatives, especially since Harry only had this upcoming tour and then one more album to fulfill his contract. Then, he'd have to decide what to do with his life.

What to *really* do.

He'd seen his uncles disband and flee Coral Canyon. It sure had seemed like it was every Young for himself for a while there. Harry didn't know, truth be told, because he'd lived in Los Angeles with his mother until she drove him to Coral Canyon and dropped him off at his grandparents.

His father had arrived the next day, and Harry had been clinging to him ever since. Even now, his daddy was his rock, his one true champion, and the voice in Harry's head.

But he had been in town as uncle after uncle came home. As they found good women to marry, and they started having more babies. He'd seen Blaze, the darkest, scariest of them all turn into pure marshmallow for Faith, and he'd been right beside Luke as the man went through a lot of anger to come out the other side a happily married man—who now had four kids he loved, adored, and would do anything for.

Harry suddenly felt very small in a very big world. He knew he'd be missed if Uncle Gabe accidentally flipped this SUV and none of them made it. But he didn't have anyone to love, adore, or care for, except himself.

"Here we go," Gabe said as he turned into the parking lot of a restaurant Harry had actually eaten at before. "I want coffee, and pancakes, and eggs, and sausage."

"Why's he so hungry?" Harry asked.

"I guess he eats breakfast at like six," Morris said. "And with your sleep schedule, he's ravenous." He grinned at Harry and patted his arm. "Don't worry, bud. I told him what you're like, and he's fine. He's eaten once already today."

"A single boiled egg," Gabe said as he pulled into a spot. "And I'm pretty sure it was going bad, so let's go." He got out of the SUV, and Morris and Harry did too. He peered over to the restaurant while his uncles came around the vehicle, and then the three of them headed inside.

He'd only taken two steps, flanked by his uncles, when a woman asked, "Harry?"

A shot of wariness bolted through him, but he couldn't stop himself from looking toward her. A woman with a face he recognized stood, waving off the other two women she waited with. He felt like he should know her, but her name had flown right out of his mind.

She had dark hair that seemed to hold some red or some purple or both, and Harry sure did like it. She touched her breastbone. "It's Emmylou," she said, and the way she dragged out those syllables in her Southern twang would make it mighty hard for him to spell should he be required to.

"I'm sorry," he said. "I don't remember...."

"I danced on your first tour." She grinned at him and moved

right past his uncle-bodyguards. Some help they were. "It's great to see you again." She hugged him, and since Harry was a human being—and fine, a little lonely—he hugged her back. "What are you doing now?"

"Oh, uh—"

"Eating," Gabe said. "Come on, Harry." He took Harry by the elbow. "You ladies have a good day now." He nodded his cowboy-hatted head at them and didn't bother to stop at the hostess station.

Somehow, they did have a table, which made no sense as plenty of people waited in the lobby. "Gabe," he said. "What was that?"

"That was me rescuing you from a woman you don't want to be involved with."

Harry looked back toward the waiting area, but he couldn't see Emmylou. "How do you know?"

"A dancer?" He shook his head.

"My daddy married a dancer," he said, raising his eyebrows. "She seemed nice. She remembered me."

"Yeah," Morris said. "But *you* didn't remember *her*."

Uncle Gabe flapped his menu at Morris like he had a point. A waitress appeared and tossed cardboard coasters on the table. "Drinks?"

"Ma'am, we are ready to order," Gabe said, though Harry hadn't even picked up his menu yet. "And I hear y'all are fast here?"

"Fast enough," she said.

"Okay, so I want the white chocolate macadamia nut pancakes," Gabe said, and Morris pushed Harry's menu closer, and he took that to mean he better be ready to order in less than twenty seconds.

He still took a couple of those to look back over to the waiting area, trying to figure out why Emmylou wouldn't just march right on out of his mind the way other women had.

20

Cecily Young peeled off another piece of provolone and laid it over the thick slice of ham already on the individual hamburger buns. Ahead of her, Jerry continued to slather on the brown sugar and mustard mix and lay down the ham.

Once he finished this fourth sheet pan, he'd circle around behind her again and spread more mustardy goodness—this batch laced with poppy seeds—on the top bun.

She'd come behind and top the sandwiches and wrap them in squares of aluminum foil. They'd perfected this dance over the years, and while they worked, the radio played throughout the condo.

When Cecily had first moved into this fifty-five-plus community, not a single one of her nine sons had lived in town. She made meals for her and her husband most days, but sometimes they went out to breakfast, and some days they fended for themselves.

Now, all of her sons lived here, and they all had wives and children. Some of her grandchildren had grown into fine young adults too, and Cecily would do whatever she had to—even make over a hundred sandwiches in a tiny condo kitchen—to have them in her life.

"Grandma," Joey called, and Cecily paused in laying down the cheese. "I'm here." She closed the door behind her and walked straight back into the kitchen. "I brought Georgia's pans."

Sure enough, she carried four more sheet pans, and Cecily smiled at her. "Thank you, dear." She leaned into Joey's cheek-kiss and added, "We'll have to use the table. I put the buns over there."

"I'm done with this sauce," Jerry said, nudging the big stainless steel bowl toward Joey.

"Okay," she said. "Hey, Gramps." She hugged him, and Cecily loved watching her tough cowboy hug his granddaughter with a soft smile on his face. All of the littles had him wrapped around their fingers, and Cecily couldn't really blame him.

Joey stepped back and smiled at both Cecily and Jerry. "Don't think I don't know that you've already made this sauce, thus keeping me in the dark as to what's in it."

Cecily smiled. "Old Young family secret," she said. "The day my grandmother let me see the recipe is etched in my mind."

"Is that day today for me?" Joey turned and started unstacking the pans and laying them out on the table.

"Oh, probably, honey," Cecily said, smiling down at her work as she peeled off another piece of cheese.

Joey gasped and turned around, a bag of hamburger buns in her hands. "Really, Grandma?"

"Well, I'm no spring chicken," Cecily said. "I should probably pass this along to someone, and well, Bryce isn't askin'. Harry's off in Nashville, and Cash has turned rodeo-pro. It's your birthright."

"Grandma." Joey rushed at her, and they laughed together as Joey glommed onto her and hugged her tightly.

"All right." Cecily laughed. "We've got to get these in the oven soon, or we won't be able to get them all cooked before tonight."

Joey nodded and went back to the table to lay out the buns. "Do you think everyone in the family understands what you do for this party-in-the-park?"

"It's not about that, Roo," Cecily said, though she had gotten older in the past few years, and making a meal for over one hundred people to eat on blankets and in chairs at the park wasn't as easy as it once had been.

"Besides," she said, echoing something Jem always said. "I asked for help this year, and all of the Hammonds are bringing side dishes to go with these sandwiches."

"Georgia said she's bringing drinks."

"Yes," Cecily said, her throat growing a little tighter. "I asked for help this year." It had taken some convincing on Jerry's part, and she deliberately didn't look at her husband as he moved by her. She still knew exactly what his face would look like and what he'd say if Joey wasn't here.

He always had her best interests at heart, and he loved her more than she even knew. He'd been a loyal and true companion, spouse, and her best friend for over fifty years now, and she loved him endlessly too.

"So I have a recipe book above the microwave."

"Yeah, we made the rice pudding out of it," Joey said.

"The ham sandwich recipe is in there," she said. "It's a lot of butter, mustard, and brown sugar. Some salt in the stuff on top, and poppy seeds."

"That's all?"

"That's all," Cecily said with a smile. "I remember thinking it should've been something more too."

"It's just so good."

"It's the combination of it with the ham and the cheese," Cecily said. "We're doing half of these with provolone, but your trays will be done with Swiss. I just know not everyone likes it, your daddy included."

"I'll mark these with the Sharpie," Joey said. "Because I don't love Swiss either."

Cecily did, but she kept it to herself. If having nine boys taught her anything, it was that every person, no matter if they were related or not, had individual tastes. They could like different things and still get along, still love one another.

She loved cooking with her grandchildren, and she was thrilled Joey wanted to be here, doing this with her. "You talk to your daddy yet?"

"No," Joey clipped out. "So I don't need you sayin' anything." She gave Cecily a look over her shoulder. "It's barely

July. I have two more months to let him know about the culinary program."

"Do you?" Cecily reached the end of the trays and started to move back to the beginning. "I thought you had to be there by August fifteenth."

"Well, yes."

"And the tuition has to be paid by the first."

"Cecily."

She looked at Jerry, who gave a single shake of his head.

"I'll talk to him," Joey promised, because she did need to. Cecily hadn't ever graduated from college, but she knew there was less than a month between July fourth and August first.

Otis didn't like surprises unless they included birthday cakes and fun trips to the beach. His oldest daughter quitting college to go to culinary school in the city? New York City, in fact. No, he would not like this.

Cecily tried to set her worries on the shelf, because Otis was reasonable and level-headed. He wanted only the best for his wife and his children, and if Joey wanted to leave Wyoming for New York, he'd do whatever he had to in order to make it happen.

He might be spitting mad about it for a few days. He'd probably come over and vent to Cecily and Jerry about it for a half-hour. She laughed inside her mind, because it would be more than an hour. And probably multiple times. And then he'd come after she left, and vent-worry over her in the city. He'd already done that when she'd gone to college, and she'd only been an hour down the road.

"Let's get these in the oven," she said as she started wrapping. "We need to be at the park by five."

"RIGHT THERE, SWEETHEART," CECILY SAID A FEW minutes past five. No one had taken their spot, and they'd probably be the only people there for the next half-hour. She'd asked everyone to have their food at the park by five-thirty, and she started setting up the folding table with Joey's help.

She'd gotten more efficient in the past few years, and it just made more sense to have the food out, so people could get it when they arrived, rather than her trying to keep track of who had eaten and who hadn't, putting off her always-starving sons and grandsons until everyone had gotten a first helping, and then trying to anticipate how many Hammonds and Whittakers would be there.

With the band in town this year—and for every year moving forward—Cecily didn't want to try to remember who had gotten what, when Bryce would show up, or why hadn't she seen Gray and Elise Hammond's eldest daughter in a while.

Jerry and Joey put the thermal warmer under the table, and she could replenish the sandwiches as they got taken. Then she stayed while the two of them returned to the truck for blankets and chairs.

"Momma," Tex said. "No matter how early I get here, you're already here." He smiled and leaned in to hug her. Cecily liked nothing more than a hug from her oldest son. He held her tightly and as long as she wanted, and she breathed in the sunshiney smell of his clothes. "Hey, baby."

"We're bringing over more chairs," he said. "Abby has the best rice crispy treats you'll ever taste."

"Is that right?" Cecily doubted it, because Abigail liked to put things in her rice crispy treats. Oreos, peanut butter, coconut. She had quite the vast collection of recipes for them, but Cecily was a rice crispy purist. She just wanted the cereal and marshmallow. Nothing more.

"I think you'll like them this time," he said. "I really do."

"I'm sure I will, son." She turned and let Jerry set up a chair for her. Tex put up a big, red umbrella, which marked the spot for anyone who hadn't been there before. At this point, Cecily wasn't sure who that would be, but it seemed like they added to their ranks every year somehow.

"Hey, Momma." Morris arrived with his three kids and his very pregnant wife, and Cecily jumped up to help him get Leigh somewhere to sit.

They came in waves then, with son after son arriving, and all of the Hammond brothers and their wives. Cecily sure did like them, and Wes Hammond was the same age as her, but his oldest was only twenty-five, as he hadn't met and married Bree until he was fifty years old.

Michael was serving in the military, and his next oldest was away at college, as was his daughter. But he and Bree had brought the biggest crock of baked beans Cecily had ever seen, along with little plastic cups to put them in.

Gray arrived with his wife and only his youngest son, and he and Elise put a big platter of fruit on the table beside the baked beans. The picnic continued to come together when Colton and Annie arrived with a literal vat of potato salad, Georgia and Otis set up what looked like a trough but was really a cooler of various soda pops, lemonades, and water bottles at the end of the table, and the Hammond brother twins brought what seemed to be the entire chip aisle from the grocery store.

Seeing them all come in their red, white, and blue made Cecily so happy. She loved nothing more than a wide open sky, a long table laden with food, and her loved ones surrounding her. She loved celebrating Independence Day in the park, with the fireworks, the bands, the chatter, and the freedom she enjoyed in her life.

"Grandma," a very familiar voice—one etched on her soul—said, and Cecily turned from setting out more foil-wrapped sandwiches.

Her beloved Bryce stood there, his hand clasped around that of a beautiful woman with light brown hair that barely dusted her shoulders. Bryce grinned at her, then darted a look to the woman at his side. "This is Codi, Grandma. Codi, my granny, Cecily."

"It's a pleasure to meet you," Codi said.

Cecily's eyes welled with tears. She knew Bryce had started seeing someone, of course. He'd put it on the family thread, with a firm warning to not make it a big deal. She'd wanted to get in the truck and drive up to his ranch in Dog Valley immediately, but Jerry had taken the keys and refused to take her.

A smart move, sure, but that didn't mean Cecily worried any less.

"Bryce," she said, her voice lodged somewhere behind the

thick part of her tongue. He stepped into her and hugged her, and it was like embracing Tex all over again. But somehow better, different, and calming. He stepped back, and Cecily reached for Codi too. "It's lovely to meet you, dear." She hugged her lightly, because she knew how much tension and awkwardness there could be when meeting family.

And they had a lot of family.

"Bryce."

Cecily's eyes moved to Graham Whittaker, and her heart seized in her chest. Just went right into full paralysis while she stood there in the park. He'd spoken pleasantly, and Bryce grinned at him as he stepped into the other man's hug.

"How are you?" he asked.

"Good," Bryce said.

"The ranch?" Graham stepped back, and his wife, Laney took his place.

"Good," Bryce said again as he hugged her. He nodded to Codi, only the slightest hitch of a swallow in his throat. "You guys remember Codi."

"Of course." Graham and Laney both hugged her too, and Cecily's heartbeat broke out of the icy box it had been in and raced now. Positively raced. They'd met her already?

And she hadn't.

She turned back to the sandwiches, determined not to let her feelings get hurt. Her grandson was cautious with his heart, and he had an enormous family. Of course he wasn't going to show Codi around like a pony, and in fact, Cecily wasn't surprised at all to watch him lead the pretty woman over to his parents, who likewise jumped to their feet like they'd been found sitting in the presence of royalty.

So they hadn't met Codi either.

"This looks amazing," Laney said, having picked up a sandwich and peeled back the foil.

"Ham and cheese," Cecily said. Her eyes caught on Laney's, and the two of them simply looked at one another.

"We ran into them picking up OJ out on the ranch once," Laney said without Cecily even having to ask.

"Probably better than here for the first time."

Laney glanced over to where Bryce and Codi stood with Tex and Abby. Their younger children had congregated on a blanket several paces in front of them, as the littles liked to do. Jerry arrived in their little circle, and they made room for him as Bryce introduced Codi to his grandfather.

"OJ wrote Bailey a birthday card," Laney said next, and that got Cecily's attention to whip back to her.

"He did?"

Laney pressed her lips together and nodded, her focus now on trying to get the baked beans into a plastic cup without spilling them everywhere. As Cecily's hands shook, she didn't think she'd be much help.

"We need to mail it by the end of the week if it's to get there on time."

"So you're going to ask everyone," Graham said, and Cecily thought it probably should be a question.

"Not everyone," Laney said, shooting him a look. She smiled at Cecily. "We're in quite the stalemate. OJ and I want to send the card. Bryce and Graham are...worried about it."

"I'm not worried about it," Graham said. "I voted no. I flat-out don't think it's a good idea."

"They're worried," Laney repeated without looking at her husband. "That Bailey won't respond at all, and that'll just break little OJ's heart."

Cecily might need a pacemaker for how wildly her pulse had been acting in the past five minutes. She didn't know what to say. "Are you asking for my vote?"

"Sure," Laney said. "If you want to call it that. I'd love to actually get your opinion. Your thoughts on the matter." She looked at Graham as he came to her side. "We both would. You and Jerry."

"What about Otis and Georgia?" she asked, always worried about them whenever the topic of OJ's genes or heritage came up.

"They helped him write the card," Graham said.

"So it's four to two," Cecily said. "Not a stalemate."

Laney shook her head as Graham popped a chip into his mouth. "They're staying neutral. They want to do what OJ wants, and they've asked us to decide what is best, since we're her parents, and Bryce is...."

"Always going to do what's best for OJ."

Cecily looked over to her handsome grandson. He didn't exactly wear a frown, but it couldn't be categorized as a happy look either. "You're asking them?"

"Yes," Laney said simply. "And I'd like to talk to your momma and daddy too."

"Bryce," someone said, and Cecily knew that voice too.

She turned as Harry himself strode off the sidewalk. Bryce

whooped and went to greet his cousin, and after they'd pounded one another on the back, both of them talking over one another, Bryce lifted Harry's hand into the air like he'd just won a wrestling match and said, "Young cousins! Look who's here!"

It took a few moments, but then a surge ran through the younger children as they realized Harry had come home, if only for tonight and tomorrow, and they converged on him and Bryce.

"We doin' announcements then?" Morris asked, and Cecily simply nodded. Perhaps she really was getting older, and she couldn't take as much excitement. Perhaps the question at hand —should OJ send his birth mother a birthday card after eight long years of no contact?—had wiped her out. Perhaps making all these sandwiches had exhausted her.

No matter what, she moved over to her chair and sank into it as Morris raised both hands above his head to calm the children and the crowd. Not many people paid him much attention, and Gabe got up to stand beside him. Blaze whistled through his teeth, and that cut through the rest of the noise.

"All right," Morris said, waving his hand. Gabe copied him completely, even raising his voice slightly in timbre to match his twin's.

Morris gave him a dirty look, and Gabe gave it right back to him. The little kids started to laugh, and Cecily could admit she loved seeing the twins together. They'd been inseparable growing up, and they'd had the hardest time with the family band. It had severed them completely from the family, and Cecily had not let a day go by where she hadn't prayed for both of them, individually and specifically.

"I have an announcement," Morris said.

"I have an announcement," Gabe repeated. One of his triplets, Brant, toddled over to him, and Gabe bent to pick up the darling boy. He looked at Morris, who bent to pick up another triplet, this one Cort.

Hilde held the third one in her lap, and Tanner didn't seem to feel the need to be up front like his brothers.

"Country Quad," Morris said. He hung there, and thankfully, Cecily already knew this news. If she didn't, then her heart would've been in arrest again, and she really might need an ambulance.

Morris looked at Gabe. Gabe looked at Morris. They grinned at the same time, faced the crowd, and yelled, "Is officially retired!"

A gasp moved through the family, and Abby said, "Praise the Lord," in a loud voice. Ev started to weep, which wasn't surprising, as she was going to have another baby soon. Georgia stood up and raised both hands above her head, her smile gleaming and glorious. And Leigh and Sterling high-fived one another.

"This is good news?" someone asked from behind her. "They're all so happy."

"For a while there," Bryce said. "It seemed like they'd never quit. Touring is hard. It's long. It's days and months on the road. So yeah, I think it's good news." He laughed, and Cecily looked over to see him hugging his father.

Codi looked a little lost, and Cecily motioned for her to come over. She did, and she took the seat beside Cecily. "Bryce is going out with Harry this fall. Maybe you'll go with and see what touring is like."

Codi smiled, and she seemed like a calm, steady spirit. "Maybe," she said. "We haven't talked about it much."

"Did you get dinner, dear?" Jerry asked, and Cecily looked up to him.

"No," she said. "Would you get me some of everything?"

"Yep." He looked at Codi. "For you?"

"Yes, please," she said, and Cecily liked how she didn't check with Bryce. She hid her smile though and simply basked in the energy in the park as the congratulations and celebration over the band's retirement died down.

"Are we sittin' here?" Bryce asked as he pulled up a chair and sat beside his girlfriend.

"Wherever," she said.

"We can try here for a minute," he said. "But I'm pretty sure I'm gonna end up on the blanket with the kids." He grinned at the dozen or so of them on the blankets one row up. Harry currently sat with two kids on his lap, and three more trying to show him something.

Oh, how Cecily loved him. She loved Bryce. She loved all her grandchildren, of all ages, and her heart grew and grew, and grew with love for them.

"Here you go." Jerry handed her a plate with beans, salad, fruit, chips, and a sandwich. He gave one to Codi too, and Bryce's eyebrows went up.

"I see how it is. You're eatin' without me."

She giggled and tucked her hair, then picked up a chunk of potato and ate it without an explanation. Yes, Cecily liked her.

Bryce did too, if the way he chuckled, kissed her cheek, and then went to get his food said anything.

And to Cecily, it did.

Bless them, Lord, she pleaded. As she surveyed her family, her friends and their children—the ones they had with them and the holes left by the ones who weren't—she added, *Bless them all.*

21

Gabriel Young locked his office door after he entered, because he worked from home in the summer. He and Hilde had five children at home, with his daughter Liesl being the oldest and about to turn twelve. She helped a lot with Canyon, who had just turned five, and the triplets, who were two-and-a-half.

Lynnie, Gabe's stepdaughter, was home between her junior and senior year of college, but she'd just returned to Colorado for a few days, and when she got back to Coral Canyon she'd have her serious boyfriend with her.

Gabe rotated his shoulders and stretched his neck. He and Hilde had never met Matthew face-to-face, though Lynnie had included him in several of their video calls. From what Gabe knew about him, and listening to Lynnie talk, he liked him well enough. Lynnie had admitted she loved him, and Matthew loved her, and both Gabe and Hilde were expecting a proposal to happen sooner rather than later.

In fact, it had been Gabe who'd suggested perhaps they should meet Matthew this summer. Lynnie had agreed, and Gabe could still see Hilde fuming as she paced in their master suite, saying, "Do you know how many times I've suggested we meet Matthew?" She'd thrown darted and dangerous looks to Gabe over and over. "At least four times, and you say it once, and whammo! He's coming to town!"

Gabe grinned at the memory, because his wife was right. Lynnie, though she'd grown up a lot, still sometimes resisted the ideas of her mother. Plus, the word *whammo* tickled his funny bone.

He had a lot going on inside his family, and a lot going on inside his law firm, and a lot going on with his brothers and their wives and children. His twin, Morris, had a wife who was due with twins at literally any moment, and Gabe was the contact person.

The moment Morris called, Gabe would be in the truck, headed the few minutes down the road to his brother's house, to pick up Eric, Rachelle, and Skip. Soon, they'd have five children too, and as Gabe sat down at his desk, he didn't feel so overwhelmed.

People had big families all the time. Tex had four kids, as did Blaze and Mav and Luke. And this year, Trace and Jem would up their kid-count to four too.

He worked through the morning, crossing off several things that needed to be done, making phone calls, and meeting virtually with his partner and staff in Jackson Hole, as well as his paralegal here in Coral Canyon.

Gabe had taken some steps back from his busy law firm by not taking on as many clients here while still supporting the busyness of the Jackson office. Both he and Cheryl, his paralegal, had families that required their attention, and Gabe didn't need the accolades his prestigious firm had brought him in the past.

He wanted to be the best husband he could be, and he never wanted to miss an event for any of his children, his nieces or nephews, or his brothers, their wives, their siblings, or his parents.

When he opened the door, he heard one of the triplets crying, and he could guess who that would be. Brant.

Sometimes the oldest triplet wore Gabe to the bone, and sometimes Gabe saw himself and all of his grumpy, fiery, go-getter genes in Brant.

He entered the kitchen to find the little boy already strapped in his highchair and clearly upset about it. He didn't have any food or snacks on his tray, and he slammed both of his chubby toddler palms onto it as he howled in clear protest.

"Hey, buddy." Gabe swept between Brant and Hilde, who had likely put the child in his seat because he'd been causing problems with the other children or in the kitchen. "Did you get lunch yet?"

"Dad-Dad-Daddy," Brant sniffled, his eyelashes so wet and his eyes so sad. "No bars."

Gabe leaned down and kissed the boy on his forehead. "Did Momma say you couldn't have a granola bar?"

"Lunch is literally five minutes away from being ready," Hilde said behind him.

Gabe turned to her and rounded the island to get the other boys out of her way. "Come on, guys," he said when he found Canyon, Tanner, and Cort amidst an array of plastic containers, brightly colored lids, and what looked like an entire family set of blue plastic utensils. Spoons, knives, *and* forks.

"Canyon, start putting all this all back in the bin. Tanner, Cort, let's help Brother *clean up*." He really enunciated the last couple of words and bent down to help get everything back in the bin where the boys could play with it later.

"Clean up, clean up," Tanner sang, the mildest of the triplets. Cort copied him, because Gabe was sure Cort had part sheep genes. He followed his triplet brothers, or Canyon, Liesl, Lynnie, or anyone really.

Gabe wasn't sure if that was good or not, but it made him a fairly agreeable two-year-old, so he didn't complain about it now. He did worry about all of his kids for various reasons, but they got the plastic kitchenware cleaned up, and Canyon ran over to the table and pulled out his chair.

Gabe lifted Cort into his arms and put him in the chair next to Brant, who looked at his identical brother like he'd been imprisoned unfairly. Once Tanner was strapped in too, tray in place, Gabe went to help Hilde get four bowls of lunch ready.

He slipped his hand along her waist and leaned in to smell the skin along her neck. She still made his cells vibrate and his pulse bump and boom a little harder. She smelled like powder and flowers and a little bit like the pesto macaroni she'd made for the boys. "This looks good," he said, reaching for a chunk of the chicken she'd mixed in with the macaroni.

"How was your morning?" she asked.

"Good," he said. "You going in to the store this afternoon?"

She scooped a spoonful of pasta and chicken into a bright blue bowl and turned to look at him. "Later, like three. I'm going to stay tonight and do that re-staging."

"Right," Gabe said. "The dining room remodel." He smiled at her and picked up two ready-to-go bowls. Hilde had put chunky plastic forks into the noodles, but Gabe suspected the boys would all use their hands at some point. Then it would be bath time for four boys, though Canyon could clean up after himself pretty well now.

"All right," Gabe said in a loud voice. "We've got pesto and pasta!" He put the red bowl of food in front of Brant first, and the child yanked at the fork immediately.

"We're gonna pray first, buddy," Gabe said as he slid a bowl onto Tanner's tray. Hilde gave Canyon and Cort their lunch, and they looked at each other.

"Canyon," Gabe said. "Will you say our lunch prayer?"

Canyon looked at him with midnight eyes, half-sober and half-scared. "You help me?"

"You try, baby," Hilde said as she slid into the seat beside him. She smiled softly at him and swept his hair off his forehead. "Momma will help you if you get stuck."

Canyon folded his little five-year-old-boy arms, and Gabe copied him and watched the triplets. Brant had put something in his mouth already, but he squished his eyes closed and pressed his palms to the tray in front of him.

"Heavenly Father," Canyon said. "We be thankful for lunch. Bless Momma that she take us to the park. Bless Daddy to unlock the door so we can play."

Gabe grinned, despite the fact that he wouldn't unlock his office door so the boys could play. He'd bring his laptop out here and finish the filing he needed to do this afternoon, and then he'd take them to the park at his parents' condo complex, so they could see the kids today and everyone could get out of the house.

"Bless the food," Hilde prompted their son, and Canyon glanced over to her.

"Bless this pasta. We love Grandma and Grandpa and Momma and Daddy and the little boys and Liesl and Lynnie and Uncle Morris and—"

"Baby," Hilde interrupted, and Canyon stopped his recitation of every family member they had. She nodded at him. "Amen."

"Amen," Canyon said. The triplets yelled the word, and Brant dove back into his food as if he hadn't eaten in days.

"Where's Liesl?" Gabe asked as Hilde got up to get something out of the kitchen.

"She was sleeping," Hilde said. "I didn't want to wake her, and I figured she could eat when she gets up."

"I'll go check on her," Gabe said as Hilde brought over two adult-sized bowls for the two of them. Liesl had been fighting a lingering summer cold, and Gabe wasn't sure when she'd lain down.

He eased open her bedroom door, and sure enough, she was

still sleeping, looking so peaceful and calm, her bright purple comforter sort of flung off as if she was hot. Gabe crossed to the bed and gently trailed his fingers along her forehead. She didn't feel too hot to him, and she didn't stir.

He watched her for another moment, the sight of her precious to him in a way Gabe couldn't describe. His stomach growled, and he turned away from his daughter and pulled the door only partially closed behind him.

His phone rang, and it was Morris's sound. Gabe couldn't get his device out of his pocket fast enough, and he swiped and said, "I can grab my keys right now."

"Grab your keys right now," Morris said. "Leigh's water broke, and I'm getting her into the car."

"I'll be there in ten," Gabe said, moving now.

"The kids have their bags ready, and they're okay here with Eric until you get here."

"Yep." Gabe entered the living room and kitchen, swiping to end the call. "Leigh is in labor."

Hilde had just put a bite of pesto pasta in her mouth, but her eyes widened. Gabe went right past the family lunch and reached for the keys hanging on the wall. "I'll be back in a half-hour with the kids."

"I don't have to go to the store," Hilde said.

Gabe paused; his eyes locked on hers. "I'm fine with the kids."

Hilde surveyed the four children at the table, looked down the hall, and then met Gabe's eye again. "You're going to have seven children here, baby. *Seven.*"

And only two of them girls. He loved his big, loud, almost-all-boy family, and he wouldn't trade it for anything. Hilde loved her furniture store, though she'd pulled way back in the past five years by hiring three full-time managers to run the place while she raised four boys under the age of five.

She found an escape in her re-staging, and Gabe would not take it from her.

"Morris said he'd leave his van for me, and we're going to my mother's." Gabe grinned at her and moved back to her and kissed her. "I'll be back in a half-hour," he said as he held his beautiful wife close, close, close to him. "Save me some lunch too." Then he turned and headed for the door that led into the garage.

"There's enough for Skip and the others," she called after him, and Gabe waved as he disappeared down the hall to the garage.

At Morris's, the minivan sat in the open garage, and he parked so he could leave his truck there and take the van back to his house at the end of the cul-de-sac.

He bounded up the steps in the garage and entered the kitchen. "Eric," he called, and he found the teen coming in the sliding glass door that led into the backyard. "Hey, buddy." He smiled and hugged his nephew. "Your daddy said you guys have bags ready." He pulled back and looked at the boy. He seemed more sullen than Liesl, but they were nearly the same age. "You're sleepin' at my place."

Eric smiled back, finally. "Yeah, we've got bags." He turned back to the yard. "Rachelle and Skip are back there. I'll go get all the bags." He left to do that, and Gabe took a look around the house.

Leigh and Morris usually kept the house clean enough, but it currently looked like a bomb had gone off, with dishes and clothes and shoes and toys everywhere. Gabe wasn't going to stay here and clean right now, but he'd tell Hilde and she'd organize some help to come get the house in tip-top shape for when Morris and Leigh brought home their new babies.

He whistled as he left the house, an effective tactic he'd picked up from Blaze to summon his brood, and Skip and Rachelle looked toward him. "Come on, guys," he said. "We're going to my house."

"Uncle Gabe," Skip yelled and jumped out of the swing. Morris's kids ran on the wild side, and Skip currently only wore a pair of beige shorts. No shirt. No shoes. Shorts, a smile, and a smudge of peanut butter along his chin.

Gabe loved him and swung the little boy into his arms while his older sister hurried toward them too. Rachelle didn't have quite the same sass as Rosie, but she could run and play with the boys just fine. "Uncle Gabe," she said. "Can I sleep in Liesl's room?"

"Sure thing, Little Miss. Let's go get shoes and a shirt for you." He grinned at Skip. "And your bags. The boys are eating lunch, and Aunt Hilde said we could set up the plastic and do the water slide."

The kids cheered, and Gabe gathered up the three kids and their overnight bags, and he loaded them all into the minivan. Then he had to run back inside the house to grab the keys. He stood there for a moment, in the quiet, horribly messy house of his twin brother, and he prayed, "Bless Morris and Leigh today. Bless the babies." He took a deep breath. "And bless me with all these kids this afternoon, and that Hilde won't kill me about the water slide."

Now, he couldn't wait to find out what name Leigh and Morris came up with for their little girl.

22

Bryce's neck hurt for how long he'd been bent over the papers on his desk or his phone, which had started blowing up. Today, his family text had gone nutso with the birth of Uncle Morris's twins.

He'd started the hullabaloo with a picture of both of them—one boy and one girl—perfectly wrapped in white blankets and cradled in Aunt Leigh's arms as she lay in a hospital bed.

He'd already given the name of the boy—Ridge Thomas—but he'd been holding out on the girl's name for several minutes now.

Bryce's uncles had started sending demands in all caps, but another text rolled down from the top of his screen, and this one had Bailey's name on it.

His heartbeat puckered and pounced, and he grabbed his phone and leaned back in his desk chair. He'd texted her almost a week ago now, and she had not answered. Bryce had learned that more texts didn't mean he'd get an answer, but that it would annoy her, so he'd left it at the one. The woman could read.

And write, as she'd said, *Did he send the card? Bryce, I don't know how to do what you do, but I would never hurt that child.*

Relief filled him from head to toe, and instead of answering Bailey, he tapped around to call Graham.

"Hey, bud," Graham answered good-naturedly.

"I'm not interrupting you, am I?" Bryce asked, getting to his feet. Everything felt knotted and tight, and he didn't know why. "You're not at work?"

"I am, but I just finished my meeting. What's goin' on?"

Bryce passed over to the open doorway of his office and turned back to the window. He breathed, and the air went into his lungs okay. Well enough. Sort of.

"Bailey texted me back," he blurted out. "I think she'll respond to OJ's card." His voice dang near broke on the last word, and he sucked at the air as he stared out over the front yard.

Graham sat on the other end of the line, silent, and Bryce knew how he felt. He was sort of without words too. And his emotions continued to surge and rollercoaster back and forth, around and around.

"We'll mail it out today," Graham said, his own voice choked.

"Do you think—?" Bryce cut off, because he couldn't ask what he wanted to. Graham and Laney Whittaker missed Bailey fiercely. They loved her, no matter that she hadn't come back to town for much longer than a turkey dinner. No matter that she'd turned away from God. No matter that she couldn't seem to communicate with them much.

Truth be told, Bryce missed her and loved her too. He wanted this simple act of an eight-year-old mailing her a birthday card to start her journey toward healing, but he simply couldn't ask Graham if he thought it would.

Bryce had tried to force his ideas and will onto Bailey in the past, and it had never gone well. In fact, it had pushed her further away, and when he'd realized that, he'd backed off.

"I've texted Laney," Graham said. "She says she'll get it mailed out today."

"It should arrive in time," Bryce said, though it didn't matter if it did or not. Someone didn't have to get the card on the exact right day to get it. And Bryce wanted Bailey to *get it* so badly. He wanted her to *see* their son for who he was, and how amazing he was, and how she could have a place—a peaceful place—in his life. If she wanted it.

"Thank you, Bryce," Graham said.

"I'll text her back," he said. Maybe he'd call. He needed to pray about it first, because he felt wildly out of control right now, and he didn't trust himself to make decisions in this state of being.

"We'll call her too," Graham said quietly. "Maybe she'll pick up."

"She has Otis's address?"

"It's the return address on the envelope," Graham said. "Are you going to tell them?"

Bryce supposed he would. He turned away from the window, this triangular relationship between him, Uncle Otis, and Graham sort of odd. Right, but a bit strange. "Yeah," he said. "I'll call him too."

"Well, I suppose it's in her hands now," Graham said.

"And God's."

"And God's."

The call ended after a brief good-bye, and Bryce turned back to his desk. He took a centering breath, focusing on the way the air felt as it moved through his nose and down into his chest. He held it, released it, and repeated the action. He sat down in the desk chair he'd spent far too much money on. But he sat there a lot, and he worked here constantly, and he wanted to be comfortable.

He looked at his phone, noting the number in the family text. Over fifty now.

He navigated to the private text with his uncle Otis and aunt Georgia and tapped out a quick message. *I heard from Bailey. I think she'll send OJ something in return. Laney is going to mail the birthday card.*

Back on Bailey's string, he typed, *Can I call you real quick?* As soon as he sent the text, he looked at the clock at the top of his phone. His heartbeat thrashed through his throat and down into his belly.

Codi would be here in only a few minutes. She'd been working afternoons on the ranch with Kassie, and she always came into the house at five-thirty. She reported to him about the horse she'd worked with that day, and he kissed her, and they made plans for their evening. Tonight, they'd finally agreed to go to the Mongolian barbecue restaurant, and tomorrow, she was coming to church with him for the first time.

The weight of so many things pressed into his shoulders, his lats, his lower back. The horses—of which Kassie had brought home two more in the past thirty days. Two. They had the boarding room for them, but even with Codi, they were at maximum capacity to rehabilitate the horses.

He reasoned that it was enough that they now had proper shelter and nutrition, but Kassie was leaving next week to visit Reggie in Seattle.

Breathing out, he released the weight of the ranch. Another exhale took Codi with it. She could wait on this. He'd tell her all about it anyway, and she wouldn't mind if he took a few minutes to deal with it. Another exhale, and with Bailey's answer—*Yes*—he tapped to dial her.

"Hey, Bryce," she said, and wow, he hadn't spoken to her in a long time. Years.

"Hey, Bay." The nickname just came out, and it was like they'd rewound time eight years and she'd walk in at any moment. "Listen, it doesn't have to be much, okay? He just—he said he's been thinking about you more, and he might want to meet you one day. That's really far down the road, okay? It's just a card."

He took a breath, because he'd delivered a lot of words in a rush of air, and his chest squeezed.

"I understand, Bryce," she said, and she sounded calm.

He wished he could see her, and he leaned back in the chair and turned so he faced the outdoors again. They'd always helped him calm down too. "Will you please send him a note or a card back? I think that's what he's looking for. He's...he's eight and half, Bay. He knows about you and me, and he sees your parents all the time. He's...curious. He wants to know more about you."

"I know."

He wasn't sure she did, but when she moved into this type of talking, Bryce had to let her have her space. He couldn't make her say more, and it wasn't an open invitation for him to lecture her.

"He's a great kid," he whispered. "He's got your spunk and intelligence and my dark hair, and I love him so much." That was Bryce-code for, *You would too, Bay.*

She cleared her throat and said, "I'm thinking of coming home—coming back to Coral Canyon for a visit."

Bryce leaned forward now, trying to see into the future though he just looked out the window. "Okay," he said slowly. "When?"

"I don't know. I have a ton of time off I can take, and I think I'll call my mom and talk to her about when would be a good time."

"That's great, Bailey," he said. "I'd love to show you the ranch I've got here, and I—well, I'd introduce you to this woman I'm seeing now."

"Bryce," she said, her voice straying into the teasing zone. "Are you dating again? Finally?"

"Yeah, a little," he said with a smile. He wanted to say he could introduce her to OJ—the OJ he was now—but he bit back the words. *One step at a time,* ran through his head, and it wasn't entirely in his voice.

"What's her name?"

"Codi," he said. "You? Who are you with?"

"No one right now," she said. "I think there are more horses and cows than men in Montana."

He chuckled and said, "Yeah, probably. Plus, you like those pretty-boy cowboy types. Not the real ranchers."

"I like the real ranchers just fine," she said with mock defensiveness in her voice.

"Hey, it's just me comin' in," Codi called from behind him, and Bryce spun away from the window and toward the door. She didn't appear there, and she'd likely gone to wash her hands in the kitchen sink.

"I have to go, Bailey. It's...really good to hear your voice. Really, really good."

"You too, Bryce. Thank you for...well, I guess for just being you. For being strong enough to do what you do with him."

He wanted to tell her she was strong enough too, but it wouldn't land well. So he just said, "You take care of yourself, and I hope to see you in town soon."

"'Bye, Bryce." The call ended, and Bryce lowered his phone and stared at it until it flashed to black.

"Hey," Codi said. "You're still in here?" She entered the office and came toward him, her snowy white hair clipped back out of her face, though plenty of it had escaped and wafted around her ears.

"Hey." He got to his feet and gathered her into his chest. "Mm, I like you."

She giggled as she wrapped her arms around him too. "Good day?"

Bryce stepped back and opened the family text. "Can you

scan that and give me a summary? I'm mostly just looking for the name of Morris's girl-twin."

"Ninety-two messages." She shook her head. "I don't think I've gotten ninety-two messages this month." She scanned while Bryce closed his notebook and cleaned up.

"How's Dragon?" he asked.

A smile filled her face. "He's going to be the best horse for someone," she said. "Kassie and I got him on the lead today."

"Wow, already?"

"He loves me," Codi said, glancing up and right back at the phone. "I bet I can get him to run in the circle too. We're gonna try after she gets back from Seattle." She gave him the phone back. "They named her Remington. Morris said he hated it for a boy, because Rem is ugly, but he sure did like Remi for a girl. So they both got their wish."

She smiled at him as Bryce tucked his phone away. "And Bailey texted twice." Codi gazed evenly at him, plenty of questions streaming between them despite her not speaking a word.

"Laney's gonna mail the card." Bryce swallowed. "Bailey said she'd respond."

"She gave dates."

"She's thinking of coming here for a visit." Bryce took Codi's hand. "She...I get all worked up over this."

"I can see that." She leaned into him and swept her fingers down the side of his face. "Why is that?"

"It's just so delicate, you know? I don't want OJ to get hurt, and I feel trapped in the middle of all of it." He pulled away from her and left the office. There seemed to be more air out in the kitchen, and he went all the way to the door and opened it. "Come on, Lucky."

His golden ran outside ahead of him, with Pentagon hot on his heels. Bryce crossed the deck and stood at the railing, gazing at the sunflowers, the barns, the sky, the Teton Mountains in the distance.

Codi came to his side but didn't touch him.

"I'm between her and him," he said. "Her and Otis and Georgia. Even her and her parents. Then I'm between OJ and the Whittakers. And OJ and my aunt and uncle. It just feels like this big, tangled web, and I'm stuck right in the middle, where all the stickiest webs come together."

"Mm." Codi let several long moments of silence simply rain down on them. "And you want room to be able to feel how you want to feel instead of worrying about how everyone else is doing."

Bryce hadn't put it in those words, but they were true. "Well said," he murmured.

"Baby, you get to feel how you want to feel with me." She laced her fingers through his. "No one else even needs to know."

He squeezed her hand and tugged her closer. "Thank you."

"So how do you feel?"

"I'm worried about OJ," he said honestly. "I want that boy to have everything he wants, and I don't want his birth mom to disappoint him."

Codi again gave him wide open silence to speak his mind, but he took some time to organize things before he just spewed everything out. "I want to show her that she doesn't have to hide from me, or you, or her momma and daddy. That she can come home anytime she wants, and we'd all welcome her."

"That's what you'd do? Welcome her?"

"Yeah," he said with a sigh. "I invited her to the ranch and everything."

Codi leaned against his bicep. "You're a good man, Bryce."

"Everyone makes mistakes," he said. "Absolutely everyone, and we all need the relief of forgiveness."

"Yes," Codi whispered. "We do."

He took a big breath, which somehow cleared everything, and said, "All right. Let's go to dinner." He called the dogs, and they both came back. Inside, he finally dared to truly look at Codi. "I'm sorry I'm a little—well, whatever I am—sometimes. I don't know how to not get worked up about Bailey and OJ, and I missed my hello kiss because of it."

She grinned at him. "Well, then, hello."

"Hello." He grinned back at her, leaned down, and touched his lips to hers. She sealed all the fissures in his soul, and Bryce felt himself falling harder and faster than he'd let himself before. She kissed him back with fervor, and he pulled away. "You okay?"

"Yeah," she whispered. "Yeah, I'm okay now that you're okay." She looked up at him, and Bryce could get lost in eyes that blue, like diving into open water and swimming with dolphins.

"You're a little nervous over something," he pressed.

"Church," she whispered as her eyelids drifted closed. "I'm a little nervous to finally be going back to church tomorrow."

"You just hold my hand, baby," he said. "I won't let you fall."

"What a promise," she murmured. "Now, I believe you said you'd feed me some amazing barbecue tonight too." She smiled up at him, all trace of her nerves gone. But Bryce had felt it in her touch, her kiss. He could *see* it in her. He liked that he could, because it indicated their connection, and he wanted that, craved it, more than anything.

"Mm, yes, I did. But first...." He kissed her again, because he could, and he wanted to, and he needed her to know that when he made a promise, he kept it.

One hundred percent.

23

Codi regretted the bright pink dress with splashy white flowers the moment Bryce opened the door. He'd been in motion, but at the sight of her, he froze. "Wow."

"It's too bright," she said.

"It's the prettiest dress I've ever seen."

"Do women wear dresses like this to your church?"

"Sure," he said, continuing out of his house now. She'd driven up to Dog Valley to meet him, because an hour-long round-trip for him before and after church had seemed ridiculous.

"Does Kassie go to church?"

"Yeah, sometimes," Bryce said. "I think she's panic-packing today, though." He smiled as he ran his hand up her arm. "You are so pretty."

Codi reached up and touched her dark wig, a little self-conscious in it. "My hair is okay?"

"It's fantastic," he said.

"The pink was so bright, and I thought the hair would help tone me down."

"Baby, you never need to be toned down." He leaned down and touched his lips to hers. He kissed her fairly chastely, but Codi enjoyed herself immensely, though he didn't let things go too far. She simply liked being held, and the nearness of Bryce, and the way he sure seemed to cherish her instead of taking from her.

"We're going to be late," she whispered.

"Can't be walking in late," he whispered back. "Everyone will be staring at us, and I'm nervous enough already."

He took her hand, his smile appearing, and he led her to his truck. He didn't speak much on the way to the chapel, and that suited Codi's nerves just fine. He could be a chatterbox, but he'd been quiet last night too, after he'd told her about OJ and Bailey and the birthday card.

Codi didn't mind his silence, because she didn't want to be reassured. She stewed in her nerves until he opened her door and took her hand again. His was so much bigger than hers, and warm and solid, and Codi absolutely felt safe in his hands.

He wore a big, black cowboy hat to go with his black suit coat over a white shirt. His tie fluttered with colorful butterflies, and he wore black slacks and black cowboy boots. "You sure look nice," she said as they climbed the steps to the open doorway. A huge stained-glass window depicting the Garden of

Eden shone down on them, and Codi started to relax at the first strains of organ music.

"Thank you," he said.

"Do you always wear a jacket to church?"

"Not always," he said, cutting a look over to her. His eyes went right back to roaming, and she wondered who or what he was looking for. "Remember how you make me a little nervous, and I want to impress you?"

"You're nervous because of me, or you're nervous because we're at church together?"

"Nervous because we're at church together," he said. "Here's one reason why." He lifted his head and pasted a grin in place. "Hey, Miss Beverly." He leaned in and kissed the cheek of a much older woman. Codi didn't even think Bryce's grandmother was this old, and she smiled as Beverly warbled something at Bryce.

"This is Codi," he said, returning to her side and taking her hand again. "Come on, sweetheart. We don't want to be found standing when the pastor starts." He led her past the older woman, who stared at Codi with narrowed eyes.

Thankfully, she didn't say anything to her, and Bryce indicated a row, and Codi stepped down it. She sat, leaving enough room on the end for Bryce, and he settled beside her. He easily lifted his arm and put it around her shoulders, and Codi snuggled into him, needing to be close to him to draw on his strength and support.

He said nothing, and when Codi looked at him, she found him with a half-smile on his face, his eyes closed, as if praying or thinking or giving his troubles to the Lord.

When the pastor stood behind the pulpit, Codi shifted, her nerves suddenly firing up again.

"Welcome one and all," he said, and Codi really felt like he was personally welcoming her to the meeting. He spoke with a big, loud voice, and he spoke with both of his hands spread wide. Codi liked him instantly, and she relaxed even more.

"Today I want to talk about Lazarus, Mary, and Martha. After Lazarus grew ill, his sisters sent for Jesus, but Jesus did not go right away. In fact, he didn't arrive until after Lazarus had died, and indeed, not even until the fourth day following his death. By then, according to some, Lazarus was beyond help. His spirit could have lingered for three days, but it was the fourth day."

Codi knew the story of Lazarus and Jesus Christ raising him from the dead. She didn't know about the customs of the Jews at the time, and her pulse fluttered as she continued to listen.

"So, despite their summoning the Savior before their brother's death, and the faith of Mary and Martha, they lamented that Jesus had come so late.

"But my friends, Jesus Christ is never late. He might not come on the first day, or the second, or the third. He might not come when we beg Him to, when we bend our will to His and summon Him in our most desperate need."

Bryce cupped his fingers around her upper arm and kept her close, but she couldn't look away from the powerful man up front. A couple of people around her nodded, but she only saw them out of the corner of her eye.

"Jesus had two men roll the stone away from the sepulcher, and then He did what only He can do: He commanded Lazarus to come forth." The pastor smiled a wide, wide smile and spread those hands again, almost like he was gathering his people to him. Codi *belonged* here, and that feeling streamed through her strongly.

"And Lazarus did come forth. The Savior was not late. He was not late then, and He is not late—for you—now. Even though it feels like He might be. Even though you may have been praying for Him to come to you, to relieve you, to help you, for a long time. I want to stand here and testify that the Savior *always* comes."

His smile rained down on all of them as he stood there in his testimony, the glory of it streaming through the chapel. Codi realized then that tears ran down her face. The pastor continued to speak, but all she could think of was that she had done her makeup beautifully that day to go with her dark wig.

Now, it would be ruined, because the pastor had borne such a beautiful testimony of the Savior.

It seemed that every hole in her face leaked, and she took a tissue from someone on her right. She hadn't even realized how much of a wall she'd put between her and the Lord. She *had* believed God had shown up too late for her mother. For her terrible relationship and engagement that at least hadn't become a wedding.

She'd felt abandoned, but now, she felt as if the Savior had entered the chapel and had chosen to come sit beside her, commanding her to come forth and live. Really live.

And Codi wanted to. She wanted to walk beside Jesus, relying on Him, talking to Him, and consulting with Him on what she should be doing with her life.

"Hey," Bryce whispered and pulled her back to him. He didn't ask her if she was okay or not.

She shook her head, trying to find her composure. He didn't insist she did, nor did he tell her everything would be okay. He simply held her while she sniffled, and Codi felt herself falling for the big, strong cowboy right there in church.

"Let your heart not be troubled," the pastor said, and Codi recognized the scripture. She knew the importance of it as Jesus said it, but for the first time, she thought she might be able to trust her heart and what it felt and said to her.

She might be able to give it to Bryce, and he wouldn't shatter it.

"He said, 'I will not leave you comfortless; I will come to you,'" the pastor said. "My friends, let Him come to you."

Codi finally found a smile emerging through all the tears, and it cleared the way for pure, divine healing to move through her too, sealing up all the wounds that she'd been suffering with for so long.

Jesus had not abandoned her. He'd just done what only He could do: He'd healed her.

A couple of hours later, she and Bryce walked hand-in-hand along a dirt road on the ranch, two horses strolling along either side of the lane with them. The breeze played with her wig, which was a little longer than the normal hair she wore.

She'd brought a sun hat, because Bryce had said they could spend the afternoon together, with the horses, and he'd invited her back to his place for lunch and dinner. So she'd brought the hat and used his sunscreen, because she knew both she and Bryce loved being outside.

Up ahead of them about ten yards, the dogs trotted along, side by side, and Codi smiled into the moment, this very day, the sky and sunshine above.

"So you liked the sermon," Bryce finally said. They'd decided to take a walk while the meat he'd put in the slow cooker finished up, and Codi expected to see Kassie later today, as well as Bryce's parents, for an early Sabbath day dinner.

He'd fed her a bowl of her favorite mixed cereals before this walk, and Codi looked over to him now. "Yes," she said. "I rather liked your pastor and his sermon."

"I really liked the reminder that Jesus always comes, even when we think He's late."

"It was a beautiful message," Codi said. "Can I come with you again?"

"Every week," he murmured, his head down, his own hat shading his face. To her right, the horse on Bryce's side of the dirt road picked up his pace, and Bryce lifted his head. "Where's he goin'?"

Vanderbilt caught up to the dogs and they both looked over to the chestnut and slowed down so he could go back to walking.

"I guess he wanted to be with them." Codi stepped closer and linked her arm through his. "Bryce, can I ask you a question?"

"Anything," he said.

"More than one?"

"As many as you'd like." He glanced over to her. He'd changed out of his slacks and suit coat and into a pair of jeans and a T-shirt that had the silhouette of a horse on it.

"Did you and Bailey want to get married?"

A beat went by, then another. "She didn't," he said, his voice somber. "I did." He pulled away from her slightly on the next step. "I mean, I would've married her." He glanced over to Codi, holding her gaze for a long moment. "It wouldn't have been right or good, but for the sake of that baby, I'd have done it."

Codi liked his honesty, because it felt like it created no gaps between them. "What about now? Would you get married now?"

He sliced a smile toward her. "Are you thinking about marriage, Miss Codi?"

"Are we dating for fun?"

"Yes," he said. "I think being with you is fun."

"Come on." She bumped him with her hip. "You know what I'm asking."

He grinned and sighed up into the sky. "Yeah, Codi, I'm looking to get married. I want kids to fill that big house with, and to gather all those eggs from the hen house, and teach to play the guitar, though I am teaching my brother now. You should see him, Codi. He is the cutest thing ever."

Bryce radiated happiness and joy, and Codi sure did like it. This summer seemed stitched of magic and growth, and she wanted these sunshine-filled days to last forever.

Of course, she'd lived through more than one winter, both here in Wyoming and in Idaho, and she knew snow and dark-ness and cold too. She'd like to watch and taste and experience

Bryce brighten the wintertime too, and she hoped she'd be able to.

"So you want children you keep and raise," she said.

"I do," he said. "What about you?"

She nodded, a smile filling her from sole to scalp. "Yeah, I'd like some kids. Maybe not like nine or anything, like your grandmother."

"Or Uncle Gabe," Bryce said with a laugh. "You never know what you'll get, you know? Some people can't have kids at all."

"Like Otis and Georgia," she said, her heart suddenly not as feathery and light.

"Right," he said.

"I'd like to try," Codi said. "I'm not super nurturing, but I'm good with dogs and horses and I figure I'd be okay with children." She nudged him again. "I've seen you with your cousins; you're a rockstar to them."

"I've had a lot of practice with little ones," he said. "That's all."

Codi had gotten the answers she needed there, and she took a few more steps, her sandals making sliding noises against the dirt road. "Talk to me about this tour of Harry's. Are you going with him?"

"Yep," Bryce said. "Yeah, I sure am. His tour starts in September, and I'm doing six or seven shows with him. We're playing a duet."

"How long will you be gone?" she asked.

"Two weeks." He slowed and turned toward her, taking both of her hands in his. "Do you want to come? My daddy traveled and toured with me and his family every time they went."

"Come with you? Do you take Lucky?"

"Yeah, he comes," Bryce said. "Kassie will be here, and my uncles come to help feed and care for the horses."

"Sounds like you need me here."

"Oh, come on," he said. "You love traveling around in a bus. You could stand riding along with me and Harry, staying in hotels, and then flying back here right before winter."

She didn't understand who would take care of the ranch, but Bryce was in charge of it, and if he thought he could leave for two weeks to tour with his cousin, then he'd handle it.

"Can I bring Penta?"

"One hundred percent." His phone went off, and he pulled it out to check it. "My parents are here with the kids. Wondering where we are." He glanced over to her. "We better head back."

"Along the way," she said. "You can tell me about this 'one hundred percent' thing and why you call your stepmom your mother."

Bryce tilted his head back and Codi waited for him to start ranting at the Lord. "She's asking a lot of things here," he said, but his voice held laughter.

She smiled to Dragon on her left, and the horse even looked over to her, as if silently saying, *You asked, and he's gonna tell you now. Good job, Codi.*

"Okay, so I worked with this guy in Louisville," he started, and Codi loved hearing stories of his life outside of Coral Canyon. She knew he'd worked at a horse boarding facility in

Louisville, where he'd met Kassie as he looked after her family's racehorse after it had ran through a fence.

"He trained me, and as I learned, I'd ask him questions, you know? So I'd be like, 'So I need to change the bandages every other day?'" He chuckled and shook his head. "And he'd say, 'One hundred percent...but no, it's every day, Bryce. We change the bandages every day. Sometimes twice.'"

"So it wasn't a hundred percent," Codi said, getting the joke.

"He did it for everything. My cabin mates and I used to ask him something wrong just to see what he'd say. It was *always* "one hundred percent," but no, It's like this...." He laughed again. "We kind of adopted it, and I've been saying it for years, obviously."

"Even after leaving Louisville," Codi teased.

"One hundred percent," Bryce threw at her, and they both laughed. Bryce took her hand, and they turned back to the main ranch. He whistled over his shoulder to the dogs and said, "Vanderbilt, Lucky, come on."

Codi checked over her shoulder to make sure Penta had started to come back with Lucky and the other horse. He had, of course, and she loved the happy, beagly look on his cute face. He'd definitely crash back at the farmhouse, as she and Bryce had been walking for a while now.

Dragon didn't immediately turn, and Codi said, "Dragon," in a certain tone of voice, and the horse plodded up onto the road as he made a wide arc. "Oh, you're going to walk over there now?" she asked, eyeing the horse. "You think you won't have to listen to him if you're over there, huh?"

"To be fair, he *doesn't* listen to me," Bryce said out of the corner of his mouth.

Codi grinned at him. "He does. He will."

Bryce grinned at her and gave her a mock-scathing look. "I think you whisper all of my faults to him, because I think he's just getting saltier and saltier with me."

As if on cue, Dragon nickered, and that set off some of the other horses in a nearby pasture.

Then, a moment later, a little voice yelled, "Bryce! Codi!"

Melissa ran toward them, and she yelled over her shoulder, "I see 'em! Come on, guys! They're out here!"

Codi grinned at the kids coming toward them at full speed, and when Bryce asked, "You ready for this?" she said, "One hundred percent."

24

Bryce didn't mind that everyone fawned over Codi, though he suspected it smothered her a little. She laughed with his momma, and she looked at every leaf and bug Pippa pointed out on the way back to the stables.

They put the horses away with his daddy while Momma took the kids around to look at the horses in the pasture and then to see the chickens.

"Codi, how's the grooming bus going?" Daddy asked, and she flashed him a smile over her shoulder without breaking the stroke over Dragon's side.

"Good," she said. "I do a dog or two each day before I come out here. Or I don't. I'm kind of enjoying the freedom right now."

"You've got enough to pay your bills?"

"Daddy, are you kidding me right now?" Bryce practically threw his brush at his father. "She's not your daughter." He looked at Codi, pure embarrassment climbing through him. "He asks me that every time I see him. It's a sheer miracle I'm alive all these years later."

He made a payment to his father for the part of the ranch he'd funded years ago. He'd never missed one, and he'd never asked to miss one.

"It's fine," Codi said. "I got some money from my momma's inheritance, and I've been living on that for a while now."

Bryce hadn't heard this, but he hadn't asked his girlfriend about her finances either. He kept his mouth shut as Codi continued working on Dragon.

"I sort of wandered in the grooming bus until I came here," she said, and she had told him this. "I did a couple of art pieces in Arizona, and I've groomed dogs all over the Western States, but I wasn't permanent anywhere." She gave Daddy a smile. "It's nice to have a place to belong."

"Coral Canyon is a great place," Daddy said.

"It made an impression on me," Codi said. "Which was why I came back here after being gone for a while." She patted Dragon. "You're done, bud. I'll put you away."

As she ambled down the aisle with Dragon, Bryce edged closer to his father. "Can you not ask anything embarrassing for like, one day?"

"I didn't realize it was that big of a deal. I thought her dog grooming did great."

"I really like her, Dad."

"I know you do. I was just making conversation." He put down the saddle he'd been polishing. "You hide her out here by yourself, and I'm just trying to get to know her too."

"I'm not *hiding* her," Bryce said. "We're busy is all. I've brought her to the house for dinners. She works here. I don't have to work hard to see her, and I don't think about *you* getting to know her." He sighed and finished up with Vanderbilt too. "Momma is probably going nuts, right?"

"She's probably hovering outside the door, with her eyes on the kids, but not even seeing them."

Bryce's eyes felt too hot, and he turned away from his father. "I hate feeling like I'm letting you down." And letting down Abby? Unacceptable. Bryce had done it before, and he worked hard not to do that. His father was right. Abby would want to know everything about Codi, and he couldn't fault her for that.

"No," his daddy said. "You're not." He moved right in front of Bryce, and he had nowhere to hide then. "You're not."

"Feels like it." Bryce gazed at his father. "I'm doing the best I can. I *like* this woman. I'm falling in love with her, and it's not going to be a fast process, okay?"

His daddy started nodding, but Bryce kept going. "So there's time, Dad. There's time for you to get to know her and Momma to take her shopping or whatever, and everyone to fall in love with her too, okay? But I think *I* should like her more than anyone before that happens."

"Yes, of course," Daddy said, his dark eyes firing with as much passion as Bryce felt moving through himself. Dad drew Bryce into a hug. "I'm sorry if I overstepped. It was an innocent question, I swear."

Bryce wrapped his arms around his father. "I know." Because he did know. His father and Abby would never do anything to upset Bryce on purpose. Daddy possessed a charm he couldn't control sometimes, and he was very good at talking to people and getting to know them.

As his father continued to hold him, he said, "I wanted to tell you about your granddaddy. He's not been feeling well, and we finally got him to go into the doctor. They're doing some blood tests."

Bryce's heart dropped to his boots, and he drew back blinking at his father. "Is he—? What do I need to do? Can I go see him?" He wanted to go right now, but he was feeding everyone Sunday dinner tonight.

Panic ran up his spine the longer his dad looked at him. "Daddy," he said, begging him to just spit it out.

"My father is getting older, Bryce," he said simply. "He's in the hospital. Only Abby and I know, because he asked us to wait until tomorrow to tell everyone else."

Bryce watched the weight of the whole Young family settle on his father's face. His dad had always been a complete rock for Bryce, no matter how stormy life had gotten. He carried everything, for everyone, and tears pricked Bryce's eyes as he saw it, felt it, experienced it.

"Dad, I'll go see him tonight after everyone leaves," he said. "Why is he in the hospital if they're just doing tests?"

"They don't like his kidney or liver enzymes, and the doctors want to go over his blood test results with us in person tomorrow. We're leaving everyone with Cheryl and Wade to be there."

"I'll be there too," Bryce said immediately. "What time?"

"Bryce."

"Dad, do *not* tell me I can't go too." Desperation clawed at the back of his throat, trying to get out. "Please, don't tell me I can't go."

"They only allow two people in the room," Dad said. "Besides a spouse. Abby and I are going to go." He spoke evenly, but he also looked like he'd aged a decade just during this conversation.

"What are they saying?"

"Nothing," he said with a sigh. He reached up and took off his cowboy hat. He definitely had more silver hair than ever before. "They're not saying anything. They will tomorrow, and then we'll know." A smile flashed across his face. "I think we should be prepared. I think everyone should pray, though the blood tests are done. They're going to show what they show."

"Prepared for what?" Bryce unclipped Vanderbilt and reached for the lead.

"My daddy is eighty years old, Bryce," he said. "He's lived a good life. He's raised nine boys and has a mess of grandkids. But bodies wear out."

Bryce didn't want to think about this right now. He met Codi coming back, and she took one look at him and paused. "What's wrong?" she asked.

He handed her the lead. "Can you put him in his stall?"

"Of course." She wouldn't look away from him, though, and Bryce simply let her study him.

"My grandpa is in the hospital," he said.

"Oh, no." A lovely look of concern filled Codi's face. She was genuine and kind and so good, and Bryce felt one more breath would shatter him. She kept the lead in her hand as she moved into him, pulling him tightly against her. "I'm so sorry. Did your daddy say why?"

Bryce held onto her like she was a new rock he'd found to cling to. "No," he whispered. "They'll get the results of some blood tests tomorrow."

"I'll take him." Dad went by them and took Vanderbilt with him.

Bryce didn't want this sadness to hover over them. He tried to smile, but it settled a little strangely on his face. Codi returned it anyway and said, "Let's go find your momma and the kids."

"Yeah," he said as he turned to go back the way he'd come. "So Abby." He released his breath. "She married my daddy in my senior year of high school. She's been there every day and every step of the way since." He pushed open the stable door to find his stepmother standing over by the fence, the kids running through a field of sunflowers with Golden Boy and a pretty horse who could probably be sold named Boulevard.

She turned toward them as if she sensed their presence, and Bryce didn't know how to explain the past decade of knotted, twisted feelings between him and his mother. He did know how to smile at Abby and lead Codi toward her. She smiled too, took one look at the pasture, and came toward them too.

Bryce had introduced Codi to his parents a couple of weeks ago, at the park right before the fireworks. It had gone well enough, considering she'd also met his grandparents, all of his uncles and their wives, all of his cousins, and then the Whittakers and the Hammonds who'd come too.

"Hey, baby," she said, though he'd already given her a greeting. He took her into a hug and held on, and Abby surely instantly knew something stormed inside him. When she pulled back, she searched his face with her dark eyes. "Bryce?"

He smiled and returned to Codi's side. He took her hand and looked at her, then focused on Abby. "Codi, I call Abby my momma, because she loves me like one. She functions as one, and she's earned the title."

Abby blinked rapidly, clearly not expecting any of that. Bryce wasn't sure how to explain it, but for maybe the first time, the Lord had provided the words when he'd opened his mouth.

"My mother lives in Boise," he said, and Codi pulled in a breath. "Yeah, remember how I've told you I don't like that city? Yeah, well, she's why. She doesn't want me."

"Bryce," Abby said, sharper this time. No questions in sight.

"It's fine, Abs," he said, using the nickname for her his father did. "It's the truth, and no one needs to deny it or dance around it." He faced Codi now, noting her wide blue eyes framed by all that dark hair. He really did like her so, so much, and he liked that she seemed as appalled by his mother's behavior as he'd been.

"I lived with her for a long time," he continued. "She did raise me, the best she knew how, but I held her back. I was a hinderance for her. I asked my daddy if I could live with him my senior year, and I've tried to keep in touch with my mother. But she doesn't want it. She doesn't want me, and so I choose—*I* get to choose—who I have in my life. And *I* choose to spend time with people who lift me up, love me, support me, and want me around." He nodded his cowboy hat back to Abby. "That's her. She's my momma. That's why I call her Momma."

Abby sniffled, and Codi nodded, and Bryce wasn't sure how today had suddenly twisted from an amazing sermon which had reminded him that the Lord hadn't forgotten about him and would always be there for him to this conversation. He supposed life sometimes pitched right and left, the way a small boat did on big waves.

"Anyway." Bryce drew in a deep breath. "What do you know about Grandpa, Momma?"

"Not much," she said. "The doctors didn't like some level of something in his kidneys, so they wanted him to come to the hospital. Gramma took him this morning, and they're keeping him at least overnight."

Bryce nodded, his chin down. He wasn't sure how to feel, but when he lifted his head and met his momma's eyes, he said, "I love him."

"Oh, I know you do, baby." She gathered him and Codi into her arms this time. "We all love him, and it will be so sad when he passes."

Bryce stood there with these two great women, and he truly felt like light from heaven shone on him. He didn't know what it meant; if his grandfather would be taken soon; if he'd heal up just fine. It didn't matter. Bryce knew that all life was held safely in the hands of God.

"All right," Dad called. "Horses are done. I can smell that beef out here." He clapped his hands together as the three of them broke apart. "Okay, who's makin' my wife cry?"

"Daddy!" Carver yelled from out in the field, his voice full of joy and excitement. "Come see this snake!"

Instead of Dad being the one to vault the fence and hustle

the kids away from the snake, Codi said, "I've got this." She ducked under the fence, that dark hair swinging, and jogged out to where all three kids had huddled around something on the ground.

Bryce stood there between his parents, and he said, "Lord, I like her so much. Prevent me from saying or doing something stupid to drive her away."

"Amen," Daddy practically bellowed.

His momma scoffed, and then laughed, and that somehow broke the tension that had seethed into the sky the moment his father had told him Grandpa was in the hospital.

"It's just a garter snake," Codi yelled, and she stood up, holding it. Actually holding a snake in her hands while the kids all looked at it or her like she'd just called down manna from heaven.

Bryce grinned and grinned, and he said, "Oh, boy. We are in troub-ble." And he meant his heart, because watching Codi with his siblings and the snake was like taking a peek into the future life he wanted...with her.

"Your girlfriend is holding a snake," Momma said. "Go help her, you insensitive cowboy."

"We'll go get dinner going," Daddy said, and that was how Bryce found himself vaulting the fence and heading out to Codi, the snake, and the littles. Life still felt a bit heavy, but the sunshine poured from the sky, and Carver wore a smile the size of the Mississippi River.

Even Melissa touched it, quickly pulling her hand away from the snaky scales a moment later.

"Can we keep it?" Pippa asked.

"No, missy," he said. "You can't keep it." He exchanged a glance with Codi, who wasn't at all worried about the dark gray snake as it tried to climb her arm. "Momma would go nuts, and I need it to keep the mice out of my barns."

"You have cats for that." Pippa stuck out one hip and put a hand on it. She looked so much like Abby, and her hair shone the reddest out of all the kids.

Bryce swept her up into his arms. "Did you hear the first part, Pip? Momma will go nuts, and we don't need to be upsettin' Momma for no reason, right?"

The little girl took a moment, and then she said, "Right."

"Right." Bryce turned toward the house. "Come on, guys. It's almost dinnertime, and Codi's got to wash her whole upper body to get all the snake juice off before she can eat with us."

"Snake juice?" Melissa sounded absolutely horrified, and she caught up to Bryce only a step later. "It didn't feel wet."

Bryce grinned down at her, and when they reached the fence, he lifted Pippa over it while Mel climbed through the rungs. He turned back to find Codi several paces behind, her hand in Carver's. The little boy looked up at her, and she looked down at him, as he said something to her. Her face held the light of a thousand stars, and when she laughed...Bryce fell a little more in love with her.

He took a couple more mental snapshots of a dark-haired boy holding Codi's hand, once again cataloging them into the *This Could Be My Future* album in his mind. When Codi reached him, he lifted Carver over the fence too and locked his eyes on hers.

"Not nurturing, huh?"

"I mean—" She watched the kids run toward the house, and then she brought her gaze back to his. "I think I said I do okay with kids."

"Mm, yeah, you do." Bryce hugged her and swayed with her, the feeling of being physically close and emotionally connected to another person exactly what he'd been missing in his life.

"Bryce!" Kassie called from the deck. "Stop kissing and come go over my packing list with me! I'm sure I'm forgetting something!"

He pulled back from Codi, whose eyes now held amusement and delight. "Duty calls," he said as he went over the fence and she went between the rungs. He caught her hand on the other side and squeezed. "I'm sure she wants you to help her with something too."

"Yeah," Codi said dryly. "How to get Reggie to kiss her."

Bryce tipped his head back and laughed, because that so sounded like Kassie. She was going to Seattle in the morning, and Bryce missed her already. But with Codi here, he didn't stand a chance of being too lonely.

No, she'd painted new life into his soul when she'd pulled up in that white bus with great big, brightly colored, cartoon dogs decorating it. He could see a future with a wife and children now that he couldn't before, because of her.

Now, he just needed his prayer to come true, and he doubled down on his pleas to the Lord that he wouldn't do or say something stupid to drive her away.

25

"Okay, I'm out of security." Kassie held her phone in front of her, with the camera angled up toward her face while she scanned for Reggie Avery.

"Is there someone standing there with your name on an iPad?" Bryce teased.

"Don't get in the car with anyone without making them show you ID," Codi said, and she meant business. In fact, it had been her idea for Kassie to video call back to Dog Valley when she got off the plane to meet Reggie.

You can never be too careful, she'd said last night, at which point Bryce had laughed.

His sister is my aunt, he'd said.

Oh, come on, Codi had argued back. *With how big your family is, a serial killer is bound to marry in at some point.*

They'd all dissolved into laughter then, and Kassie missed

Codi and Bryce more than she thought reasonable. Bryce had hugged her goodbye only a few hours ago, for crying out loud.

Her pulse sprinted through her body as she scanned left and right in the Seattle airport, and it sure wasn't hard to see Reggie standing way over by a pillar. Two bodyguards flanked him, though they stood several paces away from him. He wore a pair of sweatpants that somehow made him seem like a fashion model for sweatpants, and a T-shirt for the Seattle Stingrays, a matching baseball cap, and that smile that she'd seen on video every day for the past several weeks.

Part of her wanted to squeal, leave her rolling carryon behind, and run to him. At the last moment, she remembered Bryce would witness such a thing, and she kept a good grip on the handle of her suitcase. After all, she wasn't supposed to leave her bag unattended.

"There he is," she said, and she sounded breathless to her own ears. That came from the striding she'd been doing since she'd deplaned, nothing more. Certainly not the sexy baseball player currently walking toward her too.

"Be cool," Codi whispered.

"She is so far past cool," Bryce said. "Look at her face." He chuckled, and Kassie wanted to hang up.

"What does my face look like?" She couldn't stop smiling, she knew that.

"Like you're really excited to see him," Codi said, and she heard Bryce grunt. Kassie didn't care what they had going on back in Wyoming, because Reggie only stood two more paces from her.

She took them quickly, laughing, and she sort of forgot about her friends on the phone as she wrapped her arms around Reggie. He lifted her right off her feet as he said, "It's amazing to see you in person."

He laughed too, and as he set her back on her feet, his baseball cap fell to the floor. His sandy hair grew long enough to curl, and Kassie had been dreaming of running her fingers through it for over a month now. Reggie looked right into her eyes, his smile white and gleaming and so genuine. "Let me take your bag."

Moving past her, he collected the bag where it had stopped rolling, and then he tucked her hand into his. "I called a ride, and it should be here in a few minutes."

"Just enough time to get a soda," she said, eyeing a little store off to the left. "Can we?"

"Yeah, sure," he said, veering that way. They navigated through the other travelers so Kassie could get her diet cola, and it wasn't until she heard her phone ring that she realized the call with Bryce and Codi must've ended at some point.

"It's Bryce," she said, glancing over to Reggie.

He took her soda and reached for a bag of chips. "Get it," he said. "I'll get this stuff."

"But we're going to lunch, right?"

"Yeah, sure," he said again, and Kassie wondered if he'd just agree with her while she was here this week. She hoped not, but she'd take a soda without complaint.

"Sorry," she said by way of hello. "I'm obviously alive, and he's obviously not a kidnapper or anything."

"Codi hung up on you," Bryce said.

"I did not," Codi said. "I was preserving her privacy."

"Why would she need privacy in the airport?" Bryce bickered back, and Kassie loved him so much. "She's not going to kiss him for the first time in the baggage claim area."

"You never know," Codi said.

Kassie laughed, her back turned toward Reggie. Truth be told, the greeting they'd just had would've been perfect with a kiss. It would've been natural too, but Bryce was right. She didn't want her first kiss with him to be in the baggage claim area of the Seattle airport.

"What are you doing the rest of today?" Bryce asked. "You'll check in with me tonight, right?"

"Yes, *Dad*," she said, though she did need the check-ins. She'd only met Reggie once in person, and she did need to be careful. She hadn't told either of her parents about her long-distance relationship, nor this trip. She could imagine her mother's reaction, and it wouldn't be a supportive position.

"Kassie," he said, and she took her teasing down a notch.

"Okay," she said, watching a family pass by. "Yes, I'm going to be careful, okay? We're going to lunch, and then he's taking me to the Pike Place Market. Tomorrow, we're doing a boat tour thing, and I have everything I need."

"So you'll call me when you get to the hotel tonight," Bryce said.

"You're an hour ahead of me."

"Right," he said. "So you'll call me when you get to the hotel tonight."

"Yes, sir," she said, and she wasn't mocking him. "Thank you, Bryce."

"Have fun with him," he said.

"And be safe," Codi called.

Kassie smiled, because she wanted some good, safe fun with the pro baseball player. "Okay," she said. Reggie came to her side and handed her the soda. She took it and added, "I have to go, guys. I'll call you later."

"Bye," Bryce and Codi said together, and Kassie ended the call. She tucked her phone away and twisted the top on her diet cola. "Thank you, Reg."

He grinned at her and leaned closer, the gesture fading with every inch he gained. "Sure, yeah. My bodyguards won't leave until we get out of the airport, so...should we go?"

Kassie glanced over to one man wearing a black pair of jeans and a black polo. That wasn't intimidating or anything. "Yeah, sure," she said, echoing him. "Let's go."

"The car is here," he said.

"Do you have a car?" She stayed at his side as he navigated toward the exit, since she'd never been here before.

"I do," he said. "But I don't drive it a ton. To practice and back."

"You don't go out? Grocery shopping? McDonald's run?"

He grinned and slid her a look out of the corner of his eye. "Do I look like I eat at McDonald's?"

She nudged him with her elbow. "Why wouldn't you? Their fries are delicious."

"You want some McDonald's fries, sweetheart?"

"Yes," she said quickly. "That's what I want for lunch."

He laughed and shook his head. "Maybe tomorrow, Kass." He indicated a sleek, black SUV that looked like it belonged to a mob boss. "Today, I'm taking you to my favorite spot in the city for lunch."

"Oh, well, then." Kassie waited for a suited man to open the door for her, and then she climbed into the back bucket seat of the SUV. Her bag got put in the back while Reggie moved around to the other side and sat behind the driver.

"This is kind of weird," she said. "I've never been driven anywhere."

"Your family is like Southern royalty," he said, looking at her. "You've never been driven anywhere?"

"I have three older brothers," she said. "They're the royalty. Not me." She looked away from him as she buckled, unsure why she needed him to understand how simple her life was. "I own less than half a horse rescue ranch in Wyoming, Reg. Even if I'd stayed in Louisville, I wouldn't be someone important."

He reached over and played with her fingers, sending sparks up her arm. They lodged in her elbow and then her shoulder, and she couldn't stop smiling. "You're important to me, Kass."

The driver got behind the wheel, said nothing, and eased away from the curb without any directions from Reggie. She leaned back in her seat and gazed at him, because he'd already given the driver all of the directions, she was sure.

"Do you think you're still going to retire at the end of the season?" she asked.

His eyes flashed like aquamarine lightning. "I talked to Ev and Shawn about it a couple of nights ago."

"Thursday," she said. "Your off night." She smiled at him,

wondering if they'd be in public all day today. Her gaze dropped to his lips, and she really wanted to kiss him. *You'll be here all week*, she told herself, and she pulled her eyes back to his. She didn't have to kiss him tonight.

"Right," he said. "Ev wants me to come home, of course. She worries constantly about me here, though I've lived here by myself for over a decade." He half-smiled and shook his head.

"It's nice to have someone worrying over you." Kassie's attention moved out her side window, and despite the tinting of it, she could still see the summer sunshine over Seattle.

"Did you talk to your folks?" he asked.

She shook her head, wishing she'd borrowed one of Codi's wigs so she could change what she looked like simply by pulling on a new head of hair. She'd watched Codi do it a couple of times, and it really was amazing how her hair made her look different.

"Kass, I thought you were going to."

"I'm just not sure I see the point," she said, a sigh pulling through her whole body. "I don't have a place back in Kentucky, and I'm okay with it."

"In the business," he said. "But you're still a member of your family."

"Yeah." She turned toward him, trying to breathe through the sadness. "Can we just have a good time this week? I don't want to talk about my family."

Reggie gazed at her, his expression serious and delving way too deeply into her core. "I want you to be happy, sweetheart, and you're not. Not with this situation with your family. You can cover it up with Bryce Young Band-aids, and his rockstar uncle Band-aids, and all of his aunts Band-aids, but until you call your mother and talk to her, I don't think your wound is going to get better."

Tears burned in her eyes, and Kassie shook her head and closed her eyelids. That only squished the tears out, and she hated that she was crying within the first thirty minutes of seeing her delicious long-distance boyfriend for the first time in weeks.

"I don't want to be a Band-aid for you," he whispered. "I will, but I think you've got to do something about this festering hurt inside you." He tugged on her hand and said louder, "Can you pull over for a sec?"

The driver did what he asked, and Reggie undid his seatbelt and dropped to his knees beside her seat. "Kass."

"Reggie," she whimpered.

"Let's walk for a minute." He somehow reached past her and opened her door, then he pushed the button to release her seatbelt. She spilled from the SUV with him following close behind her. He took her hand and started walking down the sidewalk.

She had no idea where she was, and she didn't care. Reggie was with her, and she'd be okay with him. Oh, and the two bodyguards who pulled over in front of his SUV and stared at them as they walked by. Reggie may or may not have waved to them; Kassie wasn't really sure as blurred as her vision had become.

What she knew was Reggie kept her hand tightly in his, and when he stopped, they overlooked a bay. "I love this spot," he said wistfully. "Whenever I miss my mom and dad so much I can't stand it, I come here."

Kassie laced her arm through his and leaned her head against his bicep. "It's beautiful," she said. "Even in the middle of the day." A slight wind tugged at her hair, and she tucked it away behind her ear. "I feel like I can see for miles."

"Yeah," he said. "That's what I like about it too. Almost like...what I can see here on Earth isn't the full picture. There's a lot more out there, you know? The water goes on and on, seemingly endless, but it's not. Somewhere over there, it hits land again."

Kassie liked the deep rumble of his voice in her ears. She liked that he wasn't just a sports dude and nothing more. He had a good heart, and a quick mind, and he loved his family. He'd be thirty-six years old soon, and he wanted to retire somewhere quiet, where he could start a family and settle down.

He'd told her all of his hopes and dreams over the past several weeks, and she'd really opened up to him too. She'd told him things about her family, about Bryce, that she hadn't told anyone else.

"Part of me worries that if I call my mama," she said. "I'll want to go back, and then I'll go back, and me leaving will have been for nothing."

Reggie said nothing, but he did shift and put his arm around her waist, tucking her further into the safety of his side, his very soul.

After a minute, he said, "You're not gonna go back."

"You don't think so?"

"There's nothing for you there," he said, tilting his head down to look at her. "You'll go for holidays, and for your parents' fiftieth wedding anniversary, because you want to be a Goodman too—and not just on paper. But you won't go back permanently."

"How do you know?"

"Because." He smiled at her softly, the corners of his full lips barely lilting up. "I'm going to be in Coral Canyon in only a few months, and we're going to be together."

Kassie's eyebrows went up. "Is that right?"

"Mm-hm." He leaned closer. "I sure do like you, Kassie, and being with you in person is ten times better than a video call." His breath traced over her face, brushed against her lips, and made her sigh as her eyes closed.

"I'm going to kiss you now," he murmured, and before she could adequately prepare or answer, his lips touched hers. Her entire focus went to where they connected, and Kassie knew within the first second that she and Reggie were indeed going to be together. He made her heart sing, and he'd brought to life so much for her that had gone dormant by the wayside.

He knew how to kiss a woman too, and Kassie took things slowly so she could commit every—fantastic—stroke of his mouth against hers to memory. When he finally pulled away, he didn't go far, and Kassie's mind had turned blissfully blank.

"Okay," he whispered. "So I'll help you call your mama tonight then."

She nodded, because she did want the festering in her soul to heal. She wanted her parents—both of them—at her wedding to this beautiful man. She wanted to feel like she'd done all she could to smooth over the rifts she'd caused when she'd left Louisville over six years ago.

"Do you really think we'll be together after you retire?" she whispered.

"Yeah," he said. "I know we will, Kassie, because I'm already falling in love with you."

"Won't Ev and Shawn be upset? Tell you to go slow?"

"Yeah, sure," he said, gazing out at the bay again. "But they know how I am, and I don't really do anything slowly." He looked at her, oh-so-seriously. "I don't need a lot of evidence," he said. "I know how I feel about you, Kassie. I know what I want, and you're it."

Warmth moved through her from top to bottom, and though her lungs felt a bit chilled at the idea of calling her mama, she nodded. "I've never met anyone like you, Reg. I feel it too."

He nodded, apparently all he needed to hear, and said, "So I'll call my brother and sister too. I mean, might as well stir them up with two announcements, right?"

"Your retirement and that we're dating?"

"Yeah." He shrugged. "Or an engagement."

Kassie pulled in a breath, sure she hadn't heard him right. "Reggie. Really? When are you going to call them?"

He gazed at her. "When I have the two announcements." He tucked her back into his side, and they stood there together, watching the birds and the breeze and the bay. Kassie had no idea what a conversation with her mother looked like or sounded like, but when Reggie kissed her again, she could picture perfectly her life with him.

Him, her horses, her dogs, and the Rising Sun Ranch.

"Are you saying you have a diamond ring?" she whispered as they walked back to the SUV.

"Guess you'll find out." He tossed her that playful, adorable look he'd used over the video calls too, and Kassie maybe, probably, definitely fell in love with him right then.

26

Tex Young sat in the quiet hospital room, something pulsing in and out, making a machine noise that barely met his ears. His daddy wouldn't be able to hear it if he'd been awake, which he wasn't.

Abby had taken Momma to lunch, and Tex had volunteered to stay in the room with Daddy so he could rest. His thumbs already ached, and he read over what he'd typed up for his brothers, their wives and families, and other loved ones in the area. Cheryl and Wade wanted to know, of course, and he knew the Whittakers would appreciate knowing. Wes, Colton, and Gray Hammond would too. Ames and Cy as well.

Tex had several of Momma and Daddy's friends on a list his mother had given him, and the job of informing everyone of Daddy's health conditions had fallen to him.

"Dear Lord," he whispered, but he didn't know how to

continue. How did one pour all the energy of their heart into a single sentence? Or even a paragraph?

Tex couldn't, and he simply needed to get the facts out. He'd almost texted everyone last night—at least his brothers—to pray for Daddy, but in the end, he'd decided to honor his father's wishes and wait until they had more formal news.

Daddy has some kidney trouble that's been making him feel pretty terrible lately. It's stemming from his prostate, which is enlarged and cutting off the ability for his kidneys to rid themselves of the waste products in his blood.

He's been in the hospital since yesterday morning, and Trace will be making a schedule for visitors. Please don't jump in your trucks and race on over. He's not going anywhere quite yet.

The doctors have him on meds for the prostate, and they're considering a kidney surgery, but that's not certain for now. One kidney might be in complete failure, which would be bad, of course. We need to talk to a nephrologist, but there aren't any in Wyoming. The closest one is in Denver, and he does video calls, and comes up to the hospitals here only when necessary.

He's feeling better here, because he can get the nutrients and rest he needs. There's some enzyme in his liver they don't like either, and they're monitoring that. The blood work shows no cancer whatsoever.

You guys know how Daddy is. He doesn't want a fuss made over him, so we're going to make a big fuss over him. It's what we do, but let's try to do it in the most controlled way possible. Momma is a little overwhelmed, but she's taking everything pretty well, actually, and I know she'd love to be spelled from being cooped up here with Daddy at least once a day. Georgia has volunteered to arrange that schedule for anyone who wants to take her to lunch, out to the park with any kids, whatever.

Abby and I were here this morning to talk to the doctors, so we can answer your questions. Put them here, and let's not bother Momma with having to explain it all over and over. They love you, and Abby and I love you, and this is all going to be okay.

He wasn't sure on that last part, but at the same time, he absolutely was. His father might not live much longer. The doctors weren't sure he was even strong enough for a kidney surgery, at least in his current, compromised situation.

But Tex knew without a doubt that even if his father passed away, everything would be okay. He'd lose his anchor, his very solid foundation, but the world would go on. He had others he'd tied himself to, including his brothers, his wife, and his Momma. He had his knowledge of the Lord and His eternal plan for His children.

Everything really would be okay.

So he sent the text, leaned back in his chair, and closed his eyes. He hadn't slept well last night in anticipation of the meeting with the doctors this morning, but his soul and his heart and his mind felt heavy now.

Tex had silenced his phone, so he didn't hear or feel the frenzy of texts that surely were coming in. He drifted, worrying and wondering over how to be the oldest son in a family without a father.

"Dad."

He woke at the sound of his oldest son's voice, and he opened his eyes to find the young man coming into focus. Bryce wore worry on his face, a look Tex had seen in the mirror hundreds of times in the past. "Hey." He sat up, his phone clattering to the floor. "Sorry, I fell asleep."

"Momma called," he said. "Because you weren't answering your phone, and she's out with Grandma. I was getting the pets for Georgia and Otis, so I was close, and...." He trailed off and looked over to his grandfather, still snoozing in the hospital bed. "How is he?"

"He's just tired," Tex said, getting to his feet. "I can't believe I fell asleep." He slung his arm around his son's shoulders, and they stood there together, watching his daddy. After several long breaths, he stooped and picked up his phone. "I'll answer everyone."

"Okay." Bryce moved closer to the bed and took his grandpa's hand in his. He said nothing, but Bryce had always been strong and sure and confident. Even when he thought he'd lost everything, He'd forged ahead, refusing to wallow or stay stuck in the past.

Tex focused on his phone then, really regretting the quick cat nap when he saw he'd missed several phone calls from Trace and hundreds of texts from those on the string he'd created specifically for his father's health updates.

He started going through them, systematically answering questions as they arose and starring comments like, *We'll pray for him, Tex*, or *Thanks for letting us know. Hugs and prayers.*

He'd just caught up when Trace entered the room, and he looked like the dark stormcloud that would blow right through any human heart that he pretended to be on the album covers for Country Quad. "Hey," he said, softening instantly when he saw Tex standing only a few steps inside the door.

"I fell asleep." Tex wrapped his brother in a hug and held on tight. "I'm sorry, Trace. I didn't mean to. I just...I'm tired."

"I bet." Trace held him back and when they separated, his younger brother took Tex's face in his hands. "You do not have to do this alone. You could've called me last night."

Tex nodded. "Daddy didn't want me to."

Trace's eyes only turned darker. "You do what *you* need to do, Tex. You hear me?"

"Yes, sir." He smiled softly and closed his eyes, nodding to his brother.

Trace dropped his hands and looked over to their daddy. Bryce moved out of the way for him, falling back to Tex's side. "He looks okay," he said.

"I really think he'll be okay, yes." Tex met his son's eyes. "No one lives forever, though."

Bryce's jaw hardened, but he nodded. "If you can't go with me to the auctions next week, I get it."

"No, I'm going," Tex said. "I'll just make sure Trace has others scheduled." He shifted his feet, not sure if he should ask the question on the tip of his tongue. "Is Codi coming?" he managed to squeeze out anyway.

"No," Bryce said, shaking his head. "I haven't even asked her to." He looked at Tex. "Should I?"

"I don't know," Tex said. "You run that part of the ranch. I don't know what you want her to know and do."

Bryce said nothing as Trace turned toward them. "I can sit with him for a bit," he said. "You've been here all morning."

"We'll just go grab some lunch." Tex nodded to his brother and steered his son out of the room. Bryce wasn't crying, but a silent Bryce usually meant something brewing in that brain of his. Something not good.

Tex didn't know how to comfort his son in this case, and he decided that wasn't his role right now. "Did you ask Codi about going on tour with you?"

"Yep."

"And?"

"The thing with Codi is," he said. "She's really good at talking about something without committing to it." Bryce smiled, but it looked a little wary around the edges. "I'll have to pin her down to get a real answer."

"Maybe she just needs time to think about it."

"Yeah, she likes to think things through," Bryce said quietly. "She...she wants to show you and Momma something."

"Show us something?"

"Oh, and I'm babysitting all of Otis and Georgia's pets this week while they take their family to the Lion Lodge, so I'm gonna need some prayers too."

"Oh, boy." Tex chuckled. "Obsidian is going to eat your liver out while you sleep."

Bryce burst out laughing too, but Tex wasn't really kidding. Georgia's cats barely tolerated Otis, and they'd been married for over a decade now. Bryce's house, with all the traffic in and out, all the dogs, the horses, the lack of high bookshelves? Onyx and Obsidian were definitely going to claw up something, and Tex did send up a prayer that it wouldn't be his son's face or any of his vital organs.

As Bryce pulled his seatbelt across his lap and Tex started his truck to take them somewhere delicious for lunch, his son looked at him. "Codi wears wigs, Daddy. Her hair has this albino quality to it. It's pure white, and it's pretty thin, and she doesn't like it. So she wears wigs."

"Ah," Tex said. "I mean, I figured something when we saw her with that long, dark hair last night."

"She wants to show you and Momma her real hair sometime."

Tex paused in adjusting the radio and the air conditioning vents and looked at his son. Really looked. "This is a big deal."

"You'd be in the top five people who she's shown," he said. "Ever. So yeah. Kind of a big deal."

Tex's pulse thundered through his chest like the horses his son rehabilitated. "Well, you tell her whenever she's ready, we'd love to see it. I'm sure it's just fine." He smiled at his son and aimed the truck out of the hospital parking lot. "Now, where are we eatin' today? Burgers or barbecue?"

"Burgers, please," Bryce said, and Tex wasn't going to complain.

A couple of weeks later, Tex loaded up in the passenger seat of his son's truck, their roles nearly reversed. He moved the folder of information Bryce had put together on this auction, and he left his door open while he waited for his son to show up with the keys and start the truck so the air would blow.

August had come and school had started, but that didn't mean it was super cool. In fact, a heat wave had come in this week, and Tex couldn't wait for the cooler temperatures to hit Coral Canyon.

"Ready?" he asked as his son jogged out of the barn. Codi stood in the doorway of it, a smile on her face. She definitely wore a wig today, this one with blonde bangs and curls that reached for her shoulders but didn't quite make it. She lifted her hand in a wave, and Tex returned it.

He really liked her, and he liked her for Bryce, and he liked the two of them together. He'd said nothing of the sort to Abby or his son, and he wouldn't either. He'd been praying for Bryce to have the experiences he needed to have, nothing more. Nothing less.

"Sorry," Bryce said as he vaulted into the truck. "I got tied up in there."

"I can see that." Tex turned his smile on his son. "The horses are loaded up?"

"All ready." Bryce wouldn't look at him, which meant only one thing: He'd give away everything if their eyes met.

Tex gave him the space he clearly wanted, and he didn't say a word until they'd left the ranch, left Dog Valley, and were headed further north. Then they'd go east for a bit, and then dip back down south.

They'd end up at Honor Farm, where the federal penitentiary held an auction every so often to reintroduce wild horses back into working jobs.

"You got Golden Boy back there?"

"Yes," Bryce said, the word clipping from his throat.

Tex said nothing more, because Bryce loved Golden Boy and wanted to keep him. But Bryce also ran a business, and he couldn't keep every horse he happened to like. He had to sell some of them in order to keep his operation running, and Golden Boy was an extraordinary horse.

"He'll go somewhere amazing," Tex said. "Who else is ready?"

"Boulevard," Bryce said. "And A Horse Named Charlie." He glanced over to Tex. "He should go to a farm somewhere. Not law enforcement."

"You don't think so?"

Bryce shook his head. "He'll do great on a farm and giving kids rides, but he's not a workhorse. He's old. I'm not even going to show him for the law enforcement leg."

"What about Golden Boy and Boulevard?"

"Well, I'd like them all to go to small family farms," Bryce admitted. "Golden would love something touristy, because he loves people. Police work is hard on a horse."

And Bryce loved his horses. He loved the animal in general, but he gave a little piece of his heart to every equine who came through his unit.

"Well, let's see what we've got today." Tex loved riding along with his son, because Bryce demonstrated not only his horses' amazing abilities when he showed them, but his own. He maintained a level head and a calm heartbeat when with his horses, Tex liked nothing more than watching his son do what he'd been born to do.

"Any word from Bailey?" he asked as casually as he could.

Bryce looked over to him and held there, which he could do because the highway stretched long and straight—and empty—in front of them. "She wrote OJ back. Otis didn't tell you?"

Tex shook his head, something crawling up his throat and lodging there, making it hard to speak. "I think he doesn't want to burden me with more." None of the brothers did, and Tex had been finding out things via the brothers' text or secondhand since he'd distributed the information about Daddy's health a couple of weeks ago.

He did need surgery, but they'd scheduled it for next week, and Mav, Jem, and Blaze were covering the care for most of it. Tex, Otis, and Trace were planning on heading out of town for a couple of weeks as Harry's tour started, as was Bryce.

Tex suddenly knew why God had given Momma and Daddy so many sons. When they needed help, they'd have it.

"Yeah, she wrote him a real nice note," Bryce said. "OJ brought it out to the ranch, oh, last week? Something like that. She's coming to town right before we leave on tour."

"Is she now?" Tex's eyebrows stretched toward the ceiling. "And you're...are you going to see her?"

Bryce shook his head, his fingers gripping and regripping the steering wheel. "I don't think so, Daddy. She hasn't told me any of her plans. She's making all the arrangements with Uncle Otis." He looked over to Tex. "I'm really surprised he hasn't told you."

Tex swallowed against the lump in his throat. "Well, I'm not as good at everything with OJ as the rest of y'all."

"Yes, you are," Bryce said, dismissing Tex's statement instantly. "Don't be sayin' stuff that isn't true, Daddy. You handle Otis and Georgia, and me and OJ, and Graham and Laney just fine."

"But not Bailey," he said quietly.

Bryce swung his attention toward him again. "You haven't forgiven her?"

"Nothing for me to forgive," Tex said, keeping his gaze out the windshield.

"You think *I* have something to forgive her for?"

"I'm not saying anything like that," Tex said with a sigh. "I'm saying I don't know how to handle seeing her. I think Otis thinks I don't know how to handle it, so he doesn't tell me."

"Well, you haven't always agreed with what he and Georgia have decided to do."

"As I've been told," Tex said with a hint of ice in his voice. "She's still Abby's best friend, and I want to be there for Otis. I just...I don't know how to cross this bridge over and over."

"You just take the first step," Bryce said, grinning now. "That's what *you've* told me, Daddy, like, a thousand times."

"Okay," Tex said with a smile too.

"I can't believe I'm giving my father advice," Bryce said. He laughed, and it did sound joyful and happy. "This is the greatest day of my life. Just take the first step, Daddy." He spoke the last sentence in a deeper voice, and the two of them laughed together.

Tex knew he did need to take the first step, and that meant he should text Otis. So while Bryce drove, he pulled out his phone and texted the brother who was raising his grandson. Tex hardly thought of OJ like that anymore, and he knew he'd have grandchildren soon enough. *All in the Lord's time*, he thought as he sent the text.

They arrived at Honor Farm, and Bryce slipped into his professional mode. He filled out the required forms and put his horses with those the inmates had trained. Several others showed up with an equine or two, and then the auction started.

Tex climbed the stands after leaving Bryce to do his job, noting that the bleachers were really full today. He could tell the law enforcement agencies by their decorated and uniformed officers, but plenty of plain-clothes people watched too.

Bryce came out about halfway through, and the announcer said, "This is Golden Boy, trained by Bryce Young from the Rising Sun Ranch in Dog Valley, Wyoming. He's available for commercial, residential, or law enforcement buyers." He continued to outline what kind of horse Golden Boy was while Bryce ran the horse through several exercises, and when the bidding started, the auctioneer began at twenty-five hundred dollars.

Tex's face filled with a smile, because Bryce wore one, and Tex would swear in a court of law that Golden Boy did too. He loved being a horse, and he got purchased by the Jackson Hole Outbackers for just over six grand.

Tex whooped when the auctioneer called the winner, and Bryce galloped in front of the crowd with Golden Boy. The air held a certain excitement, and Tex found himself glad the glorious Golden Boy didn't have to go work with a policeman on his back. Instead, he'd take tourists up into the mountains, and he'd love it.

Tex's own spirit felt freer than it had in a while, and though his phone continually held dozens of unread messages, and he still hadn't heard back from Otis, he took a deep breath and let it all out. He loved Wyoming, and he loved his family, and he loved his life.

Everything would work out okay, because God had heard his son's prayers about Golden Boy, and even that small miracle mattered. Even the smallest person mattered to God, and He heard them.

Tex had that reiterated to him again, sitting in the stands in the August sunshine, watching his son ride another horse who got bought by a commercial family farm who needed horses to do hayrides.

He hears us, he thought, and it rang true through his whole heart and soul.

27

odi set her phone on the shelf, and said, "I love it here, Dad."

"It's drivable, Codi."

"Dad, you don't need to come."

"I haven't seen you in a few months," he said. "I want to see this amazing place you've described, and I want to meet Bryce."

Codi ducked her head and smiled, because she may have gushed over the Rising Sun Ranch and its owner a little bit. She finished cleaning the combs she'd used on the horses that day, and she turned back to Dragon, who stood still, waiting for her.

"He's pretty busy," Codi said. "But we find time for each other." Codi had tried to be strong and at Bryce's side as he dealt with his grandfather's illness and stay in the hospital, then OJ and the card his birth mother had sent him.

"He'll be on tour after Labor Day," she added. "Maybe the end of the month?" She immediately shook her head. "No, that's still harvest for you. It's gonna have to be the end of September, because we'll be gone."

"You're going on tour with him?"

"Just for one week," she said. "And I haven't told Bryce yet, so you better not try to talk to him first."

Her dad laughed, and it streamed through Codi too. She hadn't heard her father so joyful in a while. "I don't even have his number, Codi."

They sobered, and Codi stroked her hand down Dragon's neck. "I really like him, Daddy. I want you to meet him; I trust your opinion." She took a breath, and she did what Bryce said he always tried to do. Just open his mouth and let the Lord fill it with the right words.

"Daddy, I'm so sorry I didn't listen to you about Lester."

"Codi, honey, you don't need to apologize."

"I just couldn't see it," she said, her emotions wavering. "I shouldn't have *needed* to see it. I should've listened to you and Mom. I don't know why I didn't."

"You were in love," Dad whispered.

"So you've got to come before I fall all the way in love with him."

"Let me talk to your brothers, and we'll see when we can get this harvest done."

Codi nodded, though her dad couldn't see her. Dragon put his big head on her shoulder, and Codi pushed him back. "I love you, Dad."

"Love you too, Codi. We'll talk again soon."

"We will," she said, and then she moved over to the shelf and tapped the red button to end the call. She took a deep breath and watched as the screen darkened. Then she swiped her phone off the shelf and tucked it into her pocket.

"All right, Dragon," she said, facing the horse again. The very stubborn horse who wouldn't let her ride him. "I talked to my dad, and that means you're going to let me ride you."

She set about saddling the horse, which was a major accomplishment by itself. He didn't even snuffle at her for his treats as she got every piece in place.

"Come on," she said, taking the lead and walking forward. Dragon came with her, and in fact, he crowded right into her back, pressuring her to go faster than she wanted to. "Stop it." She moved slower, forcing Dragon to do the same.

Outside, she led him down the lane and past the walking rings, where she'd put Stardancer earlier. Dragon started to move toward that gate, but Codi went right on by. He plodded along after her, and he tossed his head when she took him past the pasture too, where three of his friends got to snack on grass.

Once they'd left the main buildings of the ranch behind, Codi dropped the lead and let Dragon walk where he wanted. He came right to her side, and she trailed her fingers down his side, a smile in her soul.

"I love you, Dragon," she said to him. "I don't weigh that much, and we'll just do this—walking—but I'll be on your back."

He snuffled at her, and she smiled. "It's not hard. It's this same thing. I won't make you go fast or through water, or even close to the fence. We'll just get to walk down the road together."

Dragon tossed his head, and it looked like he'd just given her permission to try getting in the saddle. Again. he'd resisted her this whole week, and Codi moved to his shoulder. "Behind me, Dragon."

He did what she asked, and she slowed until she stopped. He did too, and she turned to face him. "Okay, I'm going to get on." She'd mounted plenty of horses in her lifetime, and she only needed eight seconds to be in the saddle, ready to go.

She moved to his side, grabbed the saddle horn, and put her foot in the stirrup. She didn't hesitate. She didn't give him a moment to move. She simply pushed herself up; she swung her leg over; she landed in the saddle; Dragon didn't move.

Pure pride filled Codi, and she leaned over and wrapped her arms around Dragon's neck. "That's right, buddy. See? Ain't no thing." She heard herself repeat something Bryce said, and he claimed to have gotten it from an uncle, but Codi couldn't remember which one right now.

Because she currently sat in a saddle on Dragon's back. She pulled out her phone and took a grinning selfie, then sent it to Bryce with the words, *Guess where I am?*

He called, which she suspected he would, and since she kept her phone on vibrate while working with Dragon, it buzzed in her hand. "Let's walk," she said to Dragon, giving him a gentle nudge in his haunches. "Walk, Dragon."

The horse started to move, and Codi swiped on Bryce's call. "He's walking," she said excitedly. "I'm riding him, Bryce."

"Where you at? I want to come see him."

"Just the main road out to the pumpkin patch. It took all week, but I made a deal with him, and after I called my dad, I told him, 'All right, Dragon. I did what I said I would, and now you have to too.'"

Bryce chuckled. "There's so much to unpack there, but I just want to see you riding him. I'm saddling Violet, and I'll be on my way."

Codi laughed, and she said, "I'll be here, riding him."

Bryce hung up laughing, and Codi reached up and unclipped her wig. She removed it and tucked it into her back pocket. "Just me and you, Dragon," she said. The Wyoming breeze played with her hair, and pure joy streamed through her.

He kept walking, no complaints, and Codi wanted to have day after day like this with him, walking through the sunshine and sunflowers, and her chest turned a tiny bit tight.

Bryce rode up on Violet, a pretty gray horse, and whistled at her like she was something to behold. "Wow," he said. "Look at the two of you."

"He's the best," Codi said, grinning over to him. "Bryce, I want him."

"You want him?"

"Yeah, I want to buy him. I don't want to train him and then watch you sell him to pull a wagon on a hayride. *I* want him." Her heart thumped painfully in her chest. "How much for him?"

Bryce looked at her, clear shock in his eyes. He sighed and faced the long lane in front of them. "Where are you going to keep him?"

"Here," Codi said. "I'll pay for boarding."

He smiled and angled his head toward her. "So you want one of my horses, one who won't even let me feed him, and you want to board him here too—where I'll have to feed him."

Codi grinned at him. "Look at him, Bryce. I can't—" Her throat closed. "I want him."

"Yeah, and I want you to have him." Bryce looked forward again, and Codi let her emotions storm through her in silence. Bryce let her, and then he drew Violet closer to Dragon. "Can we get this close?"

"I guess we'll see." Codi held Dragon steady as Bryce brought Violet closer. "Hold steady."

Bryce positioned his horse right beside Dragon, and they walked along, content. He reached over and took her hand, and Codi looked at him. "You have room for him. I will drive up here and feed him morning and night."

He smiled and shook his head. "Nah, I can do it. I survived that week with the Cat Brothers and all those extra dogs."

"And a bird," Codi reminded him.

"And a bird," he said with a chuckle. "I can feed your dragon horse." He gave her a raised-eyebrow look. "Maybe you can make another deal with him. Tell your boyfriend about your call with your dad, and he'll let me feed him."

Codi giggled and ducked her head. "I'll talk to him."

"Yeah, you will," he said.

"One hundred percent." She squeezed his hand, which drew his attention back to her. He wore his cream-colored cowboy hat today, and she'd seen him in every shade over the past couple of months. "I told my dad about this ranch, and how much I love it here, and then about you."

She didn't say "and how much I love you," but it hung in the air between them anyway. "He wants to come see it all. He wants to meet you." She watched him, but Bryce didn't show any signs of nerves.

"I'll be on my best behavior," he said.

"So no puncture wounds," she said. "No cereal for dinner."

"Well, that might be going too far," he teased. "If I can't impress him with cereal, he'll never like me."

She squeezed his hand again, really liking the feel of his skin against hers. "It would be impossible for him to dislike you."

"I guess we'll see."

"He probably won't come until after the tour. It's potato harvest right now."

"Oh, sure," Bryce said. "So we've got some time."

"Loads of time."

Codi could spend hours riding horses with Bryce, holding his hand, wigless, and with the glory of the mountains and sunshine and peace surrounding them.

As she let herself feel those big things, she realized her father might not be able to meet Bryce before she fell in love with him. Especially when he held Dragon while she dismounted and then took her into his arms. "You are incredible," he said in all seriousness, his gaze on her and only her. When he kissed her, it held tenderness, passion, and...love.

28

"**D**addy?"

Otis Young turned from the notebook where he'd been working on a set of lyrics. "Yeah, Roo, come in." He leaned back in this chair and stretched his arms above his head. Whenever the world felt like it had started to shed and fall down around him, he turned to writing lyrics.

Country Quad had retired, but Harry still needed songs, and Otis had been selling songs to record labels, individual artists, and bands for decades now.

"What's up?"

His daughter sat precariously on the ottoman in front of the black leather couch where Otis sometimes brainstormed ideas with Trace. Joey's hands went round and round, her tell of nerves.

"Are you nervous about dinner with Bailey?"

"A little," Joey said. "But Daddy, there's something else."

Otis's heart slipped from its rightful place behind his ribcage, and down into a more vulnerable position. "Okay," he said. "Whatever it is, it's fine. Just tell me, and we'll work it out."

Joey had turned nineteen this past winter, and she was a gorgeous, talented woman. Otis could hardly believe she was his daughter, and love filled him from head to toe. No matter what Joey said, he'd still love her. A smile touched his mouth, and Joey exhaled.

"I'm not going back to college in Jackson Hole," she said. "I've put my tuition on a credit card, and I'm moving to New York City in three weeks."

Otis took a breath, trying to process everything all at once. "I told you I'd pay your tuition, Roo."

Her bottom lip quivered. "But I don't want to go to Wyoming State. I want to cook. I'm really good, Daddy, and I got into the Culinary Institute." She wiped her eyes, and Otis didn't understand why she was upset.

He left his chair and moved over to the ottoman too. He was too big to sit there with his grown daughter, but he mashed himself onto it anyway. "Roo," he said as tenderly as he could. "I love you to the moon and back. Always."

He gently reached and held her chin in his hand, turning her to look at him. "Why didn't you just tell me?"

"I didn't think you'd let me go to the city," she said. "You freaked out over that guy I dated in Jackson, and he was nothing."

Otis would not apologize for his overprotective behavior. "You can always talk to me," he said. "That's what I want. I want to make sure you're okay, and that guy had a...bad name."

"I know." She sniffled. "So I can really go to the Institute?"

Otis didn't want to say yes, but he absolutely couldn't say no. He had no idea what it took to get into a prestigious place like that—or how much it would cost—but one look at his lovely, fair daughter, and Otis's heart told him what to say.

"Yes," he said. "Do we need to go find somewhere to live?"

"I got a dorm at the Institute," she said. "It's behind a coded door, and I, uh, got a private room. I can pay for the first semester from my savings this summer, but I—well, I'll need some help for the second semester."

Otis had gobs and gobs of money in the bank, and he wouldn't even need to ask his wife if they should fund this. Everything in the heavens and inside Otis told him he should.

"Okay," he said. "I need to see a budget sheet."

"I have it." Joey rose to her feet, her tears nearly gone. "I'll just grab it, okay? Can Georgia come in?"

Otis stared at Joey. "Did you tell her already?"

She shook her head and wiped her eyes again. "No, but she'll want to know what's going on, right? We can go over all of it together." Joey looked so hopeful and so angelic in the sunlight coming in from the window.

"Of course," Otis said. "Let's meet back in the kitchen."

Joey smiled and headed for the door while Otis got to his feet. She turned back and rushed at him. "Thank you, Daddy." She collided with him, and he grunted as he wrapped his arms around her.

"I love you, Roo. You don't have to be afraid to tell me anything, ever." He pulled back and looked at her. "We've never kept secrets from each other, have we?"

More tears filled her eyes as she shook her head. "No," she said in a near whimper. "I'm sorry. I didn't know how to tell you."

"You just come in and tell me," he said. "You are the most important thing to me."

"The door is open," OJ said as he appeared in the doorway. "He's not workin', Momma."

Otis kissed Joey's forehead and then turned to his son. "Hey, bud. What's up?" The boy held his guitar, and Otis sure did love the sight of OJ. "Is your lesson over?"

"Yeah, and I want to play my song for you." He looked at Joey. "Can I?"

"Yeah, we're going out into the kitchen." Otis shooed the boy back out of his office, and Joey followed them. She turned toward her bedroom while OJ led the way back into the main part of the house.

Georgia worked in the kitchen, because Bailey McAllister would be joining them for dinner that evening, and the whole house had held a certain tension since she'd called and set up the meal.

She wanted to meet OJ, and the boy had excitement for blood in his veins. They'd taken him to two counseling sessions this week, so he could work through his expectations and feelings for meeting Bailey, and he'd go first thing on Monday too.

"Hey, baby." Otis joined Georgia. "Joey has some news," he murmured in her ear. "Can you spare fifteen minutes?"

Georgia looked at him with alarm on her face. "News in only fifteen minutes?"

Roo appeared with a notebook in her hands and pure fear

shining in her eyes, and Otis looked at her. Georgia followed his gaze, and said, "I'll put a timer on this dough. Let's see what we can go over in fifteen minutes."

Otis grinned as Joey advanced toward them, and then he turned toward OJ. "First," he said. "OJ is gonna play his song for us. Then, we're going to hear Joey's plans for the fall."

OJ wiggled his way up onto a stool and positioned his guitar in his hands. "This is called—"

"Momma! Daddy!" Ana burst through the back door. "There's a black and white cat out here, and—"

"No," Georgia said firmly, and Otis secretly beamed as she went closer and scooped the five-year-old into her arms. She'd be six next week, and to Otis, she was a miracle child. "No more cats, Ana. Now come on, we're listening to Brother play the guitar."

OJ looked at Otis, and he nodded at his son. "This song is called *Under the Bridge*." His fingers started to move across the strings, and Otis couldn't contain the smile that filled his whole face. He played well for an eight-year-old, and when Otis closed his eyes, he could see Bryce sitting on the stool, playing the guitar for him, for his other uncles, for his daddy.

And now, a generation later, OJ was doing it.

Otis clapped harder than anyone when the song ended, and he swarmed OJ with Georgia and Ana and Joey. "She's gonna love it," he promised his son. Now, he just had to pray that Bailey would give the boy the reaction he needed to be healthy and happy and whole.

So he did that, with every fiber of his being, every ounce of energy in his soul, every beat of his heart.

THE DOORBELL RANG, AND GEORGIA GASPED. "SHE'S HERE."

"It's fine," Otis said as his wife whipped off the apron she'd been wearing all day. "Think of her. Think how hard it is for her on the other side of the door."

He couldn't even imagine what it took to drive here, park outside, walk up to the door. He had no idea what it had cost Bailey to call them in the first place. She'd been kind and polite, and she'd been accommodating to their schedule.

Otis took Georgia's hand and looked over to OJ. He wore a pair of navy blue shorts and a collared shirt in pale yellow. It had an insignia embroidered on the chest, and Otis reached for him too. "Are you ready, my son?"

His emotions rose and rose and rose, causing a burning, stinging sensation in his nose as he fought to keep his composure.

"I'm ready," OJ said. "She's going to be so nice, I just know it."

"We're ready," Joey said, and she held Ana's hand. They both wore a dress in pink and stripes, and while it wasn't a matching pattern, and they only shared Otis's genes, he saw two sisters when he looked at them.

"We're ready," he said. "This is just dinner, okay? We are this family, and a single dinner doesn't change us." He looked at Georgia, who nodded resolutely. He looked at Joey, then OJ, then Ana. "We belong to each other. Always."

"Always," Joey whispered.

"Always," Georgia echoed.

"Always," OJ and Ana said together.

Otis nodded, and he knew they were all waiting for him to lead them to the door. To lead them everywhere; they'd follow too, because they loved him. They trusted him.

"All right," he said. "Let's go greet her like she's a member of our family, because she kind of is." He grinned at his son, and then he took the first step toward the front door—and Bailey McAllister.

29

Bailey McAllister fought every flight response in her body. She'd taken a plane here. She'd spent last night with her parents, and it had been one of the most beautiful evenings of forgiveness and love she'd experienced in her life, ever.

Help me, she thought, and it sounded dangerously like a prayer in her head. She wasn't sure if she should ring the doorbell again or not, but it felt like she'd been standing on this well-decorated stoop for half her life.

Finally, the door opened, and Otis Young stood there, his hand secured in his wife's. Georgia smiled, the radiance of it beaming straight into Bailey's heart. Tears already clung to Georgia's eyelashes, and they rushed into Bailey's eyes too.

She looked at the stunning blonde next to Otis, but she'd forgotten the girl's name. She held the hand of another little girl who had to be close to five or six years old, and then Bailey's eyes landed on OJ.

Her son.

He had *her* DNA in his veins, and Bailey dropped to her knees right there on the cement and reached for him. "Oh, I see you," she said, not sure where the words had come from.

Without any encouragement from his parents, he stepped into her outstretched arms, and Bailey wept as she hugged her little boy.

She didn't want to make a scene for too long, so she pulled back and wiped at her face. "You must be OJ, the boy who wrote me the *nicest* birthday card I've ever gotten."

"That's me," he said. "And you're my birth mom." He looked back to Georgia, who nodded. "Bailey." He turned to face her again, his smile now curving up that mouth that looked so much like...hers.

"Yes." She took a big breath and reached for the gift she'd brought. She'd dropped it upon first sight of OJ, and she righted the blue and white striped bag. "I brought something for you." She held it out, her smile finally feeling like it belonged to her.

She'd been smiling a fake smile for nine years, since the day she'd found out she was pregnant with Bryce Young's baby. But faced with that baby—now grown to an eight-year-old boy—her smile had returned.

She wasn't sure why she'd put this off for so long, but she suspected it was because she hadn't known how healing mending all the bridges she'd set on fire and walked away from would be.

Guilt gutted her, but she held her head high as she extended the bag toward OJ.

"We didn't get you a gift," he said as he took the bag.

"Being able to see you is my gift," Bailey said, and she put her hand in Otis's and let him help her to her feet.

"Come in and open it, baby," Georgia said, and OJ did what she said. "Bailey, not sure if you remember Joey. And our youngest is Ana."

"Joey, yes," Bailey said, the name coming to her with clarity the moment Georgia said it. She stepped into the girl and hugged her. She carried absolutely no extra weight, but Bailey certainly did. "And Ana." She beamed down at the little girl. "I got you something too."

Her face lit up like Bailey had flipped a switch. "You did?"

"Momma!" OJ yelled. "Look! It's that magnet building set I wanted."

"Oh, wow, buddy," Georgia said. "Look at that."

"Can I open it?" OJ handed the box of magnets to his father, who took it. "We're eating first, bud. Remember? Momma's been cooking all day."

More guilt piled into Bailey's stomach, where she couldn't digest it fast enough to ever feel good again. "I'm sorry," she said, not sure why she felt like she needed to apologize. "I could've brought dinner."

"Oh, no, no," Georgia said. "It's no problem." She seemed so regal and polished, in a pair of black slacks and a black and white sweater that had elbow-length sleeves and a wavy pattern in the stripe.

"Come on back. We're almost set."

"Momma," Ana whined. "I didn't get my present."

"Oh, right." Bailey dug into her purse and pulled out a tiny stuffed animal. They were all the rage in Montana, but she really didn't know if the little girls here cared about them. "It's a Tiny Pet. They come with names, and you can get teeny clothes for them, but they don't need them."

She presented the fluffy sheep to Ana, whose eyes grew and grew and grew. She reached for it reverently, and Bailey bent down to be more on her level. "I take care of animals in my job," she said. "And I love the sheeps the best. This one is fluffy and rainbow-colored, which isn't real, but I thought you might like it."

"What do you say?" Otis prompted.

"Thank you," Ana said with pure awe in her voice. "Momma." She turned to Georgia. "She got me a Tiny Pet sheep." The little girl burst into tears, and Bailey wasn't sure what to do about that.

"I—she doesn't have to have it."

"Are you kidding?" Georgia let her daughter cry into her knees. "She's been begging me for a Tiny Pet for weeks now." She patted Ana's back and stroked her hair down.

Bailey looked at Joey and smiled. "I got you a lame gift card, but." She shrugged and pulled out the envelope that held the coffee gift card. "I figured one of my favorite gifts is a gift card."

"Thank you," Joey said pleasantly. "You know, you didn't have to bring presents." She studied Bailey in a way that made her feel like fleeing again.

"I know," she said. "But I felt so awkward coming without anything, and getting these little things helped me calm down."

She smiled at Joey, who pulled her into a hug. "We have missed you in our family."

That simple statement undid Bailey and all of her carefully gathered strings. She sobbed into Joey's shoulder and blubbered, "Thank you. I'm sorry I stayed away so long."

"Okay," Georgia said several moments later. "We are not crying all night, okay? This is a happy thing. This is good. This is a *happy* night for you, and for us, and for OJ. Okay?" She spoke with enough authority that Bailey started to lace back together her emotions.

She nodded and wiped her face. She stepped over to OJ. "I deliberately didn't look at any pictures of you before I got here," she said. "But my mom said you play the guitar, and maybe you'd play for me."

"Yeah," OJ said, plenty of enthusiasm in his expression. "Daddy, should we play first? Or are we eatin'?"

"We're eating," Otis said. "We can do our talent show after dinner."

"I get to do mine during dinner," Joey said, her smile pretty and oh-so-accepting. "I made the appetizer, Bailey." She moved further into the house, into the kitchen. "Come try this hot chicken dip. It's *so* delicious."

"Joey is going to culinary school," Georgia said with a smile. She'd picked up Ana, and she transferred her to Bailey, so she could go into the kitchen to get the food.

Bailey froze, the little girl in her arms. "Do you like the sheep? Did you check the name tag?"

"Her name be Shelly," Ana said. She looked at Bailey with somber eyes. "Thank you for her. I take so good care of her."

Bailey grinned at her. "I'm sure you will."

"Bailey," Otis said. "Come sit down, okay?"

"Yep," she said, remembering how Bryce would say that all the time. She'd done her best to drive the handsome cowboy from her mind, but she hadn't been able to do it. Alcohol didn't do it. Other men didn't do it. Her job didn't do it. The only relief she'd found from him, her biological son, and Coral Canyon had been pretending like they didn't exist.

But she was done with that now. She needed to be here, and she needed to feel the love these people had for her—for OJ. She'd only ever wanted him to feel loved. Wanted. Accepted.

She wanted those things for herself too, and she'd realized that until *she* accepted herself and the situation, she would never be whole.

She'd fly home in two days, and between now and then, she had to find one more well of courage. She had one more person to see, to talk things through with.

Bryce Young himself.

30

Bryce laughed as Lucky snapped at the butterflies. "Get 'em," he said through his happiness. But the dog couldn't get them. He wouldn't even know what to do with one if he did. It would flap around in his mouth, and he'd spit it out.

He bent over to get more carrots out of the ground, and then he'd go back down the length of his garden to get the peas that were ready. He had to gather the eggs too, and he couldn't wait to make ham fried rice for Codi that night. It was one thing he could do pretty well, and he'd brought home plenty of rice from their dinner out last night.

Lucky barked as he continued to jump and chase the hoard of butterflies that had decided Bryce's sunflowers were the place to gather, and then the golden retriever retreated to the deck once he'd decided the game was no fun.

Bryce worked through the late afternoon sun, finally

taking everything inside. He ran the water in the sink to wash the produce, and looking at something he'd grown and cultivated made a sense of pride and accomplishment rise up within him.

His doorbell rang, and that got Lucky off his mat near the back door. He barked once and then trotted for the front of the house. Bryce reached for a towel and took it with him as he dried his hands. He didn't get many people stopping by out of nowhere, and he wasn't expecting any visitors today.

He and Codi had gone to church that morning, but she'd gone back to Coral Canyon to take a nap. She'd been feeling a tiny bit under the weather lately, and she wanted to get Penta and bring him up to the ranch for dinner.

Bryce opened the door, and all the air in the world got sucked away from him. He knew the woman standing there as if he knew his own face, but he couldn't vocalize her name.

Bailey.

"Ah, I found it." She smiled at him and her hair had gone back to its normal blonde. She didn't wear dark eye makeup, and in fact, Bryce couldn't see makeup on her face at all.

"I'm—" she started to say, but Bryce had found himself again. He stepped out of his house and took her into his arms, silencing her.

"You're here," he whispered. "It's so good to see you." He knew he held her too tightly, but he couldn't make himself relax. She clung to him too, and this interaction was so different than their last few since they'd held their baby and then given him to Uncle Otis and Aunt Georgia.

"You're blonde, and you're perfect, and you're here." He

stepped back, pulling in a deep breath. "What are you doing here?"

Bailey's tears streamed down her face, and she made no effort to wipe them away. "I met our son," she said.

Bryce reached for the doorway to support himself, pure shock flowing through him. Words once again escaped him as he studied Bailey's face, desperate for the story. One tiny, pinching part of him whispered, *Without me? She went to see him without me?*

He drove it away, because it was a selfish thought. He wanted to be there to protect OJ from a woman who he didn't need to be protected from.

"Come in," he managed to say. He pulled Lucky back away from his sniff-fest at Bailey's knees. "Come on, Lucky-Lucks. She's comin' in. You can say hi in here."

The dog came, and Bailey smiled shyly at him as she stepped up and into his house too. He closed the door, feeling like he was living someone else's life.

"I don't want to stay long," she said. "I fly home tomorrow, and I'm having dinner with the whole Whittaker clan at the lodge tonight."

Bryce's memories fired at him, and he could remember meals with Bailey and her parents, her siblings, all her cousins, and aunts and uncles. Her family wasn't as big as his by any means, but he'd enjoyed a family meal or party up at the Whiskey Mountain Lodge when they were together.

He smiled, and it felt so good to do that in her presence. "Your favorite."

"I'm actually looking forward to it," she said as she took in his living room. "Being here has been...." She exhaled and brought her gaze back to his. "Good. Bryce, it's been really good for me."

"Come tell me about OJ," he said. "I'm making dinner for Codi with veggies I grew in my garden."

She beamed at him. "Look at you, Bryce. You're doing it."

"Doing what?" He led the way back into the kitchen and family room, Lucky at his side.

"Living your dreams," she said. "A horse rescue ranch? It's exactly what you've always wanted." She looked out the back wall of windows. "Wow."

"You want to see it?" He moved to the sliding door and opened it. She came outside with him, and the last of the shock of finding her on his doorstep faded into the sky, almost like the towering Tetons in the distance absorbed it all.

They stood side-by-side at the railing, and he said, "There it is. I've got horses, ducks, chickens, cats, and dogs."

"It's beautiful," she said. "Is Codi a ranch hand or your girlfriend?"

"Girlfriend," he murmured. His heart suddenly jumped and pumped and *ba-bump-boomed* in his chest. "She'll be here soon. You can meet her."

"Oh, I won't stay that long," Bailey said. "I just wanted you to know...I don't know what." She faced him. "I wanted you to see me like this. To see me when I'm not broken and ruined and unhappy."

Bryce looked right at her. "You saw OJ?"

A smile bloomed on her face. "On Friday night. He is your twin. A mini-Bryce." She laughed lightly and shook her head.

"Georgia and Otis and Joey were extraordinarily kind to me, and—" Her voice broke and she did brush at her eyes now. "OJ and I are going to stay in touch." She nodded through the emotion and faced the ranch again. "I'm trusting you, Mister Young, that this will get easier and I'll feel better and better."

"You will," he promised.

"I already feel so much more like myself," she said. "I wanted to apologize to you."

"Bay."

"No, let me say it."

He nodded and looked back at the ranch too. His designer chickens warbled in the distance, and the breeze didn't seem to mind the two of them standing on the deck.

"I'm sorry I left you here to do all of this yourself. I'm sorry I wasn't strong enough to be a support for you when I'm sure you were hurting."

He nodded, but he really didn't need this apology. Something inside him told him this wasn't about him. This was about Bailey doing what she felt she needed to.

"I'm making things right with my parents," she said. "I know you've carried that burden for a long time, and I love you for it." Her voice cracked again, but she kept going. "They adore you, and it's easy to see why. OJ loves you, and again, it's easy to see why. I'm so glad you have this ranch, and I want you to know that I'm seeing a therapist, and I'm doing really good at work, and maybe one day, I'll be strong enough to start dating someone again. For real. Dating someone with the intent to fall in love and marry them and have kids with them."

"You will, Bay."

"Is that Codi for you?"

"Could be," he said, because he wasn't going to deny how he felt about her. "We're only a couple of months in."

Bailey reached over and took his hand in hers. "I wish the best for you."

"I pray for the same for you," he said.

She nodded, squeezed his hand, and said, "Well, I better go, or I'll be late, and I'm trying really hard not to let my momma down any more than I already have." She flashed him a beautiful smile, and Bryce hauled her back into his embrace.

"You are welcome here anytime, day or night."

"Thank you, Bryce." With that, she stepped out of his arms, and with a semi-sad look on her face, she ducked her head and turned back to the house.

He went with her back to the front door, and she continued on to a sedan. He waved to her from the safety of his front porch, and only when he realized she'd been gone for a while and he still stood there did he return to his house.

"Lord," he said out loud. "Bless that woman with what she needs. I don't know what happened with OJ, but it sounds like it was positive." His own emotions surged and stormed and splashed all over. "I just want him to be happy. Her too."

They are, Bryce.

Tears pricked his eyes as he started peeling carrots, because he knew he'd just had his own personal Lazarus moment. Jesus had come to Bailey, and while it had felt like He'd come late, He hadn't. He'd done what only He could do, and that was call her back from the dead to live again.

31

T race Young pulled his guitar from the oversized luggage rack and nodded down to another compartment. "Yours is down there, brother."

Otis went to get his guitar, and while Trace was officially retired from the family cowboy boy band, this felt all too familiar. Traveling with bags and instruments and Otis.

Tex and Luke were not with them, and in fact, Morris was still home with his twins too.

He and Otis were taking the first month of Harry's tour so Morris could enjoy his family. Tex and Bryce would join them next week, and then they'd all be back in Coral Canyon by the first of October.

"Momma texted," Otis said as he shoved his phone in his back pocket and moved to get his guitar. Trace's chest tightened for a moment. His momma and daddy had been going through some things regarding Daddy's health recently.

He'd put off the surgery until Tex and Trace would be home from the tour. Of course, only Tex and Trace knew that, because they'd gone to dinner at their parents' condo and been told that. Momma and Daddy didn't want the other boys to know, and Trace hated keeping secrets from his brothers.

But Otis had a lot going on with OJ, his daughter's health, and he'd just taken Joey thousands of miles across the country to the Culinary Institute in New York City. Otis would be at Daddy's side in a moment if he needed him, and everyone knew it.

Blaze would too, and he didn't have a ton going on—besides his three children under the age of five. With Tex and Trace gone, the oldest brother mantle fell to Blaze, and he could shoulder it well. Momma and Daddy didn't want him to.

With Bryce coming out on tour next week too, Blaze, Jem, Luke, and Mav went up to the ranch to take care of the horses. So they had their hands full with kids, equines, and a multitude of other things.

Luke had a mess of kids too, and Gabe and Hilde with their triplets, and Morris had literally canceled the first month of his time with Harry on his tour so he could be with his family.

So Daddy was waiting on the surgery, and it was with a heavy heart that Trace pulled out his phone and looked at the text from his mother. If Otis had gotten it too, it wouldn't be that bad, surely.

Daddy's blood levels are normal! Praise Jesus. Thank you for all the prayers, and I'm making sugar cookies to celebrate. Anyone who wants some can stop by after dinner, or Bryce and Codi have volunteered to deliver them.

Trace smiled, because this was good news. He met Otis's eyes. "Next time you say there's a text from Momma, maybe don't sound like you're the Grim Reaper himself." Trace shook his head as Otis laughed, and they left the oversized baggage area to get their regular sized bags from the belt.

Over the past several years, Morris had really refined the process of traveling on tour, and he had everything booked right down to the littlest detail. So Trace and Otis had a driver holding their names on a card, and he helped them with their guitars and baggage. Soon enough, they rode in an air-conditioned SUV toward Trace's son.

His pulse seemed to enlarge with every turn of the wheels, and before he knew it, the driver turned into an arena Country Quad had played in a few years ago.

An *arena*.

Trace shook his head again, still awed and humbled by the rapid success of his son. It had taken the band over a decade to get to where Harry found himself in only a few years. Maybe two decades.

Harry's tour for this album spanned arenas, regular concert halls, and even some tiny joints that barely seated a hundred people.

As they neared the arena, Harry's face loomed above them. He played the silent giant too, with zero trace of a smile anywhere on his mouth. His eyes looked like midnight orbs under that black cowboy hat, and his mother had been his wardrobe consultant for the past few years, and she'd put him in a dark brown shirt that had some sheen to it.

His son was as handsome as the day was long, and Trace

loved him with every fiber of his being. He played a mean guitar, and his voice hadn't lost an ounce of smoothness. He worked dang hard, doing everything from workouts, to singing lessons, to guitar lessons—to this day.

Trace wondered how long he'd stay in this business, because while Harry was a rare talent, Trace uniquely knew how heavy being a country music rockstar could be.

And Harry didn't love performing. He loved playing, singing, and writing, and there were a lot of opportunities for that which didn't require him to live so far away and put so much of himself out there.

You'll talk to him about it, Trace told himself. He'd brought it up a time or two before, but the conversation hadn't yielded anything.

"He's incredible," Otis said.

"Yeah, you want your son to do this?"

"I wouldn't mind it," Otis said, taking his gaze from the big banner of Harry that covered the whole building in the middle of the arena. "We had a good career."

"Yeah, I know." Trace didn't sigh. "I'm grateful for it. I am. I just worry about him. He's so young, and he's not having the experiences other young people his age have."

"Why do you think that's bad?" Otis asked.

"It's hard to have a normal relationship."

"Yeah," Otis said. "We all managed, even Blaze." He chuckled, and Trace could smile with him.

"Yeah, but we were all out of the lifestyle first," Trace said. "And now Tex and I are raising babies in our fifties."

"Harry has a good head on his shoulders," Otis said. "He might surprise you."

The SUV came to a stop as Trace said, "I'm sure he will." He got out and stretched his arms above his head as his son burst out of the door ahead of him. Harry called, "Daddy," his smile huge as he jogged toward Trace.

Happiness exploded through Trace, because he loved this boy with his whole heart. He wrapped his son in his arms, both of them laughing, and when he pulled back, he cupped Harry's face in his palms. "You okay, son?"

"I'm good, Daddy." Harry knew what Trace was asking, and Trace knew Harry wasn't all the way good, but that he was good enough. The young man had plenty of money, a good manager, and good people around him.

"I've got a surprise," Harry admitted as Trace dropped his hands.

"I love surprises," Trace said dryly.

"Yeah, that's why Ev texted me to say y'all are havin' another girl." Harry grinned at him. "This is a girl too, Daddy." He swallowed, an edge coming into his eyes that Trace saw plain as day. "A woman."

Harry got interrupted by Otis, who came around the back of the SUV with their bags. "Uncle Otis."

Trace took a moment, because Ev had not told him they were having a girl. He'd known she was going to the doctor today, but he couldn't change his flight, and she couldn't get in sooner.

Joy filled his soul, because he loved his daughter, Keri. Clay had come along only eighteen months after her, and then he and Ev hadn't been blessed with any more children. Until now.

"Harry, my boy." Otis laughed and hugged Harry too, and Trace sure did enjoy the way his brothers and their wives loved Harry so much. Behind them, the door Harry had come out of opened, and Trace looked that way. A pretty woman with long, shiny, black-like-oil hair came outside. She had other people with her—two men and another woman—but Trace only saw her.

Because Harry would only see her.

When he separated from Otis, he turned toward them, and he extended his hand back. Sure enough, that pretty brunette slipped her hand into Harry's, her smile already stretching across her whole face.

"Daddy," Harry said with the same sort of lovesick smile on his face. "This is Iriana Goldstein."

What a mouthful, Trace thought, but he minded his manners. He reached up and tipped his hat at the woman, wondering now how old she was.

"Iriana," Harry said. "This is my daddy, Trace, and my Uncle Otis."

"It's so amazing to meet you," she gushed. "I grew up listening to Country Quad, and my brother is going to *flip out* when I tell him I met you." She reached out with her free hand, and Trace shook it. Otis did the same, and he looked a bit dumbstruck. Trace hoped his face didn't look like that, so he looked to the other people who'd come out.

"I'm Trace Young," he said, extending his hand to them.

"Oh." Iriana laughed, and Trace could admit it wasn't the

most annoying thing he'd heard. "Sorry. These are my band-mates." She rattled off their names, along with the name of her band, and Harry grinned and grinned and grinned.

"They open for me," he finally said after all the intros, and Trace put the dots together.

Another band.

That didn't sit well in his gut, and Ev would be so proud of him for not saying anything. Not even a growl came out of his mouth.

In fact, it was Otis who said, "Should we get inside and get set up? Go through our songs a couple of times before dinner?"

"Sure, yeah," Harry said, and he turned to lead them all inside.

Trace exchanged a look with Otis, and he grumbled under his breath, "I didn't know about her," when everyone else was way out of earshot.

"She's pretty," Otis muttered back.

"So was Val." Trace cocked an eyebrow, needing to talk to Harry about his mother too. She'd definitely been more involved in his life since the first tour, and Trace hadn't heard if she'd be in-person on the tour to help with his wardrobe. Just the fact that his twenty-three-year-old son needed a wardrobe consultant seemed insane, but Trace remembered the days when he had someone telling him what to wear too.

He'd loved that life once. Now, he wouldn't trade Ev and the kids for anything, and inside, he quickly got out his phone and texted her.

1. You told him we're having a girl. 2. He's got a girlfriend he failed to mention. 3. I didn't say anything embarrassing. 4. I'll call you after dinner. 5. I love you endlessly. I wish you were here, and I miss you and the kids every moment I'm gone.

He sent the text, not caring that if anyone ever saw it, they'd realize he wasn't as menacing and dark as he pretended to be. He didn't have to hide anything from Ev, from Harry, Keri, or Clay, and he couldn't wait to welcome another baby girl to their family.

Looking up, he did finally let the sigh come out of his mouth. As Otis unpacked his guitar, Trace realized he couldn't wait for one more thing.

Harry to come home.

32

Harry checked on his father a couple of times before Daddy looked up from his phone. Judging the man's reaction was impossible, and while Harry was still good at it, he hadn't been able to get an accurate read of what his dad had thought of Iriana.

"Did you get those songs I sent you?" Uncle Otis asked, his fingers lazily strumming across his guitar's strings.

Harry yanked his attention back to his uncle. "Yeah, thanks, Uncle Otis. I'll go over them on the way to Jacksonville."

His tour started tonight, and Harry's nerves had been buzzing through his whole body for days now, like he'd been hooked up to a caffeine drip and couldn't get off. First, being on stage did that to him, and second, he had someone to impress now.

He looked over to Iriana, who'd gone back with her band, Petals and Pines, into their recording room.

Harry reached for his personal guitar, not the one he played on stage. Just the feel of it soothed him, and his dad said, "You're playing this one tonight?" as he approached.

Harry shook his head. "No, I just like the feel of it in my hands." He didn't have to hide anything from Daddy. "It calms me down."

His father nodded and sat on the third stool nearby. "How long until dinner?"

"An hour," Otis answered, and Harry was glad, because he didn't know. Uncle Morris had arranged everything, and when the driver walked in to take him to dinner, he'd go.

"Let's talk now then." Daddy cleared his throat and glanced over to Otis. "He can stay or go, Harry. Up to you."

"He can stay," Harry said, because he knew what his father had burdening him. The same things had been weighing heavily on Harry's mind too, and he truly was his father's son, because he kept it all bottled up until it fizzed out the top and he couldn't keep things silent any longer.

"I have to finish the contract I have," he said. "It's another album, Daddy."

"It has no tour requirement in it," he said. "Are you going to renegotiate that?"

Harry nodded, his throat tight. He'd had plenty of grown-up conversations with his daddy, and that was one of the reasons he loved him so much. He didn't have to hold back, and he knew Daddy wouldn't either.

"You don't like touring," Otis said as if it had just occurred to him.

Harry shook his head. "It's part of the job, but not one I

particularly like." He glanced around, but no one lingered nearby. No one would overhear them. "I feel like God's been calling me somewhere else," he said quietly. "But He won't tell me where. When I see pictures of the cousins or kids, I'm so homesick, it feels like someone is pulling my stomach out through my belly button."

Harry looked down, a stream of shame moving through him for a reason he couldn't name. "I have no right to be unhappy or discontent. I'm really struggling with the Lord right now, trying to be grateful for what I have while I wish for something else?" He shook his head, his thoughts tangled and jumbled like always. "It doesn't make sense."

Daddy stayed silent, and Harry just wanted him to *say something.*

"Maybe you try coming home," he finally said, and every word carried significant weight, like he'd carefully measured them before he said them. "Uncle Tex has a recording studio there. You and Otis and I can work on your songs for the third album. We recorded from there for years, Harry. Maybe you can too."

"To complete the contract." Harry looked up. "I don't want to get another one, Dad. Isn't that dumb?"

"Why is it dumb?" Daddy just watched him, and Harry wished he could just transfer his thoughts from his head into his father's.

"People work their whole lives to get where I am, and I don't want it?" Harry shook his head, feeling stupider and stupider by the moment.

"It's not about that," Daddy said.

"You have to follow your heart," Uncle Otis said. "You'll never be happy if you don't, and it's really hard to hear the Lord when you're not doing what He wants you to."

Harry looked back and forth between the two of them. "I love you guys." His voice choked in his throat, and Harry couldn't remember the last time he'd let his emotions this close to the surface. He slid from his stool and stepped into Uncle Otis and Daddy at the same time, hugging them both as he ducked his head between theirs.

"I hate that I haven't seen Grandpa. I hate that I can't go spell Grandma, or go help Bryce with the horses, and see the mountains and all the littles."

"Well, son," Daddy said, and Harry had heard so many sentences that started that way. "It sounds like you already know what you want. Now you just have to be brave enough to do it."

Harry's muscles tightened, but he nodded. "Yeah, I know." He moved back and picked up his guitar. "Can we play now? Got everything out you needed to say?"

He gazed at his daddy, such love flowing between them. He should say it, but he didn't, and Daddy bent to get out his instrument too. "Let's play," he said, and Harry and Daddy could usually say what they needed to without words.

"What are we playin'?" Uncle Otis asked.

Harry grinned at Dad, and he smiled right on back. "*When She Comes Home*," they said together, and Harry started the opening notes of the song, everything suddenly right in the world—all because he was playing and singing a song he and Daddy had written for Ev years ago.

Hours later, Harry bounced on the balls of his feet. Petals and Pines had just finished and would be coming off-stage. Harry had everything in place, from his shiny silver belt buckle—courtesy of Uncle Blaze—to his pressed dark wash blue jeans to a brand-new T-shirt his mother had commissioned just for him.

It had a stick-figure band on the front, with one cowboy out in front of the others, and he liked that it didn't label the band or himself. He liked that it spoke to his quirky T-shirt style, and he loved that his mother had known enough to get it for him.

"Opening night," he said to himself as the band started coming toward him. They seemed to be riding a high, and Harry knew what that felt like too. Nothing compared to the energy a live audience could provide a performer, and he fed off them as they went by.

"Good luck, Harry," they said. "You'll slay it, Harry," and "They're a really great crowd."

Iriana came last, as she was the lead singer of Petals and Pines, and Harry liked her smooth voice that seemed to be a siren's call to his weary and lonely heart.

"You were great," he said, though he didn't come out of his room until ten minutes ago. He slid one hand around her and brought her flush against him. "We'll meet up later?"

"If you're not busy with your daddy and uncles."

Harry would be, he knew. He'd have to call Ev too, or she'd be livid with him. "Maybe breakfast tomorrow, since we don't have to break-down and move for another day."

"By breakfast, you better mean lunch." Iriana smiled at him and leaned in. Harry kissed her, because they'd been dating for a couple of months now, and this wasn't the first time he'd touched his mouth to hers.

She had introduced a ray of sunlight into his life, and he did enjoy spending time with her. He hadn't told his father that she was a decade older than him, nor that she had a five-year-old daughter.

Dad would freak out, and truth be told, Harry wasn't sure how he felt about any of it. He liked being with her, and he wasn't looking for anything too serious right now, so he simply pushed away the things that made him uncomfortable to deal with later.

"Harry," someone said, and he pulled away.

"See you later," she whispered, and Iriana faded into the blackness backstage before the stage manager came forward.

"We've got you set up," he said.

Harry nodded, his game face slipping into place. Yes, he'd smile and wave at the crowd, but he wasn't the country musician who told jokes and charmed little old ladies. He had a set script he pretty much stuck to, because someone smarter than him made him into the personable, down-to-earth rockstar that everyone loved.

"Ready?" the stage manager asked.

"I'm ready," Harry said.

"Just a sec." His father emerged from the shadows, Uncle Otis right behind him. Daddy pulled him into a hug and whispered, "Enjoy this, Harry. It's a good experience, and you'll think of it fondly once it's over."

Harry clung to his father, because he wanted that to be true. He didn't want this to feel like work. He did want to enjoy this, and he wanted everyone who'd paid to come see him to get a good show.

The best show he could give.

"Love you," Daddy said as he pulled back.

Uncle Otis held out his fist, and Harry bumped it. "We'll see you in a bit."

Harry nodded, because they'd come on-stage in about an hour and do a trio, and then he'd do a duet with his father and one with Otis while they talked song-writing and growing up in small-town Coral Canyon.

Harry had even turned in childhood pictures of himself for a slideshow, and he couldn't wait to see what his production team had done with them.

Quiet excitement built within him, and he nodded to his father and Otis. "All right," he said. "I think I'm due on stage."

He took his guitar from the stage manager and followed him down the narrow walkway that led to the entrance. The stage manager held back the curtain, and the noise from the arena filled Harry's ears.

He still couldn't believe all these people—tens of thousands of people—had come to see him.

Him.

Simple Harry Young, who had nothing in his own life sorted out.

"Lord," he whispered to the flickering lights he could see at the front of the stage, where he'd be in another few moments. "Bless me to provide for them the escape, the healing, and the experience they need to have. I will be Thy mouthpiece."

Then he took one last deep breath, held it, and exhaled as he walked toward the light.

He stepped into it, smiled for all he was worth, and lifted his guitar into the air.

The crowd rippled and moved, seemingly like ocean waves coming ashore. Their voice rose up and up and up, until they were all cheering for him.

Him.

Harry Young, who strode over to the mic in the middle of the stage, leaned it, and said, "Howdy, Atlanta!"

"Howdy, Harry!" they chorused back, and just like that, his second concert tour kicked off.

33

"I'm so nervous," Codi said to Penta as she pulled everything out of her suitcase for the second time. Which was ridiculous. She was going to Texas, Arkansas, and Louisiana, not the moon. She didn't need any special equipment and if she forgot her toothbrush, she could go to a store and buy another one.

Bryce had been gone for a week, and he'd be picking her up in Dallas later that day. She'd been working with a few of his uncles for the past week, and they'd all been nothing but kind to her. In fact, Maverik had brought a container of cookies for her and Bryce that his wife had made. Codi sure did like all of the members of his family she'd spent time with.

A knock sounded on her door, and she spun from the mess of clothes and toiletries she'd just strewn across her bed.

"It's me, Codi," Abby called, and she hurried to the door and down the hall. Bryce's momma stood there with little Pippa, and Penta went to greet them both while Codi slowed and froze.

Abby smiled at Codi while Pippa cooed at the beagle and then looked up at Codi. "Can I take him outside, Codi?"

"Sure," she said. "His ball stuff is on the table there." She grinned at the little girl. "You been workin' on your whistle?"

Penta would come back when Codi whistled now, and Pippa sure had liked that when she'd shown the four-year old. She'd been trying to whistle through her teeth too, but she couldn't do it. Number one, she only had one front tooth. Number two, she was four years old.

"I been workin' on it," Pippa said, and she made a horrible raspberry noise as her lips flapped together, barely a whistling noise in sight.

Codi laughed through her tension, glad the little girl could do that for her. "Keep working at it. He should come back if you put some treats in your pocket."

Abby helped her get all the things she needed, and she said, "Pip, look at Momma." The little girl did, and they were so cute together. "Tell me the rules for you going out with Penta alone."

"Stay in the yard," Pippa recited to her mother. "Come get you if I lose Penta." Abby nodded encouragingly. "Don't go into the trees alone."

"Good girl," Abby said. She pressed a kiss to Pippa's forehead and nodded her out the door. "I'm going to leave this open, so you can yell for one of us, okay?"

Pippa said, "Okay," grabbed the ball and launcher, and skipped out the door like she didn't have a care in the world.

Penta went with her without a whistle at all, because Pip had the ball, and Penta loved balls.

"We can open my window too," Codi said. "It's right against the back yard."

Abby nodded at her and smiled. "How are you, dear?" She drew Codi into a hug, and Codi could admit she sank right into it. She'd spent quite a bit of time with Abby and Tex and their family this summer, as she and Bryce had dated. When she'd mentioned she was nervous about going on tour a week after him, all alone, Abby said she'd come help her pack.

Codi had wanted to resist her, but she hadn't. She'd simply said, "I'd like that," and here Abby stood.

"I've packed twice, and I just pulled it all out," Codi admitted as she led the way down the hall. "Again. I don't know why I'm so keyed up."

"You'll be traveling with your boyfriend," Abby said behind her. "It's a big deal."

Codi entered her room and took in the mess on her bed. "You know what? It does feel like a big deal for me and Bryce."

Abby looked at her with something sharp in her eyes, but Codi didn't know what that meant. She picked up a sundress and held it up. "This is okay, right?"

"Of course," Abby said. "What you'll really want is a great pair of pajama pants. Loungewear."

Codi looked at the mound of clothes she'd pulled out. "Really?"

"It's a lot of travel," Abby said. "You'll change into your cute sundresses for dinners and such, but then, when it's just you and him? You'll want to be comfortable."

Embarrassment squirreled through Codi. "I don't have pajamas."

"At all?"

"I wear a nightgown to bed," she mumbled. "For this, I thought I'd just wear sweats and a T-shirt." She did pick up the pair of navy blue sweat pants and the ratty tee with a cartoon potato on the front of it.

"Perfect," Abby said with a smile. She took the pants and started to roll them into a tight cylinder. She put them in the suitcase and reached for the T-shirt.

"Perfect?" Codi repeated.

"I don't see jeans here," Abby said.

"I—Bryce said it would still be hot down there."

Abby nodded and said, "Yeah, probably. But Codi, I've watched you all summer. You wear jeans every single day." She picked up the sundress and folded it in half and then half again before tucking it into the suitcase. "You don't have to change who you are for this tour."

"I didn't think I was."

"They'll be photographed a lot," she said. "You'll probably be in some of the photos. That's why you want the dresses. I get that. I do. But you get to be you on this trip too. It'll be more fun if you are."

Codi nodded, thinking of her wigs. Both Tex and Abby knew she wore them, and she picked up the bag of the ones she'd packed for the tour. "So I probably don't need six of these."

Abby looked at them and then up to Codi's hair. "It's up to you."

Codi swallowed. "Do you want to see my hair?"

Abby swallowed and nodded. "Bryce told us it's white, and that you'd show us when you were ready."

"I don't wear them around him all the time," she said. "But the wigs still serve their purpose, because I used to get so many questions and so much staring."

Abby gave her a soft smile, and for a moment, Codi saw her mother's face superimposed over Abby's. Her heartbeat flailed, then settled again, and she reached up. "I can just slide this one off. I have a headband on that it clings to."

The wig came off easily, and Codi swiped the headband back and off too. Her hair wisped around her ears, and she refrained from brushing it back. Abby pulled in a breath, her eyes wide. She reached up and pushed Codi's hair behind her ear. The gesture felt maternal and tender, and Codi's eyes filled with tears.

"Codi, you are so beautiful," Abby said. Her smile spread in such a genuine way that Codi felt so loved and accepted by her. "No wonder Bryce is smitten with you."

Their eyes met, and Abby added, "Beautiful inside and out."

"Does Bryce talk about me when I'm not there?" she asked.

Abby's smile faltered. "No, not really."

Codi pressed her lips together and looked back at the clothes on the bed. "My ex-fiancé did. He said the cruelest things, and I didn't know it."

"Do you think Bryce would do that?"

Codi shook her head. "No, I don't really worry about that with him. I don't know why I asked." She looked at Abby again.

"Let's take a selfie and send it to him." She smiled and took out her phone as Abby moved to stand next to her.

They both grinned into the camera, and Codi held her phone out and snapped the picture. "I'll send it to you."

"Yes, so I can send it to Tex."

Codi nodded, only a slight tremor moving through her at the thoughts. "Maybe I'll tell Bryce he can put it on the family thread. Then everyone will know about my hair."

"It's unique," Abby said. "But nothing to be ashamed of."

"I'm not ashamed," Codi said. "That's not the right word." She tapped and swiped to get the texts pulled up and the picture attached. "It's more like an avoidance thing."

"You don't need to avoid who you are," Abby said.

"Yeah, you're probably right." Codi finished with the picture and faced the packing again. "So if I'm going with who I am, I need my boyfriend jeans."

"That's right," Abby said as Codi went over to her dresser to get the jeans. "Oh, we are the cutest ever. I'm sending this to Tex, and if you're really okay with it, I can put it on the family text."

Codi remembered what Bryce had told her about his parents wanting to get to know her, and how much Abby wanted to be involved in his life. "Sure," she said, and by the beaming smiled on Abby's face, Codi felt like she'd just made her year. She could only hope that a single picture of her wouldn't cause hundreds and hundreds of texts.

"Codi!" Bryce called, waving his arm above his head. As if she couldn't spot him and Harry standing together in the airport. They both stood over six feet tall, wore huge cowboy hats, and had a throng of people gathered nearby, some of them taking pictures.

Codi walked faster, her backpack bouncing on her shoulders as she did. Bryce came forward too and swept her off her feet as he hugged her. "Hey, hey, hey," he said among his laughter. "For a minute there, I wasn't sure you'd get out of Jackson."

"We sat there *forever*," she said. "I hope I'm not delaying you guys."

"No concert tonight," he said. "We can eat anytime. Ain't no thing." He took her bag from her and put it on his own shoulders after adjusting the straps. "Come on. There are a lot of people here, and Harry left his security with the car." Bryce looked right and left and crossed the few steps back to Harry.

"Hey, Harry." Codi stepped into him and hugged him. "Thanks for letting me come on tour with you."

"Thanks for loaning me Bryce for a few days." Harry grinned with all the power of the sun, and it wasn't hard to see why he charmed so many.

"I have a bag," she said. "I think it's at carousel eight."

They got it, and Harry walked in between her and Bryce as they left the airport. Codi had no idea where to go or even where she was, but a man wearing black from head to toe stood next to a shiny black SUV, and Codi assumed it was for her as Harry nodded to him.

"This is James," he said. "He's our driver and security here in Dallas, and he's even coming to Arkansas with us, right?"

"Yes, sir," he said, smiling at Codi. "I'll take your bag."

"Thanks," she said, and Bryce held the door for her to get in first. Codi had toured around the western states in an old school bus that had been retrofitted into a dog grooming facility. This SUV probably cost more than anything Codi had ever been inside, including Bryce's house.

Fine, probably not his house, but this was a very nice car. Codi wasn't sure how she felt about sitting on the black leather, especially when Bryce opened the other door and slid onto the seat behind the driver. Harry followed her, and Codi found herself sandwiched between the two broad-shouldered cowboys.

Bryce took her hand, and Harry said, "We're headed to dinner. Then we'll go back to the hotel."

"Reservations at Wild West," James said. "I called and said we'd be there in forty minutes. Miss Goldstein is on her way as well."

Codi looked at Harry, who nodded and turned toward her too. "Who's Miss Goldstein?" she asked.

"His girlfriend," Bryce said, leaning forward. "He's bein' real sly about it."

"Sly?" Harry half scoffed and half laughed. "I'm just not talking about her non-stop, like some people."

Codi turned to Bryce, her attention volleying to him now. "I haven't been talking about Codi non-stop."

"Pretty much," Harry said, and Codi whipped her attention back to him in time to catch a smile.

"Fine," Bryce said. "I won't say another word about her." He settled into his seat and looked straight forward, but something tickled inside Codi.

She leaned toward him and didn't try to keep her voice down as she mock-whispered, "You're talking about me to your cousin? Good things, I'm sure, like how I've kept your horses fed and happy this past week and how I've entertained your uncles flawlessly."

Bryce looked at her out of the corner of his eyes, his mouth twitching dangerously close to a smile. "Yeah, all of that."

She laughed, as did Harry, and Bryce finally relinquished his control over his smile and let it loose. He chuckled too and said, "I'm so glad you're here now." He leaned toward her and kissed her quickly. "Sorry the flight was a nightmare, but dinner should be amazing, and wait'll you see Harry on stage tomorrow night."

"She can wait for that," Harry said in a bored voice.

"No, I can't wait," Codi said, once again volleying her gaze over to Harry. "You're incredible, and Bryce is going to be playing. I've seen him on stage before, but only in a video, and I can't wait for the real thing."

"No pressure," Bryce said with a chuckle.

"There's none," Codi told him. She pulled out her phone. "Now, let me show you these pictures of the Bookmobile. I think your momma loved it...."

THE FOLLOWING EVENING, CODI WORE HER CUTEST sundress. It bore splashy flowers in gold, orange, and yellow against a black background and she felt like the epitome of autumn in it. She'd brought one wig, and despite the fact that Abby's text had indeed garnered hundreds of texts from the Youngs—all of them supportive and complimentary—she continued to wear it in public.

She'd styled it as prettily as she could, and she wore more makeup tonight than she had all summer long. They'd gone to dinner again, and she'd posed for pictures with Bryce, then Bryce and Harry, then Harry and his opening band, Petals and Pines.

She was sure those would be on social media by now, but since she was a nobody, it didn't affect her too much.

What did was the fact that Harry had just finished a song, and Bryce had given her the set list. She expected to hear Harry call him out onto the stage at any moment, and she found herself with her thumbnail in her mouth, chewing away.

"And now," Harry said after he'd taken a long drag from a water bottle. "This is where you're gonna wanna put your hands together for the amazing talent I come from. Up first, I'm gonna play a duet with my amazing cousin, who's been gracing stages like this...." He paused, grinning from ear to ear as the crowd grew in intensity.

They obviously knew what was coming, and Codi grinned as she made out what they'd started to chant.

"Bryce! Bryce! Bryce!"

He hadn't told her about the marketing campaign for Harry's album tour, but Codi had the internet and knew how to use it. She'd seen the flyers with Bryce on them, standing next to his cousin, with his concert dates and cities on them.

She joined in, calling, "Bryce! Bryce! Bryce!" as Harry

yelled, "*Bryyyyyyyyce* Young!" into the mic.

And then, her gorgeous, tall, dark, talented cowboy boyfriend ran out on stage, his charisma surely reaching all the way to the very furthest concert-attendee. He high-fived Harry, picked up a guitar, and moved to stand in front of his own mic.

"Hello, Dallas!" he yelled, and they responded by cheering even louder. As they settled down slightly, he leaned in again, his fingers already picking over the strings. "Last time I played here, your daddy had sprained his finger, and I had to really up my game to cover up for it."

"I remember that," Harry said with a laugh, and while Codi suspected this conversation was staged, it didn't sound or seem like it. He joined his guitar to Bryce's, and they grinned at one another. "My daddy is one of the best guitar players in the world, and don't you worry." He turned toward the crowd. "He's here tonight, and he doesn't have a sprained finger."

"We're gonna play a duet Harry wrote for the two of us last summer," Bryce said into the mic, his whole person shining like gold. Codi couldn't wait to see him sing and play in person, because everything he did radiated life, and she loved basking in it.

"It's called *Back to Where I Belong*," Bryce said. "Since we all eventually find our way back to where we belong, whether that's into the arms of a family member, a friend, or the Good Lord Himself."

Harry nodded and they moved right into the music together, not a missed beat and no way for Codi to tell how Bryce knew to do what he did. The drummer, piano player, and bass guitarist had left the stage, leaving just the two cousins, and Codi swayed from the second row as the two cowboys wove their voices together into the most beautiful harmony she'd ever heard.

The next few minutes held magic and music, and Codi found herself pressing her hands to her heart as it boomed and bellowed that she loved Bryce Young.

34

Graham Whittaker pulled up to Pancake Power and glanced toward the well-worn entrance. Sighing, he put the truck in park and headed inside. Otis Young wasn't hard to find, but he raised his hand from the corner table anyway.

Graham nodded to the hostess and headed in Otis's direction. He slid into the chair across from him. "Good morning."

"Morning." Otis reached for his coffee and took a sip. He smiled, because Otis acted like a duck—lots of things simply rolled off his back.

"Morning, Graham," Jean said as she put a mug in front of him and filled it with coffee. "You cowboys ready to order?"

"I'll take the Western omelet," Otis said. "Buttermilk pancakes with that real maple syrup Jem's always bragging about." He grinned at her, and Jean then turned to Graham.

"I want the three-egg breakfast," he said, as he'd been to

Pancake Power plenty of times and didn't need a menu. "Scrambled eggs, and I want the pumpkin pancakes with the cinnamon syrup."

"Oh, boy," Otis said with a chuckle. "I didn't even know that was an option."

"Pumpkin pancakes all of October," Jean said. "Do you want to switch?"

"No, I'm sticking to my pure pancakes," he said. "Real maple syrup."

Jean smiled and shook her head. "You Youngs and your obsession with maple syrup," she said as she walked away.

Graham could ask about Georgia, or how Joey was doing in New York City, or OJ. He could mention something about Harry's tour, or Laney and the ranch, or the lodge. Instead, he gave Otis a smile, and said, "Thanksgiving is coming up."

"Yeah, it sure is." Otis gave nothing away, but Graham had given him zero details about this breakfast date.

"Bailey is going to be in town." Graham looked down and rearranged the silverware on the table. "We'd love to host dinner at our house, up at the ranch." He looked up. "If the weather isn't too bad, of course."

Otis offered him a warm smile. "I'll start praying that the snow stays away."

"We'd like to have you and your family there," he continued. "I'm going to invite Bryce and Kassie, and Tex and his family. Then us. I think that's three full families, plus Bailey and Bryce, and it will be big enough with that." He cleared his throat, the invitation out.

"I'm sure you have plans with your family," Graham said. "It'll pull you and Tex away from everyone else."

"We don't always have a big family meal for Thanksgiving," Otis said. "We do smaller units, and sometimes we eat just by ourselves." Otis waved his hand. "We can come." He leaned forward. "We'd *love* to come."

"It might be really awkward," Graham said. "Ronnie's bringing home a girl we've never met, and Bailey has a lot of catching up to do."

"Trust me," Otis said. "In a family as big as mine, we always have a lot of catching up to do. Things change by the minute, and it's honestly exhausting." He laughed, and Graham finally reached for his spoon and started stirring his coffee. He poured in some sugar and then reached for one of the cream containers.

"What do you think Bryce will say?"

"I think Bryce will move the Tetons to be there if necessary." Otis grinned at Graham, his head ducked so he could barely see past the brim of his cowboy hat. "That boy has a heart made of marshmallow and diamonds."

Graham knew that, and it made him emotional every time he dwelled on it too long. So while Otis was probably trying to be funny, Graham actually thought he'd just paid Bryce an amazing compliment.

"He's a unique individual."

Jean returned with their food, naming it all as she set it down in front of them. Once she'd left, as Otis salted his omelet and spread butter over his hot pancakes, he said, "Graham, don't forget to invite Codi."

Graham startled, because he hadn't named her. "Of course,"

he said. "I guess she was just implied with Bryce." He scooped up a bite of his eggs. "They're getting along?"

"As far as any of us know," Otis said. "Bryce doesn't say much about her, but if you haven't seen them together in a while...." He took a bite of his omelet, something glinting in his eyes. After he finished chewing and swallowed, he asked, "How will Bailey take seeing them together? She's ready for that?"

"She says she wants him there, and she knows they're together."

"Maybe make sure she knows what that *actually* means," Otis said. "Because when you see them together, it's pretty obvious they're in love."

Graham's whole soul filled with a smile. "I'm so happy for him. He has come such a long way." He wasn't expecting such a keen sense of hope to run through him, but it did. "It makes me hopeful for Bailey, that she can move forward too. That maybe she can find someone perfect for her too."

"She will, brother," Otis said, and Graham sure did like being called his brother. It meant something, as he well knew, as he had three brothers of his own that he loved dearly and had spent a lot of the past two decades with right here in Coral Canyon. "She will."

Graham nodded, his faith getting restored again and then again while he and Otis chatted about Georgia, Joey in New York City, and how OJ was doing with the transition to having his birth mom in his life.

Graham left the Rising Sun Ranch, his heart lighter than it had been in years. "Do you want the radio on, bud?" He glanced over to OJ, who looked over from his passenger window, where he'd been waving good-bye to Bryce.

"Sure."

Graham reached to adjust the volume, and the country music playing through the speakers made OJ cheer. "That's cousin Harry, Grandpa Graham. Can you turn it up?" He reached for it, but Graham drove a huge SUV and OJ couldn't quite get to the volume button.

He got it turned up, because yes, this was Harry Young. The young man still toured around the country, but Graham understood he'd be home for the holidays. Not the Thanksgiving Day holidays, but Christmas.

The Youngs had a lot going on at Christmastime, including OJ's birthday. It was on the same day as the annual tree-lighting ceremony at Whiskey Mountain Lodge, which Graham owned and which a couple of his brothers ran.

He'd turned sixty-three years old this year, and he was ready to retire from the family energy company he'd moved back to Coral Canyon to run over two decades ago. He and Laney only had one child together, and Robbie still had another year to go on his business degree, but then he planned to start working at Springside, and Graham would train him up and leave him the corner office in favor of more time on the ranch he also helped Laney run.

She'd had Echo Ridge in her family for years and years, and while they didn't need the money from the cattle anymore, she still kept up the land, raised a few cows and goats and horses, and enjoyed country life.

The song ended, and Graham reached to turn down the radio. "OJ," he said.

"Yeah?" The boy possessed so much innocence, so much charm, and boatloads and boatloads of trust.

"Grandma Laney made raspberry jam," he said. "She'll have a jar of it for you and your family."

OJ grinned like he'd won something magnificent. "Great," he said. "I love raspberry jam on toast."

"She does too," Graham said with a smile. Their communication with Bailey had improved in the past few months since OJ had mailed her a birthday card, but she still had a lot to work through. She'd wanted to put together the Thanksgiving Day dinner, but in the end, she'd finally called Laney and asked her to do it.

"Did your daddy tell you about Thanksgiving?" Graham gripped the wheel and looked over to OJ.

"No." His smile faded. "What about it?"

"Your birth mom is coming," Graham said. "We'd like you guys to come up to Echo Ridge and have dinner with us."

"Yeah, sure," OJ said in that carefree, cowboy way he had. "Is that what you were talking to Bryce about when I came in?"

So he hadn't missed that. "Yeah," Graham said, seeing no reason to lie about it. "He's going to come with Codi."

OJ nodded and looked out his window. "Do you think Grandma Laney will make the pumpkin chocolate chip cookies?" He returned his attention to Graham, who had to pay attention on the apple highway, as it had plenty of curves, twists, and turns as it led out of Dog Valley and back to Coral Canyon. "She told me once that she hates pumpkin pie, so she never makes it for Thanksgiving. She makes cookies instead."

Graham chuckled. "That's totally true," he said. "Grandma Laney is adamant that we don't have pumpkin pie on Thanksgiving."

"She brought me some cookies last year. They were good."

"She's a good cook," Graham said. "I talked to your daddy about coming. He thinks y'all will be able to."

"Okay," OJ said.

"When's the last time you talked to your birth mom?" he asked.

"Uh, I don't know." OJ looked out the window again. "I think she sent my mom a text last week? On Sunday maybe." He turned back to Graham, his face lit up. "It totally was Sunday, because it was my turn to pray, and I thanked God that she'd called." He grinned, obviously proud of himself for remembering such a thing.

Graham couldn't help grinning back. The little boy had so much *life*, and because Graham had raised Bailey from the time she was six years old, he could see some of her spunk in him. "That's great, bud," he said. "That's really great."

He quit questioning OJ then, because he didn't need to know what he and Bailey talked about. He just needed to know that his daughter was following through on her promises. *Sounds like she is*, he thought, and he hated that trust took so long to build, and even longer to rebuild after it had been broken.

Bailey's a good woman, he thought next, and the words

didn't entirely belong to him. Graham's heart opened, and shooting rays of forgiveness spilled out. He immediately pulled to the side of the road, saying, "I just need to send a quick text."

Once stopped, he grabbed his phone and typed a text to Bailey. *I just want you to know that I think you're a good person. Not only that, but I'm driving with OJ right now—your mom made raspberry jam for him—and I had this distinct voice tell me how good you are. Love you, Bay. Can't wait to see you at Thanksgiving.*

He sent the text and got back on the road. She'd only been home once since her summer birthday, but Graham had been praying for her return for almost ten years. *Ten long years* he'd listened to his lovely wife weep over her daughter. Ten years they'd knelt together and prayed for her. Ten years they'd loved her from afar, constantly worrying over her, and holding onto each other when they'd lost the last thread of hope that they'd ever see her again.

And now? Now Graham held so much hope, it overflowed. It poured out of his heart, his head, his hands, as he had no room to hold it. "Thank you, Lord," he murmured, his gratitude starting to overflow with his hope.

"My grandma says 'Praise Jesus!'" OJ said, really yelling the last two words. "At least that's what she's been saying about Grandpa lately. He's having surgery soon."

"Yes, I heard," Graham said. "Did you want to say a prayer for him?"

"Yeah, okay." OJ folded his arms and bowed his head. Graham couldn't help watching him and letting his goodness settle between his ribs. Yes, he'd listened to OJ pray before, and the boy could rattle on and on and on.

Graham didn't mind; he actually liked it, because he got to hear the inner feelings of the boy's heart when he prayed.

So he grinned when OJ said, "Dear Lord, we thank Thee for medical professionals in the world."

He'd so gotten that from someone older and wiser than him, but Graham didn't care at all. OJ was pure, and good, and fun to have around, and Graham *praised Jesus* that he got to see and spend time with him.

Now, he just had to put in a few more hours and days of prayer that Thanksgiving dinner would go off without a hitch.

35

Hilde Young set a couple of ladles in the middle of the table and stepped back. She'd never in a million years thought she could fill a dining room table this size with just her family. For so long—almost sixteen years—she'd only had Lynnie.

Now, her daughter would be walking in at any moment with her boyfriend, Matthew. Hilde knew what was happening even if neither one of them would say so out loud. After all, it was a random weekend in early October. No holiday. No break in their school or work schedule. And yet, Hilde had spent most of the afternoon yesterday preparing the pumpkin curry soup, buying the rolls, and rearranging her furniture store in anticipation of this Sabbath Day dinner.

Lynnie and Matthew would be gone again tomorrow, and she suspected Lynnie would be wearing a diamond ring. She'd thought Matthew would propose over the summer, when he'd first come to meet her and Gabe. But he hadn't.

Hilde had seen how much in love her daughter was with Matthew, and how good he treated her, and though every time she thought about her twenty-two-year-old getting married, she shivered with worry, she actually believed Lynnie and Matthew would be okay.

She'd put them side-by-side on the far side of the table, with Liesl beside them. Hilde would sit on one end, with Brant next to her. Then she could give the boy whatever necessary to keep him agreeable. She'd put Canyon next to Brant, because he was older and could do so much more. Then the other two triplets— Tanner and Cort—and lastly, Gabe, on the opposite end from her.

He'd be able to wrangle the almost three-year-olds from his end, and she'd be able to communicate with him silently simply by looking down the table.

Behind her, the door leading into the garage opened, and she knew it was Lynnie though she couldn't see down the hall and into the mudroom. This house had seemed huge when she and Gabe had purchased it almost ten years ago, but now, it barely fit all of them—and they hadn't invited anyone else to dinner today.

Gabe worked with a lot of his brothers, and Hilde loved to entertain. They were closest to Leigh and Morris, but they had over Blaze and Faith, Luke and Sterling, Trace and Ev, and Mav and Dani all the time. Jem and Sunny came often too, because Rosie and Liesl had always gotten along incredibly well.

Liesl struggled in school, but Gabe got her every assistance she needed. Rosie had a mouth on her and would defend Liesl to the death, so Hilde didn't worry about her too much anymore.

"Mom," Lynnie called, and Hilde's heart expanded to fill her whole chest. Her daughter appeared in the mouth of the hallway, her gorgeous auburn hair flowing across her shoulders in curls. She wore a hint of mascara and lip gloss, a bright purple sweater with pretty cable knit that really brought out her green eyes and highlighted the color of her hair, and a pair of skinny jeans that accentuated her curves.

She moved into Hilde and hugged her tightly. "Hey, my girl," she murmured.

Matthew came behind her, towing a single suitcase, and Hilde stepped out of Lynnie's arms and into Matthew's. "Hello, Matthew."

"Hey, Hilde." He hugged her too, and while Hilde had resisted him in her daughter's life in the beginning, because her heart had increased in size tenfold, he had plenty of room to fit now.

"Where is everyone?" Lynnie looked around the silent kitchen, dining room, and living room. "I expected a triple threat, plus Canyon."

"Daddy has them in the backyard, finishing up with the leaves."

"Smart," Matthew said as he moved away from Hilde. "Tire them out before feeding them."

"I don't think Canyon or Brant ever get tired," Hilde said. "They have too much of their daddy in them." She smiled at the young couple in front of her. "I'll get them, though. Dinner is ready."

"We're ready whenever." Lynnie exchanged a look with Matthew, and he wound his arm around her waist and pressed a kiss to her cheek. Hilde wanted to stay and ask them a bunch of questions, but she didn't. Lynnie wouldn't mind, but if Hilde's suspicions were correct, she didn't want to disrupt Matthew's plans.

She opened the back door and found Gabe holding open a black garbage sack as their boys and Liesl played more in the leaves than did anything to get them off the lawn.

"They're here," she called. "Let's eat."

Gabe looked toward her, his handsomeness punching her in the chest all over again. She would never get tired of being with him, and he was the best dad in the whole world.

"Go on," he said, but it wasn't necessary as the boys had started running toward her the moment they'd heard her voice.

"Momma, Momma, Momma," rang through the air, and Hilde loved moments like this. She bent down to receive her babies, and with all four little boys in her arms, she said, "Lynnie and Matt are here. Go say hello, and then everyone has to wash before dinner."

They clamored their way into the house, and Lynnie started exclaiming over how big this one had gotten, and how that one had lost a tooth, and how another could now tie his shoes.

Liesl smiled at Hilde as she rose to her feet, and Hilde drew her into a hug too. "Did you guys get any leaves off the ground?"

"Yeah, three bags." Liesl indicated them piled against the side of the house and then stepped past Hilde to go in and greet Lynnie and Matt too.

Hilde moved out onto the porch to have a moment with her

husband, because she'd steal those whenever she could. She helped him finish up the last pile of leaves and watched as he tied the bag.

"So, did it look like he had a diamond ring with him?" Gabe asked, a smile on his face. He'd been such a good father for Lynnie, though she still saw and talked to her biological dad.

"He had a suitcase," Hilde said. "It was impossible to tell."

Gabe hauled the bag of leaves over to the others and dusted his hands off. "I'm starving."

"Thanks for doing the leaves," she said, because sometimes the enormity of household and yard work tasks overwhelmed her. Gabe never seemed to get overwhelmed with anything but his job, and Hilde loved that about him. She loved that she still had the furniture store to escape to as well, even if her role there wasn't what it had once been.

"Mm, you smell good." Gabe pulled her close and kissed her, despite the easy viewing from anyone inside. "Thanks for making lunch for us."

"I just want him to propose," she said. "The waiting is killing me."

"Think how Lynnie feels."

"I just don't get what he's waiting for."

"Were you nice to him?" Gabe teased.

Hilde swatted at his chest and pushed by him. "I've always been nice to him." She went back inside and found complete chaos in the kitchen as Liesl and Lynnie tried to get four little boys washed up at the same time.

"Go on," Lynnie said to Brant. "Take the towel and go." He did, and Liesl got Canyon out of the fray next. Gabe started helping the boys into their seats as they arrived at the table, and Hilde went into the kitchen to get the soup off the stove. She didn't see Matt anywhere, but everyone else bustled around her until they all made it to the set and ready dining room table, with Hilde putting the big pot of soup in the middle of it.

She found the girls settling down, and Gabe finishing with Tanner, and she moved behind Brant and reached for a roll in one of the baskets she'd already put out. She pinched off a piece and put it on his plate without making it a big deal.

She sat and looked over to Lynnie. "Where's Matthew?"

"He got a phone call from his mom," she said, looking into the living room, toward the hallway that led toward the formal front living room and entrance to the house. Hilde only used it to answer the door if someone came over, but most people simply walked in, and her family used the garage entrance.

"I can check on him," Gabe said, and he shot to his feet and left the table before Lynnie or Hilde could move.

"Momma," Cort said from the other end of the table. "I have roll too."

She didn't want to throw bread to her babies like they were ducks, so she nodded to Liesl, who got a roll and gave some to both Cort and Tanner. Hilde gave more to Brant and some to Canyon, though he didn't complain about eating the way the triplets did.

She watched her boys for a moment, her eyes getting drawn back to the mouth of the hallway over and over. The hair on the back of her neck stood up when she thought she heard the front door open. Why would someone be going outside?

Or coming in? she wondered.

"Maybe I should—" Lynnie started, but she cut off with the first strains of a guitar. Gabe could play the piano beautifully, and Lynnie looked at Hilde as the piano joined the guitar.

They said nothing as they both launched themselves out of their seat. Liesl did too, and the three of them bustled into the front room, where Gabe's grand piano stood proudly. Liesl played incredibly well, and Hilde loved listening to Gabe teach the kids to play.

She arrived in the formal living room last to find Gabe at the piano, Bryce standing next to him with his guitar in his hand, and Matt beside them both—something glinting prettily in his hand.

Liesl moved to Gabe's other side and smiled at him. Lynnie had frozen, and Hilde moved past her and pulled out her phone. Thinking quickly, she started recording from a vantage point where she could see everyone—and Lynnie, whose face had started to turn bright red.

Let her enjoy this, she thought, and then Bryce and Liesl started to sing. They both had perfect pitch, and it became obvious to Hilde within the first two seconds that they'd rehearsed this.

Her feelings pinched, but she pushed past them, because this wasn't about her. They'd planned this amazing thing for *Lynnie.*

"You and I go together like the sun and moon," Liesl and Bryce sang. "Like peanut butter and jelly, like left and right."

The song didn't last very long, and thankfully, Lynnie's face had settled back to a normal shade. As the piano and guitar still wove their sounds together, Matt dropped to both knees and held up the diamond ring. "Lynnie, I'm so in love with you. I will do anything I can to make you happy and build a life together that we'll both love. Will you marry me?"

She nodded, and Hilde's chest tightened with emotion too. Love permeated the room, and Lynnie took the few steps to Matthew, Hilde following her with the camera. Gabe's parents would love to see this, and she'd send it to Ethan, Lynnie's father, too.

"Yes," she whispered, and Gabe turned on the piano bench.

Grinning, he said, "I don't think he heard you, bug."

"Let's do the outro again," Bryce said, his grin also filling his whole face.

Gabe put his fingers on the keys and he and Bryce played through a few more bars of music.

"Yes," Lynnie said loudly. "I love you, Matthew. Of course I'll marry you."

"Yes!" Liesl yelled and started clapping. Gabe and Bryce whooped, and the little boys came running into the room. They mobbed Lynnie as Matt slid the ring onto her finger. He stood, and Lynnie took his face in her hands and kissed him.

They laughed, and Hilde finally stopped the recording and lowered her phone. She moved over to Gabe's side, and he pressed a kiss to her temple and pulled her close, closer. He knew she needed the support now that her daughter would be building her life independently of Hilde's.

"All right, all right." Lynnie yelled, wiping at her eyes. "Boys, back to the table. Go on. Go back to the table." She started herding the little boys out of the room, and Liesl followed them.

"I'll wrangle them."

Lynnie turned back to Hilde, and she stepped into her open arms. "Congratulations," Hilde whispered in her daughter's ear. "He's wonderful, and you two will be so happy."

Gabe pounded Matthew on the back, and then turned to Bryce. "Where's Codi?"

"She was talkin' to her daddy," he said. "I'll grab her. She probably didn't want to interrupt after we'd started." He ducked out the front door, and Hilde took Gabe's hand and led him back into the kitchen, leaving Lynnie with Matthew to celebrate quietly and privately for just a moment.

"Help me get two more places set," she said.

"I told him it would be okay." Gabe took the two bowls Hilde handed him. "Liesl suggested Bryce and the guitar, and it really brought the song together."

"How long have you been planning that?"

"A week or so," Gabe said. "Not long." He leaned closer. "It's time with Bryce and Codi too."

"I'm not upset they're here," Hilde said. "I love Bryce and Codi." She'd no sooner said the words before both couples entered the kitchen, the four of them chattering as if they'd been best friends for years.

Gabe moved himself around to the side of the table with the boys and put Bryce on the end with Codi sort of straddling the corner and sharing a space with Liesl. She wasn't wearing a wig, and as Hilde put the silverware next to the bowls Gabe had set down, she said, "Codi, you look lovely."

She took the woman in a hug and gave her a quick squeeze.

"I hope you're ready to dine with these little boys. It can be a bit of an adventure."

Codi grinned at her and let Bryce pull out her chair for her. "I like adventures." She sat, and Bryce did too. Hilde reached over and squeezed his shoulder, and he put his hand on hers.

Then she returned to the head of the table and looked at Gabe. He looked around the table, pure joy streaming from him. "I love every one of you so much."

He looked at Bryce, then Matthew, then Hilde again. "Liesl, will you pray?"

"Yes, Daddy."

Hilde closed her eyes and listened to her sweet daughter thank God for all the blessings in their lives, and Hilde kept adding her own gratitude and thanks for the thing she prized most: Family.

36

Leigh Young strapped Remi into her seat and smiled down at the little girl. The twins were three months old now, and she remembered Hilde saying that if Leigh could make it to six months, she'd have figured out how to deal with more than one infant at a time.

Leigh had some serious doubts, because Hilde always had everything more put together than Leigh did. She was a decade older, and Leigh often felt like she was fumbling along behind the other wives, Hilde included.

She got in the front seat of the minivan and glanced in the rear-view mirror at her five children. Morris was out on tour with Harry right now, after delaying his departure by over a month. Trace and Tex had gone, as had Otis, but they'd all been home for a few days now.

Leigh took a deep breath and said, "All right, guys. Let's get up to Auntie Hilde's. She's going to show a movie tonight and everyone is sleeping over, even me."

She'd requested to be put on the rotation to help with Cecily and Jerry, and no one had given her anything. She couldn't stay cooped up in the house with five kids, and she'd called Abby, then Dani, and then Faith until they took her seriously enough to give her a dinner slot.

She'd meet Dani there, and they were taking in dinner for Jerry and Cecily that night. His surgery had happened two days ago to fix one of the tubes leading from his kidney to his bladder, and it had gone well. The kidney wasn't doing well, but the doctors had cleared out all the toxic waste and all the old blood, and everything existed in a state of hope.

"I'm always there," Leigh muttered to herself as nursery rhymes bled through the van. She just *hoped* she could make it to lunchtime. She *hoped* she could get Eric to talk to her about his day at school. She *hoped* Skip wouldn't throw a ball in the house and hit one of the twins in the face.

Tonight, she *hoped* to enjoy herself, talk to adults, and provide some relief for Cecily.

At Hilde's she gave Ridge to Eric and carried Remi in her arms as the six of them advanced toward the front door. "Rach, just go right in," Leigh said. "Hilde is expecting us."

She'd almost taken the kids to Mav's, but then Hilde had volunteered her house and she'd recruited Bryce and Codi and Kassie and Reggie to help her with the ten children she'd have at her house that evening.

Leigh would come back here afterward, and she'd sleep in one of the guest bedrooms with the twins. Then she wouldn't have to go home in the dark or worry about trying to get everyone out of here and back to their house and immediately into bed.

Heck, if she stayed out late enough, all of the kids would be in bed before she returned.

"Aunt Hilde," Eric called, but it was Codi who appeared at the end of the hall and relieved him of the baby boy.

"Hey, Ridge," she cooed at him, and the little boy did a whole body shake down. Leigh grinned at Codi as the other woman giggled at Ridge.

"We're upstairs in the loft," Hilde called. "Boys, go help Aunt Leigh with all the kids and their bags."

Before Leigh knew it, Kassie had taken Remi, and Bryce and Reggie had both followed her back outside to the driveway to help with the bags.

"The twins will eat again in a couple of hours," she said to Hilde once she got back inside. Codi and Kassie both sat on the couch with the babies, and all of Hilde's boys had climbed up in between them to see them. Leigh's heart warmed and warmed at the sight of all those boys, and then Remi.

"I love them," Hilde said, and Leigh found her looking at them too. She took a big breath and said, "We'll be fine here, okay? I have enough adults to be one-to-two for each child, and that includes Liesl and Eric, and they don't need much help."

"Depends," Leigh grumbled. "Sometimes I have to get after Eric for the most minor things."

Hilde gave her a smile. "Oh, I hear you. Liesl sometimes throws a fit over practicing the piano, something she's done for years and years."

"If I could get Eric to turn in his homework, I'd fall down on my knees and praise the heavens." They smiled at one another, and then Leigh went to kiss her kids good-bye. "Momma will be back soon," she told all of them. Skip alone wore worry on his face, though Leigh had left him with Hilde before, as well as Denzel and Michelle. They had two children now too, and Leigh always marveled at how Michelle strapped her baby girl to her chest and took her to the coffee shop at five-thirty in the morning.

You've got to stop comparing yourself to everyone, she told herself.

"Thank you for helping, Bryce." She looked over to Codi and Kassie. "Codi and Kassie, thank you."

"I could hold this baby forever," Codi said, as Ridge was a lot like a bag of flour. He would mold back into whoever held him and just lounge there, not even bothering to try to hold up his own head. He currently laid like that against Codi's chest, and she beamed down at him.

Leigh caught the way Bryce watched her too, and she wondered if they'd have another engagement in the family soon enough. Lynnie had set a date to be married in May, and she and Matt would be coming here to tie the knot after their semester ended.

She looked away as Bryce glanced over to her, and then he got up and came over to hug her. "We'll make sure they stay alive, Aunt Leigh."

"That's all I'm trying to do," she said against his broad shoulder. "Thank you, Bryce."

"Warn Grandpa that it's a guy's night tomorrow, would

you?" He grinned at Leigh as he pulled back, and she smiled back.

"I'll tell him." She left, and driving away without a single child in her car felt like the oddest thing she'd done that year. She tapped to call Morris, but he didn't pick up. She wasn't exactly sure where he was today, but she knew Harry had a concert, so he was probably in the throes of set-up, testing mics, or tracking down event managers to fix something that wasn't right.

She arrived at the hospital and went inside. She navigated her way to Jerry's room, and when she opened the door, she found him there by himself. Asleep.

That sounded absolutely heavenly to her, and she wondered what she'd have to do to land herself in the hospital where she could sleep.

Smiling at the ridiculousness of the idea, she padded over to the recliner and sank into it. She closed her eyes and toed herself back and forth, enjoying the steady silence in the room and the low hum of machinery.

She didn't fall asleep, but her mind softened enough to allow a sense of calmness and peace to course through her. In soft moments like these, she allowed herself to think through all the amazing things the Lord had done for her.

"Oh, she is here," Dani said, and Leigh opened her eyes.

It took a moment for Dani and Cecily to come into focus, and when they did, they both wore a smile. Leigh got to her feet and went to greet them near the door. "I brought all the things," she said as she hugged her mother-in-law. "But if he's asleep—"

"I'm not asleep," Jerry said, and they all turned toward him in bed. Leigh returned to him, her smile curving her mouth up. "Howdy, Leigh."

"Jerry, you sweet thing." She bent over and hugged him. "How are you feeling?" Maybe she'd tell the boys they couldn't all converge on him tomorrow night. Sometimes they listened to her. If she could get through to Luke or Blaze, they'd kick everyone out if things got too rowdy. The problem was, sometimes Blaze and Luke were the *cause* of the rowdiness.

"Good," he said as he tried to push himself up into a seated position. Leigh picked up the remote and sat up the bed further to help him.

"The food will be here in five minutes," Dani said. "Should we get set up?"

Leigh turned to her bag, which she'd set on the floor. "Absolutely." She pulled out a blanket and draped it over Jerry's legs and the end of his bed. "This is a quilt from the shop where Cecily and I hang out sometimes." She shot a look toward Cecily. "One of our friends named Christine made it for your recovery, and we're going to have a picnic here with you."

"You girls are so sweet," he said as someone knocked on the door.

It opened a moment later, and Dani turned to get the bucket of fried chicken and bag of sides from a nurse. "You didn't see this," Dani said, and the nurse asked, "See what?"

She faded away, and Dani closed the door again. "We're also not telling the men about this little dinner." She eyed everyone until Jerry started to chuckle.

"I won't say a word," he said, and he wouldn't. He loved fried chicken, and while the nurses hadn't specifically said he couldn't have it, Leigh suspected it wasn't on the approved diet list.

Dani and Leigh got out all of the food and served Cecily and Jerry, and then Leigh picked up a piece of chicken while Dani pulled out a couple of folding chairs from the closet in the corner. They barely fit in the room, but Leigh would rather sit with her knees against the end of the bed than stand to eat her fried chicken.

"Tell me how the twins are doing," Jerry said. "I miss those babies."

She glanced over to Cecily, who nodded once. "They're amazing, Jerry," Leigh said. "And I wanted to ask you something...." She reached for a napkin and wiped her hands and lips.

"I need help at the house while Morris is gone, and I was thinking you and Cecily could come stay with me. Then I can help you recover from the surgery, and you can help me by holding the babies." She smiled at him, and while he was normally a pretty stoic cowboy, she saw the emotion stream through his expression.

"Momma?" he asked, and he wanted to know if they could do that. Leigh loved the way they spoke to each other, as it was always kind and both Cecily and Jerry would do anything for any member of the family.

"I can come help you pack up a few things," Dani said, as she was in on the plan. She'd been coming to help almost every day, as her youngest was now in kindergarten.

"It would be fun," Momma said. "I could hold a baby all day long."

"So we'll come stay with you after I'm released," Jerry said, the decision made.

Relief sagged Leigh's shoulders. "Thank you," she said. "Morris will be gone for a couple more months, and most days, I feel like I'm drowning." She glanced over to Dani, who wore a look of sympathy. She reached over and patted Leigh's hand, and that nearly undid her composure.

She sniffled and she took another bite of her chicken. She wouldn't be upset that she had five healthy, happy children and a husband who loved her and his family.

Morris was just gone right now, and Leigh needed a little extra support. That was all.

When she arrived home the following morning, Michelle's SUV sat in the driveway. Leigh knew what that meant. Her house would be cleaned from top to bottom. Denzel would be sitting in the hot tub, and lunch would be ready whenever she wanted it to feed the kids.

Gratitude flowed over her, and she pulled into the garage with the words, "Uncle Denzel is here, and we will not mob Scout." She put the van in park. "Promise me, Skip."

"Puppy," he said.

"You pat him," Leigh said. "You don't wrap your body around him."

"I'll help him, Momma." Eric looked over to her from the passenger seat.

"Thank you, my boy." She smiled softly at her teenager and wiped his long hair off his forehead. "I love you."

"Love you too, Momma." He smiled, and Eric was so handsome, just like his daddy. "I'll get Ridge."

"Yep." Leigh sighed as she got out of the van. She'd get Remi, and she'd herd Skip inside while Rachelle wouldn't even realize they'd arrived at home.

She got everyone out and then everyone in, and sure enough, she found her house clean and the scent of something browned and creamy—with coffee—hanging in the air.

Michelle sat on the couch and watched her two kids play in the living room, and she got up when Leigh entered the house with Remi on her hip. "I'll take her," she said, though Remi on Michelle's lap would cause her two-year old to start whining and crying for Michelle's attention.

Hazel looked up with her eyes of the same color as her name, and she abandoned the toys she'd been playing with.

"Hazel," Skip said as he ran toward her. Leigh transferred Remi to Michelle and looked around for Daniel and Scout.

"Where is everyone?"

"Outside," Michelle said. "Denzel said you guys didn't mind if he used the hot tub."

"Of course not," Leigh said, finding Dan in the tub with him. Scout stood at the sliding door, his nose pressed against the glass, his tail wagging. Leigh moved over to let him in, and the German shepherd trotted over to Skip immediately.

"Scout!" Skip threw himself at the dog, wrapping his skinny arms around the dog's neck and front end.

"Thank you for cleaning my house," Leigh said. "You don't have to do that."

"I know." Michelle gave her a smile. "But I don't mind, and I know you have a lot going on. How's Jerry?"

"He's doing well," Leigh said. "They're watching his potassium right now, and as soon as his blood levels are right, they'll release him. He and Cecily are going to come here and help out while he recovers."

"So your plan worked." Michelle grinned at Leigh, and then she stepped into her and hugged her. "You look tired, Leigh. If you want to go lie down, Denzel and I can handle the kids."

Leigh wanted to tell her no. She didn't want to be weak. She also knew Michelle and Denzel wanted more kids, and she'd be there to help them when they needed it. Denzel had continued to get better and better over the years, but he still couldn't walk very far without a cane, and he couldn't lift his kids once they reached twenty pounds.

"You know what? I'd love to have lunch and then take a nap."

"We'll stay and help with the kids so you can." Michelle reached out and tucked Leigh's hair behind her ear. "You don't have to do everything. Who told me that?"

Leigh ducked her head. "Okay, I got it."

"Yeah, but who told me that?"

"I did," Leigh whispered.

"So we'll have family nap time after lunch."

Leigh nodded and went to say hi to her brother. "Let me talk to Denzel for a minute."

"Sure, I'll get the pot pies heated up." Michelle moved into the kitchen with Remi on her hip, and Leigh slid open the door and stepped outside.

"How's the hip?" she asked her brother, because she knew that gave him the most trouble these days.

"Feels good in here," he said with a smile.

"Howdy-ho, Daniel," she said to her nephew. "Are you swimmin' like a fish?"

"Yeah, but it hurts my nose," he said.

"That's because it's not a swimmin' pool, bud," Denzel said dryly. He loved his kids—and Michelle—with the same level of intensity he did everything else. Denzel only knew two speeds—fast and slow, and he almost never operated on slow.

"Well, lunch is almost ready," Leigh said. "Thank you for coming over, Denzel." She didn't want to admit how lonely she was with Morris gone, but she didn't have to say it for her brother to know.

"Come on, Danny," he said to his boy. "Momma's got lunch on, and Skip will be inside if Aunt Leigh is home."

"Skip!" Danny yelled, and he sloshed over to the steps to get out of the hot tub. Though Denzel's accident was over a decade old at this point, Leigh still hovered nearby in case he needed help climbing out of the hot tub. He didn't, and he toweled off and laughed with his son as he dried him too. Then they all went inside to get lunch.

And that nap Leigh sorely needed.

37

Bryce could hear the party in his grandfather's hospital room from down the hall. An internal groan started in his stomach and rose through his chest until it leaked out of his mouth.

The scent of marinara and rosemary hung in the air, along with the yeasty scent of bread dough. That meant Uncle Blaze and Uncle Jem had indeed smuggled in the pizza they said they would. Before Bryce could reach the door to the right room, it opened, and Uncle Luke walked out.

"There you are," he said, the growly-bear look on his face smoothing away when he saw Bryce. He pounded Bryce on the back in a quick man-hug, and then turned to face the door as a round of laughter burst out before it could close all the way.

"I feel like we're going to get chastised," Bryce said, shooting a look down the hall toward the nurse's station. "I don't want to get yelled at tonight."

"It's kind of a circus in there," Luke said. He grinned and looked over to Bryce. "It's your daddy's fault. He's got Otis, Blaze, and Gabe riled up over that yogurt they like."

Bryce shook his head, but his mouth curved up too. "At his age, he should know better."

"I don't get the allure of yogurt at all," Uncle Luke said dryly, and that struck Bryce as funny. He laughed, because Luke wasn't kidding.

"So where were you going?"

"Bathroom," he said.

"If you escape without taking me with you, I'll never let you come ride Baconator again." Bryce raised his eyebrows, and Luke did too.

"You think I'm going to escape?"

"I think you could text Sterling a safe word, and she'd call and tell you the kids needed you at home. She'd probably pinch that cute baby of yours just to get her to squeal and squawk over the line for proof."

Luke blinked at him. Then he tipped his head back and laughed and laughed and laughed.

"You laugh it up," Bryce said, though he semi-laughed too. "That's how I know I'm right."

"If I try to escape, I will take you with me." Luke made an X over his heart and headed down the hall.

Bryce took a deep breath and entered the hospital room. Grandpa stood now, holding onto a tall pole for extra support. Uncle Trace and Bryce's dad stood very nearby, both of them tensed like panthers about to pounce.

"Bryce," Uncle Blaze said, and Bryce was sure he didn't

mean to bellow. When the brothers got together, it was almost like they forgot how to use indoor voices. They forgot they weren't in competition with each other. They forgot their manners, just a little.

"Hey, Uncle Blaze." Bryce hugged his uncle, because Blaze had come to help with the horses while Bryce had been on tour with Harry. So had Jem, as he boarded his three horses at Bryce's ranch.

He moved over to Mav next, who grinned at him and said, "Welcome. There's pizza over on the counter."

Bryce saw it, and his stomach growled though the pizza looked a little cold. He had come late, because he and Codi hadn't wanted to say good-night so early. She'd actually gone to Kassie's so Bryce could come here.

Now that the baseball season had ended in Seattle—Reggie's team hadn't made it into the World Series—he'd moved to Coral Canyon to be near to Kassie. The four of them had been spending a lot of time together, and Kassie had been training Reggie how to work with horses, with the fields, and anything else out on the ranch.

"How'd your garden come in?" Mav asked.

"Amazing this year," Bryce said as he watched Gabe join the group surrounding Grandpa. "We've got one more crop of corn to put up, and then the pumpkins."

"Can I bring my kids out to the patch this weekend?"

"One hundred percent," Bryce said. "I'll put it on the family text. Then I'm gonna take them all to the Farmer's Market in Dog Valley and hopefully get rid of them."

"Grandma might want some. She was talking about making

pumpkin pie from a real pumpkin this year." Mav smiled and lifted his can of cola to his lips. "She's at Leigh's right now and has that great big kitchen."

"Definitely an improvement over her condo kitchen," Bryce said.

"Hey," Uncle Gabe said as he turned toward Bryce. "I didn't see you come in." He hugged him and smiled around the room at everyone. "Codi didn't want to come?"

"Codi wasn't invited." Bryce cut a look at his uncle. "Do you see any other women here?"

Gabe only grinned, but Bryce wasn't going to take this bait, just like he hadn't last night either. He was aware of his own feelings for Codi, but that didn't mean he had to broadcast them to anyone who dared to ask.

Bryce *really* liked her. Beyond anyone he'd dated before, and in the moments when he prayed while he waited for his toast to pop up in the morning, he recognized the absolute fear that plagued him over his feelings for Codi Hudson.

The only other woman he'd ever liked like this, he'd lost. He couldn't stand the thought of being shattered and left alone the way he had been with Bailey, and Codi now held more of his heart than Bailey ever had.

He pressed his lips together and folded his arms. "How's Morris doing on tour?"

"Good," Gabe said. "I've got your third quarter profit and loss statement done."

"Oh, thanks, Uncle Gabe." Bryce looked over to him then. "How bad was it?"

"Well, you should've sold Dragon for a lot more, but your

extra hay sales last month made up for it." He gave Bryce a raised-eyebrow look, and Bryce grinned as he ducked his head.

"Codi wanted Dragon," Bryce said. "What? I'm going to tell her no?"

"No," Gabe said with a chuckle. "I don't suppose you are."

"Would she tell you no if you asked her a special question?" Mav asked.

"Are you guys tag-teaming me?" Bryce asked as his father looked his way. His stomach vibrated, but he grinned at his daddy. "If he comes over and piles on this, I'm leaving."

"It's not a tag-team," Gabe said. "You two sure seem to like each other."

"You usually do when you date," Bryce said. "Hey, Daddy." He leaned into his father's arms.

"Why are you all tight over here?" He looked at Gabe and then Mav. "Did you ask him about the—?" He cut off. "Nope, I'm not walking into this again."

"We didn't ask him."

"Ask me what?" Bryce looked at his uncles, then his father.

"Heya, Bryce," Jem said as he joined their group. "My kids are dyin' to come get a pumpkin, and they want you to do that spooky pumpkin walk again. What are the chances of that?"

Bryce had carved two dozen jack-o-lanterns last year and set them up in his corn stalks, which he'd tilled under to make an aisle. He'd invited the kids out to the ranch for a little Halloween celebration, and he honestly hadn't thought about it this year.

Not with everything already going on with Codi, and Kassie

and Reggie, and the long harvest, and Grandpa in the hospital, and Harry's tour.

"I don't know."

"Can we come up to the ranch for a Halloween party?" Gabe asked. "That's what we were going to ask. You wouldn't have to do much, except provide the space. The wives will plan it all."

Bryce met his father's eyes, and Daddy nodded. "Okay," Bryce said. "And if I can get some pumpkins carved, I'll do the spooky pumpkin walk."

"Rosie said she'd come help," Jem said.

"I'll send you my teenager too," Gabe said.

"Same," Mav said.

Bryce loved the teens in the family, and they told him things they didn't tell their parents. He couldn't say no to them either, and he rolled his neck to stretch it out. "All right," he said. "Let me pick a date, and I'll have them all out to carve."

Uncle Luke slipped back into the room, and Uncle Blaze came over to Bryce. "How's Cash doing?"

"Good," Blaze said, a pair of shutters going over his eyes. Bryce wondered if his father had ever answered like that about him. Most likely. "You guys, Daddy's tired. Let's wrap this up, okay?"

Bryce moved over to hug his grandfather and chat with him, and once he'd left, he sat in his truck and texted Codi. *How good are you with carving a pumpkin?*

I mean, I can make circles for eyes, she said. *Why?*

Bryce told himself he didn't have to hide anything from her.

She knew about his big family. She'd helped with all of his littlest cousins just last night, and seeing her with that brunette baby on her lap...that smile in her eyes...that sexy, maternal instinct?

Bryce could admit right there in the cab of his truck that he'd fallen in love with her. He'd dreamed of having a family with her last night.

But he couldn't say it out loud yet, and he simply needed more time. At least that was what he was telling himself for now.

"I'm here," Codi yelled several days later as she walked in the back door of his house. She waited for Penta to enter too, and then she pulled the sliding door closed.

"We're right here," Bryce said, poking his head out of the freezer, where he'd just put a stack of bagged corn kernels. Codi wore her usual jeans and a long-sleeved shirt with pink, green, and blue swirls, no wig, and a pair of sunglasses.

"Codi," Grandma said as she turned from the huge boiling pot of water she'd just pulled the last few cobs of corn out of. "How are you, dear?"

"Good." Codi grinned at her and moved to hug her first. "You're not done with the corn yet?"

"Last batch," Bryce said. Codi turned toward him, and he took her into his arms and kissed her, right there in front of Grandma. "How's Houndstooth?"

"He doesn't like me," Codi said with a sigh. "I think Kassie is going to take him back, because he's just not making progress with me."

"I could take him once we get the pumpkins in and Halloween done with."

"Kassie said that too." She moved to sit at the bar, because she'd probably been running since this morning.

Bryce got out a bottle of water and handed it to Codi, who gave him a grateful smile. She took a long drink from it, and Bryce moved over to the bowl where Grandma had sliced off the blanched kernels. He bagged them, and several minutes later, he and Grandma finished with the corn, and she put it in his freezer.

"Do you still want to go get the pumpkins?" he asked Codi.

"Yep," she said. She glanced out the windows at the back of the house. "We better get going, though. It's already starting to turn dusky."

"Let's go." Bryce waited for her to put her sunglasses on again, and then he opened the door for the dogs and followed them out. He held Codi's hand as they walked through the afternoon sunlight, and he didn't have to say anything to be completely comfortable with her.

He'd hooked up the trailer to his truck already, and he and Codi climbed in before he rumbled off down the lane toward the big pumpkin patch he planted every year. It wasn't exactly easy work to slice them from their dry vines and load them into the back of his truck and trailer, but he did love pumpkins.

Once at the patch, he handed Codi a pair of gloves and then a knife, and she looked at it. "I have to cut them off?"

"Sometimes it's easier," he said. "Depending on how big they are."

She stood on the edge of the field of pumpkins, and he joined her as he pulled on his own pair of gloves. The leaves of the plants had started to brown and wilt, which made it far easier to find and collect all the pumpkins.

Bryce looked at the acre of pumpkins he'd planted, and he suddenly felt incredibly tired. He looked over to Codi and asked, "How hard would it be to put this off a day?"

She looked back at him. "You know more than me. Will they get ruined? It might freeze tonight."

"Some of them, maybe," he said. "But they'll be fine." He honestly wasn't sure he cared if they all went mushy. He could till them all under and he wouldn't even have to plant the patch again next year.

Then, he wouldn't be able to do the teen carving day this weekend, and all the younger cousins wouldn't be able to come to the ranch and do their spooky pumpkin walk.

Bryce pulled off his gloves and took Codi's knife from her. "Let's do it tomorrow." He gathered her into his arms, really enjoying the way her smile lit up her face and a teasing look entered her expression.

"You want to play hooky."

"I want an hour off in the glorious afternoon sunshine with my gorgeous girlfriend." He lowered his head and kissed Codi, and she kissed him back. His pulse pittered and pattered until it finally settled back into a normal rhythm, and he didn't even mind that Codi still wore her gardening gloves as she ran her fingers through his hair.

"Come on," he murmured. He left his truck and trailer right where it sat, and he led Codi to the edge of the pumpkin patch and into the shade of a towering aspen which stood there. The leaves on it had turned a glorious shade of gold, almost tangerine, and Bryce believed aspens to be the most beautiful tree in the world.

He sat down on the ground, groaning as he did, and Codi joined him. He laid all the way down and put one hand behind his head as he gazed up into the sky. Waves of blue rose above him, and he exhaled. "I love the sky," he said.

Codi cuddled into his side, and he curled his arm around her, his long enough to hold her wrist. "I love being here with you," he said, getting dangerously close to three little words he hadn't said to a woman since he'd lived in Montana and Bailey got bigger and bigger with his baby.

He had loved her, on some level. But this thing with Codi had surpassed that a long time ago, though they'd only been dating for four and a half months. This thing with Codi meant the world to him, and if that wasn't love, Bryce didn't know what was.

"My daddy will be here tomorrow," she said. "Maybe he can help us with the pumpkins."

Bryce's breath stalled as it filled his lungs, because he'd semi-forgotten about Codi's daddy coming to town tomorrow. "I'll harvest them in the morning."

"I don't have any dogs," she said. "I'll come help you."

"Codi." He didn't know what else to say. Words had always been Bryce's friends, even when the right ones didn't come right away. He closed his eyes and listened to his inner thoughts, his gut, and God.

He felt the earth hurtling through space, and his awareness zoomed in and out and back in again.

"Codi, I'm falling in love with you."

"Are you?"

"Completely," he whispered. "Hopelessly. It's...it's unreal. It's this thing I've never felt before, and I don't know what to do with it."

Codi snuggled closer and wrapped her arm across his midsection. "Bryce, you don't have to do anything with it. You can simply feel it, and that's okay."

"Okay," he said.

"I promised my daddy I wouldn't fall in love with you before he could meet you," she said. She cleared her throat. "I think I'm kind of failing, and I'm hanging on by my fingernails."

A smile came to his face, but it wasn't one of his wide, winning ones. It was a smile filled with awe and then love, and he let it stream through his soul as he ran his fingers up to her shoulder and then back down to her wrist.

He turned, and instead of saying *I love you* in words, he matched his mouth to hers and kissed her tenderly, hoping the big things he felt could be communicated without words.

38

Codi had her phone up as loud as it would go, because her daddy had been texting her all morning, since the moment he'd left the potato farm at five o'clock that morning. Yes, she'd heard the notification, because she hadn't slept well, her nervous anticipation of seeing her father for the first time in several months keeping her restless and awake.

Since she didn't have a dog to bathe and clip, she'd run Penta at first light, and she'd come out to the Rising Sun Ranch to help Bryce with the pumpkins. They'd finished those, and he currently had hundreds of them in the bed of his truck and filling his trailer.

Jem and his wife Sunny had just arrived with Blaze, Luke, and Mav, and Bryce's aunts and uncles had brought all of their kids. Well, Jem only had Rosie and Ladd with him, and Blaze had his wife and two girls and his toddler son, who currently rode on his shoulders. Cash lived in Las Vegas, but Codi had learned he'd be home for the Thanksgiving Day holiday.

Luke had brought everyone with him, including his baby girl, who Kassie held while the other kids climbed over pumpkins and handed them down to their daddies. Mav only had his younger two with him, but he had a whole pile of pumpkins to take home. Dani hadn't come either, as she was working at the flower shop that day.

Codi could admit the pumpkin-carving fever had caught fire in her chest too, and she was planning to attend this Saturday's teen carving festival here at the ranch. Kassie and Reggie would be there, and apparently everyone in the Young family trusted the four of them to be responsible adults around the teenagers.

Bryce had joked that he could call nine-one-one just fine, and his aunts and uncles had sent laughing emojis—at least on the messages he'd shown to Codi about this weekend's activity.

Her daddy would only be here today and tomorrow, as he then had to get back to Idaho and the potato farm that consumed him almost all the time.

"Nothing yet?" Bryce asked as he came to her side.

Codi shook her head, and when one of the littles started to cry, she turned toward the sound. Blaze dang near dropped his son, Tyrone, as he removed him from his shoulders, and Codi went to take him.

"Can I have him?"

"You can have him all day long." Blaze looked like he might seriously leave Tyrone with Codi as he handed him over. He bent to pick up his cowboy hat, and he smoothed his hair down before putting it back on.

"Hey, little boy." Codi looked at the dark-haired boy and rubbed her nose against his. "Let's go get some crackers, okay?"

"Da-da," he said.

"Yeah, go on, bud," Blaze said as Faith arrived at his side. "You can have some crackers."

Codi smiled at him, glad when Bryce's darkest uncle returned the gesture.

"You sure you're okay with him?" Faith asked.

"Yeah, of course," Codi said. "I'll be right back with him."

"If you bring crackers out, everyone will love you," Sunny called after her, and Codi smiled as she twisted to look at her over her shoulder. Inside the quiet warmth of Bryce's house, Codi pulled down the crackers from where they sat on top of the fridge. He had several boxes in a few varieties, and she held one tiny fish cracker for Tyrone until he could grab it with his chunky fingers.

She'd never considered herself to be very nurturing or maternal, but the more she interacted with Bryce's cousins, the more that perception of herself disappeared. Standing in his kitchen, Codi realized she wanted it to be her kitchen. She wanted this baby on her hip to be her cousin, if only through marriage. She wanted babies of her own to love, care for, raise, and hopefully feed goldfish-shaped crackers to one at a time when something made her anxious or afraid.

When she'd slowed her thoughts enough, she took the box of crackers with her, grabbed another one, and put Tyrone on his feet. "Okay, buddy, you can walk with me." He toddled along, moving at about the speed of a snail, but they made it back to the side of the house where Bryce had parked the pumpkins.

"Crackers," she called to the kids still climbing all over the pumpkins. She only saw Mav nearby, and even then, he picked up a pumpkin and started toward the front of the house, where they'd all parked, supposedly to put the pumpkin in his truck.

North whooped, and Codi could admit he was one of her favorites. He catapulted over the side of the truck, stumbled as he landed, and her heart stalled in her chest. "North," she said, having no idea how she'd tell Luke and Sterling their son had just broken his leg.

But the boy came up just fine, and he jogged over to her. "Don't jump like that," she said. "You scared me."

He blinked at her and asked, "Can I have the two sides?"

"Yeah, sure." Codi put a stack of crackers in his hand, and by then, several of the kids had managed to get out of the truck and trailer and were lining up in front of her. She saw Bryce lift Celeste over the edge of the truck and set her on her feet, then turn to get Grace.

She smiled at him, and he smiled at her, and it sure felt like love to Codi. She resisted the thoughts, burying them until after her father arrived. If he would ever get here.

She handed out crackers until every child had something. Their moms and dads returned, and they started loading up to leave. Sterling stopped in front of Codi and said, "Thank you, Codi." She stepped into her and hugged her. "You're the best."

"Thanks, Codi!" Jem called, saluting her with one hand

against the brim of his cowboy hat as he kept a good grip on his son's hand.

Sunny hugged her too, her bulging baby belly between them. "Next time, you don't have to harvest *all* the pumpkins."

"It was fun," Codi said.

"You sure you want the teens this weekend?"

"One hundred percent," Codi said, copying Bryce. Sunny grinned and waved as she followed her husband, and Luke arrived to help Sterling with Ryder and North, whistling for his dog to go with them.

Blaze stepped in front of her. He took Tyrone from her and smiled at his son. "You happy now?"

"Dad-dad-dad-da."

"You don't pull Daddy's hair," Blaze said, giving the boy a sharp look. It softened completely when he looked at Codi. "Thank you for rescuing me."

"I think I was rescuing me," she said, glancing over to Faith as she sidled up to Blaze and took their son from him.

"Yeah?" Blaze's eyebrows went up now that he didn't have anyone but her to focus on. "Anything I can help you with?"

"Just waiting for my daddy to show up," Codi said. "He's meeting Bryce and Penta and Dragon for the first time."

Faith watched her with a neutral expression, but her smile was kind and reassuring. "He's going to love Bryce."

Blaze's smile roared to life on his face. "Which one of those are you most nervous about?"

"Honestly?" Codi looked over to where Bryce stood talking to Mav, little Emilia in his arms. "Probably Dragon."

Blaze chuckled, and Codi grinned, and he hugged her with

Tyrone between them too. "He's going to love Bryce." He faced him too. "Everyone does."

"Yeah," Codi said. "They do."

"Do you?"

Codi didn't know what to say, but she didn't want to lie. She thought of their conversation from the previous evening, as they lay in the prairie grass, the shade above them and the sky so blue and so beautiful.

"I think I'm getting there," she admitted. "But don't you dare tell him." She focused on Blaze again, seeing his ridiculously clownish smile. She looked over to Faith. "Do you have any control over him?"

"I promise he won't tell a soul," Faith said. "Will you, Blaze?"

"Oh, honey, hasn't anyone told you?" Blaze grinned at Codi. "I'm the secret-keeper of the family." With that, he squeezed her hand and left with Faith too. Codi wandered over to Mav and Bryce, who put his cousin on the ground.

"'Bye, Codi," Emilia chirped. "Thanks for the crackers."

"Of course," she said. Her phone bleepity-buzzed, and her heartbeat mimicked it. She pulled out her phone to see a text from her daddy.

Almost there.

"Thanks, Codi," Mav said. He hugged her good-bye too, and then he left. Codi showed her phone to Bryce, who lifted his eyes to hers.

"I'll go start lunch," Bryce said. "Do you think he'll be hungry? Or do you think he stopped somewhere?"

"Knowing my dad?" Codi grinned at Bryce. "He'll be starving."

Bryce nodded, his mouth set in a tight light and his jaw locked. She reached up and said, "Are you nervous?"

"Yes," he said. "What if he doesn't like me?"

"Here's what Blaze just said," Codi said. "He said everyone loves you, so my daddy will too." She tipped up onto her toes, balancing against his chest, and kissed him. "But I'm nervous too."

They started for the back of the house, but Codi heard tires crunching over the gravel out front. Mav should've been gone by now, so Codi looked at Bryce as they paused. "Could that be him?"

She turned and strode toward the front of the house now, her legs using the adrenaline pumping through her to propel her forward quickly. Since Bryce was so tall, and his legs so long, he kept pace with her easily. They emerged near the garage, and sure enough, a dirty, brown truck sat there, Codi's daddy emerging from it.

"Daddy," drifted from her mouth, and Codi's hand shot up. She waved at him and called louder now, "Daddy."

He looked in her direction, his smile suddenly shining toward her like she needed it on a dark night. She jogged toward him, squealing when he caught her in a hug. "You made it."

He laughed, and Codi hadn't heard him do that in a while. Her father got the job done. He didn't have much time for endearments or compliments, but Codi knew he loved her. "I found it easy," he said. "Lost service a bit there in the apple orchards, but I just kept driving."

Bryce's footsteps sounded behind her, and Codi turned toward him. As he'd introduced her to various people over the months, he'd always stood beside her. So she moved to his side and took his hand in hers. "Daddy," she said. "This is my boyfriend, Bryce." She grinned and grinned and couldn't stop.

"Bryce, this is my daddy, Randall Hudson."

"It's my pleasure to meet you," Bryce said, extending his hand. "Codi has told me all about you, your sons, and your farm in Boise."

"Oh, wow." Daddy chuckled, his eyes stuck to Codi's for a moment. He shook Bryce's hand and said, "I suppose she's said a lot about you and your family too."

"Well, we're a zoo, so that's not hard to believe." Bryce smiled as if he met his girlfriend's father all the time. "We were just going in to start lunch. Are you hungry?"

"I've been on the road all day," her father said. "I'm starving."

Codi beamed, because she'd been right. They rounded her father's truck and headed up the front sidewalk to the house. Bryce told him about the pumpkins they'd harvested that morning, and what chores he still needed to get done that afternoon. "But Codi has the whole afternoon off," he said. "We've got some great horses for you to ride, because she wants to show you Dragon."

"He's the best horse," Codi said.

"He is now," Bryce said. "But he is the one who gave me a puncture wound."

"Codi told me about that," Daddy said. "She's pretty handy with a first aid kit."

"She was that night," Bryce agreed. He opened the fridge. "All right, what do we want? I have quite a few things from the garden. Green peppers, onions." He pulled the produce out as he named it. "Eggs, ham. Omelets?"

"Quick and easy," Codi said.

"And delicious," Bryce added, smiling.

Codi felt the weight of her father's eyes on her as she looked at Bryce, but it still took her a long moment to pull her attention away from him. "You like omelets, right, Daddy?"

"I love an omelet," he said. "You can cook that?"

"Sure can," Bryce said as he pulled out his multi-colored eggs.

"He gets the eggs from his chickens," Codi said. "He grows all his produce. He made me the best zucchini bread ever a couple of weeks ago."

"That was my grandma's recipe," he said. "It's about the only thing I can bake." He put a pan on the stove and a bowl on the counter.

"Where did you learn to cook?" Daddy asked.

"Out of necessity," Bryce said. "When I left home after high school." He spoke easily, though Codi knew when he'd left and why.

Her beagle came over, and Codi bent down to pat him. "Daddy, this is Pentagon." She picked up the solid dog, something she didn't do very often. He didn't squirm, but he did look at her with a fierce side-eye that made her want to put him down as soon as possible.

"He's cute," Daddy said, about the best praise Codi could've hoped for when it came to her dog. "Is the golden retriever Bryce's?"

"Yep," Codi said. "His name is Lucky. He was my first customer here in Coral Canyon."

"How is the dog grooming going?" Daddy asked.

Codi bent to put Penta back on his paws. "It's okay," she said. "To be honest, I don't even try to get customers. I like working out here all the time."

"But you're not getting paid for a full-time job out here." Daddy pinned her with his bright blue eyes, and Codi found herself squirming though she had no reason to. Bryce glanced over to her, but Codi could handle this.

She pushed her hair out of her face, and her daddy said, "You're not wearing a wig." His eyes widened, and he added, "Why didn't I notice that the moment I saw you?"

"I don't need it here," Codi said lightly. "The wigs are hot out on the farm."

"Your momma always said you didn't need to wear them."

Momma wasn't the one enduring junior high with pure white hair either, but Codi didn't say anything like that. Daddy pushed her hair back off her face, his smile so soft and so loving. "I've missed you Codi-girl."

"I miss you too, Daddy."

He glanced over to Bryce, but he'd busied himself with cracking eggs. "I don't suppose you'll ever come back to Boise."

"No." Codi shook her head. "I can't, Daddy." He knew that, and she didn't need to explain more than that. "I love it here. I want to live here."

Daddy leaned closer. "With him?"

Codi gave him a closed-mouth smile and nodded, though she also shrugged one shoulder, not fully committing to the idea of settling down with Bryce Young on this ranch.

"He's great," she whispered. "Don't you think he's great?" She looked over to Bryce who lifted the cutting board and poured the cubed ham and diced red peppers and onions into the eggs.

"He has a very good spirit about him," Daddy admitted. "But I want to see him with Dragon."

"Daddy." Codi shook her head. "Dragon is my horse, not Bryce's."

"A good man can handle his girlfriend's horse." He hadn't kept his voice down, but Codi didn't know what Bryce had heard. Hopefully not the challenge her father had just laid at his feet, and she prayed through the making of the omelets and the eating of the omelets and the cleaning up of the omelets.

Jesus, she thought. *It's time to come and calm Dragon for Bryce. Just for a few minutes, please.*

She wanted her daddy to like Bryce, because she trusted his opinion, and she wanted to listen to him this time.

You can listen to your heart too, she told herself, and that was true too. Before she knew it, they'd agreed to go meet Dragon, and Bryce opened the back door and stepped onto the deck first.

"Here we go," Codi muttered, and then she followed Bryce and her daddy out onto the Rising Sun Ranch.

39

Bryce held Codi's hand on the way to the stable where he kept his personal horses. His uncle Jem boarded his equines there too, and Codi had moved Dragon into a nice stall that she worked on every day. Bryce had left her roses one morning last week, and then he'd left her one of his momma's snickerdoodles a few days later.

He wasn't usually overly sentimental, but their five-month anniversary was coming up at the end of the month, just before Halloween, and he'd started planning a quiet, romantic evening for the two of them.

Right now, Randall talked about his farm and his sons, and Bryce smiled and nodded, laughing when appropriate, and asking another question to keep the man talking. If he did, then Bryce didn't have to.

He pulled open the stable door, the familiar scent of horse-flesh, straw, and leather filling his nose. He loved the chill in the air, though it was after lunchtime, and while Bryce didn't love the feet of snow that Mother Nature could drop with a single storm, he did love experiencing every season in powerful ways.

One of the horses inside nickered, and Bryce smiled about that too. He let Codi go in first, and then he smiled Randall on in too. He wasn't sure what Codi's daddy thought of him, but he'd managed to make lunch with the two of them talking quietly nearby. He didn't know what they'd discussed, but Codi wore a bright smile as she turned back to him.

"Do you want to go riding?" she asked.

"Sure," Randall said. "Then I can see this ranch you love."

Codi faced forward again and went down the aisle to Dragon's stall. "Bryce, will you take him out for me?"

"One hundred percent," he said.

"Then I can get Daddy a horse."

Bryce went by Randall at the end of the aisle and joined Codi in front of Dragon's stall. He had his head over the half-door that was open, as did most of the other horses there. "Who are you going to give him?"

He reached out and put his hand against Dragon's nose, and the horse didn't move a muscle. That was progress for Bryce, but he and Codi had gone riding plenty of times over the past several weeks. She took Dragon, because he still had a lot of work to do in order to be "the perfect horse," and Bryce liked using him to train other horses too.

"Maybe Wooden Soldier?" Codi guessed. "He's good with Dragon, and he hasn't been out in a couple of days."

"Sure," Bryce said. "You get him, and I'll take Dragon out."

He looked over his shoulder to Randall, who watched them. He ducked his head and murmured, "Do you think he likes me?"

"Yes," Codi whispered back. "Pretend he's Blaze or Luke. You know, grumpy without a cause? Soft inside, once you break through that outer shell?" She smiled at him and swept her lips across his cheek. "He's like that."

Bryce nodded, and he unlatched the lock on the stall. "Come on, Dragon."

Codi looped a lead around the horse's neck as he emerged from the stall like a princess would from her royal carriage. Dragon really thought highly of himself, and he was a gorgeous horse. Bryce smiled at him and let him crowd right into his chest, his forehead against Bryce's shoulder.

"You gonna be good today?" Bryce murmured, standing strong against the push of the equine. "Codi's daddy is here, and she wants to show you off, okay?"

Dragon stopped pushing, and Bryce took that as horse-code for, *Okay, Bryce. I'll be good for Codi's daddy.*

Bryce smiled and faced Randall. He led Dragon that way, half-expecting the horse to buck and body slam him against the wall. Again. Different stable, but a similar situation. He didn't, thankfully, and Bryce took the horse outside. He looped the lead over the nearby post, and said, "Great job, Dragon. I'll be right back, okay?"

He waited for Codi to lead out Wooden Soldier, a deep, dark chestnut, whose mane and tail and coat all matched. He almost looked like he'd been auburn once, but had been dipped in oil. Bryce loved him, and he trailed his fingers along Soldier's ribs as the horse plodded by.

"I'm gonna get Smokestack," he said as Randall came out. "He's in the yellow barn. Did you want to come with?" He watched Codi loop Soldier's lead over the post too. "Codi can saddle up here and come get us."

"One hundred percent," Codi called, and Bryce looked at Randall, well aware of what he'd just done. He'd given the man a chance to be alone with Bryce, to ask him anything he wanted, without Codi there as a buffer.

Bryce smiled though his insides quaked a little bit.

"Sure," Randall said. "Tell me about the colors in the stables."

"It's just for organizational purposes," Bryce said. "Our Red Stable is our newer horses. Ones that need more care. They've either just arrived, or still need to gain a lot of weight, or won't let anyone touch them." He glanced over to Randall.

"Codi has been amazing here. She has such a calm spirit. The horses love her."

"Does she work in the Red Stable?"

"Kassie—she's my business partner and the lead trainer here —assigns horses to specific people. Codi has a couple in the Red Stable right now, yeah. Almost all of my horses are in the Red Stable. I only have this one in Yellow, and then I deal with all of our permanent horses too."

"Wow," Randall said, and he sounded impressed. Bryce wasn't sure, as he'd met the man an hour ago. "How many horses do you have?"

"Right now, let's see. I sold a couple last week who were ready...Kassie went and picked up three that we just started with...I think we have thirty-one. That includes our permanent residents."

Randall smiled and entered the Yellow Stable first, after Bryce opened the door and held it for him. "Seems like you have a good operation going here."

"I love it," Bryce said. "I trained in Kentucky, and then Kassie and I moved here, bought this place, and...yeah. Now this is what we do."

He looked past Randall as he heard footsteps, and he caught Reggie emerging from the aisle. "Hey, Reg."

Reggie smiled and hooked his thumb over his shoulder. "I can't get Sunflower out. Can you help me?"

"One hundred percent." Bryce went to do that, telling Reggie as he passed, "We just moved her from Red to Yellow, so she's just being stubborn." She might need more time too, and Bryce went all the way to the end, where he'd housed Sunflower. "Hey."

The horse—a pretty all-black beauty—didn't come out of the corner to greet him. "I'm comin' in," he said. "You have to go out. Reggie is here for you. He's just going to move you over to the pasture for a few hours."

He unlocked the stall door and swung it wide. He stepped inside as Reggie arrived, and he said, "Just wait there for a second, okay?"

"Yep." Reggie and Randall watched from several paces away as Bryce continued toward Sunflower.

"Why don't you want to go out? You're stuck in this corner stall until you can play nice with the other horses, and I'm pretty sure Thelma is out in the pasture already." He glanced over to Reggie, who nodded.

"You like Thelma," Bryce said, continuing to use a soft, soothing voice as he took slow, measured steps toward the horse. She didn't stand very tall—his cowboy hat would probably reach as high as her head—but horses weighed a lot, and they spooked easily, and he didn't need any hoof prints anywhere on his body.

He stopped and reached out his hand. "Come on, Sunflower. You don't want to spend all day in here. When it starts to snow, you'll have to, and then you'll be upset you didn't get your pasture time right now." He smiled at the horse and reached into his pocket.

Her ears flipped and fluttered, but she made no noise. She shifted her weight off one back hoof, and Bryce knew he had her. He pulled a small slice of dried mango from his pocket. He made these tasty horse treats himself, in a freeze dryer he kept on the kitchen table. No added sugar. Nothing but the dried fruit itself.

Sunflower blinked lazily, but Bryce knew she saw the treat. She came forward a step, and he said, "Good. Come on. Another one." She started to move then, as it seemed like it took horses a moment to get all of their legs lined up and working properly.

Bryce backed out of the stall at the same pace she moved forward, and when she stood all the way out in the aisle, he let her take the dried fruit. He ran one hand down the side of her neck, feeling the tension in her muscles there.

"Reggie is going to take you," he said. "He's really great, and all you do is walk along behind him." Bryce grabbed a rope from the peg on the wall and looped it around her neck. He moved her around so she faced the right way to exit the stable, and he handed Reggie the rope and another piece of mango from his pocket.

Reggie nodded to him, then smiled at Sunflower. "Come on," he said, giving the rope a little tug. Again, Sunflower took a step, paused, and then finally got walking, and Bryce watched Reg take her all the way down the aisle and outside.

"She might need to have that right front leg looked at again," he said. "Let me make a note of that, and then we'll get Smokestack saddled."

"Daddy?" Codi called into the stable. "Bryce?"

"Right here, sweetheart," Randall said. He looked at Bryce for a long moment, nodded, and then turned to go meet his daughter.

Bryce let out the breath that had been caged in his lungs, and then he pulled out his phone and opened the recording app. "Sunflower wouldn't get out of the stall for Reggie. She would for me and some dried mango. Watching her walk down the aisle, she's still favoring that right front leg, and you need to maybe call Doctor Hershey and get it looked at again."

He ended the recording and followed everyone outside. Codi had Dragon and Wooden Soldier saddled already, and Bryce retraced his steps to grab his saddle for Smokestack. "Sorry," he said as he passed the saddle to Codi. "I'll get him right now."

Bryce hurried to get out his horse before he remembered there was no hurrying when dealing with these horses. So he calmed himself in front of Smokestack's stall, the horse's breath wafting over Bryce's face.

"Yeah," he whispered. "I'm a little rushed and a little on-edge." He opened his eyes and looked at the magnificent creature in front of him. Horses had always held such a special place in his heart, and he smiled as he reached for Smokestack's face.

"Codi's daddy is here, and I'm just trying to impress him. Do I need to do that? I am who I am." Bryce could change; he'd done it in the past. But if Randall didn't like him, Bryce wasn't sure he could do anything too quickly to adapt.

His heartbeat slowed, and he got Smokestack out of the stall. Outside, Codi had left his saddle for him, and he quickly put it on the horse. Once he sat in the saddle, he looked into the October sunshine and said, "Lord, thank you for this beautiful day. I don't know why I've been so blessed to own this land, and run this ranch, but help me do it well."

His throat closed a little bit as his emotions spiraled and pinched through him. "I think I'm in love with Codi, Lord. I want her father to like me, because if this works out, I'm going to be the one keeping her here."

She'd told him multiple times she would never go back to Boise, but as Bryce sat in the saddle, he had the thought that the two of them should make the trip back to Idaho.

Together.

40

Kassie carried in another pumpkin, this one heavy enough to make her take short, stilted steps as quickly as she could. She dropped the gourd on the folding table Bryce had set up, and it made a loud booming noise through his kitchen and living room.

"Whew." She wiped the sweat from her face as Bryce looked over to her. "I think that's the last one."

"Uncle Gabe just texted to say that Beth and Boston have picked up Liesl and they're on the way." He smiled and brought over a couple of carving kits. "I ordered the pizza, and it should be here in about forty-five minutes."

"Pizza and pumpkins," Kassie said with a smile. "What could go wrong?"

"You forgot to mention the *seven* teenagers we have coming." Bryce gave her a smile and then turned back to the kitchen. "When's Reggie coming in?"

Kassie watched him, but she didn't see anything on his face when he turned back to her. They hadn't talked much about Reggie, and Kassie walked into the kitchen and leaned her hip against the end of the peninsula. "You like him, right?"

"Reggie? Sure." Bryce's gaze wouldn't land on hers, and oh, Kassie didn't like that.

"He'd good with the horses."

"Yeah, he sure is."

"He's going to put in his retirement papers by the end of the year."

Bryce finally looked at her. Really locked eyes with her. "Kassie, I don't...it's not my business. If you ever want to sell your part of the ranch, that's all I need to know."

"I don't want to do that." She folded her arms. "And of course this is your business. We've always told each other everything about our lives. It's what makes us...us."

Bryce nodded, something a little afraid in his eyes. She narrowed hers at him. "Bryce. I know that look."

"No, you don't." He turned away from her and went over to the sink to wash his hands, something he'd just done.

Kassie followed him, really getting in next to him at the sink. "Bryce, what's going on?"

"I'm not talking about this right now," he said.

"Why not?"

He huffed out his breath, which meant he really was irritated. But Kassie had had plenty of discussions with Bryce. Tense discussions. Happy discussions. Serious, professional discussions. This would be no different.

He turned toward her. "Do you want me to ruin this for you?"

She blinked, because she hadn't been expecting that. "Ruin...what for me?"

"What are we talkin' about?"

Kassie searched his face, trying to put all the dots together. "Reggie," she said slowly.

"If you want me to talk about this, I'm going to ruin something for you. You won't like it." The sharpness in his eyes softened. "Kassie, just...of course I like him." He reached out and touched a wisp of her hair that had fallen out of her ponytail. "*You* like him, right?"

Kassie's chin quivered for only a moment. "Yes," she whispered.

"He's good to you?" Bryce asked. "Like, really good? Like, remember when we drove way out in the middle of the fields in Louisville, and we just watched the clouds roll by?"

"Yes," she said again, knowing the exact day he referenced.

"You said you wanted a man who adored you. Who would let you buy as many horses as you wanted, and who would be okay with you in tattered shorts and bare feet and too many dogs."

Kassie's eyes filled with tears.

"And it would be nice if he cooked," Bryce said. "But that wasn't a deal-breaker for you. Do you remember what the deal-breaker was?"

She nodded and swiped at her eyes. "He can't treat me the way my daddy treats my momma."

"Right," Bryce said. "He doesn't own you. You don't have to

do everything he says the moment he says it. It's not a dictatorship. You want a marriage that's give and take. A partnership."

"Like what we have on the ranch," Kassie said. "It's really too bad we had no spark." She smiled at Bryce, who smiled right on back.

"Is Reggie okay with us being...us?" He gestured between the two of them. "Because if he's not, I will back off. I'm not going to get in the way of you two."

"You're not?"

"Absolutely not," Bryce said firmly. "And I could tell you why, but—" He cut off as the back sliding door opened and Reggie himself walked in. "Go on," Bryce murmured, but Kassie met his eye.

Bryce nodded at her, straight-faced; Reggie said, "Whew! The wind out there tonight is *howling*."

Kassie moved away from Bryce to go see her boyfriend, and while she still wasn't sure what Bryce was going to say, she was glad she hadn't forced him to say something that would ruin anything for her.

"Hey, baby." She stretched up and kissed him. "Maybe we won't be able to do the spooky Halloween walk if the wind doesn't die down."

"If you want a Young Family Riot, cancel the spooky Halloween walk," Reggie said dryly. "My sister's been talking about it for a week." He grinned at her and slid his hand along her waist, pulling her closer to him. Kassie loved being close to him, and she couldn't believe the way they'd connected and grown together in the past few months.

It's only been a few months, she told herself. But at the same time, she and Reggie knew so much about one another. She loved spending time with him, and he seemed just as smitten with her. Even now, as he gazed down at her, the whole world fell away until it was just the two of them.

"We're here!" someone yelled, and that definitely brought back the reality that they weren't alone.

She turned away from Reggie to find Rosie, Cole, and Corrine coming into the kitchen. They each carried something, and Bryce looked at the stuff in their hands. "What's all this?"

"Daddy wouldn't let us leave without bringin' something," Rosie said as she handed him an oversized bag of candy.

Bryce looked at it dumbly. "So your daddy wants me to get you all hopped up on candy and then send you home?" He looked at Rosie, and then Cole, who carried a twelve-pack of Diet Mountain Dew. "Is this some sort of sick joke?"

"Wait, aren't we sleeping here tonight?" Corrine asked.

Kassie dang near tripped over her feet as she practically ran to Bryce's side. "You're not sleeping over," she said. "Are they sleeping over?"

"No," Bryce said darkly. "I'm calling Uncle Luke right now."

Corrine laughed, and foolishness rushed through Kassie. "I'm joking." She held out a bag of candy corn. "Daddy says this is your favorite."

"The candy is for you, Bryce," Cole said. "Daddy said you like those little Kit Kats."

Bryce looked at the candy, clearly shocked his uncles had sent him candy gifts. Kassie smiled to herself and leaned back into Reggie as he came up behind her. "Huh."

"It's for you, Bryce," Kassie said, grinning at him. "Better hide it in your secret candy cupboard." She took the case of soda from Cole. "I'll put this in the fridge." She moved away from everyone to do that, and while she ripped off the end of the box for Bryce and slid it into a bare spot in his fridge, another group of teenagers arrived.

Kassie stayed out of the way, though she knew Beth, Boston, Liesl, and Eric just fine. Boston was a senior this year, and he'd been working out on the ranch after school since he'd started back to school this fall. Bryce had him doing hard labor, like moving hay bales and checking fences, and she loved watching him hug his cousins.

In so many ways, he seemed like their uncle, as his closest cousin in age was Harry at twenty-three. And he wasn't here.

Reggie came toward her. "You hidin' over here?"

"No," she said, lacing all ten of her fingers with all ten of his and smiling up at him. "Did you see Codi out there? She hasn't come in yet."

Reggie blinked a couple of times, and he cleared his throat. "I, uh, haven't seen her."

Kassie tilted her head. Her heart pounded in her chest, and she could just see her momma in her head. She would not be like her.

"Reg, I don't think you've ever lied to me before." She delivered the line with an almost clinical tone. Pride moved through her, because she didn't want a man who lied to her.

"Kass," Bryce said, but she held Reggie's gaze. He at least had the courtesy to flush a deep red and drop his head.

She stepped away from him, wondering if there was something going on with Codi. No, that made no sense. Codi was with Bryce, and she'd never cheat on him. Never. Kassie had seen how Codi looked at him, and she knew Bryce loved her too, whether he'd told her yet or not.

Do you think he knows you love Reggie?

Kassie couldn't believe her thoughts as she crossed the kitchen and stood beside Bryce.

"Did you want to give the instructions for picking the pumpkins?" Bryce asked.

"Yeah." Kassie reached up and tightened her ponytail. "All right, guys," she said. "We brought in an array of pumpkins, but you don't just get to pick the one you want."

"What if we don't want any of these?" Eric asked.

"There's more outside," Kassie said. "We want everyone to do at least two tonight, so we can use them in the spooky Halloween walk this next week."

"My word," Rosie drawled. "You should hear Ladd talk about the spooky Halloween walk. He won't be quiet about it."

"All the boys at my house are excited about it," Liesl said.

"My brothers are too," Corinne said. "Daddy says if they don't help Momma with the dishes, they won't be able to come."

Kassie smiled to herself, because getting a different view of the tall, tough Young men sure was interesting.

"Sorry, I'm late," Codi said breathlessly as she came in the front door, not the back. Kassie sure had enjoyed getting to know her, but now her mouth had a strange taste in it. One she couldn't identify. "Did any of you drop something outside?"

Everyone turned toward her, almost all of them saying, "No," or "I didn't," or "What was it?"

She met Bryce's eyes, her smile blinding. "Well, there's something out here. I think someone lost something."

Penta sat at her feet, panting, and Kassie went to say hello to the dog she'd once owned. When she straightened, Codi still stood there. Something playful glinted in her eyes. "Maybe it's yours, Kassie."

"Mine?" Kassie never used Bryce's front door. "I doubt it."

"I think it belongs to a girl," Codi said.

"I'll check," Rosie said, and the rail-thin girl with plenty of attitude and confidence strode past Codi, Kassie, and Pentagon and opened the door. Kassie couldn't help edging closer to the door too. Darkness fell earlier and earlier these days, and she didn't want Rosie out there alone.

Only a few seconds later, Rosie said, "Holy cow! Come look at this!"

Everyone moved now, including Codi and Bryce and Reggie, but Kassie wasn't sure why her feet didn't take her with them. She did make it as far as the doorway, and she stood there and looked out.

Two trucks had been pulled up onto the lawn, making an L as the front of one met the back of another at an angle. Kassie frowned, because Bryce liked to keep his lawn impeccable. Then she realized what had been taped to the sides of the trucks.

Letters.

Letters that read: *Will you marry me?*

All of the teens had made a huddle, with Codi and Bryce behind them. Was he going to propose to Codi tonight?

For some reason, that surprised Kassie. One, she'd figured

Bryce would come to her for help with a proposal, and she'd heard nothing of this

A couple of people giggled, and then Kassie's eyes landed on Reggie because he walked toward her with his head down, looking at something in his hand. Something which glinted in the porch light trying to reach way out into the night.

Kassie's heart leapt and dipped and pirouetted in her chest. Bryce wasn't proposing.

Reggie was.

"Kassie," he said when he reached the bottom of the steps that led up to the porch. "I did lie to you just now, but it was the very first—and last time." He nodded over his shoulder, his sandy curls moving with his head. "Codi was out here, finishing up the letters on the trucks, but I didn't want to tell you that."

He faced her again. "I know it's fast. I know I haven't met your parents. I know there are a million reasons why we shouldn't get married or that I should wait to get to know you more. But there's also one really big thing weighing on me."

Kassie had never imagined what getting proposed to would look like or feel like. Her body felt semi-numb and frozen to the spot, but she asked, "What's that?"

Reggie grinned, that sexy, soft, playful, happy, beautiful grin that Kassie loved. "I love you," he said. "And I don't care that it happened fast. Just because it didn't take forever doesn't mean it's not real."

He held up the glinting diamond ring, pinching it between two fingers. He dropped to his knees on the bottom step and looked up at her with pure hope streaming from his bright eyes. "Will you marry me?"

Kassie bounced on the balls of her feet, pure giddiness moving through her. "Yes," burst from her mouth. "Yes, yes, yes!"

Reggie chuckled as he got back to his feet. He ambled up the steps to her, and she stuck out her left hand so he could put the ring on her finger. He did, and their eyes met.

"I love you," he whispered, and Kassie had heard those words before, but when he said them, they meant so much more. They carried so much weight. They'd been bathed in special-ness, and Kassie let her eyes drift closed so she could continue to hear the echo of those words in Reggie's voice.

"I love you too," she said, and a moment later, he touched his mouth to hers. Cheering and applause came from behind him, but Kassie barely heard it.

For she was kissing her fiancé.

41

Codi walked through the corn field Bryce had left up. He'd carved a path through it by tilling under some stalks and leaving tall ones on either side. They'd taken the twenty-five jack-o-lanterns that the teens—and Codi, Bryce, Kassie, and Reggie—had carved over the weekend and placed them along the path for tonight's spooky Halloween walk.

Bryce had arranged for everyone to come out after dark, after all of their trick-or-treating would be finished. Codi didn't really dress up for Halloween, but Bryce had worn a big, puffy pumpkin costume all day long. Some of the horses hadn't liked it, but he'd called it a "training exercise."

Everything about him excited her, and she couldn't wait to spend Thanksgiving with him and his family. She wanted to see how he celebrated his birthday, and what he'd make for dinner on the first big snowfall of the season.

She reached the next pumpkin and bent to switch on the "candle" inside. Instead of using candles, which tended to get blown out by the wind and could be a fire hazard with dry corn stalks nearby, Bryce had bought battery-operated candles that flickered almost like the real thing.

With her phone shining light on the candle, she switched the button from left to right, and it started to glow. She put it back in the pumpkin and put the lid back on, smiling at the growling pumpkin as she straightened.

She couldn't believe Kassie and Reggie had gotten engaged already. They'd met after she and Bryce had started dating. "Sort of," Codi said to herself. Kassie had met Reggie before, at big Young family functions, as his sister was one of Bryce's aunts. The Youngs invited anyone and everyone into their fold, and Codi now knew what he'd meant by "honorary aunts and uncles and cousins."

"They'll be here soon," she said as she came out of the stalks to find Bryce setting up a big bowl of candy on an overturned bucket.

He looked at her and smiled. "You put on a costume."

Codi looked down at herself. "This is a black dress."

He rose to his full height and approached her, a playful smile pulling at the corners of his mouth. "And a witch hat." He reached up to touch it, and Codi watched him.

"It's Kassie's," Codi admitted. "I'm not much into Halloween."

"You put that shark fin on Penta." Bryce took her into his arms and started dancing with her right there in the corn field.

"Mm, yeah." She closed her eyes and pressed her cheek to

his chest. "Do you think it's a little wild Reggie proposed to Kassie?" Both of them had known it was going to happen. All of the teenagers had been involved too, because they'd made and cut out the letters.

"A little," Bryce said. "But I know Kassie, and she really loves him."

With her eyes closed, Codi felt like she was falling. "I feel like I'm in love with you," she murmured. Then she realized what she'd said, and she sucked in a breath and straightened. Her eyes popped open, and she looked at Bryce in the darkness. Only a partial moon hung in the sky, and the only reason she could see him was because her eyes had adjusted to the darkness.

"You think you love me?" Bryce spoke in a higher pitched voice than normal, and Codi didn't know what to make of it.

He'd heard her. She couldn't take it back or stuff it away or pretend it hadn't been said. She couldn't run away, and the longer she looked at him, the more she wanted to stay.

"My daddy really liked you," she said. Her voice came out froggy and low, and she cleared her throat. "He said he thought you'd treat me real well for my whole life, and he didn't have a single bad thing to say about you."

"That's great," Bryce said, his voice barely louder than the crickets chirping in the night.

"I trust him." She leaned closer to Bryce. "I trust you."

"What would you say if I said I think I'm in love with you?"

Codi smiled and tilted her head back. "I'd say you better kiss me, so I can *feel* it."

Bryce did just that, and oh, he sent stars and sparkles

through her bloodstream. He never went too far or too fast, but the passion and quiet, restrained enthusiasm spoke of how he wanted to. He pulled away and licked his lips. "Well?"

"I don't think you're a liar," she whispered.

"Maybe we should talk a little bit about marriage," Bryce said. "Kids. All that."

"We should, probably, yeah."

Before that very serious conversation could begin, a series of honking horns filled the peaceful night. Bryce sighed, but Codi didn't mind the interruption. She needed to wrap her head around what she'd said, what Bryce had said, and what their next conversation needed to be.

"They're here," Bryce said needlessly. "I told them to come back and park at the barn." He turned that way, taking her hand as he did. They took a few steps together before he asked, "Do you want like, a summer wedding?" He looked over to her like he'd just asked her to do something terrible.

She grinned at him. "I think summer or fall," she said. "Autumn is my favorite season, especially here."

The sound of chattering children met her ears, and Codi looked forward. Ryder, North, and Corrine stood near the front hood of their family's oversized SUV, because Luke would not drive a minivan. Codi loved Sterling and Luke, because they'd always been so accepting of her. Luke also acted like things bothered him, but they really didn't, and Sterling was seriously the nicest woman on the planet.

"All right," Bryce said as he lifted both hands out to his sides. "We're going to line up here before the spooky stalking begins." He stopped behind a folding table they'd set up and then draped a dark tablecloth over the contents of it.

"Are you a Ninja Turtle?" Codi asked Ryder, Luke's oldest boy. He ran to her, and Codi crouched down to touch his green shell. "Wow, look at your face mask."

"I couldn't wear it to school," Ryder said.

"But you can here." Codi gave him a hug and rose to find Corrine standing there in a scary skeleton costume. "Oh, wow. I'm so underdressed."

Corrine grinned and said, "My daddy doesn't even dress up."

"Halloween is for kids," Luke said grumpily, his right arm full of a baby in a bright pink dinosaur onesie and his left hand holding his wife's. Sterling wore a clown costume, right down to the bright red curly wig.

Codi laughed at her, and then she moved over to hug her, then Luke. "Can I take her?"

"She's fussy," Sterling said. "Fair warning."

Codi took the chubby baby anyway, and Mattie looked at her with round eyes and her dino hood up over her ears. She stayed next to Bryce as more and more of his uncles arrived, and when Tex and Abby got there, Codi went over to say hello to them.

"He's not just letting us go?" Melissa asked as she slid from the back seat of the truck. "Codi, why are we waitin'?"

"Bryce has something for all the kids," she said. "Then we can do the spooky walk." She pressed her palm to Mel's back as she hugged her, and then she took in Carver's Dracula costume.

"Wow, your face is so white," she said. "Did your momma

slick your hair back like that?" It sure looked like it had taken a whole tube of gel too.

"Daddy did it," Carver said, his face full of a grin, thus negating his evilness. She grinned at him as she took in Pippa, the spunkiest girl in the family—in Codi's opinion.

"I'm a princess," Pippa said as she spun in a circle. She wore a bright pink, sparkly dress, and carried a silver wand in one hand.

"Oh, you have Mattie." Abby kissed the baby girl and slid her out of Codi's arms. "You won't be able to take her during the walk."

"Heya, Abby." Codi leaned in for a hug and when she pulled back, she met Abby's eyes.

"What happened?" she asked immediately.

Codi's smile faltered. "What do you mean?"

She looked over to where Bryce stood with ghosts, cowboys, princesses, and various animals. Abby whipped her attention back to Codi. "Something happened."

Codi wasn't sure she wanted to tell her just yet, but the way Bryce's momma just knew things was a little unnerving. "We maybe started talking about marriage," Codi said. "But don't you make a big deal out of it."

Abby's face lit up as her eyes widened. "Tex," she said.

"Abby."

"What's up?" Tex looked over to Bryce and back to Codi and Abby. His expression changed in an instant too. "Everything okay here?" He scanned Codi to her feet and back.

"Yes," she said in a normal voice. "Absolutely fine." She hugged Bryce's daddy and added, "My daddy wished he could've spent more time with you guys. Next time he's in town, we have to get together, okay?"

"Of course," Tex and Abby said together, and Codi left baby Mattie with Abby as she went to rejoin Bryce.

"Is everyone here?" he called into the night. "Who are we missing?"

Everyone looked around, and Codi still had to count all the Young brothers on her fingers. Tex and Abby were here, along with Abby's brother Wade. Cheryl carried their youngest, a little girl who'd just turned two. Their other two children—Bennett and Wyatt—stood closer to Abby than their mother.

Trace was the second oldest, and he stood very close to Ev, who looked like she might go into labor at any moment, though she wasn't due until December. They stood with their son, Clay, and their daughter, Keri. Her brother had come too, and Shawn held his wife's hand as she held their one-year-old dressed like a sheep.

Blaze and Faith were there with their three children, and Otis and Georgia had brought a couple of dogs along with OJ and Ana.

Mav and Dani had their family—Boston, Beth, Lars, and Emilia.

Jem stood next to Blaze, with Sunny over by Sterling, and Cole, Rosie, and Ladd waited near the front of the crowd for the spooky walk to begin. Luke had arrived, and that only left the twins.

Morris was still on tour with Harry, but Leigh stood with her brother, Denzel and his wife, Michelle. Between the three of them, they manned seven children in various capes, boots, and masks.

Gabe and Hilde had their four boys right in front of them, and as Codi went to stand beside Bryce, she didn't see Liesl. She had to be here somewhere, but she said, "They're all here, baby."

Kassie and Reggie hung out near the back of the crowd, and Codi was surprised they weren't off spending a quiet evening together in her private cottage. Surely no trick-or-treaters would come out here.

Bryce smiled at her and looked out over the mass of cousins, aunts, uncles, and honorary aunts and uncles. His grandparents had decided not to come, as Jerry was still a tiny bit unsteady on his feet, and they'd literally be walking through a field lit with jack-o-lanterns.

"Tonight's spooky Halloween walk got a little upgrade," Bryce said, his smile as wide as the sky. Codi wanted to bask in it forever, and now that the door had been opened to marriage and family and long-term love and commitment, she thought she might actually have the chance to do exactly that.

Lord, she thought. *Thank you so much for guiding me here.*

"It's more than just a walk through the cornfield," Bryce continued. "There are twenty-five pumpkins in the field, and I've also hidden three special keys. If you find one, you get to open one of the treasure chests."

Codi whipped off the tablecloth with perfect timing, and a gasp and *oooh* went through the crowd.

"It's not a race," Bryce said. "So no running. No pushing.

You big kids be mindful of the littles." He looked at Codi. "What am I forgetting?"

"This is fun," she said in a loud voice. "Everyone gets candy no matter what, so just try to have fun." Some of the little-little kids wouldn't even care about the keys, but Codi saw the competitive glint in Mel's eyes, as well as Lars and OJ. Those tween kids, who hadn't been invited to carve the pumpkins, but were certainly old enough to find a key in a corn field.

"All right," Bryce said, gesturing to the corn stalks behind him. "Let's do our spooky Halloween walk!"

Everyone surged forward, and Codi loved being caught in the tide of them. The Young family sure possessed plenty of energy, and she fed off of it, enjoying the enormity of the people, their personalities, and their positivity.

Bryce took her hand and they followed at a slower pace with some of the other adults. She'd walked this path before, but it seemed more magical now, with all the pumpkins lit, and little boys looking behind stalks of corn to find a key to a treasure chest.

Codi squeezed Bryce's hand and while his family surrounded them, when he looked at her, they had an entire conversation. That had always been a dream of Codi's, and she moved her hand around Bryce's arm. As he looked at her, she hugged his arm and grinned at the spooky pumpkin that had a big round O for a mouth as he screamed perpetually into the night.

42

"They're driving themselves," Abby said as she entered Carver's bedroom. Tex sat on the bed with their son in front of him, lifting his pajama shirt over his head.

"I figured they would," Tex said. "Bryce will want to stay as long as he wants, or leave when he wants to."

Abby nodded and turned to get out Carver's clothes. She'd let the kids stay in their pajamas all day today, because it was Thanksgiving. She'd made pancakes, bacon, and eggs, and Cheryl and Wade had come over for a gratitude breakfast.

Then, while the wind howled, and Mother Nature threatened to leave some snow behind, they'd cuddled together on the couch here in the basement of the farmhouse and watched movies.

Abby absolutely loved her life. She loved her husband, and she met his eye as she turned toward him with Carver's long-sleeved shirt. She handed it to Tex and sank onto the bed beside him.

"It's going to be fine," Tex said, reassuring her though she hadn't said anything. "We've eaten with the Whittakers before."

"Not with Bailey there."

"Sure we have," Tex said. "That first time, when we found out she was pregnant."

Abby remembered that summer night, and it wasn't an experience she wanted to repeat. She'd told Tex that Codi had mentioned that she and Bryce were talking about marriage, but almost another month had passed since Halloween night, and there had been no announcements on the family text, no discussions about marriage and weddings between Bryce and Tex or Abby, and no diamonds in sight.

Tex got Carver dressed and told him, "Go find some socks and your boots, buddy. We have to get goin' soon."

The six-year-old ran off to do that, and Abby couldn't help smiling at him. "I love him so much," she murmured as she leaned her head against Tex's shoulder.

"They know you do." Tex put his arm around her. "I love *you* so much. This is going to be fine."

Abby appreciated that he still told her how much he loved her. He took care of so much around the house and farm without complaint. He brought her doughnuts and her favorite soda when he went to town and she stayed out on the farm. In every way, Tex completed her, and she tried to push away her worries about the forthcoming dinner.

She groaned as she got to her feet. "I'll check on Mel." Most likely, the girl would be lying in bed, listening to something on her new earbuds. They weren't really new, but Kassie had been getting rid of them and had offered them to Mel. Since Mel adored Kassie and thought the woman walked on water, she'd taken them and had hardly removed them from her ears since.

She didn't have a phone, because Abby wasn't ready to monitor it yet, but she had an iPod that Tex had helped her load with her favorite songs, and with the introduction of this new pair of earbuds, Mel had been walking around the house listening to music more than ever before. She fed the horses and Franny while bee-bopping around, and Abby drove her and Carver to school while chattering with Carver and Pippa, because Mel was so absorbed in her earbuds.

"Mel." She pushed open her daughter's bedroom door, surprised to find her sitting at her desk. The brunette turned toward her, and Abby put one hand on her hip. "What are you doing?"

Mel whipped back around, but Abby had already seen the makeup on her face. She entered the room and moved over to the bed, which sat directly next to Mel's desk. "Where did you get that?"

"It's just a little eyeshadow," Mel said.

Abby didn't tell her she was ten. Mel knew how old she was. She'd be in sixth grade next year, at the middle school, and Abby supposed some of the girls there would be wearing makeup. *The eighth graders*, Abby thought.

She had no idea what to say to her daughter. Abby hadn't been super girly growing up, and she hadn't started wearing any makeup at all until high school. Even then, she couldn't be bothered to do much more than swipe on some mascara and use Chapstick as she ran out the door.

What do I do here? she wondered. *Lord, I need help here.*

"Where did you get it?" she asked as gently as she could. Sometimes she and Mel butted heads, and Abby didn't want that. She wanted her daughter to come to her with anything, as the next few years would bring a lot of changes to Melissa's body and life.

"Nowhere." Mel zipped up the case and reached for a tissue. She started to wipe the makeup away, which only smeared it.

"Baby." Abby pressed her eyes closed and begged God to help her. *Please. Just give me the right thing to say here. Help this bring us closer, not divide us further.*

"You'll need a special wipe to get it off," Abby said softly. "I have some upstairs in my bathroom."

Mel finally turned and looked at her, her gorgeous brown eyes wide with anxiety. "I just wanted to see what it looked like."

Abby smiled at her and reached out to gently tuck her hair behind her ear. She looked so much like Tex in her facial features, but she had Abby's thick hair and somewhat spicy spirit. "Makeup is so personal," she said, not sure where the words had come from. "Usually, you choose it based on your own skin coloring and the look you're trying to achieve."

She dropped her hand back to her lap. "What are you trying to look like?"

"I don't know," Mel said. "Aunt Cheryl had thrown it out,

and I...took it." Mel dropped her head, because she knew she shouldn't have done that.

She already knows echoed through Abby's head, and she took a breath to give herself another moment to find the right words.

"Well, when you're a little older," Abby started carefully. "We'll go shopping together and find the just-right makeup for you."

Mel looked up, hope in her eyes now. "Really?"

Abby nodded. "Really."

Mel picked up the zipper case and handed it to Abby. "Do I have to tell Aunt Cheryl I took it?"

"Where did you take it from?"

Mel dropped her chin again and mumbled, "The trashcan in her kitchen."

"I think it's probably fine," Abby said, though she'd definitely made Melissa confess her misdeeds in the past. "She was throwing it out. She probably doesn't even know you took it." And Abby could talk to Cheryl later, just to let her know.

"Now." Abby took a big breath. "Come give your momma a hug, and let's get dressed for dinner. We have to leave in only a few minutes."

Mel stood and moved into Abby's arms. She held her daughter close to her heart and said, "I love you, Mel. I am so thankful I get to be your mom." She pulled away and smiled at her little girl. "You're growing up so fast."

"I love you too, Momma." She looked down at her dress. "I'm dressed. Will you help me with the makeup?"

"Of course." Abby stood and took Mel's hand in hers. "Let's

grab Pippa too, and then maybe we can beat the boys to the truck."

Mel possessed a mean competitive streak, and that got her moving upstairs ahead of Abby. Several minutes later, Mel had a makeup-less face, and Abby had both girls in the truck ahead of Tex and Carver.

She grinned at Tex as he got behind the wheel, and he gave her a raised-eyebrow look. "Later," she murmured, and he got the truck started so they wouldn't freeze in their own driveway.

On the way across town and then up the canyon, Abby simply looked out her window, a steady stream of prayers running through her mind. She'd been begging for a miracle for so long, and as Tex made the turn and they went past the brightly lit Whiskey Mountain Lodge, Abby stopped.

"It's in God's hands," she whispered to herself. And it was time for her to exercise her faith and rely on the Lord to take care of everyone congregating at Graham and Laney Whittaker's house that evening.

She couldn't control the situation. She couldn't make anyone there act a certain way—except maybe Carver. Even Pippa already had her own mind and exercised it. She responded much better to Tex than Abby, as had Mel.

Tex pulled into the driveway, and both Bryce's and Otis's trucks already sat there. With their truck in park, Tex looked over to Abby. "Ready?"

"Can we pray first?" she asked.

"Sure." He swept his cowboy hat off his head and looked into the backseat. "We're prayin', guys."

Carver and Pippa had started to unbuckle their seat belts,

but they settled back down, and Abby's heart filled with love for them. Pure, unadulterated love. She realized then that that was what she needed to do tonight.

Love others.

"Mel, will you say it?"

"All right." Mel cleared her throat and said, "Dear God, we are glad we were able to drive up the canyon without any snow. Bless us tonight to have a good time."

She paused, and Abby thought that was the perfect prayer already. Gratitude for safety. A request for a good time.

"We love Thee, Lord, and we're grateful for our family." She paused again, and then said, "Amen."

"Amen," Abby murmured along with her other family members.

"I didn't know what to say," Mel said. "Was it okay?"

Abby twisted to look at her, and she reached back and covered Mel's hand with hers. "It was perfect, Mel."

"Let's go," Tex said. "I think we're the last to arrive, and we don't want to hold up dinner." He got out of the truck, and the kids started spilling from the back doors.

Abby looked to the ranch house where she'd been many times before. She didn't pray. She gripped her faith and got out of the truck.

Tex guided Abby up the steps, and she had Mel, Carver, and Pippa in front of her. His four-year-old went right to the door and knocked on it, of course. That was so Pippa. She wasn't worried or nervous about anything that might happen here. To her, it was just dinner, and Tex wished he could be more like that.

As it was, he had a nest of snakes in his gut as he waited for the door to open. When it did, Bryce stood there, and a grin sprang to Tex's face.

"Hey." Bryce stepped back. "C'mon in, guys."

"Bwyce, you hold me," Pippa said, and her older brother swooped the little girl into his arms. Watching him, Tex, had the distinct impression that he'd be the greatest dad ever.

"In, in," Abby said. "We're letting out the heat."

His family piled in, and Tex closed the door behind him. He took Abby's coat and Mel's, and he hung them on the hooks near the door. Bryce had receded into the house, and Tex let everyone go in front of him again.

By the time he got into the large living area at the back of the house, where Graham and Laney had a living room with two couches in it, a dining room with a table already set for a feast, and a big, remodeled kitchen, hugs and hellos were being exchanged.

He hugged Otis and Georgia, then moved over to Graham and Laney, and finally stepped into Codi.

"How are you?" he murmured in her ear.

"It's a little weird," she confided, and he liked that she'd tell him the truth. As she stepped back, she added, "Like, I don't know my place here."

"Your place is with Bryce," Tex told her, looking straight into her eyes. "Okay? *You* hold that spot."

She nodded, her smile hidden safely away. Tex nodded, as

he couldn't really say more right now. He turned and picked up Ana to give her a squeeze, and he shook Robbie's hand. Graham and Laney's son would come back to town once he finished college. Tex knew him to work at the lodge up the hill, which Graham owned with his brothers, as well as do some horseback riding lessons from here at Echo Ridge.

The plan was for Robbie to take over Springside, the energy company that had been in the Whittaker family for generations.

At last, Tex came face-to-face with Bailey. He hadn't seen her when she'd come to town previously, and his pulse streamed through his body with barely a beat in it.

The snakes in his stomach struck; his mouth turned too wet, and then as he swallowed, too dry.

"Bailey," he finally managed to say, and he put Ana back on her feet and vaguely heard Georgia tell her to come back over to her. Tex met Bailey's eyes, and all he felt was pure forgiveness. Pure love. Pure acceptance. He pulled her into a hug and held her tightly as she wrapped her arms around him too.

"You look good," he said into her ear, because none of the dyed hair or dark makeup remained. He pulled back, his smile coming back. "How are you? How's the job in Helena?"

Bailey swiped at her eyes and sniffled briefly. "I'm good, Mister Young."

"Oh, no." He shook his head. "You don't have to call me Mister Young. We're all friends here."

Bailey looked over to Abby, and Tex extended his hand toward his wife. She came to his side, and she too looked at Bailey for a long moment. Abby could be fiery and stubborn, slow to apologize and to forgive. But she always did both eventually, and he admired her so much for bucking against her natural human instincts as she tried to become more Christ-like.

"Happy Thanksgiving, Bailey," Abby said. She moved in to hug her too, and Tex got to watch as Bailey's eyes closed in relief while she embraced Abby in return. "I'm so grateful you're here."

Bailey smiled and asked, "Are you really?"

Abby pulled back and took Bailey by the shoulders. "If you knew how much your momma has prayed for this, you'd understand that yes, I'm grateful you're here, if only for her."

Bailey nodded but said nothing.

"She is so happy." Abby nodded, her smile a little wobbly. "She loves you so much." She looked over to Tex and stepped back to his side. "And so do we."

He nodded, because Abby had said everything he'd felt and didn't know how to say. She often did, which was why he loved having such a good woman at his side. She could say and do things he couldn't, and sometimes he carried that same burden for her.

"Let's eat," Laney said, and their trio-huddle broke up. The tension seemed to break too, and Tex took a deep breath as Bryce moved to Bailey's side and said, "OJ wants to sit between us." He wore a look of apprehension and he glanced to Tex, Abby, and then over to Otis and Georgia. "I'll go talk to Uncle Otis."

Tex knew exactly what would happen. Otis had told him a long, long time ago that he and Georgia knew they had to share OJ with a lot of people, and they were prepared to do that any and every time they needed to. So OJ would sit between Bailey and Bryce, and Tex stood out of the way until someone told him where to be.

He ended up between Pippa and Abby, who had the other two children on her side. Georgia sat by Mel and she had Ana and then Otis surrounding her. Codi took the next spot, and then Bryce sat next to her, and then OJ—the human bridge between them all—climbed onto the chair between him and Bailey.

Her brother sat next to her, and then Laney and Graham brought the oval back to Tex and Pip.

Everyone settled down and all eyes turned to Graham. He smiled, and Tex sure did love him too. He reached over and covered Graham's hand. The two men looked at each other, a strong, strong unspoken bond between them. They were both grandfathers to OJ, but they didn't quite get to play that exact role in his life.

OJ called Tex *Uncle Tex* the way he did for Trace, Blaze, or Mav. He called Graham *Grandpa Graham.*

"Thank you so much for coming," Graham said. "This means so much to us." He looked over to his wife, and Laney was a strong, almost stoic woman, but tonight, she wore her emotion right out in the open for all to see.

"I'd like to pray, and then we'll eat. We have a little gratitude game for later."

"Oh, brother," Robbie said, but he didn't make much more of a fuss. Tex thought he was supposed to have his girlfriend with him, but he didn't, so he wasn't sure what had happened.

Graham took Laney's hand and Tex switched his to Pippa's, and they all bowed their heads.

Tex sent up his own personal prayer that things would unfold exactly the way Graham and Laney needed them to, and then he released his breath and relaxed his muscles, ready for whatever the next couple of hours brought.

Codi found herself right at Bryce's side the way Tex had said she should be. She held his hand and Otis's, feeling strange that she was only one person between him and his son.

"Lord," Graham Whittaker said, his voice rough and husky. "We come before Thee as Thy children in humility and gratitude. We recognize the beauty around us in the mountains, trees, and the goodness of our land. We acknowledge Thy hand in our lives, in organizing us into families that have such strong bonds."

He paused, and Codi missed her momma more than ever. Tears filled her eyes, because her emotions lingered so close to the surface today. She'd spent the morning with Penta and Kassie, Reggie, and Kassie's dogs. They'd done their holiday chores, and then she'd gone to Bryce's for a simple lunch of turkey and stuffing leftovers that he'd gotten from his grandmother's pre-Thanksgiving meal she'd invited all the adult grandchildren to.

Joey had been there, and she'd done a lot of the cooking. Cash had come home for a moment in time, and Codi had met the rodeo star for the first time. Harry was still on tour, and he and Morris had sent pictures of the two of them and Harry's band and dancers at a restaurant in California, where they currently were. He'd play tomorrow and Saturday, and Codi didn't envy his lifestyle at all.

"We love Thee Lord, and we trust Thee in all things," Graham said, and Codi sure did like that. "We want to do better, and we ask Thee to guide us to the people who need us. Inspire us to say the right things to bring them back to Thee. Help us to open our mouths and speak when necessary, and give us the courage to forgive those who have hurt us in any way."

"Amen," Bryce whispered beside her, but Graham hadn't finished his prayer.

"Bless this food," Graham said. "Bless everyone here to feel of our love for them, and Thy love for them. Amen."

"Amen," chorused around the table, and as Codi pulled her hand back from Otis, he leaned into Georgia and gave her a side-hug.

"I love you." He pressed a kiss to her temple, and Georgia simply nodded at him, her throat working as she swallowed and smiled.

Codi watched Tex and Abby share a chaste kiss, and Graham pulled Laney into his chest and kissed the top of her head.

Codi turned to Bryce, wondering if he saw the same love and affection moving around the table that she did, and she found him holding Bailey's hand and tugging her closer. He pressed his lips to her cheek and said something to her that Codi couldn't hear.

Horror snaked through her and her lungs turned cold. Air

felt like liquid nitrogen, and her next breath would shatter everything inside.

They separated, and Codi quickly turned away from him, her tongue stinging and then turning slightly numb. Her fingers tingled, and when Otis looked at her, she wanted to run from the house.

But she hadn't driven herself here. She'd come with Bryce. They'd had to heave themselves off the couch and smooth the wrinkles out of their clothes and rub the sleep from their eyes to come. Codi couldn't believe that slow, easy, comfortable, perfect afternoon had happened only a few hours ago.

"You okay?" Otis asked.

She nodded and stood. "I think Laney left something over here." She walked into the kitchen, her back to the table as conversations broke out. The weight of someone's gaze on her bowed her shoulders, and she scanned the countertop for something, anything, she could take back over to the table.

Her eyes landed on a beautiful butter sculpture of a turkey, and she picked up the china plate it sat on. She couldn't turn around though, despite the fact that her lungs had unfrozen.

Bryce had chosen to show his affection for Bailey instead of her, and Codi was more confused than ever. She really didn't belong here, and as she saw the group gathered at the table in her mind's eye, she wished her seat could be taken out and the circle could just close around it.

Then where would you go? she asked herself.

Kassie and Reggie were celebrating Thanksgiving with Ev and Trace, as well as Mav and Dani. All of Bryce's other uncles were gathering at Blaze's house at the mouth of the canyon, but

Codi would never go there. Why should she find shelter with *his* family?

Because she had no one else.

Because she had no one else, and they'd all welcomed her with open arms as if she already belonged to them.

A sob heaved through her stomach, but she managed to keep it down inside.

"Hey," Bryce said, his voice tender and soft. "What's—are you okay?" He came around to stand in front of her, and Codi couldn't hide from him. Their eyes met, and she had no idea what he saw. His expression changed, and he took the plate of turkey-butter from her and slid it back onto the counter.

"Come on." He took her hand and started to leave the kitchen.

"Bryce," she said, her cells shaking and her feet feeling like wooden lumps on the end of her legs.

"We'll be right back," he called to the group, and then he pulled her into the garage.

BRYCE KNEW SOMETHING WAS WRONG WITH CODI, BUT HE didn't know what. She'd been worried about tonight's dinner, and he'd done his best to assure her that she'd been invited, that of course she'd go with him, that they were together. What he did, she should do too.

The garage held a winter chill, and Bryce shivered as he went down the steps to the larger area where he could stand more easily. He turned to face Codi, who'd remained up on the stoop. "What's going on?"

She shook her head, her lovely blonde hair brushing her shoulders. "Nothing. The last thing I want to do is cause a scene tonight."

"You were frozen in the kitchen," he said.

Codi's eyes narrowed slightly, and she said, "You don't see it, I know. I don't want to talk about it tonight. Can we just go enjoy dinner, and I'll tell you later?"

He'd always given her space and time when she asked for it, and Bryce didn't see another option here. At the same time, he wanted to know what he didn't see that she did. He started up the steps, stopping a couple down as he came to Codi's height. "You'll tell me later? For sure?"

He took both of her hands in his and watched as their fingers slid between one another. "Whatever it is, I'll fix it."

"I don't know if you can," she said. "But again, this is a far longer discussion than we can have in this garage, on Thanksgiving Day, with your family waiting for us inside." She pulled her hands away. "We'll talk about it later."

She turned and opened the door, and Bryce could watch her walk away, or he could follow her. Since it was Codi, and he wanted to be with her, he followed her into the house.

All eyes came to them, and Bryce knew Codi wouldn't like that. She said, "Sorry, everyone. Everything is fine," as she sat down and fluffed her napkin over her lap. "Oh, someone filled my plate. Thank you."

Bryce sat down, watching her, and he caught the light streaming from her face as she smiled at Uncle Otis.

He asked her something, and Codi engaged in a conversation with him and Georgia while she ate her turkey, mashed potatoes, and creamed corn.

OJ took Bryce's attention, and Codi turned and talked to him as well. Whatever had forced her from the table didn't show at all, as she laughed with Bryce and OJ, asked Bailey about her veterinary practice in Montana, and even went into the kitchen to help get coffee for everyone once the meal ended.

But Bryce knew something was wrong, and he thought and thought and thought about what he couldn't see and what Codi had.

He came up blank.

43

Everly Avery handed a cup of coffee to Kassie Goodman, the woman who would soon be her sister-in-law. She was almost a decade younger than Ev, but she brought a brand new energy to Reggie Ev hadn't seen in her brother in a while.

"Do you think he's really going to retire?" Ev sank onto the ottoman as Kassie smiled at her.

"Thank you." She lifted her coffee mug to her lips and took a tiny sip. "He better. He's planning to live in my little house and work the farm with me. I don't see how he can do that from Seattle."

"He'll have to report in February."

"We're going to be married by then," Kassie said.

Ev's eyebrows lifted. "You are?" She hadn't been aware of a date for her younger brother's wedding. "Are you getting married here?"

Kassie reached over and set her mug on the end table. She looked outside, where Trace and Reggie had gone with Keri and Clay. They also had Skip and Rachelle with them today, and Ev rested her hand on her enormously pregnant belly, so ready to welcome another little girl to her family.

She and Trace had their first two children very close together, and then she'd struggled to get pregnant again. She'd almost given up hope when she'd learned she was carrying this baby, and she and Trace had agreed it would be their last. Ev was forty now, and Trace older than that. He loved their kids and family, but he didn't want to have babies into his fifties.

"I'm going to get married in Kentucky," Kassie said. "I called my momma, and we have this amazing gazebo, and Reggie says he doesn't care where we get married, as long as we do." Kassie smiled, and Ev sure liked the soft, loving look on her face. She obviously loved Reggie, even if their relationship still seemed new to Ev. She'd fallen hard for Trace, though it had taken them years to truly be together. Everyone had a different path to happily-ever-after, and if Kassie and Reggie had fallen in love quickly, Ev wasn't going to question it.

"That's great, Kassie," Ev said sincerely. She didn't know all the details, but Reg had told her that Kassie hadn't been home to Kentucky since she and Bryce had moved here and taken over the horse farm. "So what date should I put on my calendar?"

"The wedding is going to be on February first," Kassie said.

Ev tapped on her phone and typed it in. "We'll be there." She grinned over to Kassie. "Have you told everyone? Shawn? Bryce?"

Ev had enjoyed Thanksgiving with her brothers and their

significant others. Shawn had announced that he and Enid were expecting another baby, and they'd all enjoyed good food, good company, and amazing desserts.

Now, a couple of weeks later, Ev only had three days until her due date, and she and Trace had invited Kassie and Reggie over for a Sabbath Day lunch and given Leigh a break after church with her kids.

Morris and Harry would be home in another week, and the family would be gathering here to welcome him, eat, and celebrate.

Ev wasn't sure how she'd do that with a newborn. She might still be in the hospital for all she knew. She'd put the celebration in Trace's capable hands, just like she did so many other things, her own heart and life included.

"I don't think he's told anyone," Kassie said. "I just talked to my mom this morning."

"I can put it on the family text," Ev said, her fingers poised to do just that.

Kassie nodded, and Ev's heart grew wings and soared. She smiled as she quickly tapped out the news about Reggie and Kassie. She'd no sooner sent the message and set her phone on the ottoman beside her before her baby stretched and kicked.

She pressed back against the baby, and the next thing she knew, her water broke. Pain shot from her pelvis up to her throat, and she gasped.

"What?" Kassie asked.

"My water just broke." Ev tried to stand, but she couldn't get her feet under her. A contraction started, and it felt like the baby inside her had just thrown out both legs and arms and was trying to push her uterus out as it constricted in.

Kassie shot to her feet. "I'll get Trace." She ran to the back door and opened it. "Trace! Ev's in labor!"

She'd passed out before, and Ev took a long deep breath through her nose. She'd done this before. She was going to be okay. Trace would get her to the hospital, and they'd bring their baby girl into the world.

"Ev," Trace said, his hands landing on her arms. "Look at me."

She opened her eyes and said, "We're going to need a new ottoman."

"Good thing your best friend owns a furniture store," he said without missing a beat. "Let's go. Reggie and Kassie will stay with the kids."

Ev nodded and let her husband help her to her feet. She grabbed her phone, glad the first contraction had subsided. But she knew more were coming, and she hoped she could make it to the truck before that happened.

"She's perfect," Trace whispered as he gazed down at his newborn baby girl. He took her over to Ev, who looked exhausted. Still, she shone in a way that only new mothers could, and he slid their daughter into her arms. Ev wept quietly and said, "I think Avery fits her perfectly."

"Me too." Trace pressed his lips gently to Ev's forehead and then to his daughter's tiny cheek. "I'll go tell the nurses."

"I'll see if she'll eat," Ev said, and she lifted herself up and moved the bed to support her.

Trace had a week before his eldest son would be home, and he said, "Thank you, Lord," because now he had a week to get everything ready, and Ev wouldn't be in the hospital for the party. Since it was at their house, all she'd have to do is get dressed. There would be plenty of people to hold the baby, and they'd all bring food that would last for weeks.

Trace loved his big family, and he couldn't wait to see Harry again. Morris had texted that he had a meeting after the New Year about Harry's next album and tour, but Trace just wanted his son to rest.

Touring was hard work, and while Harry was young, traveling, singing and playing, and being a public celebrity took a great toll on anyone.

Later that evening, he sat reading the scriptures on his phone while his girls slept, and he looked up from his phone when the door opened.

"It's dark," Bryce whispered. "Let's be quiet." He herded Keri and Clay into the room, and Trace set aside his phone to receive his kids.

"Daddy," Keri said as she saw him awake.

"Come on," he whispered. "Come meet your sister." He picked up his five-year-old, and Bryce picked up Clay, and they stood at the end of Ev's bed, where Avery had been bundled and slept in her little bin-bed.

"We named her Avery," he whispered. "Isn't she so cute?"

"I kiss her," Clay said, and he practically flew out of Bryce's arms as he leaned over. Thankfully, Bryce caught him and held him while the little boy kissed his baby sister.

"Hey, my babies," Ev said, her voice a bit scratchy. "Come see Momma."

"Momma, you okay?" Keri asked as Trace lowered her to Ev's side. He took Clay from Bryce and crowded him into the bed too, and then he picked up Avery and went around the bed. He passed Ev the baby and perched on the edge of the mattress with his family.

"I'll take your picture," Bryce said, and he held up his phone while everyone smiled. At least Trace hoped so. With little children, he couldn't predict what one of them might be doing.

Bryce smiled at his phone and said, "I'll send it to you."

"Where's Codi?" Ev asked as baby Avery gurgled.

Trace stood to give her more room to feed the baby, and he walked toward Bryce as the young man's face hardened.

"At home, I guess," he said.

Trace frowned as he came to stand in front of his nephew. "You guess?"

"She's...." He sighed and shook his head as he dropped his gaze to the floor. "She needs a lot more time to think through things and process them than I do," he said. "I just blurt things out, and there's—"

He looked up, his eyes blazing in the dim room. "We're working through some things."

"What things?" Ev asked.

"Ev," Trace said over his shoulder. "He doesn't want to say."

"I don't even know," Bryce said miserably. "Something happened at Thanksgiving, and she said she'd talk to me about it, but she hasn't yet." He wandered away, then turned and came back, as there wasn't really anywhere to go. "She sort of disappeared like this when I told her about OJ."

"Sit down," Trace said, indicating the only chair in the room. "Tell us everything about Thanksgiving, and we'll help you figure it out."

Bryce did sit, but he didn't blurt out anything despite his proclamation that he did. He flipped his phone over and over and over. "I miss her. We used to spend all our free time together."

"She surely misses you too," Ev said.

Trace nodded, because he'd seen Codi and Bryce together, and they were *good*. He'd thought Bryce had finally found his One True Love, the way Trace had found Ev.

Bryce sighed as he got to his feet. "Kassie and Reg had to take the other kids back to Aunt Leigh. I said I'd bring your kids here to visit real quick, and I can take them home with me."

"Yeah?" Trace said. "You hear that, kids? You want to go sleepover with cousin Bryce?"

His kids cheered and Clay slid out of bed and jumped up and down as he yelled.

"Quiet, bud," Trace said with a smile.

"Hilde will come get them in the morning," Ev said. "She'll get Keri to school and keep Clay with her."

"I'll just sleep at your place then," Bryce said. "I can crash in Harry's bedroom, right?"

"Day or night." Trace pulled his miserable nephew into his arms and held him tightly. "You'll figure out what to do about Codi, I'm sure of it."

"I hope so," Bryce said. He pulled away, and Trace recognized this sullen, withdrawn version of the man. He hadn't seen him for a while, and he didn't like witnessing it now. "Let's go, guys."

"'Bye, Momma," Keri said. "I love you so much." She cuddled into Ev, who grinned at their daughter. With everyone ready to go, Trace walked them all to the door, and he watched them walk down the hall. Well, Bryce walked. Keri and Clay skipped or ran or slowed down to look at something and then had to hurry to catch up.

Trace turned back to Ev, and he slid into bed with her while she nursed Avery. "I am the luckiest man in the world to have you," he murmured.

She laid her head against his and said, "I love you too, baby."

Gabe angled his phone toward Trace, who scanned the text. *Ten minutes out*, Morris had texted his twin, and Trace's anticipation of seeing his son kicked up a notch.

"Ten minutes," he called throughout the house. Every one of his brothers—besides Morris, of course—had come for this homecoming celebration. For the past several years, Country Quad had returned home to Coral Canyon to a big family party like this, and Trace had made sure Harry enjoyed the same thing.

He prayed this would be the last one he'd have to plan and coordinate, but Trace would do anything for his son.

The minutes passed, and before Trace knew it, the front door opened and Morris yelled, "We're here."

He and Harry came down the hall and into the back of the house, where everyone had gathered. Tears flooded his eyes at the sight of his tall, broad-shouldered, beautiful son.

"Four months on the road!" Harry yelled as he raised both hands above his head.

"Four months on the road!" everyone chorused back to him, and then Trace moved forward to hug his son first.

<h1 style="text-align:center">44</h1>

Bryce folded the flap on the metallic blue wrapping paper and ripped off a piece of tape to secure it. OJ's birthday party was this afternoon, and Bryce had spent the morning at his desk, working through finances, horses that needed to go through their final tests before he tried to sell them, and putting in any orders he needed for January.

Bailey was once again in town, and Bryce had never been more conflicted. "You don't want to be with her."

That had never been truer. He wanted Codi.

He sighed as he finished wrapping the present, and he picked up his phone. He'd invited Codi to OJ's birthday party, which would be one of the first events they'd gone to together since Thanksgiving. But she hadn't said yes. Worse, she'd said she might be out of town.

But she wasn't, as she'd worked with a horse named Pepper that morning. She came in for lunch only sometimes now, when she used to drop by every day. He still kissed her, but she never let him hold her anymore, and Bryce was sure that if he didn't make her talk or figure out what he'd done wrong and fix it, Codi would break up with him.

He pressed his eyes closed and leaned back in his chair. "I can't do this, Lord," he said. "I can't lose her. Help me."

"Bryce," a woman called and for a moment, he thought it was Codi. But it was Kassie who appeared in his doorway. "You hidin' in here? I thought you were going to take the yellow horses for a herd ride."

"I ran out of time," he admitted. He gestured for her to come in. "Can I ask you something?"

Kassie entered the office and sank onto the couch against the opposite wall. "What's up? You never run out of time."

Bryce had not discussed his relationship with Codi with anyone, but Kassie knew something had splintered. Everyone knew, and Bryce had to do something, or he'd never see his heart again. He'd never *live* again.

"Something happened with Codi, and she promised me she'd tell me, but she hasn't yet."

Kassie nodded. "Yeah, she's been over at my place a lot lately."

Bryce hesitated, and then plowed forward with the only question in his mind. "Has she said anything to you?"

Kassie sighed and looked down at her hands. That was Kassie-code for *yes*. "Not much," she said. "But Bryce, I'll just say this: you need to figure out what you want."

"What do you mean?"

She leveled her gaze at him. "Codi is amazing," she said. "If my ex, who I'd slept with *and* had a baby with, had come back into town, and I had a boyfriend, I'd want to make sure that boyfriend knew exactly where I stood."

Bryce blinked, sure he wasn't interpreting her correctly. "She thinks I want to get back together with Bailey?" That was laughable. And impossible. "Before Thanksgiving, we started talking about getting married. Me and Codi. Married. Surely she doesn't think that."

"I don't think you've done as good of a job as you need to in reassuring her that you want to be with *her*. That you want to marry *her*."

His chest constricted. "I can't lose her, Kass."

"Then don't."

Bryce ran his hand through his hair. "It's OJ's birthday party in like, an hour. I can't miss it."

"She doesn't expect you to miss stuff for OJ," Kassie said. "But." She got to her feet and came over to the desk. She put both palms on the top of it and leaned toward him. "Bryce, I love you. You know that. You're my best friend in the whole world, and Reggie says it sort of bothers him, but we're still getting to know each other. So he hasn't overtaken you yet. But Bryce, baby, he will, because while I love you, he's more important to me now than you are."

"Great pep talk," Bryce said dryly, smiling at her.

She smiled back at him. "The reason I say that is because you have to figure out what you're doing with Bailey. You don't have to be there for her. You don't have to make sure OJ's birthday is perfect *for her*. If you want Codi, go get Codi."

He looked at the wrapped birthday present, his mind whirring. "Where is she?"

"I saw her leave the ranch about twenty minutes ago. My guess is she went home."

Home.

Bryce wanted his home to be Codi's home.

Christmas Eve was tomorrow, but Otis and Georgia were celebrating OJ's birthday a day early so they could have their holidays to themselves. Bryce had no plans with Codi for the holidays, though they'd talked about eating breakfast with his family at the farmhouse.

It seemed all they did was talk *around* things. They never landed on *doing* anything definitive, and Bryce had to do something about all of this. Right now.

"I can't believe I've let us get to this." He got to his feet and picked up the birthday present. "Kassie, tell me I haven't ruined this."

Please, please, he prayed, begging God for the same assurance.

She smiled at him and moved around the desk. She cradled his face in one hand. "Bryce, you don't know who you are or what power you hold over others, I know. It's one of the greatest things about you."

He simply looked at her, because no. He didn't feel like anyone special, and he certainly had no power over anyone.

"If you show up at Codi's and just open your mouth, your heart will come out, and she'll forgive you."

"I'm so sick of relying on just opening my dang mouth."

Kassie grinned at him and said, "Go on, now. Don't call me

later, because you'll be cuddling with your girlfriend after you've made up." She walked backward for a couple of steps, and then turned and left his office.

Bryce followed her, a plan forming in his mind—but no words coming.

Of course.

He'd have to go into this blindly, as usual.

45

odi poured the hot water over the pairing of one beef bouillon cube and one chicken bouillon cube, the steam rising up to greet her. She felt semi-robotic tonight, simply moving here, then moving there.

Open the drawer. Get out a spoon. Stir the broth.

Penta had curled on his doggy bed, and Codi felt somewhat human as she smiled at the beagle.

That was what her life had become. Broth on a Tuesday night, alone, while she smiled at her only friend. She sank heavily into the couch and stared at the blank TV. She had no plans for Christmas Eve tomorrow. No plans for Christmas Day.

She leaned her head back and closed her eyes. She just wanted to get in her bus and drive. She and Penta could run away together. Since she'd been working for the past six months, she had money. She could buy some hamburgers on the way out of town and just go.

What was holding her here?

Bryce came into her mind, and that only made tears gather behind her closed eyelids. "Bryce is holding you here," she whispered. She opened her eyes and leaned forward to put the broth on the table. Knowing her, she'd start to drift off, and then she'd spill piping hot liquid all over herself.

She sniffled as she picked up her phone. It was time to talk to Bryce. He'd asked her once or twice about what she'd seen at Thanksgiving, but she'd put him off. Then he'd stopped asking. He still acted thrilled to see her every time she stepped into his house, and guilt pulled through her.

If she didn't tell him, she couldn't expect him to fix it. Feeling like a coward, she typed out a quick message to him.

I know it's OJ's party tonight, but if you have a second afterward, could we talk?

She felt like she'd been plunked down in the middle of a teeter-totter. If she moved an inch in one direction, she'd break-up with Bryce, pack everything she owned, and flee Coral Canyon. But if she went even a fraction of an inch in the other direction, she'd be on the road to happily-ever-after.

And the biggest problem was, she didn't know which way she wanted to move.

Bryce had been openly affectionate with Bailey, right in front of her. It was like he carried some mantle for her, and he wanted everything to be just right for *her* as she tried to build a relationship with the son she'd left behind nine years ago.

Codi would like to build that same relationship with OJ, but only if she was going to be in Bryce's life long-term.

"I don't know what I want," she complained to Penta, but that was only because if Codi truly admitted that she wanted Bryce, it would hurt far too badly if she couldn't have him. Needing some noise to drown out her thoughts, she reached for the remote and tapped to turn on the TV when someone knocked on her door. It sounded at the same moment her thumb touched the button, and she thought her finger had made that noise.

She jumped slightly as the screen blared to life and the sound flowed from the television. She hurried to turn it off, and then she looked toward the only entrance to her apartment.

"Codi," Bryce called. "It's me, and I have to talk to you." He knocked again, and Codi jumped to her feet and scurried toward the door. Her heartbeat zoomed and boomed at her, because he hadn't even answered her text.

Heck, she'd only sent it three minutes ago.

She opened the door to find the handsome cowboy standing there in his white cowboy hat, a denim jacket, and a delicious pair of jeans. He wore pure anxiety on his face and sexy cowboy boots on his feet.

Codi had no idea how to talk to him, and she hoped he and his usually big mouth would do most of the talking.

"Can I come in?" he started with, and she nodded as she stepped back out of the way to allow him entrance. She closed the door behind him while he paced into the kitchen and then back toward her.

He swept his cowboy hat off his head and held it in his

hands. "I'm sorry for just showing up," he said. "But I can't stand—" He swallowed. "I can't lose you. This past month has been absolutely awful, because we're not us, and I need *us* to be *us*."

Codi folded her arms and studied him. He had always been real and genuine with her, and she didn't detect anything other than that in him now. "Do you know what I saw at Thanksgiving?"

"I one hundred percent do not," he said miserably. "I've gone over it and over it, and I don't know. I'm sorry I don't know. Please tell me, and I will do whatever I have to do to fix it."

She stepped toward him and took his hat from him. He didn't stiffen and growl at her like he had the first time. She laid it gently on her kitchen table and wove her fingers through his. "After the prayer, I looked around and I saw Otis proclaiming his love for Georgia, and Graham holding Laney, and your parents kissing."

That few moments had plagued her for so long, and it had barely been a month. "When I looked at you, I guess I thought you might want to kiss me too." Her voice turned tinny, but she kept going. "Instead, you were kissing Bailey."

"I did not," he said roughly. Immediately. His eyes narrowed, and he shook his head. "No, Codi. Absolutely not."

"You're like, obsessed with her," she said, though that wasn't the right word for it. "Or rather, you're so concerned about how OJ is going to handle her in his life. It's like you want to be there to make sure everything is okay, and I'm not stupid. I know you loved her, and she still loves you, and it just feels like...maybe you should be trying to work things out with her and not me."

"No," he said again. "Just no. No." He shook his head again, those eyes blazing at her.

Codi released his hands and moved back over to the couch. Bryce jumped in front of her and sat down before her, pulling her onto his lap. She emitted a yelp of surprise, but oh, how she'd missed being held by him. She'd missed his touch, and she'd missed being so close to another person.

"Codi," he said huskily. "I acted really stupid at Thanksgiving. You're right. I do want everything between OJ and Bailey to be smooth sailing. Having her in his life makes me nervous, because I only want the best for him, and historically that's not Bailey."

She nodded and ducked her head, so her forehead rested against his temple. His hands encircled her waist and felt so warm and so right. "I don't know how to get past that," she said. "I was already feeling strange about being there, like I didn't belong, and you essentially proved to me I was right."

"I'm so sorry," he whispered. "Without you, I feel like I can't breathe. Nothing in the world is right, and I'm lost. I'm just... lost." He breathed in with her, and Codi could admit she liked what he'd said.

"I love you," he said next. "I want only you. I maybe have been too involved in Bailey's reuniting thing with OJ, and...I'll stop. I've already stopped. I just dropped off his gift this afternoon and talked to him for a minute, and then I came straight here."

He lifted his head and met her eye. "Codi, I am not whole without you. There is nothing—less than nothing—between me and Bailey."

"What did you say to her on Thanksgiving?"

"I honestly don't remember," he said. "Probably something about how I was glad she'd finally come home."

Codi nodded and watched herself fiddle with the big metal buttons on Bryce's jacket. "I still don't know how or where I belong with you."

"Then we'll keep spending time together and dating until we figure it out," he said. "To me, you belong with me. I'm all yours, and I'm begging you to forgive me and please, please don't make me go."

He gently lifted her chin until her eyes had to follow, and she looked at him. "I don't want to do anything without you at my side. You're who I want on the ranch, in the stables, at home with me. You're who I want to be the mother of my children, and the sexy goddess at my side when we go to church, and the rock and foundation of everything I am."

His words blitzed through her, the absolute truth of them sinking deep into her heart. "You sure know what to say," she murmured.

"It's all true," he said, a smile playing with the corners of his mouth. "One hundred percent."

She grinned then and slid her hands inside his jacket and around to his back. "I knew that would eventually come in."

He didn't smile for long, and his dark eyes searched hers. "Codi, I need you to say one of those things we always say."

"What's that?"

"You know, when I say, 'Hey, sorry I'm late; that horse wouldn't get out of the stall,' and you say, 'Ain't no thing, Bryce.'"

"Mm, I see."

"Or when I say, 'I love you so much it hurts when we're not together. Do you love me like that?' and you say, 'One hundred percent.'"

She tucked herself against his chest just so she could hear his heart beating. It sure did seem to be spelling out her name, and Codi never wanted to experience another moment without him.

"Or, I might say, 'I'm sorry about acting so stupid at Thanksgiving, and I will never, ever do it again. I don't like Bailey; I don't want to get back together with her; I will find clear boundaries for my relationship with her and OJ, because you're all that matters, Codi,' and you'll say...."

"Ain't no thing, Bryce," she whispered. Pure forgiveness flowed out of her, and it cleansed her from head to toe in one of the most wonderful ways of being washed she'd ever experienced.

"I love you so much it hurts when we're not together. Do you love me like that?" He swallowed, the movement touching her head and the sound of it echoing in her ears.

Codi lifted her head, and instead of saying "One hundred percent," she said, "I love you with my whole heart, Bryce."

His smile could've blinded her, but she closed her eyes and basked in the glory and light of his happiness.

"I'm going to kiss you now," he murmured.

"One hundred percent you are," she managed to get out just before his lips touched hers.

46

odi woke on a clear, crisp morning a couple of days after Christmas. Spending the holidays with Bryce and his family had been the highlight of her life so far, and she rolled over and picked up her phone.

The clock hadn't struck seven yet, but she fired off a text to Bryce that said, *Happy birthday, baby! I will have coffee and breakfast pastries for our drive today.*

She'd already told him that Joey had come over last night to make said breakfast pastries, and she got out of bed to go get the coffee started. They had a seven-hour drive to Boise to complete that day, and Codi had a feeling sweets and coffee would be the least of the things they'd consume to get themselves across that city border.

On Christmas Day, once they'd opened gifts at his parents' house, and eaten too many chocolate chip pancakes and then driven to Kassie's to celebrate with her and Reggie, Bryce had taken Codi back to his house.

He'd walked her through all the bedrooms, including his —*theirs* once they got married—and then he'd said, "I have something I have to do, and I really, really want you to be at my side when I do it."

He'd laid out the story of his mother, who lived in Boise. He'd clenched his jaw through parts of it, and when he'd told Codi that he hadn't spoken to his mom in over six years, she'd wept with him.

"I just have to clear the air there," he said. "I want to do it before the New Year. I think we both have baggage we need to leave in Boise, and then we can move into next year together."

She'd agreed, and she'd packed last night while the cream cheese Danishes had baked. Joey had helped her, and she'd told more stories of Bryce and his mother.

Codi fed Penta, humming to herself in a very human way this morning. Gone was Robot-Codi, and she still puttered around the apartment in her pajamas when Bryce showed up. Only slightly embarrassed, she let him in and said, "Let me get dressed real quick."

"Mm, no." He grabbed her hand and pulled her back to him. "Let me kiss you first, and then you can get dressed real quick." He grinned at her, but when he united their mouths, he kissed her with all the straight-mouthed passion of a man in love.

Codi had never, ever been kissed like that, not even by the man she'd loved and been engaged to. Her fingers shook at the idea of going by Lester's today, but she'd committed to doing it. She and Bryce had a deal, the way she made bargains with her horses, and Codi never backed out of a deal she'd made.

"Okay," he murmured. "Go get dressed. I'll get our coffee in thermoses."

She hurried to pull on jeans and a sweater in a splashy brown and black leopard print. In the bathroom, she grabbed her wig and then paused. She never gave much thought to her hair, because it took a few minutes to put on a headband and secure a wig in place and she was good to go.

But today, she carefully put down the wig. She'd been wearing it less and less, especially around the ranch where she never wore it. But to see Bryce's mother? Perhaps Lester?

She'd arranged to have dinner with her daddy and brothers that night too.

"Sweetheart?" Bryce stepped into the doorway of the bathroom, and their eyes met in the mirror. He said nothing, and Codi drew courage from his strength.

"I'm ready." She turned into him and ran her hands up his chest. "Maybe we should just go get out that pair of horses Kassie got yesterday. It'll be just as brutal of a day."

Bryce didn't look away from her, his expression staying serious. "I will be at your side."

He might as well have said he loved her, which he had said every day since he'd shown up at her apartment instead of going to OJ's birthday party. He'd *chosen* her, and that meant the world to her.

No one had ever chosen her before.

"And I'll be at yours," she said, and then she left the wig sitting on the bathroom counter as she went to get the bagged Danishes she and Joey had prepared for this drive to Boise.

47

Bryce's throat narrowed and he reached for Codi's hand. "Only one more turn," he murmured.

"Your daddy said she's still there?"

He could only nod. He'd told his momma and daddy about this trip, and while neither of them had wanted him to take it, they also understood why he had to. For him, it felt like the only thing holding Bryce in the past, where he could get hurt endlessly, was his mother.

And he was done being held back.

He wanted to step into and build a new future with Codi, and he felt like he couldn't if he was dragging along these old hurt feelings, this horrible last encounter with his mom.

He made the turn, his muscles feeling like someone had turned his blood into super glue and it had just hardened throughout his body. "It's that one right up there on the left."

He knew that sounded stupid. Right up there on the left? At least six houses sat on the left side of the street.

Bryce eyed the pale blue one, though, where he'd stood on the stoop and let his mom deny he existed. He hadn't called to arrange anything this time. Daddy had checked to make sure Corrie hadn't moved, and she hadn't. Her work still listed her home address as this one where Bryce had lived before moving to Coral Canyon with his daddy.

In fact, her car sat in the driveway. He recognized it, because his mother was a lot like him and a pure creature of habit, and she obviously hadn't bought a new car in years and years. He didn't see the point of buying new things just to have new things either, and that was just another thing they had in common.

Or maybe she'd taught him that, as she had raised him for the first seventeen years of his life.

He pulled up to the curb instead of in the driveway, and he looked out his window at the house. "Her name is Corrie," he told Codi.

"You said that," she gently reminded him. "Let's just go say hello. Five minutes, right?"

"Right." They'd agreed that they each only had to endure this terrible, no-good thing they didn't want to do for five minutes. Then he could return to his truck, jam his foot on the gas pedal, and get away.

Of course, it would take longer than that, as he collected Lucky's leash, hooked it to his dog's collar, and then let the golden retriever out. Snow littered the ground in Boise, which wasn't surprising for late December, but Lucky had gotten used to the cold and slush since they'd moved to Wyoming.

He found a spot he deemed good and took care of his business while Codi took Penta down the sidewalk a ways to do the same thing.

They came back together, the two of them and their dogs, and Codi put her gloved hand in Bryce's. "I'm right here."

"And you love me."

"One hundred percent."

Sufficiently reassured, Bryce led the way up to the front door. He rang the doorbell and settled back onto the heels of his cowboy boots. Surely his mom would recognize him, though it had been quite a while since he'd darkened this doorstep.

"I just hope she's sober," he muttered as they continued to stare at the black-painted door.

It opened only a moment later, and Bryce knew instantly that Corrie was sober. She wore a pair of dark slacks and a white blouse with black polka dots on it. Her eyes widened when they landed on Bryce, and he said, "Hey, Mom."

His gaze slipped to her left hand, but she didn't wear a wedding band this time. Her dark hair barely made it to her chin, and she actually looked better than Bryce had seen her in over a decade.

"Bryce." The name held mostly shock and air, and her eyes had never been wider. They darted over to Codi, and Bryce pulled her closer like he could protect her that way.

"Are you married still?" he asked.

His mother's eyes filled with challenge, and then regret. "No."

He chin-nodded to Codi, as he hadn't found a way to look away from his mom. "We're just passing through for a minute, and I wanted to—" He cut off, because no, he hadn't *wanted* to see her.

He'd *needed* to see her. Big difference.

"This is Codi," he said. "I'm in love with her, and she loves me, and we're going to get married this year."

His mom nodded and hugged herself, probably against the cold. "That's great news, Bryce."

"If you want to come," Codi said, sending surprise through Bryce. They hadn't rehearsed anything before they'd arrived. He'd told her as much as he'd been able to about his mom and why he felt the way he did about her, and they'd made the drive.

Five minutes.

He only had to be here for five minutes.

"You can," Codi said. "But Bryce is this amazing, hard-working, incredibly talented man, and the guest list will be small. We're only inviting our *closest* family and friends."

Hint: If his mom wanted to come, she had to put in some effort to be in Bryce's life.

"It's happening on this ranch I own in Coral Canyon," Bryce said. "But again, the guest list will be really small." He looked at Codi then, and she wore a big, beautiful smile just for him.

"Bryce," his mom said, and they both looked back to her. "You have no idea how sorry I am for what happened."

Bryce tilted his head at her, a measure of sassiness flowing through him. "Which time, Mom?"

She looked like he'd thrown a bucket of ice water in her

face. He sighed. "I'm not interested in discussing it all right now," he said. "We stopped by unannounced, and you're clearly working from home." He looked at Codi. "We have another stop to make, don't we, baby?"

"Yes, we do," she chirped.

Bryce backed up a step, tugging on Lucky's leash to get the dog to stand. "Come on, Lucky-Lucks. We've gotta go."

Codi turned first and let Penta go down the steps ahead of her. Bryce followed, and his boot had just touched the sidewalk at the bottom of the steps when his mom said, "Bryce." She came flying out of the house toward him.

He barely had time to catch her before she landed in his arms, and he grunted against her weight. Then, because she was his mother, and he was her son, he hugged her tight, all the tension in his muscles simply disappearing into the atmosphere.

The bond between parent and child couldn't be described. Though he wasn't raising OJ, it was the same strong, binding, everlasting connection Bryce felt with him.

"I have a new number," she said through tears as she pulled away. "Take it, okay? Could I—could I call you sometime, maybe?"

He nodded, his throat once again swollen shut. She recited her number, and Bryce was so emotional, he let Codi type it into her phone. "Got it," she said. "It's great to meet you, Corrie."

She put her hand in Bryce's and said, "Come on, baby. It's really cold out here."

He looked at his mother for another long moment, and then he nodded, turned, and let Codi get him out of there.

He stood numbly as the dogs got in the back of the truck; Codi unclipped their leashes and asked, "Do you want me to drive?"

Bryce nodded and went to get in the passenger seat. Once Codi had driven them away from the blue house, and once he'd started to warm up from the heater blowing so hard, he looked away from the houses and landscape blurring past him. "That wasn't so bad."

"No, but we didn't want to stay, remember?" She glanced over to him. "You've already initiated so many things, Bryce."

"Yeah." He nodded his agreement. "Yep. I just—I wasn't expecting that. I almost don't know what to do with it."

"Well, I'm a little peeved she gave you her number and didn't ask for yours, because now, *you'll* have to be the one to reach out first. Again."

Bryce thawed the rest of the way at the discontent in her voice. "Someone's overprotective of me."

Codi's shoulders did a little shimmy and shake. She kept her gaze solidly out the window as she said, "One hundred percent."

Bryce laughed then, because it sure felt good to be with someone who wanted to protect him. His parents were like that, as was Kassie, but with Codi, it stemmed from a different kind of love.

A healing love.

A peaceful love.

A stunningly beautiful and passionate love.

"I can't wait to get married," he said. "Are you still stuck on September?"

Codi cut him a look out of the corner of her eye now. "The ranch is beautiful in September."

"You haven't even seen it in the spring," he said. "It's gorgeous then too. Wildflowers for miles."

"I might be persuaded to move the wedding up," she said. "You know, if I had an engagement ring." She made a big show of looking down at her left hand. "Oh, but look at that." She held out her hand as if he couldn't see it. "I don't."

Bryce chuckled. "All right, all right. Point taken." Now, he just needed to find a ring, plan the perfect proposal, and ask her to be his wife.

Oh, and they had to make it through Codi's uncomfortable baggage drop-off too.

Codi strangled the steering wheel as she drove, every mile the wheels turned somehow churning through her gut too. She cut a look over to Bryce, who had his head buried in his phone. "What are you lookin' at?"

She didn't want him messaging his mother right now.

"Diamonds," he said, and that only made every cell in Codi's body glow. He looked at her. "I'll put it away. Sorry." He tucked his phone under his leg and looked out the windshield and then his passenger window. "Hey, thanks for getting me out of there."

"Of course," she said. "You're going to do the same for me."

"I thought we were eating dinner with your family and staying at the farm tonight."

"We are." Codi shifted in her seat. "It's not that I'm worried about." She cleared her throat. "Lester's house is on the way."

Bryce swung his attention to her. "Are you stopping? I didn't realize we were stopping."

"If he's outside, I said we'd stop," she said, rotating her shoulders up near her ears. "I mean, I told myself that, and now I'm telling you."

"What are the chances that he'll be outside in the four seconds when we drive by?"

"He liked to sit outside," she said. "It could happen." Especially since they'd been traveling all day, had stopped to eat lunch, and the work day was almost over. In fact, since the sun had already started to go down, it was highly likely that Lester would be home and sitting on his porch.

Dear God, Codi thought, but she didn't know how to finish the prayer. "Do you ever just start a prayer and hang there?" she asked.

"Every morning while I'm waiting for my toast to pop up." Bryce simply said the words like everyone in the world had the same raging indecision inside them that Codi did. He reached over and took her hand from the wheel. "You're sort of squeezing that thing really hard."

He lifted her hand to his lips, and Codi settled for a moment as his skin touched hers.

"If he's sitting outside," Bryce said, "You get five minutes to say whatever you want to him. I'll be right at your side."

"Maybe I'll just show you where he lives."

"He's still there?"

Codi squeezed his hand at the same time she clenched her

teeth. "Warren said he was. Said he'd moved on to another farm, and then another, and then another. It's his fourth or fifth since working for my daddy."

Bryce nodded, but he didn't ask anything else about Lester. Codi had told him her ex-fiancé wasn't a nice man and hadn't treated her well, but she hadn't gone into too many other details.

"He stole from us," she blurted out, glancing over to him. "Almost ten thousand dollars. I didn't believe my daddy when he told me." Her chest shook as she realized what a terrible deal she'd made with herself. "I can't do it, Bryce. I don't want to see him."

"Okay." Bryce spoke calmly and easily. "Codi, he's not your daddy or your brother, the way my mom is. If you don't want to see him, then you don't have to see him."

"Every time I think of him, I think of all the mistakes I made," she said miserably. "That I didn't listen to my daddy. That I made excuses for the things Lester would say about me, to me. That I didn't value myself enough to stand up and say something until it was almost too late."

"Hey." Bryce tugged on her hand. "Pull over for a second."

She did so—pulling her hand back to the steering wheel—without questioning him, her tears so close to the surface. "Just answer a couple of questions for me," he said gently. "If you want to pass, you say pass."

She nodded, her eyes fixed on her hands gripping the steering wheel.

"How long ago did you break up with him?"

"Almost eight years," she said.

"Have you made things right with your daddy?"

"Yes."

"What have you done wrong that still needs to be fixed?"

Codi opened her mouth to say something, then looked up and out the window. Boise was white from sky to ground, as another storm system sat heavy in the sky. The black highway stretched in front of her, the only contrast to the blinding whiteness around her.

"Nothing," she said, turning to look at Bryce.

He smiled at her, and it held so much joy. "So we're going to leave all the Lester baggage right here on this highway. You have nothing to apologize for. You have nothing to fix. Not anymore. You did that. It's done."

"It's done," she repeated.

"You can point out his house as we drive by, and I'll toss your baggage onto his lawn." He chuckled. "Deal?"

Codi nodded. She took a deep breath. "Yeah, that's a good idea." She gazed at the tall, dark-haired cowboy sitting in the passenger seat. She reached for him and drew his face closer to hers. "I love you," she whispered. "Thank you for this."

"I'm right here, baby," he whispered. "At your side. Always." He touched his lips to hers, and Codi enjoyed the slow, sweet kiss on the side of the road. He pulled away, and she kept her eyes closed for another moment.

Then she too faced the front again, ready to leave everything that she'd been carrying for too long right here. As she put the truck in drive and eased back onto the road, she did exactly that.

Another three miles down the road, she pointed toward Bryce. "That's his place right there. Comin' up on the right."

Lester had a red brick house that sat about thirty yards down a dirt lane. The front yard had been fenced, though Codi didn't see any animals. "That fence is new."

"That big truck looks new too," Bryce commented.

"His step-mom manages a car dealership in town," Codi said. "He's always got something new."

Bryce simply hummed, then he mimed like he was throwing something out of the window, like a hook shot a basketball player might make, launching the ball in a sideways arc over his head. Codi grinned and then giggled.

"All gone," he said.

"Yeah." She threaded her fingers through his. "This trip was a good idea. I didn't think so at first, but I'm glad we came."

"Me too," he said. "I've got to meet your brothers anyway, and I'm so ready for the New Year now."

"So am I," Codi said, and she definitely had more sunshine filling her now. Her shoulders didn't ache quite so much, and she smiled the rest of the way to the potato farm where she'd grown up. As she made the turn onto the land, she said, "This is it."

"Looks like a lot of nothing," Bryce teased.

"You should see it in the summer," she said. "It's rows and rows of greenery for miles and miles and miles."

"Oh-ho," he said with a chuckle. "You sound like you actually like the potato farm."

"I didn't hate it," she said quietly. "I hated everything Boise had become for me after my momma and daddy got divorced. It was a prison here. I was trapped, and I didn't know how to get out."

"I know, sweetheart." He put his hand on her thigh. "It's a good thing you finally got that bus done, so you had a way out."

She smiled as the dormant, snow-covered fields rolled by and the farmhouse came into view. "Rand built a place here. Daddy still lives in the house. Warren has a cabin a little further out. They all run the farm still."

"Randall, Rand, and Warren," he repeated. "Got it."

"And my sisters-in-law are...?"

"Rand's wife is Rachel," Bryce said without missing a beat. "They have two kids named Ryan and Riley, and it's more R-names than anyone should have in a single family." He grinned at her. "Warren and Sierra just got married, and they don't have kids."

Codi grinned at him. "So when we have kids, we won't stick to one letter?"

"I would prefer not to," he said.

"You're B and I'm C," she said. "Our first kid could be named...Diana or something. D, then E, then F. We could go in alphabetical order."

"Oh, brother," he said with a groan. "No to all of that. Just no."

"So what do you want to name one of our kids?"

"I don't know," he said. "My uncle Blaze said they had a couple of names picked out before their baby was born, and when they saw her, they just knew one was right. I think it'll be kind of like that."

Codi sure did love talking about their future with him, and she pulled up next to her dad's rickety old truck. "Okay," she said, and she started to get out of the truck.

"Codi."

She turned back to Bryce, who wore a glinting, almost dangerous look in his eye. "Do you want babies right away? Or are we waiting after we get married, or...?"

She blinked at him, a touch of surprise in her thoughts. "I'm thirty-two, Bryce. You own a ranch that we'll work together. I'm ready as soon as that diamond gets purchased."

A delicious smile curved his mouth, but she still asked, "What about you? Do you want to wait to have kids?"

"I do like just being with you," he said. "Just me and you. No distractions."

"Mm, yes, I can see that life too." She gazed out the windshield, unsurprised to see the curtains fluttering in the front window as she thought about her and Bryce, alone but together on the ranch. Working there. Living there. Riding horses there, and gathering eggs, and planting pumpkins.

She took a deep breath and held it for a moment. "I suppose we'll see what the Lord will bless us with." She looked at him as she exhaled and then she kissed him quickly. "Come on. They're waiting for us."

As she walked inside, she realized that she didn't need to fear coming to Boise anymore. Lester didn't own a single piece or particle of her heart, because she'd reclaimed it all and then given it to Bryce—and he took very, very good care of the things he cared about.

48

"N o, no, no," Blaze Young said as Morris practically trampled him. "Do you know your left from your right? We said you'd go left and Gabe would go right." He glared at Morris and then Gabe, though he'd done the move correctly.

"Reset it," Mav called, as if he were a real band dance choreographer instead of a pretend one.

Blaze honestly had no clue how Morris had coordinated everything for Country Quad, or how he'd played professional football, when he couldn't even do a few simple dance moves.

"Ready?" Jem asked, and Blaze nodded to him. He held a guitar in his hands, because yeah, they could all play. No, he, Jem, Morris, and Gabe had never been in the family band. That was what had broken them all up years ago.

Fine, Blaze had left town for Las Vegas the very moment he could. That hadn't helped either.

He started playing, as did Morris, with Gabe on the piano for a few bars. Then he got up, and Morris went the right way this time, sparing Blaze's toes. They completed the song, dropped into their predetermined poses, their arms up and splayed left and right. In that moment of time, Blaze didn't think it was half-bad.

Their audience today consisted of Mav and Luke, both of whom stared at the four of them in their ridiculous pose, Very Serious expressions on their faces. Finally, Luke broke into a smile and said, "That's perfect, guys. He's gonna love it."

"It's not about him," Gabe said as he got to his feet. "It's about whether *Codi* will like it."

"I think Otis is going to lose his mind," Luke said with a laugh. "Tex will too."

"Trace might murder us in our sleep," Jem said as he set his guitar on the stand. They'd taken over Jem's basement to practice for the New Year's Eve talent show that Momma was making everyone participate in. Literally everyone who could walk and talk had to do something, even if it was something simple like breathe in and out. Fine, it was more than that, and Blaze might've possibly been in a surly mood tonight.

He'd be sure to iron it all out before tomorrow night's party, but Faith had been bribing all three of their kids to sing songs Blaze couldn't get them to *stop* singing just to have something for Grace, Celeste, and Tyrone to do.

Cash was home now that the rodeo season was in a break, and he'd agreed to do some yodeling. Blaze didn't even want to know what that sounded like, though the thought of his son always made him smile.

Upstairs, he found his oldest with Faith and Sunny in the kitchen, and they turned as the brothers crowded into the space. "Done already?" Sunny asked, her very pregnant belly coming between her and Jem as he leaned in to kiss her.

Cole and Rosie loitered in the living room, along with the only child Jem and Sunny had together—Ladd. They'd have another girl come February, and Jem had been praying she'd be sweet as apple pie since Rosie seemed to bathe in saltwater.

Blaze loved the twelve-year-old fiercely, because she reminded him of himself. She had a strong mind, and she spoke it. She questioned her daddy relentlessly, and Jem needed to be pushed. He'd become an excellent father and husband in the past several years, and he hadn't slipped once in his sobriety.

"It's a lame dance number to a song we've been singing since we were boys," Jem said. "How long did you think we'd be down there?"

"Longer than fifteen minutes," Faith said, giving Blaze a look he knew well. One that said he better practice some more, or else. A questioning look he didn't like.

"It's for Bryce's proposal," Sunny said. "Maybe you should show it to us."

"No, I don't think so," Gabe said.

"I have to go," Morris said.

"I thought everyone was staying for dinner." Sunny raised her eyebrows and looked at Morris, who'd clearly just been caught in a fib.

"I'm not doin' it again," Blaze said darkly. "It's a family party, at a coffee shop that can barely hold us all and happens to have a teeny tiny stage in the corner." He turned away from his wife, because her eyes now told him not to be so grumpy. "Momma and her ideas."

He sighed as he retreated to the dining room table. Cash joined him, and Blaze looked at his son. "Are you really going to yodel?"

"Well, I couldn't get Grandma to bring in one of those electronic bulls that buck, so yeah, I guess so." He grinned at Blaze and pulled Celeste onto his lap as she tried to climb up on her own. Blaze looked at his two kids, their ages so far apart. Cash would be twenty-two in another month, and Celeste had just turned six. Sometimes he felt like he was living two halves of the same life, because he actually was.

And this one, he'd worked really, really hard to get. He leaned over and cuffed his son on the back of the head. "I love you, boy."

"I love you too, Daddy."

"You're not hurt anywhere? You sure you don't need to go to the doctor?" Blaze had rode the rodeo for a long time. The off-season was for healing and then working out to be as strong as possible for the next go-round.

"Dad, I'm fine."

"Okay," Blaze said, accepting the answer. "But the moment you're not, we go to the doctor." He pinned Cash with a fierce look. "You don't want to be me and having surgeries every other day."

Cash grinned and shook his head. "It's not every other day, Daddy."

"Yeah, I know," Blaze grumbled as Faith put a big casserole dish on the table, a long, wide potholder underneath it. He met her eyes again, and this time he smiled. She came over to him and leaned down to kiss him.

"Do I need to make you practice your part at home?" she asked.

"No, ma'am," he assured her. "Bryce's proposal is going to go off without a hitch." He met Morris's eye, and he nodded.

"Totally," he said.

"Yeah, I believe you," Leigh said with a giggle. "Michelle said y'all can get into the coffee shop early tomorrow night if you want to practice on the stage."

"Maybe we should do that," Gabe said.

"Go get Daddy," Hilde said from the front of the house, and the next thing Blaze knew, Gabe's four boys ran into the room, all of them shouting and clamoring over one another. Hilde lifted her hand as she came into the room with Liesl, and in Blaze's opinion, she looked one breath away from collapsing. "We're here."

Gabe shone with pure light as he picked up his boys—all four of them—and somehow had lap space for each of them. The triplets all talked over one another, and Canyon held out a blue bouncy ball without a word.

Jem sat beside Blaze, also watching Gabe. "See why we waited five years to have another baby?"

"But it still could've been you if Sunny was having multiples," Leigh said. "It's not like you *plan* to have triplets." She looked over to her own multiples. "I praise the Lord every day that we only had two."

She grinned, because while Blaze knew Leigh loved her kids, he also knew how hard it was to be so outnumbered.

"All right," Gabe finally said above the chaos. "Everyone ten and under to their table." He and Morris got up to get all the kids where they needed to be, because they were mostly their kids. Cash helped Grace and Celeste, and Faith held Tyrone on her lap, because the boy wasn't quite two years old yet.

"Want me to take him, dove?" Blaze started to take the little boy from his wife, and Tyrone smiled at him.

"Da-Da-Da," he babbled. And those really were the best words in the English language.

As all the adults and older kids settled at the table, Blaze did look at Gabe and Morris and Jem again. "Fine," he said. "We'll meet at the coffee shop at six to go over the stupid dance again."

Jem grinned at him, and Gabe said, "Perfect. I'll tell Bryce," with his fingers already flying over the screen to do exactly that.

Bryce knew the moment he'd been preparing for had come when he saw Uncle Mav and Uncle Luke with headsets on. He grinned and grinned and moved away from Codi's side. "I'll be right back," he said.

She started to say something, but he rushed away from her before she could keep him at her side. Aunt Dani gestured to him from a crack in the black plastic door that led into the kitchen area of the coffee house, and Bryce ducked through it.

"Here you go," she said, handing him the diamond ring. He hadn't even seen it yet, at least not in person. He'd ordered it, and he'd gathered together a group of his uncles to help him ask Codi to marry him.

She loved his family, and Bryce wanted to give the non-band brothers a chance to perform. Luke had volunteered to be the band manager, but Mav had said he actually had experience with that and would rather do that than be behind a mic.

He stared at the diamond Aunt Dani had picked up for him last night, sure this wasn't real. "I can't believe I'm doing this."

"You're not backing out now," Aunt Dani said with a smile. It faltered a little as she glanced over to Aunt Sunny. "I mean, you still want to marry Codi, right?"

"Yeah, of course." Bryce swallowed and looked at his aunts. Sunny hadn't even been around during everything, but she wore such happiness and love on her face. "I just...this doesn't feel real, you know? Like, who gets a second chance like this?"

"Everyone does, honey," Sunny said. "God gives *everyone* a second chance."

"Sometimes a third and fourth chance," Dani said.

"She's too good for me," he said as he heard the first strains of guitar music from out in the coffee shop. Unsurprisingly, they'd been listening to a lot of guitar playing at tonight's New Year's Eve talent show. Heck, he and Harry had already done their duet, and Kassie had strummed a ukulele while Reggie moved his hips left and right in some sort of strange baseball-player-hula dance.

"She's perfect for you," Sunny said with a smile. "Now go on. I can't even imagine the wrath of Blaze if he's doing this and you're not out there."

"Good point." Bryce kissed her cheek and then Aunt Dani's. "Thank you, you guys." He pushed back out into the coffee shop, the air much hotter out here due to all the bodies. He was pretty sure the maximum capacity sign near the door had said sixty-eight, and they definitely had more people than that.

"What's going on here?" Bryce's dad asked as Jem ran onto the stage first, just the way Daddy usually did. He was followed by Blaze, then Gabe, and then Morris. They didn't have a drum set, but the way Morris stood in front of Jem and roared at the crowd with both of his hands up clearly told everyone these four brothers were imitating Country Quad.

Otis started to laugh, and all the kids cheered, and Bryce took the opportunity to slide behind Denzel and Michelle and hide between Aunt Hilde and Aunt Leigh, who'd both agreed to make a screen for him, and the wall.

"Ready, baby?" Hilde asked, and Bryce nodded at her.

Morris ripped off his plaid shirt, and Luke whooped like this was the greatest show of his life. Bryce peered past Leigh, who held Remi in her arms, and found his father laughing too. He and Abby sat at a small table right up front, and Bryce immediately started looking for Codi.

She held Pippa on her hip, the two of them grinning like mad too. Good.

Okay, he thought as he took a deep breath and Blaze started playing the guitar. *Lord, I could use all the words in the world right now.*

He closed his eyes and listened to Fake Country Quad play through a love song all the Youngs knew, because Grandma had told them all—multiple times—how she'd met Grandpa at a church dance, and their very first dance was to this song.

They'd removed all the verses except one, and as the chorus

came to a close, Bryce edged even further forward, the gold band he pinched between his fingers starting to hurt.

He watched as Morris and Gabe switched sides, and then all four of his uncles dropped to their knees on the last few words. "I'd love you forever."

Their arms went up, and Bryce's heart froze. His feet froze. Everything in the world, for him, froze.

The coffee shop crowd around him went wild. Absolutely wild for Fake Country Quad and the old love song from fifty years ago.

"Bryce," Blaze growled, and his eyes locked on his uncle's.

He moved then, every cell in his body on fire. He stepped to the front of the stage, which was only raised about two feet from the main floor of the coffee shop. Michelle had said she hosted poetry nights and sing-ins on the weekends.

He dropped to both knees too, and Aunt Faith appeared with the mic, holding it right up to his lips. "Can I get Codi up here, please?"

That quieted everyone down, which made Abby's words of, "Oh, Tex, he's doing it," loud enough for everyone to hear.

The crowd turned and parted, and Codi stood there, her eyes wide and her mouth wider. She slipped Pippa into Kassie's waiting arms, and then she walked to the front of the coffee shop, mere feet from where Bryce knelt with four of his uncles behind him in the same pose.

"I love you," he said into the mic, and he'd sort of bellowed it in all his nerves, causing a screeching sound of reverberation to fill the coffee shop.

Groans and cries filled the air, and Aunt Faith pulled the mic back a few inches. "Sorry," Bryce said. "I'm so nervous."

Codi smiled at him and said, "Bryce, baby. Look right at me."

He did, and he hadn't even realized he hadn't been looking at her. She wore a wig tonight, and why she chose to wear them sometimes and not others, he didn't know. He didn't know everything about her yet, and he wondered if he ever would.

"Codi, I know I'm in love with you," he said steadily, no yelling quality in sight. "I want you out at the farm permanently with me and Lucky and a whole mess of horses and pumpkins and chickens, and I would be the happiest and luckiest man in the whole world if you would be my wife." He held up the diamond ring, his question-that-wasn't-a-question ringing in the now-silent coffee shop.

Codi wiped at her eyes and said, "Wow, you've silenced even the babies."

"We get a rare ten seconds every now and then," Bryce said, grinning at her.

She took another step toward him and looked at the diamond ring. "I suppose you want to get married in the spring."

"It's better than the fall," he promised. "I swear you'll love it."

"I love you," she said, and several of the women ahh'ed. "Of course I'll marry you."

"Praise the heavens," Blaze called just before the cheering from the over-capacitated coffee shop started. Bryce slid the ring onto Codi's finger, sure liking the way it looked and what it meant.

She was his.

He was hers.

"Help me up," Blaze complained. "If I'd have known I'd be down there for half my life, I wouldn't have agreed to this."

Codi dropped to her knees as the clapping, cheering, and yeehaw-ing continued around them. He could only see her, though plenty of the noise around him streamed into his ears.

"Yes, you would've," Aunt Faith said. "Look at them."

Bryce leaned forward and kissed Codi, not caring who saw, because he didn't have anything to hide, from anyone. "I love you," he murmured, beyond grateful he'd hung on for one more day, rebuilt and renewed his faith, and kept trying until this miracle could occur in his life.

It wasn't too late for him, just like Jesus Christ never arrived too late to perform the miracles required of Him.

"I love you too," Codi said, and then she kissed him again. Pure love filled him. Love for Codi. Love for his family. Love for the gift of forgiveness and repentance.

Love, love, love—and that meant something to Bryce, who'd once thought that he'd never be loved again, by anyone on Earth and certainly not by God.

She pulled away from him, and Bryce got swept into the arms and congratulations of his momma and daddy, their love for him the anchor that had kept him safe for so long.

Yes, Bryce was so thankful for the gift of love, and he couldn't wait to marry Codi and start his lifelong love affair with her.

～

Read on for a sneak peek at HARRY, the next book in the Young Brothers series. Can he figure out where he wants to be? **If you'd like to direct me in how HARRY goes, become a SMALL TOWN RESIDENT by scanning the code below with your phone.**

You'll also get exclusive extra chapters that hit the cutting room floor from BRYCE, as well as a continuation of the Young Family Saga!

Harry will be written slowly, over time, with _reader feedback_! It will then release on retailers. If you'd just like to know when the full book is out, SIGN UP BY SCANNING THE CODE BELOW, and I'll email you when HARRY is ready!

Sneak Peek! HARRY Chapter One:

Harry Young didn't exactly love the snow. But he did love sitting with Keri, Clay, and Avery cuddled around him while the flakes fell. He loved making hot chocolate for himself and the kids, and he loved watching movies while keeping the dark night and cold wind at bay.

In short, he loved being home in Coral Canyon, and since he didn't have to be in Nashville until after Valentine's Day, he'd chosen to stay in Wyoming after the holidays. It sure felt nice to have someone else looking after him. Someone making coffee in the morning, and someone filling the fridge with food.

After four months of touring, Harry was *tired*, and he didn't even want to think about having to do another album and another tour. He honestly wasn't sure how his father had done this ten times now.

With his bone-weary exhaustion plaguing him, it was no

wonder he scrolled through his social media feed while a cartoon movie of a princess played in front of him and the kids.

"Holy cow," he murmured, but Keri nor Clay cared. He paused on a particular post and picture. "Sarah Endman got married."

His high school girlfriend. The only girl he'd ever confided more in than his father, than anyone. *What?* he asked himself as he stared at her beautiful face. *Did you think she was waiting around for you?*

Of course she wasn't. She'd gone to college when he'd left for Nashville. The caption on her wedding photo read, *Reid and I have been together for four years, and I'm so happy we're finally man and wife!*

Four years.

Harry shoved his phone under his leg and folded his arms, a keen sense of loneliness filling him. Sarah had been his only girlfriend in high school. He'd only dated one other person since her, and well, Harry didn't want to go into what a terrible relationship he'd had with the lead singer of a band who'd toured with him recently.

He let his eyes drift closed, and before he knew it, he fell asleep during the kids' movie. "Harry," Keri whispered at some point. "It's over."

"Okay," he said, opening his eyes to look at the little girl. It took a moment for her to come into focus, and she looked at him with Ev's blue eyes and Dad's dark hair. "Time for bed, little lady."

He looked over to find Clay sound asleep, his face mashed into the couch cushion. Harry had put Avery in her swing, and the baby was zonked out too. He got up and stretched, yawning as he did. He loved staying up late, and as he scooped Clay into his arms and followed Keri down the hall, a second round of energy entered his body.

He laid Clay in his bed and bent down to kiss his forehead. He covered him up and left the room to help Keri with her teeth and nightgown. Once the seven-year-old had been tucked in, with properly brushed teeth, and promises of Harry being the one to drive her to school in the morning, he left her bedroom too.

Avery didn't have her own bedroom upstairs, and she still slept in a bassinet in Harry's parents' room. He collected the baby and took her in there, wrapping her up tight so she wouldn't wake up. He'd just left that bedroom when Daddy and Ev returned home, and he met them in the kitchen.

"How'd it go?" Ev asked.

"Just fine," Harry said, indicating the mess he'd left behind in the kitchen. "I think you can see everything we did right there."

Ev took in the electric kettle, the mugs, the bowl of popcorn which only held un-popped kernels and the excess fake yellow butter powder Harry loved. "Mm, yes, I see."

"I'll clean it up," Harry said. He had a bedroom in the basement, but he'd been staying out at Bryce's a lot in the past couple of weeks since his cousin had gotten engaged. "I'm staying here tonight, because I promised Keri I'd drive her to school." He smiled at Ev and moved around the island and into the kitchen.

She went down the hall to assumedly check on the kids and

get ready for bed, but Daddy plopped himself on a barstool and looked at Harry. That wasn't good.

"Uncle Morris said he's still negotiating a tour."

"Yeah, yep, right," Harry said. He'd told Morris, who acted as his manager, he didn't want to do a tour. He wanted to write the songs, record the songs, and have Rebel put out the album. The end.

"He also said you've asked him—well, he said you told him you didn't want another contract."

Harry turned his back on his dad as he put the half-full mugs in the sink and flipped on the faucet. "That's right," he said.

"What's your plan, then?"

A sigh moved through Harry's whole body, but his muscles felt like they'd been bound and tied. "Do I need a plan, Dad? I have like, millions of dollars in the bank. What if my plan is to sleep in the basement forever?"

"I'd say that's a terrible plan," his father said.

Harry dumped out the undrunk hot chocolate and pulled open the dishwasher. He loaded the mugs and spoons, then turned to get the bowl of popcorn. He met his father's eye, the storm inside him blowing out instantly.

"I want to write songs," Harry said. "I can do it from anywhere. You and Uncle Otis song-write. He makes good money writing songs for people who just sing them."

Daddy nodded, his dark eyes not quite all the way into Serial Killer Mode yet.

"I'm a really good songwriter," Harry said. "I can make more than the average person with one social media video than some people make in a month. With songs. With a guitar. I thought I wanted a life and a career in country music, but I don't."

Harry turned and took the bowl to the trashcan, where he dumped out the unpopped kernels. He set the bowl in the sink and let it start filling with water. He swept the trash from the hot chocolate packets and the popcorn bag off the counter and into the garbage, and still his father sat there, silent.

"Just ask it," Harry said.

"Are you going to move back here?"

Harry scrubbed the popcorn bowl, trying to find the right answer. Or at least an answer that wasn't, "I don't know."

But he didn't know.

He just wanted God to shine a light on the path he was supposed to be on. He hadn't been to church in a while, and he needed to go. He missed having a heavenly influence in his life, plain and simple.

He straightened his shoulders when he realized how slumped and folded in on himself he was. He finished rinsing the bowl and set it in the dish drainer to dry. As he faced his father, he grabbed a towel from the stove to dry his hands.

"You know what? I don't know, but I'm just going to be bold and try to act like an adult and say, yeah. I want to move back here."

Dad's lips twitched, but he didn't smile. "Harry, you can do whatever you want."

"Daddy, you know that's not true."

"Otis writes from here."

"Otis isn't under a contract." Harry turned back to the sink and picked up the washcloth. He flipped the sink back on for the third time and started rinsing it out. "And he's proven himself. And he's awesome."

He started wiping the counter and found a carton of cream he'd left out from the hot chocolate construction. He picked it up and put it back in the fridge, and when he faced his father to wipe down the island, he paused. "I want to have music in my life, Daddy. But I don't want to be a country music star in the way I have been. I don't like touring. I like writing, and plucking through my strings, and singing, but...I just don't think the traditional path is for me."

"No one's saying it needs to be."

"Why don't you just say what you want me to do?"

"I want you to be happy."

Harry started wiping the counter. "You know what makes me happy? Babysitting the kids so you and Ev can go out." He'd really, truly been happy tonight.

"I'm hearing someone wants a wife and a family."

"Yeah." Harry didn't mean for the sigh to slip from his throat, but it did. "I can admit I'm lonely. It's insane, but even when I'm surrounded by tens of thousands of people, I'm all alone." His chest hitched, and Harry clamped his teeth together to keep himself from saying another word. If he did, his voice would crack, and then Daddy wouldn't sleep. He'd be too worried about Harry, and that was the last thing he needed.

"Is Morris going to try to get Rebel to let you work on the album from here?"

"Yes," Harry clipped out. With the counter clean, he returned to the sink once more. He washed out the cloth and laid it out to dry before turning back to his dad. "I won't live here, and I won't live with Bryce. No matter what, Dad, I want to come back here. There's something about this place, and you're here and everyone is here."

He couldn't catch the emotion before it bled into his voice, and with his eyes locked on his daddy's, he decided he didn't have to hide anything. He wasn't "the" Harry Young here. He was just his father's son, and he could be himself.

"I miss everyone. I seriously don't know how Bryce lived away from here for so long. I miss so much, and I feel like a stranger to everyone where I live, a stranger to everyone who likes my music, and a stranger when I come home." He shook his head. "I know it doesn't make sense."

"It makes perfect sense," Daddy whispered.

"I'll get my own place," Harry said. "I can afford it, and it'll be here for me whenever I can be here too. One day." He rounded the island and sat next to his dad. "For good. Permanently. That's the goal."

Dad nodded, his chin down toward the countertop. "It's a good goal, Harry."

"Do you think I can find someone—you know—who's just...normal?"

Dad looked at him. "You mean a girl?"

"Yeah, Dad." Harry smiled at him, though the gesture felt a little tired on his face. "I mean a girl."

"All of us managed to find normal women," Dad said. "And we're big rockstars."

"True," Harry mused, but he thought it was a little different. He didn't want to call his dad old—or any of his uncles—but none of them had dated in their twenties. Daddy had been forty when he'd met Ev and started dating her. It wasn't the same as the younger culture, the younger crowd.

Maybe you'll find someone older than you, he thought, and Harry didn't hate that idea. Uncle Gabe and Aunt Hilde were quite far apart in age, and maybe it wouldn't be too big of a problem.

Especially here in Coral Canyon, where Harry wanted to be.

"Will you help me look for a place?" he asked.

"Of course I will," Dad said. "You want something big or small?"

"I'm thinking small," Harry said. "Nondescript. Normal. Average. I just want *average*, Daddy."

Dad chuckled. "All right. I'm sure we can find something in one of the older neighborhoods, where you'll have a little old lady bringing you banana bread every Sunday."

Harry grinned and leaned into his father's side-hug. "Sounds perfect," he said, and he wasn't lying. Not even a little bit.

The big city life wasn't for him. The hustle and bustle of fame didn't suit him. He did have quite a bit of money, and he'd get two more disbursements from the tour, and then two more during the making of the third album.

He had money. He had savings. He had a retirement fund already. He could find a way to do what he loved and keep making money.

Now, what he needed was someone to spend it on. Someone besides himself he could focus on.

He needed to surround himself with the goodness of nature, and of his family, and of God.

And he really, really wanted to find someone to share his life with the way Bryce had, the way his daddy had, the way seemingly everyone around him had.

HARRY ROLLED OVER IN BED, SOMEONE POUNDING ON THE door and refusing to go away. It took him a moment to remember he wasn't in his apartment in Nashville, but at home in Coral Canyon. Due to his staying-up-late-at-night habits, he wasn't surprised to find the clock on his nightstand blaring out a time of ten-twenty-four.

He was surprised that his daddy wasn't home to get the door, and as he got to his feet, he grabbed his phone and saw a text that said they'd taken the kids to Uncle Tex's for a holiday breakfast, and he should come out to the farmhouse whenever he woke up.

"Sheriff's Department," a woman yelled as Harry crested the stairs and entered the hallway leading to the front door. "Is anyone home?"

"Yeah, I'm home," Harry said as he reached the door and unlocked it. He pulled it open only to receive a nasty shock of bright sunlight glinting off the snow and streaming straight into his eyes.

A blast of cold air punched him in the chest, reminding him he wasn't exactly wearing a shirt.

As he shielded his eyes and tried to contain the chatter in

his teeth, the woman standing there said, "I'm Belle Graves of the Teton County Sheriff's Department. Can I ask you a few questions?"

Harry's eyes adjusted to the blinding light. Or maybe it all came from Belle and how angelic she was, standing there on the porch in black pants and a black shirt. An angel of darkness, maybe, but an angel nonetheless. She wore her dark brown hair long and down, and Harry wanted to run his fingers through it.

She'd done her makeup and while he'd never considered a Sheriff's Department vest to be a particularly sexy piece of clothing, on her, it sure was. Her dark eyes devoured him, sliding down to his bare feet and back to his face.

A flash of a smile stole across her face, and Harry had to make that happen again. Next time, for longer and aimed at him for something funny and clever he'd said to her.

"Do you live here?" she asked before he could ask her for her number.

"No," he said. "I mean, sort of."

The beautiful Belle tilted her head at him. "You *sort of* live here?"

"It's my parents' place," he said. "I'm just staying here for a while." He leaned into the doorjamb and rested his shoulder against it. "Do you want to come in? It's freezing out here."

Her eyes dropped to his bare chest. "Probably best if I do come in," she said as she squeezed up onto the step with him. "And you probably wouldn't be so cold if you had clothes on."

With that, she slipped by him and into the house, and all Harry could do was turn his head and watch her walk down the hall away from him, his heartbeat positively thrashing at him to *go with her! Answer her questions and then ask her one of your own.*

So he closed the door and followed the lovely Belle into the house, all thoughts of joining his family for a late breakfast completely and utterly gone.

Sneak Peek! HARRY Chapter Two:

Belle Graves took in the house, her keen eye finding and noticing details a lot of people probably wouldn't. At the sound of footsteps behind her, she turned and found the gorgeous man who'd answered the door coming into the big multi-purpose room at the back of the house.

He hadn't given his name, and Belle didn't normally just enter people's houses. Of course, men wearing only gym shorts didn't answer the door and stand there in the frigid weather in the middle of January either.

"Give me a sec," he said, and he turned left and went down the hallway, presumably back into the bedrooms. Belle reminded herself as she caught sight of the muscles in his back and shoulders—it was really just the cop in her that saw the little details—that she hadn't come here to get a date.

She had someone to find, and for all she knew, Cowboy

Cutie who'd answered the door could have Steven Bastian hidden in the basement.

"Sorry 'bout that," the man said as he returned. He had a cowboy accent, but she wasn't sure if he was from Wyoming or not. He'd said this was his parents' house, not his, and he could've been visiting from anywhere.

He now wore a dark purple shirt with four dancing potato chips on it—and they had eyes and mouths—those gray gym shorts, and a cowboy hat as he padded into the kitchen. "Coffee?" he offered in that smooth, deep voice of his.

"No, thank you," Belle said, clearing her throat and eliminating the questions about his T-shirt from her mind. She had *other* things to ask while she was here. "I'm a Missing Persons Investigator for the Teton County Sheriff's Department. I'm looking for your neighbor to the west there. Steven Bastian? Do you know him?"

"No," the man said. "Like I said, I'm just visiting my folks."

"What's your name?" she asked.

"Harry Young," he said, and he watched her for a moment.

To Belle, that sounded pretty bland, and she pulled out her notebook to write down a few things. "Who are your parents?"

"Trace and Everly Young." He pulled out the coffee pot, which already had coffee in it, and dumped it down the drain. He started to fill it with fresh water, and he looked over to her while he did. "They probably know their neighbors. Especially Ev. She runs the dance studio in town, and she knows everyone. My daddy's a bit more of a...keeps-to-himself kind of guy."

Belle scribbled something in her notebook she probably

wouldn't read later. She just liked getting it down, because then she remembered it. "Have you ever seen Steven before?"

"Probably," Harry said as he measured grounds into a filter. "I lived here for several years before graduating high school."

Belle didn't even want to know, but she asked, "How long ago was that?"

"Uh, let's see."

Well, if he had to think about it, that meant it was a while ago. Belle found herself holding her breath for a reason she couldn't name. She *really* wasn't here for a date. In fact, her whole dating-men history was pot-holed at best, and she didn't need to be trying to add another reason she crashed and burned to her personal failure resume.

Remember Buck, she told herself.

Lord, it would be great if I could focus here, she thought next. But every time she blinked, she could see Harry's well-defined abs, those broad pecs, and as she'd moved by him—sure, she could admit she'd gotten in close to him—she'd gotten the slightest scent of his cologne.

"Almost six years ago now," he said.

Belle pursed her lips. "Hm." She wrote down the year, doing the math quickly, and then she wrote a 24 and circled it a few times. Was a twenty-four-year-old too young for a twenty-nine-about-to-be-thirty-year-old?

"You?" he asked.

"Excuse me?" She looked up from his age on her notepad, pure surprise coloring her thoughts.

"When did you graduate from high school?" He dipped his

head into the fridge and came up with a couple of bottles of flavored cream.

Belle eyed those with extreme interest, because one of them was caramel, and she happened to have a very weak spot for cowboys with caramel cream in their big hands. "Uh, a while ago," she said. "Longer than six years ago."

"Like, a whole lot longer than six years ago, or just a few years more than six years ago?" Harry grinned at her, and Belle got the distinct impression he was flirting with her.

"Double the six," she said. "You know what? I'd love some coffee."

His smile only got brighter, and he turned to get down two mugs from the cupboard. "How long have you been a cop?"

"Eight years," she said. "I just moved into—" She cut off, because he'd completely reversed their roles here. The house felt so hot, and Belle really needed to regain control of the situation.

"How long have you been staying here?" she asked as she moved to the end of the counter. It was wintertime; that was why the house felt so stuffy and hot. It had absolutely nothing to do with Belle's traitorous pulse springing throughout her body.

"'Bout a month," Harry said.

"Wow, you don't have a job?"

He cut her a look out of the corner of his eye, his grin fading all the way to nothing. "I have a job," he said evasively.

"Work from home?"

"I'm on a break right now," he said.

Belle sensed something there, all of her cop tingles sparking at the same time. "So you might have been around to see your neighbor. He lives there alone. A little older gentleman. He's fifty-six."

"I've seen him," Harry said. "While we were shoveling snow, and when the kids wanted me to help them build a snowman."

"Yes, I saw that out front." Belle smiled at him, hoping to bring back the charm and charisma the cowboy had already shown her. But he'd shut down a little, and while his mouth tipped up, his smile certainly didn't hold the same wattage as it had before. "Your kids?" she asked, returning her attention to her notepad to madly scratch out some more items of interest about this Harry Young.

Search about him, she wrote as he said, "My daddy's. He got remarried, oh, I don't know. About eight or nine years ago. He and Ev have three kids together."

"I see, okay." She looked up, the question burning through her throat stuck there. She absolutely would not ask him if he was married or had ever been married. What would that have to do with Steven?

"Do you remember the last time you saw Steven while shoveling or building the snowman?"

"Well, it hasn't snowed in what? Four days?" Harry half-smiled, and oh, that was just as playful and sexy and bright as the full thing. "I swear, I love Coral Canyon, but when it snows, I do miss Nashville."

"Ah, Nashville," she said. "Is that where you live?"

"Sort of," he said.

"You have a lot of sort of's."

"I have a place there, yes," he said, giving her another sharp look. "But I'm buying a place here too."

He must be famous, she thought, and she knew the type who had two homes—one of which was in Nashville.

Men who thought they ruled the world because they could play a guitar. Well, Belle could do that too, thank you very much.

"So have you seen Steven in the past four days?"

"We built the snowman on Thursday afternoon," he said. "While Ev was teaching. I'm pretty sure I saw him then. He came home, and he was carrying in a couple of bags of groceries." He nodded like his memory had just kicked in. "Yeah, that's right."

"What time on Thursday?"

"I don't know. It was light. Afternoon. Keri was out of school, and she's in first grade. Four?"

"Four, okay," she said, writing it down. "And nothing since?"

"I don't think so."

"Did you notice any cars coming and going?"

Harry poured the coffee as he considered her question. He set one mug in front of her and nudged the caramel cream carton closer to her, as if he knew that was why she'd decided to change her mind and accept his offer of coffee.

"I don't recall," he said. "To be honest, I don't sleep here every night, and I was out at my cousin's on Thursday and Friday nights. I came here for the weekend, because my parents went out and I babysat, and then we went to church yesterday, and today's a holiday, so...." He trailed off then, his face suddenly blooming with the most adorable blush Belle had ever seen on a man.

Harry also had a hefty five o'clock shadow, probably because he'd shaved for church yesterday and then not again since. Belle liked the square jaw with stubble, the large, capable hands, the broad shoulders.

The potato chip T-shirt? She wasn't sure about that, but as a cop, she'd learned a long time ago not to make too many judgments too early on.

"I didn't see him on Saturday or Sunday," Harry said. "I didn't notice him at church, but I don't know if he normally goes or not."

"Because you don't live here."

"Right," he said. "And, in complete transparency, I don't really pay much attention to what's goin' on around me. My job —well, my job has trained me to focus on what's right in front of me and not much else. He may have been there, and I wouldn't have seen him."

He stirred coconut cream into his coffee, no sugar, and lifted the mug to his lips at the same time his pocket rang. Well, his phone inside his shorts pocket rang, and he pulled it out. "It's my daddy," he said with a sigh. "I'm late for a family breakfast."

"I won't keep you," Belle said. She did splash a bit of caramel cream into her coffee, and she took a hearty gulp of it as Harry slid the call to silent. "Thanks for the coffee, and thanks for answering my questions."

She dug into her vest pocket and pulled out her card. She hated her photo on this thing, but until she ran out, she couldn't get new ones. The county didn't just replace perfectly good business cards because she'd pulled her hair up on picture day and now looked bald in the photo.

"If you see him, please call me. His daughter reported him missing, and we really need to locate him." She handed Harry the card, took another sip of her coffee, and headed for the front door.

She'd rounded the corner and entered the hall when he called, "Belle, wait," in that delicious voice. Hens and feathers, now he'd said her name, and she'd never be able to hear it in the same way again.

She turned just as he came skidding around the corner, his coffee cup still in his hand. His shoulder bumped the wall, and he grunted, and then he came to a stop in front of her. Belle raised her eyebrows as he seemed to pant in and out a couple of times.

"Yes?" she asked.

"If I wanted—I mean." He cleared his throat and pressed his eyelids closed over those dreamy, dark eyes. "The number on this card." He opened his eyes and held up the card in the hand not holding his coffee cup. "If I call it, you'll answer?"

"Yes, sir," she said. "Day or night."

"So it's a work number."

"Yes," she said slowly. "It's my cell phone."

"Personal? Or one the Sheriff's Department issued to you?"

She cocked her head at him again, trying to get a read on him. He seemed to be putting off a very flirty vibe, but his face didn't show it, and she couldn't quite reconcile him.

"Where is the Teton County Sheriff's Department?" he asked.

"Jackson," she said. "I live there."

"Ah, I see."

"We come out to the surrounding towns as needed," she said. "It's a pretty drive, even in the winter."

"So you wouldn't be interested in maybe getting dinner with me?"

There it was, and Belle could admit that warmth seeped through her whole body. Despite the ugly, black khakis she had to wear for the job, despite the bulky vest she wore identifying herself, despite letting him steer this Q&A for a few minutes, he'd found something he liked about her.

What, she wasn't sure, but could she give him dinner to find out?

"Depends," she said.

"On what?"

"It seems to me, Mister Young," she said. "That you don't really have roots. You're here, you're there, you're in Nashville. I'm in Jackson, and that's not here, there, or Nashville."

"It's just dinner," he said.

She shook her head, feeling a little flirty and reckless herself. "I don't date for 'justs,'" she said. She nodded to the card in his hand. "If you see Steven, please call me immediately." With that, she turned and exited the house she never should've entered in the first place.

Harry didn't call for her to wait again, and Belle gave herself an extreme amount of credit for striding down the front side-walk to the driveway, and then back to her SUV, which she'd parked in front of the house next door, all without looking back once.

Only then did she eye the light gray house where Harry Young had answered the door. She made a few more notes, and then took out her phone to do a quick search for the man. Horror filled her with the half-sentence that came up under the first search result.

The prodigal son of country music sensation, Trace Young, Harry has taken the nation by storm with his—

"His what?" Belle asked herself, but she already knew.

Country music sensation, Trace Young.

Harry had a home in Nashville. He was "on a break" in his job.

She tapped and opened the link, the picture there making her breath catch and her pulse sprint.

Sexy, young, brilliant Harry Young on a stage, a guitar in his hand, that radiant smile blasting out to the whole world as he sang for them. He wore a pair of jeans, not gym shorts, and a T-shirt with a volcano on it that had a conversation bubble above its head that said, "I lava you."

The cowboy boots, a big shiny belt buckle, and that black cowboy hat completed Harry Young into Cowboy Perfection, not Cowboy Cutie. She quickly scanned the article about him, and he sure seemed like a superstar in his own right.

Belle looked over to the house again, but Harry wasn't there. She didn't have his number, and she would never humiliate herself by walking back to the door and telling him she'd changed her mind about going to dinner with him.

"It's *just* dinner," she said with a scoff. She'd done the casual dating scene, and it had sickened her. No, she was ready for serious, and Harry didn't even live here. Even if he did, an hour drive and fifty miles separated Coral Canyon and Jackson Hole, and Belle could barely keep up with her job, watering her plants, and feeding her cat.

She most certainly didn't have time for Harry Young.

Before she could shelve him the way she had other handsome cowboys that didn't fit into her life, her phone chimed. She pulled it out and swiped to get to the text.

This is Harry Young. My near future is a tiny bit up in the air at the moment, but I'd still love to take you to dinner. It wouldn't be JUST dinner. It would be us getting to know each other to find out if we have something.

"Something?" she wondered.

Another text came in as her eyebrows puckered.

Because I felt something between us, and I want to explore it. If you didn't, that's fine, and I will pray with everything I have that I don't see Steven so I don't have to call you and see you again, because wow, how embarrassing, right?

He'd included a smiley face, and honestly, Belle wasn't even sure how he'd typed all of that so fast. The man did have nimble fingers to be a country music star and—what had that article said?

"He's one of the best and rarest talents on the guitar," she said aloud, the words right there in her memory, as if her cop-brain knew she'd need them later and had catalogued them.

Let me know. I'm in town for at least another month.

Belle wanted to say yes, but she wasn't sure she should. What she did know was she had a debriefing meeting in seventy minutes, and she needed to make the drive back to headquarters.

She started her SUV but stalled in putting the vehicle into gear when she saw the front door of that gray house open and Harry himself jog down the front steps to the truck parked in the driveway. He launched himself behind the wheel, backed out of the driveway, and drove off.

Belle wanted to follow him. She wanted to text him back and say she'd go to dinner with him. She wanted to keep her job, which meant she had to get to her meeting.

And yet, she sat there on the side of the road, trying to decide what to do. Text Harry, follow Harry, or get on back to work?

Realistically, she couldn't sit there and she couldn't follow Harry. So, she started the drive back to Jackson and headquarters, a new dilemma in her mind now.

Go out with Harry? Or ignore his texts completely?

Oooh, what will Belle decide to do?

Guess what? YOU CAN HELP ME DECIDE! **If you'd like to direct me in how HARRY goes, become a SMALL TOWN RESIDENT by scanning the code below with your phone.**

You'll also get exclusive extra chapters that hit the cutting room floor from BRYCE, as well as a continuation of the Young Family Saga!

Harry will be written slowly, over time, with _reader feedback_! It will then release on retailers. If you'd just like to know when the full book is out, SIGN UP BY SCANNING THE CODE BELOW, and I'll email you when HARRY is ready!

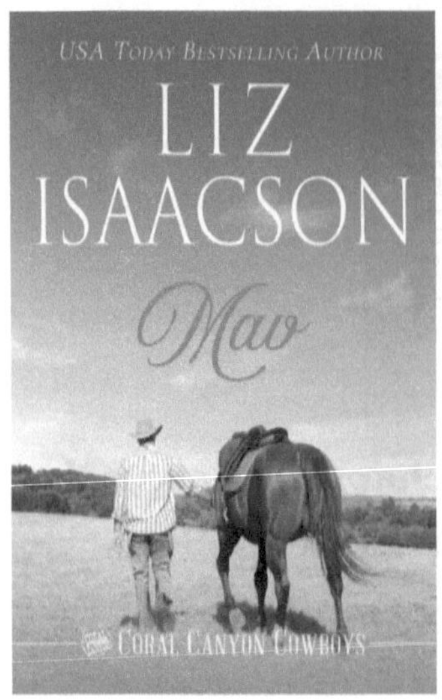

Mav (Book 0): Meet Maverik Young, the cowboy country music star ready to hang up his guitar strings in favor of being a father.

Oh, and he'd like a good woman to settle down with in Coral Canyon too, please. :)

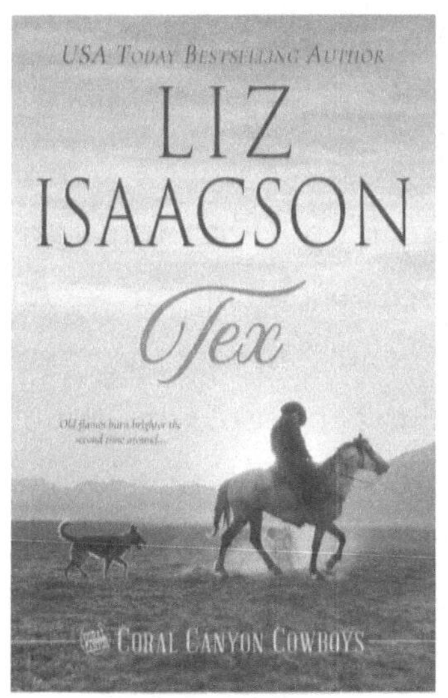

Tex (Book 1): He's back in town after a successful country music career. She owns a bordering farm to the family land he wants to buy...and she outbids him at the auction. Can Tex and Abigail rekindle their old flame, or will the issue of land ownership come between them?

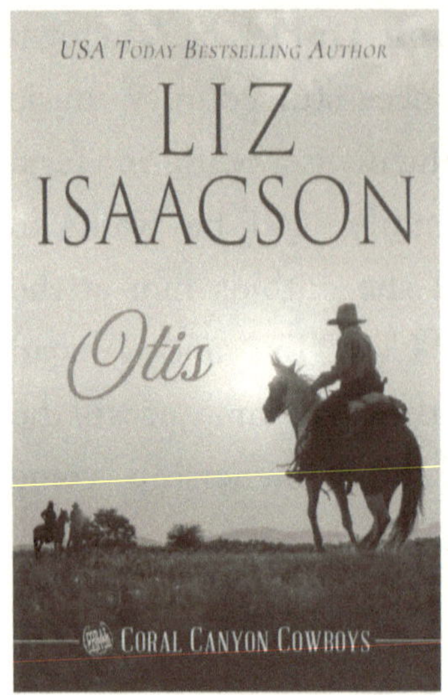 **Otis (Book 2):** He's finished with his last album and looking for a soft place to fall after a devastating break-up. She runs the small town bookshop in Coral Canyon and needs a new boyfriend to get her old one out of her life for good. Can Georgia convince Otis to take another shot at real love when their first kiss was fake?

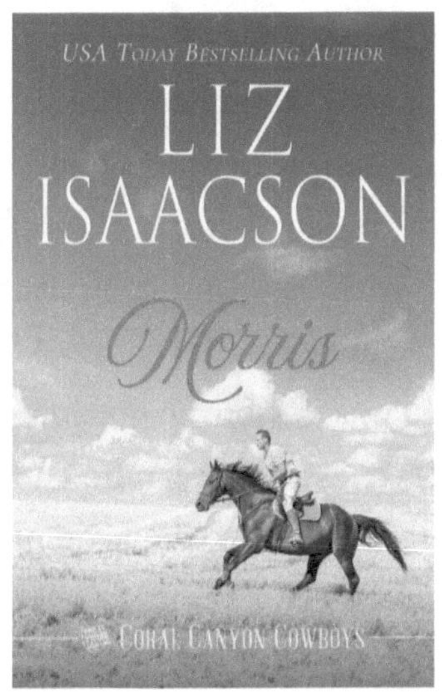

Morris (Book 3): Morris Young is just settling into his new life as the manager of Country Quad when he attends a wedding. He sees his ex-wife there—apparently Leighann is back in Coral Canyon—along with a little boy who can't be more or less than five years old... Could he be Morris's? And why is his heart hoping for that, and for a reconciliation with the woman who left him because he traveled too much?

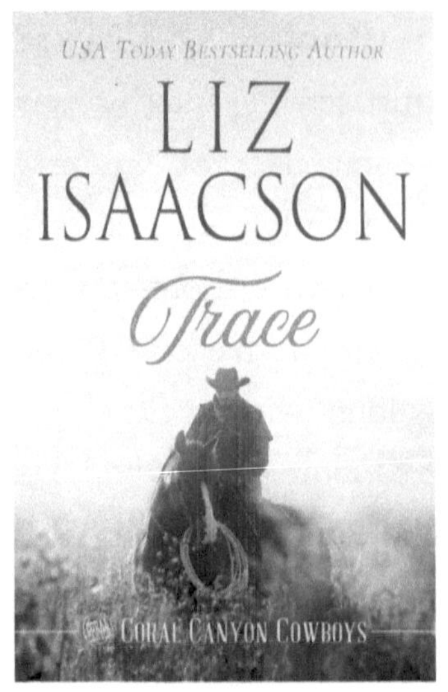

Trace (Book 4): He's been accused of only dating celebrities. She's a simple line dance instructor in small town Coral Canyon, with a soft spot for kids...and cowboys. Trace could use some dance lessons to go along with his love lessons... Can he and Everly fall in love with the beat, or will she dance her way right out of his arms?

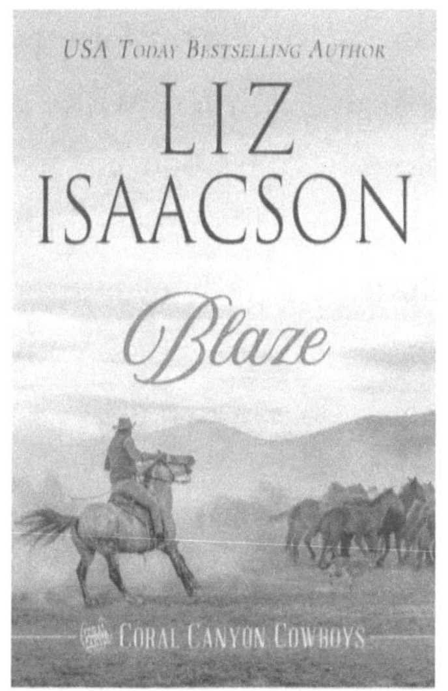

Blaze (Book 5): He's dark as night, a single dad, and a retired bull riding champion. With all his money, his rugged good looks, and his ability to say all the right things, Faith has no chance against Blaze Young's charms. But she's his complete opposite, and she just doesn't see how they can be together...

...so she ends things with him.

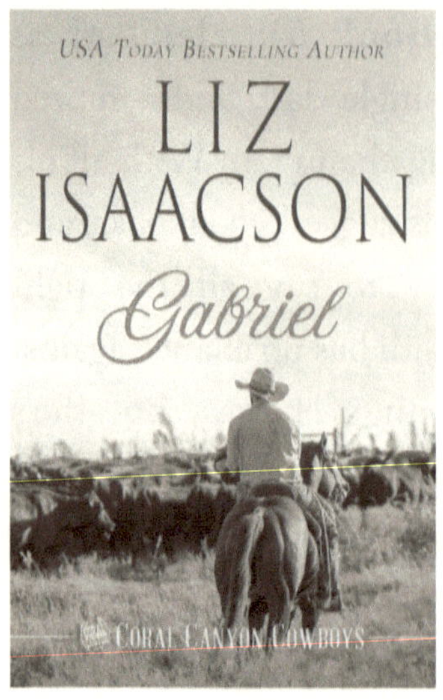

Gabe (Book 6): He's a father's rights advocate lawyer with a sweet little girl. She's fighting for her own daughter. Can Gabe and Hilde find happily-ever-after when they're at such odds with one another?

Jem (Book 7): He's still healing from his vices, and Jem has dedicated everything he has to his two kids. At least he's not mourning his divorce anymore, and in fact, he might be ready to move on. She's his former best friend, and once he breaks his wrist, his nurse. Can Sunny somehow rope this cowboy's heart?

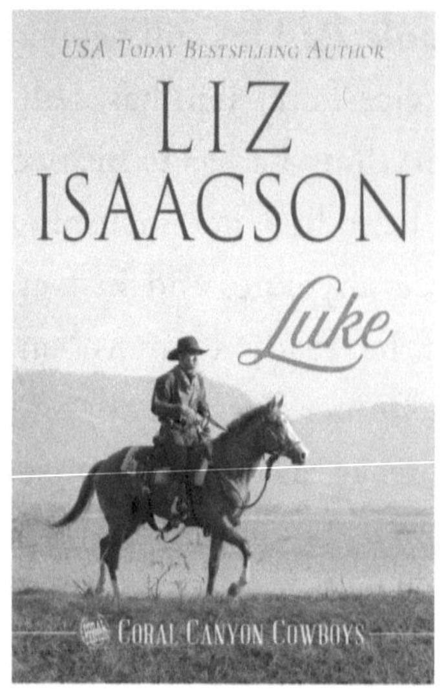

Luke (Book 8): He swore off women when his ex told him he might not be their daughter's father. But a paternity test confirmed he is, and Luke Young has dedicated his life to his little girl and his brothers' band. There hasn't been time for a girlfriend anyway. He's tried here and there, and the women in small-town Coral Canyon are certainly interested in him.

But he's been thinking about his massage therapist for a while now. Can he ask Sterling out when all they've ever been is professional? Oh, and there's the fact that she's seen practically every inch of his body... Awkward, right?

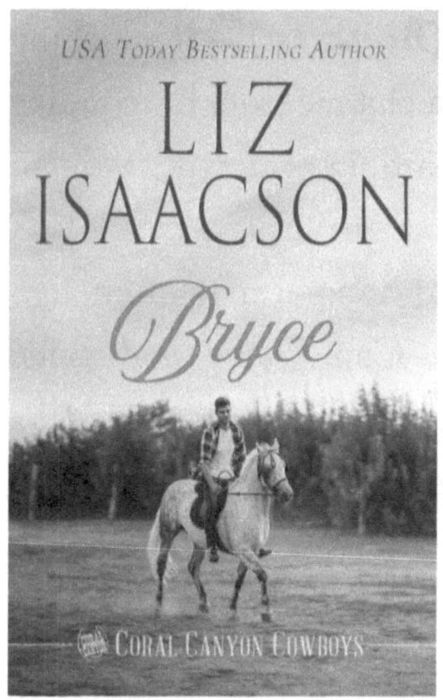

Bryce (Book 9): Bryce Young has been broken and drifting for years. After giving up his son for adoption, he left Coral Canyon and hasn't returned...until now.

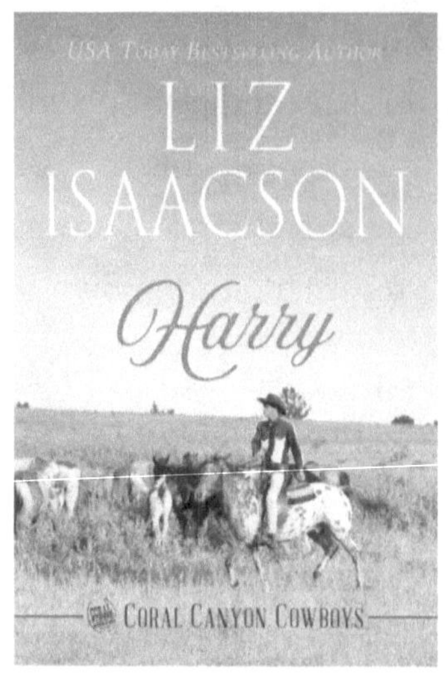

Harry (Book 1o): He's looking to make a change from his country music stardom, but the woman who's caught his eye isn't convinced he's permanent enough for her... Can Harry and Belle work out their differences to find a happily-ever-after?

Books in the Christmas at Whiskey Mountain Lodge Romance series

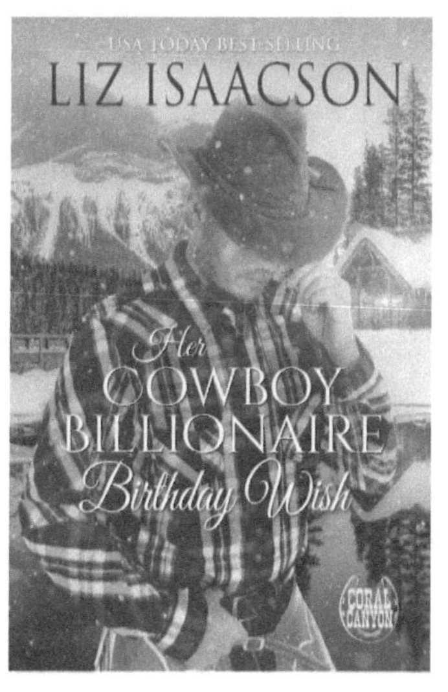

Her Cowboy Billionaire Birthday Wish (Book 1): All the maid at Whiskey Mountain Lodge wants for her birthday is a handsome cowboy billionaire. And Colton can make that wish come true—if only he hadn't escaped to Coral Canyon after being left at the altar...

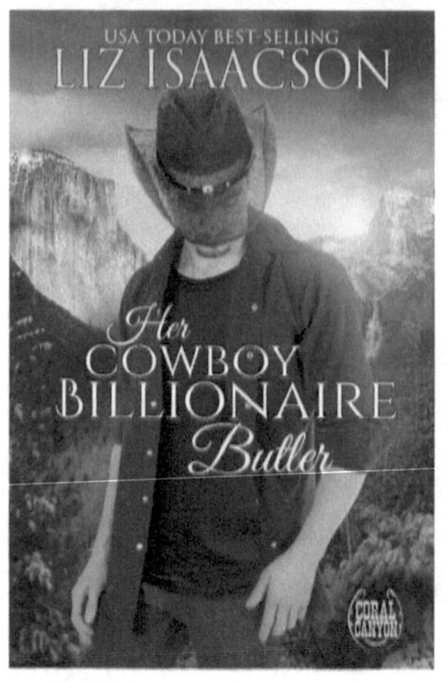

Her Cowboy Billionaire Butler (Book 2): She broke up with him to date another man...who broke her heart. He's a former CEO with nothing to do who can't get her out of his head. Can Wes and Bree find a way toward happily-ever-after at Whiskey Mountain Lodge?

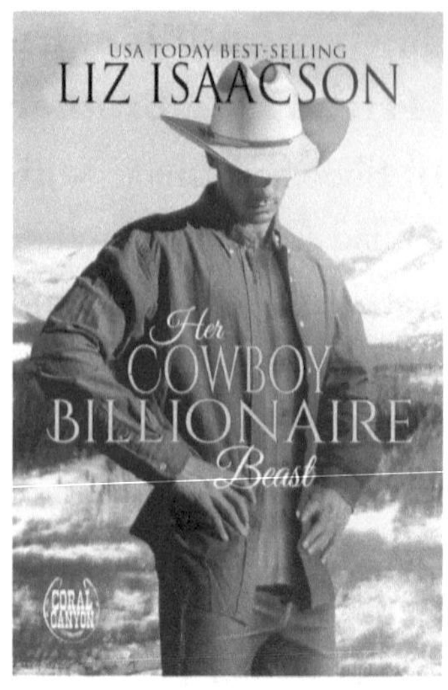

Her Cowboy Billionaire Beast (Book 4): A cowboy billionaire beast, his new manager, and the Christmas traditions that soften his heart and bring them together.

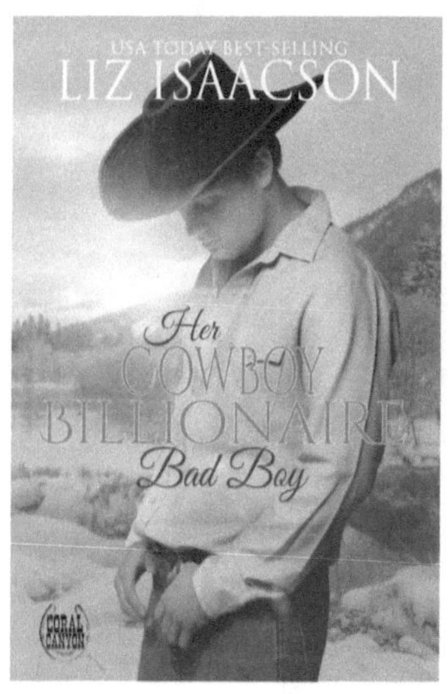

Her Cowboy Billionaire Bad Boy (Book 5): A cowboy billionaire cop who's a stickler for rules, the woman he pulls over when he's not even on duty, and the personal mandates he has to break to keep her in his life...

Books in the Christmas in Coral Canyon Romance series

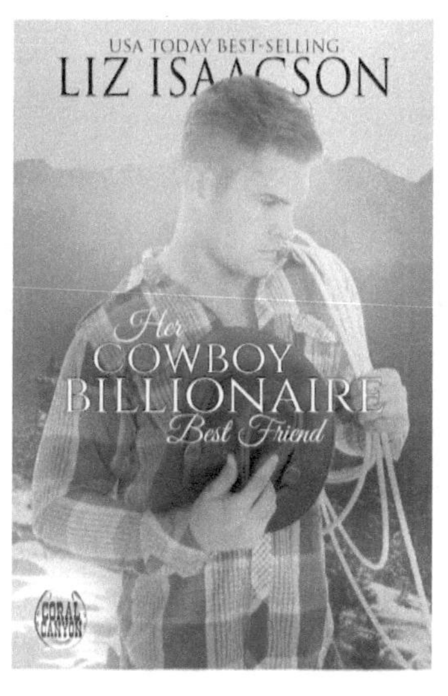

Her Cowboy Billionaire Best Friend (Book 1): Graham Whittaker returns to Coral Canyon a few days after Christmas—after the death of his father. He takes over the energy company his dad built from the ground up and buys a high-end lodge to live in—only a mile from the home of his once-best friend, Laney McAllister. They were best friends once, but Laney's always entertained feelings for him, and spending so much time with him while they make Christmas memories puts her heart in danger of getting broken again...

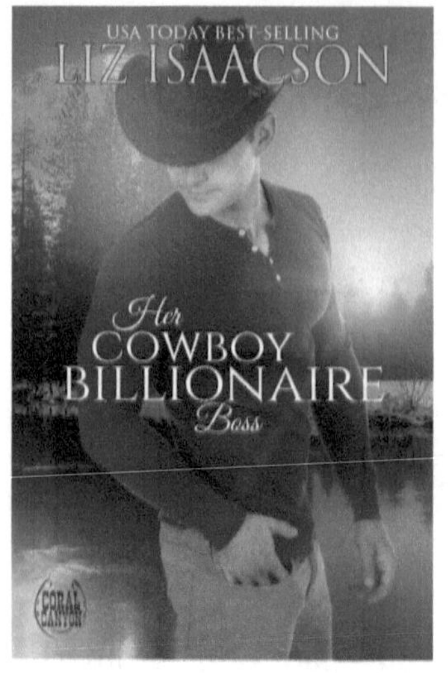

Her Cowboy Billionaire Boss (Book 2): Since the death of his wife a few years ago, Eli Whittaker has been running from one job to another, unable to find somewhere for him and his son to settle. Meg Palmer is Stockton's nanny, and she comes with her boss, Eli, to the lodge, her long-time crush on the man no different in Wyoming than it was on the beach. When she confesses her feelings for him and gets nothing in return, she's crushed, embarrassed, and unsure if she can stay in Coral Canyon for Christmas. Then Eli starts to show some feelings for her too...

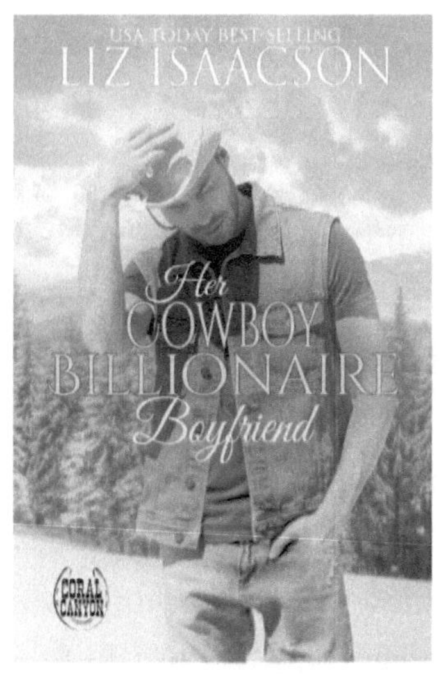

Her Cowboy Billionaire Boyfriend (Book 3): Andrew Whittaker is the public face for the Whittaker Brothers' family energy company, and with his older brother's robot about to be announced, he needs a press secretary to help him get everything ready and tour the state to make the announcements. When he's hit by a protest sign being carried by the company's biggest opponent, Rebecca Collings, he learns with a few clicks that she has the background they need. He offers her the job of press secretary when she thought she was going to be arrested, and not only because the spark between them in so hot Andrew can't see straight.

Can Becca and Andrew work together and keep their relationship a secret? Or will hearts break in this classic romance retelling reminiscent of _Two Weeks Notice_?

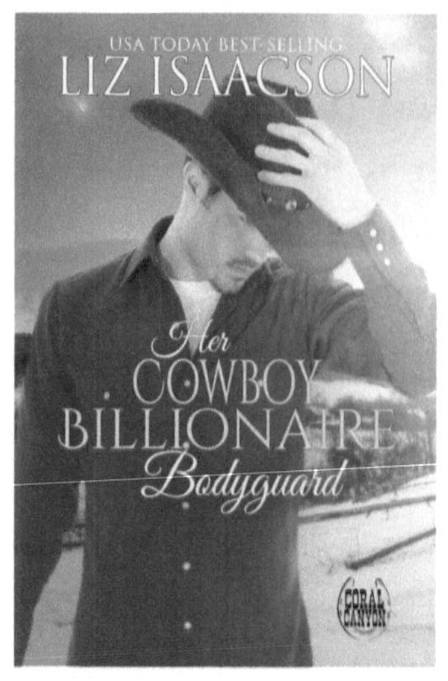

Her Cowboy Billionaire Bodyguard (Book 4): Beau Whittaker has watched his brothers find love one by one, but every attempt he's made has ended in disaster. Lily Everett has been in the spotlight since childhood and has half a dozen platinum records with her two sisters. She's taking a break from the brutal music industry and hiding out in Wyoming while her ex-husband continues to cause trouble for her. When she hears of Beau Whittaker and what he offers his clients, she wants to meet him. Beau is instantly attracted to Lily, but he tried a relationship with his last client that left a scar that still hasn't healed...

Can Lily use the spirit of Christmas to discover what matters most? Will Beau open his heart to the possibility of love with someone so different from him?

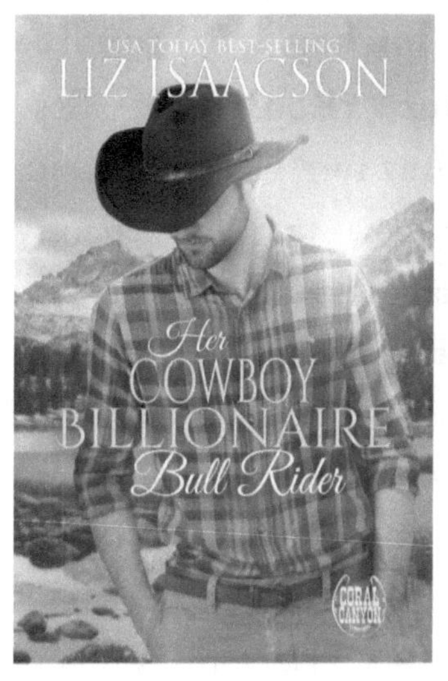

Her Cowboy Billionaire Bull Rider (Book 5): Todd Christopherson has just retired from the professional rodeo circuit and returned to his hometown of Coral Canyon. Problem is, he's got no family there anymore, no land, and no job. Not that he needs a job--he's got plenty of money from his illustrious career riding bulls.

Then Todd gets thrown during a routine horseback ride up the canyon, and his only support as he recovers physically is the beautiful Violet Everett. She's no nurse, but she does the best she can for the handsome cowboy. **Will she lose her heart to the billionaire bull rider? Can Todd trust that God led him to Coral Canyon...and Vi?**

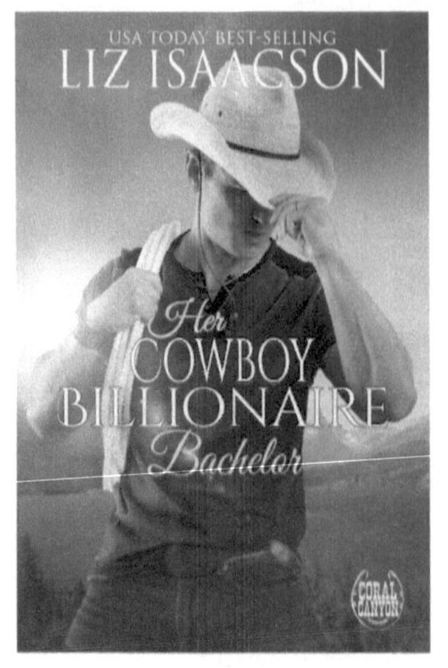

Her Cowboy Billionaire Bachelor (Book 6): Rose Everett isn't sure what to do with her life now that her country music career is on hold. After all, with both of her sisters in Coral Canyon, and one about to have a baby, they're not making albums anymore.

Liam Murphy has been working for Doctors Without Borders, but he's back in the US now, and looking to start a new clinic in Coral Canyon, where he spent his summers.

When Rose wins a date with Liam in a bachelor auction, their relationship blooms and grows quickly. **Can Liam and Rose find a solution to their problems that doesn't involve one of them leaving Coral Canyon with a broken heart?**

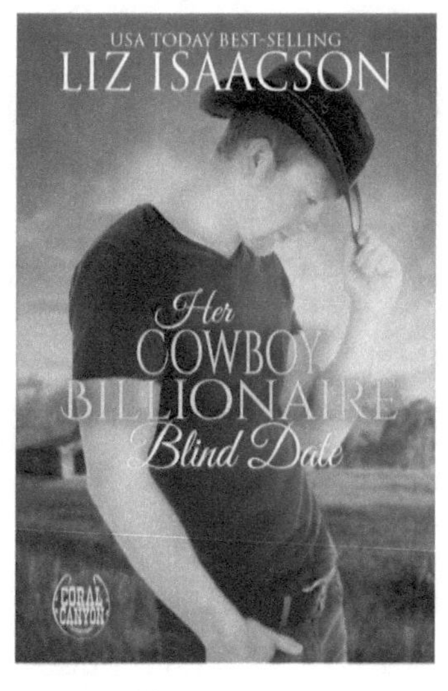

Her Cowboy Billionaire Blind Date (Book 7): Her sons want her to be happy, but she's too old to be set up on a blind date...isn't she?

Amanda Whittaker has been looking for a second chance at love since the death of her husband several years ago. Finley Barber is a cowboy in every sense of the word. Born and raised on a racehorse farm in Kentucky, he's since moved to Dog Valley and started his own breeding stable for champion horses. He hasn't dated in years, and everything about Amanda makes him nervous.

Will Amanda take the leap of faith required to be with Finn? Or will he become just another boyfriend who doesn't make the cut?

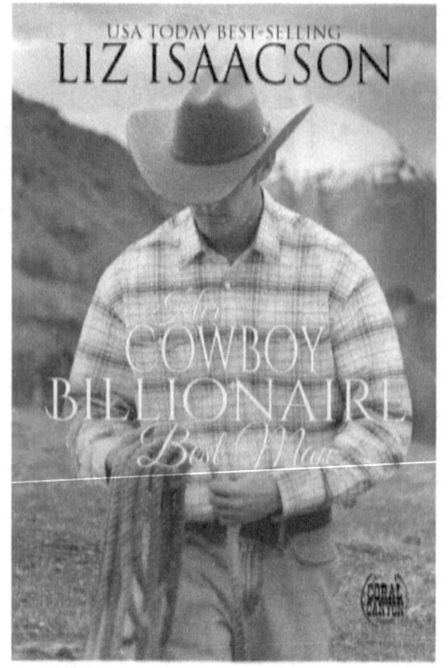

Her Cowboy Billionaire Best Man (Book 8): When Celia Abbott-Armstrong runs into a gorgeous cowboy at her best friend's wedding, she decides she's ready to start dating again.

But the cowboy is Zach Zuckerman, and the Zuckermans and Abbotts have been at war for generations.

Can Zach and Celia find a way to reconcile their family's differences so they can have a future together?

About Liz

Liz Isaacson writes inspirational romance, usually set in Texas, or Wyoming, or anywhere else horses and cowboys exist. She lives in Utah, where she writes full-time, takes her two dogs to the park everyday, and eats a lot of veggies while writing. Find her on her website at www.feelgoodfictionbooks.com.